RAVE REVIEWS FOR RICHARD LAYMON!

"I've always been a Laymon fan. He manages to raise serious gooseflesh."
—Bentley Little

"Laymon is incapable of writing a disappointing book."
—*New York Review of Science Fiction*

"Laymon always takes it to the max. No one writes like him and you're going to have a good time with anything he writes."
—Dean Koontz

"If you've missed Laymon, you've missed a treat."
—Stephen King

"A brilliant writer."
—*Sunday Express*

"I've read every book of Laymon's I could get my hands on. I'm absolutely a longtime fan."
—Jack Ketchum, author of *The Girl Next Door*

MORE PRAISE FOR RICHARD LAYMON!

AFTER MIDNIGHT

RICHARD LAYMON

LEISURE BOOKS NEW YORK CITY

A LEISURE BOOK®

March 2006

Published by

Dorchester Publishing Co., Inc.
200 Madison Avenue
New York, NY 10016

ISBN 0-8439-5180-X

Visit us on the web at www.dorchesterpub.com.

This book is dedicated to
Tom Corey
Friend, Photographer, Musician,
Construction Guru
and the Builder of Alice's Garage
&
To Donna, René and Amina
his special gals

Introduction

Hello.

I'm Alice.

I've never written a book before, but figured I might as well start by saying who I am.

Alice.

That's not my real name. I'd have to be an idiot to tell you my real name, wouldn't I? Identify myself, then go on to write a book that tells more than anyone should ever know about my private life and adventures and passions and crimes.

Just call me Alice.

Sounds like "alias," doesn't it?

I'm somebody, alias Alice.

Anyway, names are the only things I'll lie about. I'll make up names for *all* my characters, because they're real people—or were—and I don't want any trouble. If I start giving true names, no telling where it might lead.

Obviously, that'll have to go for *place* names, too. Not just people. I don't want to give away *where* stuff happened, or someone might start putting two and two-together.

Except for the names of people and places, everything else will be completely true. I promise. I mean, why bother to write my story if I'm not going to tell the truth? What would be the point?

For that matter, what is the point?

Why am I sitting down to write this book?

I'm not doing it for the money. I *would* do it for the money, but how can you get paid for a book without letting someone know who you really are? How do they make out the checks? I haven't figured that out yet, but I'm working on it.

I'm not doing it for fame, either. How can I make myself famous if nobody knows who I am?

But I want to write it anyway.

My story only happened about six months ago, but I already feel it starting to slip into the past. If I don't hurry and get it down the way it was, I'm afraid I'll lose it.

I'll never forget the main stuff, but little pieces are sure to fall away and others will change on me.

I want a record of how it *really* was. Every detail. So when I read it, later on, I'll have a way to live it all over again.

Also, it might come in handy if they ever try to prosecute me. It'll give the complete truth about my side of things, and might help me off the hook.

Or maybe it won't.

I might be better off burning it.

Anyway, here we go.

1

IT STARTS

I've already explained, my name is Alice (but not really). I was twenty-six years old when all this took place last summer, and living in a comfortable little room over the garage of my best friend's house.

That was Serena.

She had it all. Not only the huge old house at the edge of the woods, but a husband named Charlie and two kids—a four-year-old named Debbie who was every bit as beautiful as her mother, and a baby named Jeff.

Some people have all the luck, don't they?

I mean Serena, not me.

What it mostly boils down to is genes. Serena was hugely, incredibly lucky in the genes department. Which is to say, she was born beautiful and smart. When you've got that going for you, everything else is a whizz. It was only natural for Serena to marry a handsome, wealthy fellow, move into a great house, and have a couple of terrific kids.

I didn't make out quite so well in the genes department.

My parents were a couple of duds. Good, hard-working people, but duds. Not that I hold it against them. It wasn't their fault; they came from duds, themselves, and couldn't help it. Just as I can't help who *I* am.

And I don't resent who I am.

You can't do anything about your genes, so you have to do the best you can with what you've got.

I did all right.

This isn't meant to be an autobiography, so I won't bore you with the details of my youth. This is supposed to be about what happened because of the stranger who showed up on that night last summer, so I'll skip to there.

As already stated, I was living in the room over Serena's garage. I paid a monthly rent. She had tried to talk me out of paying (she really had no use for the money, anyway), but I insisted. Even though I was between jobs, I had some savings. I was glad to part with it, so as not to be considered a freeloader.

Even if a person doesn't look like a beauty queen, she can still keep her dignity.

Am I giving you the impression that I'm an ugly, pathetic cow?

Writing is harder than it looks, I guess. Especially if you want to tell something the way it really is and not mislead people.

The fact is, I'm not and never was ugly. My face doesn't stop clocks. But then, it doesn't stop traffic, either. People have said I have a "sweet" face, and I've been called "cute." Not many people have ever used the term "beautiful" in connection with me. Those who did—like my parents—were either blinded by prejudice in my favor, lying outright to spare my feelings, or hoping to lay me.

George Gunderson used to call me "beautiful" and "gorgeous," but you should've seen George. I was probably the only gal in the history of his life who didn't run away screaming. Besides, he was just flattering me to get in my pants. Guys are that way, in case you never noticed.

Anyway, I'm not exactly beautiful or gorgeous. I just have an ordinary, fairly pleasant-looking face. My natural hair color is brown, but I tint it a nice, light shade of blond. My eyes are brown. So are my teeth.

Just kidding about the teeth.

Maybe I shouldn't joke around like that. After all, this is supposed to be a serious book. People do tell me, though, that I've got an interesting sense of humor.

My two greatest attributes, if you listen to what other people say, are my sense of humor and my smile. They also say I'm a "nice" person, and that I'm "caring." But what do they know?

Though I'm nothing special in the face department, I do have a damn good body on me. I'm large for a woman (five-foot ten), and used to be on the husky side. Hell, I was fat and dumpy. But my first year at college, I pulled myself together and got into shape. Ever since then, I've stayed fit. I look great in a swimsuit—and even better out of one.

But mostly, I keep my main assets well hidden. I don't like for guys to see what I've got.

Back when I was dumpy, they never wanted to look at me or be seen with me. After I got into shape, though, I had to fight them off. Just about all of them were total jerks. They didn't want to know me or have fun. All they cared about was the fact that I was "built."

According to several charmers, I was "built like a brick shithouse."

I don't even know what a brick shithouse *looks* like.

What the hell is a brick shithouse? Why would anyone want to compare *me* to one? It's not only crass, but it doesn't even make sense.

When you come right down to it, most guys stink. By the time I was twenty-six and living above Serena's garage, I'd pretty much given up on them.

But then came the night the stranger showed up.

It was a hot night in July. Serena and Charlie were off on a vacation with the kids, and wouldn't be coming back for a week. In the meantime, I had the entire house to myself. They always encouraged me to stay in the real house whenever they went away. They said it made the house look "lived in," so it wouldn't be a target for burglars. Maybe they believed what they were saying. Personally, though, I think they were just being nice to me. They figured I would much rather spend the week in their house than in my room above the garage.

They were partly right. They had a wonderful kitchen, a master bathroom with a sunken tub that was absolutely heavenly, and a den with a thirty-five-inch television. Whenever I had the run of the house, I prepared great meals for myself, lounged in the bathtub, and spent hours watching the big-screen TV.

In the master bedroom was a king-sized bed about three times the size of my bed in the garage. The walls and closet doors on both sides of it were lined with mirrors, and another huge mirror was fixed to the ceiling directly above the mattress. Serena told me they were Charlie's idea. They probably were. Serena must've like them, too, though. The mirrors wouldn't have gone up if she hadn't approved. She and Charlie were both a couple of gorgeous specimens, so it's hardly any wonder that they liked to watch each other—and themselves.

The first time I ever stayed overnight in the house, I tried out their bed. I looked pretty good in the mirrors, myself, but I also looked very *alone* sprawled out in the center of that enormous mattress. And then I got to thinking about Serena and Charlie, and how this was *their* bed. Time after time, they'd probably made love right in the very place where I was lying. Right on the very sheet. But now it was me on the sheet, not Serena, not Charlie. To make a long story short, my imagination ran wild and nothing could stop it. Even after I finally fell asleep, my mind wouldn't settle down. All night long, I thrashed about and sweated, plagued by feverish dreams—or hallucinations—so vivid they seemed real.

When I woke up the next morning, I was so worn out and ashamed of myself that I vowed never to spend another night in Serena and Charlie's bed. From then on, I always returned to the garage for bedtime.

It suited me.

As much as I liked their kitchen and bathroom and television, I often got the willies at night. The place was too big—more rooms than you could use, a hallway that ran from one end of the house to the other, windows all over the place and too many doors. You always had to worry that someone might be peering at you through a window—or already inside, hiding and ready to jump you.

Not at all like my small, cozy place above the garage.

My place was about twenty-five feet square, a single room with a kitchenette and "half a bath"—meaning I had a fully equipped bathroom, minus a tub. From the middle of the room, with the bathroom door open, I could see every door and window. I could also hear the slightest sound.

After entering my quarters, I never failed to look around to make sure nobody had crept in during my absence. And I listened. An intruder might hide motionless and holding his breath, but I figured I would be able to hear his heartbeat.

I always felt very safe, back in my own room.

But *getting* to it could be hard on the nerves.

On that hot July night when the stranger came, I'd stayed in the house until after midnight. Normally, I would've left earlier. But this was the first day of Serena and Charlie's vacation, and I hadn't had the house to myself since their spring trip to San Francisco. As a result, I'd forgotten the wisdom of early departures. So I stayed too long in their house that night.

Overdid it.

Serena and Charlie have a lovely swimming pool in the back yard. With no other houses nearby and a wild forest behind their property, the pool is like a private, woodland pond.

A pond that I avoided like a swamp.

Except when I was house-sitting, nobody around to look at me or interfere.

The day everything started, Serena and Charlie didn't get away until early afternoon. In the driveway, I gave everyone goodbye kisses, wished them a great time, then waved as Charlie backed his car toward the road.

As soon as they were out of sight, I celebrated my new freedom by running up to my room, throwing off my clothes and jumping into my new, two-piece swimsuit. I'd already packed a small bag with things I might need during the day. I grabbed it and hurried down to their house.

First, I made myself a Bloody Mary. Then I went out to the pool.

Slick with oil and gleaming with sunlight, I spent all afternoon relaxing on the lounger, drinking this and that drink, reading a paperback mystery, daydreaming and napping. Now and then, when I grew terribly hot and drippy, I went into the water for a chilly, refreshing swim.

It was a luscious afternoon.

I drank too much and slept too much and got too much sun and loved it.

Later, I barbecued a steak on the outdoor grill. I ate it by the pool. After supper, I figured I'd had enough outdoor living for one day, and moved inside. I took a long, hot shower, soaping myself all over to get the oil off. When I rinsed, my skin gleamed. It had a warm coppery glow from the sun.

My tan was great, but it made me look a little silly in the bedroom mirrors. That's because of the places where I *wasn't* tanned. I looked as if I were wearing a swimsuit made from the skin of someone else, a stranger who'd never been out in the sunlight.

I used some of Serena's skin lotion to keep myself nice and moist. Then I slipped into Charlie's blue silk robe, went into the den, and watched television. I just loved their big-screen TV. It made everything look huge.

Their house was too far out of town for cable, so they had a satellite dish. The little TV in my own room was hooked up to the same system, so I knew how to work it.

You could get a zillion shows.

I found a movie that started at eight. While I was watching it, night came so I had to get off the couch and shut the den curtains. I don't like curtains being open at night. Somebody might be out in the dark, looking in. You can't see him, but he can see you. It really gives me the creeps.

That particular night, I felt more edgy than usual. It was probably a case of first-night jitters. Or else a premonition.

I turned on a couple of lamps to make the den bright.

I'd planned to take a long bath by candlelight after the movie. When the time came, though, I changed my mind. I much preferred to stay in the bright den with the television on, its volume good and loud. I'd lost every desire to go wandering through the dark house or to sit all alone in the hot water, surrounded by silence and flickering candle flames and shadows.

With the change of plans, I wanted popcorn—at least until I thought about the long journey to the kitchen. There were windows all along the way—enormous windows and sliding glass doors and walls of glass—every one of them facing the pool area, the back lawn and the woods. If only I'd remembered to shut those curtains before dark!

With the curtains wide open, it would almost be the same as if the house didn't have any rear wall, at all.

I had walked that particular gauntlet before.

That's true. I'd often walked it at night when the curtains were wide open and I was all alone in the house. Sometimes, I hadn't even gotten a case of the jitters. Usually, though, I found myself hurrying along, goosebumps from head to toe, afraid to even *glance* toward the windows, absolutely certain that someone horrible must be gazing in at me.

Tonight, I was already feeling too damn jumpy.

The popcorn wasn't worth a trip that might scare me half out of my wits, so I went ahead and watched the next movie without any.

It ended a little after midnight.

Which was late. Normally, eleven o'clock would've been about the right time for letting myself out of the house and hurrying to my room above the garage.

As late as it already was, I didn't feel the least bit sleepy. Maybe because I'd taken all those naps beside the pool.

So why not stay and watch one more movie?

Why not? Because if I watched another, I would have to make my trip to the garage at 1:30 or 2:00.

Way too late.

My swimsuit was still in the master bathroom. I decided to leave it there. Since I had nothing else to put on, I stayed in Charlie's robe. I liked wearing it, anyway. It was very light-weight, and felt slippery and cool against my skin. Also, it made me feel funny, sometimes, knowing it was his. Funny in a good, familiar sort of way.

My purse was with me on the sofa, so I didn't need to go searching for it. I didn't have to wander around the rest of the house to make sure all the doors were locked, either. I'd taken care of that before the sun went down. I'd also made sure that every light was off except for those that were sup-posed to stay on all night: the one in the foyer and a couple out in front of the house.

Serena and Charlie never lit up the rear of the house—the deck or pool or yard—except when they were out there. (And sometimes not even then.) I never asked them why. If it was me, though, I would've kept them off because of the woods.

Who knows what they might attract? There were things in the woods that might see the lights and come over to inves-tigate. Nasty, wild things that belonged in the deep woods, not in your back yard. Not in your house.

2

THE STRANGER

Midnight.

I wished I was already back inside my safe little place above the garage.

Before I could *be* there, though, I had to *get* there.

Getting there was the bad thing about staying in Serena and Charlie's house. It was the price that had to be paid. Not a terrible price, really. I'd always been willing to pay it for the luxury of using their house.

I mean, it was my choice to stay after dark, to stay until midnight. I *could've* returned to my place before sundown, or even kept out of their house entirely and avoided the whole problem.

Or, having stayed late, I could've avoided the return trip by *remaining* in the house.

But here's the deal.

It only takes me two or three minutes to step outside, hurry over to the garage, climb the flight of stairs to my door, unlock it and get inside. If I'm *really* scared, I can probably do it in less than a minute.

The trip always frightens me, but it doesn't last long. If I avoid it by spending all night in the house, however, I end up being tormented for hours and hours, not a few minutes.

It makes sense to me.

I do things my own way, that's the thing. If enjoying the luxuries of the house means I have to make a scary rush back to my own place in the middle of the night, so be it. I'll pay the price.

Anyway, it was time to go. Past time.

So I shut off the television, then turned off all the lamps in the den. After that, there was only darkness except for a dim, gray glow of moonlight that seeped in through the curtains. I opened the curtains. The glow brightened a lot. I stepped up close to the glass door and looked out.

With the den dark behind me and the area behind the house spread with moonlight, I felt invisible.

I took my time, gazing out. I wanted to be completely sure it was safe before unlocking the door and stepping into the night.

Impossible, of course.

You can *never* be sure it's safe.

The full moon, that night, was very bright. It laid a dazzling silver path across the surface of the swimming pool. The concrete around the pool looked gray like dirty snow. The lawn beyond the concrete was as dark as the water. Like the water, it had a path of moonlight. The path on the grass was as dim as old iron, but led straight to the brilliant path that came over the pool toward me.

At the far end of the lawn, the forest started. The tops of the trees looked as if they'd been misted with silver spray-paint. Below their tops, the trees were completely dark. So dark they looked *gone*. They cast a black shadow over part of the lawn.

I saw nobody.

But there was so much blackness.

Someone might be lurking at the border of the woods, or even closer than that.

In the pool, for instance.

The water level is a foot or more below the rim, so the far wall casts a shadow along its entire length. A dozen faces—*two* dozen—might be hidden in that strip of blackness . . . all of them watching me. The near side of the pool could provide another hiding place, not because of any shadow but because the concrete edge, itself, blocked my view of whatever might be waiting beneath it.

If he preferred to stay dry, an assailant might simply wait for me, nearby but out of sight, with his back pressed to the very wall of the house. I wouldn't be able to spot him there until I'd opened the door and leaned out. And that might be the end of me.

Or he might position himself around the corner to jump me in the space between the house and the garage.

Do you see what I mean about safety?

I stared out the door for a very long time. Even though I saw nobody, I couldn't quite force myself to move. I kept thinking about all the places where someone *might* be.

My breath kept fogging up the glass. I guess that's because the air conditioner was on in the house. Every now and then, a milky white cloud would ruin my view. I had to sway to one side or another, or crouch, in order to find some clear glass. Sometimes, I wiped away the fog with my hand or forearm or the front of my robe.

The way I'm telling it, you must think I was standing there forever and that I'm a hopeless coward.

It sort of *felt* like forever, but it probably wasn't more than fifteen or twenty minutes.

And even though I'm not the bravest person in the world, it's a fact that I'd made the trip from the house to the garage many times in the past, often at very late hours of the night. Serena and Charlie did a lot of traveling. I'd lived above their garage for three years, and I *always* came over when they were away.

Sometimes, I hardly gave a glance out the door before sliding it open and walking out. That was rare, but it happened. More often, I spent five or ten minutes. A couple of times, I'd been so spooked that it had taken me more than an hour to work up my courage to leave.

But I'd *always* gone, sooner or later.

So I wouldn't call myself a hopeless coward.

I'm a *hopeful* one.

Finally, you decide it's time. You *hope* nobody's out there waiting to jump you, because you can't be sure. Then you take a deep breath, flip open the lock, roll open the door, and go for it.

That night, the time finally came.

I was trembling quite a lot by then. Also, my robe was hanging open because I'd been using it to wipe the glass. I pulled it shut, tightened the silk belt, took a deep breath that trembled on its way in, and unfastened the lock.

I pulled, and the door rolled away to my right.

Things looked so much clearer, suddenly.

Just at that moment, before I'd even had a chance to step outside, someone crept out of the blackness at the edge of the woods.

I almost made a sudden break for the garage. But I held back.

If I darted out and ran, he would see me for sure.

And do what? Chase me down?

Holding my breath, staying absolutely motionless except for my right arm, I slowly reached sideways and found the door handle. I pulled gently, easing the door along its tracks. It made a soft rumbling sound, which the stranger didn't seem to hear.

As I slid the door shut in front of me, I kept my eyes on him.

If he noticed me, he gave no sign of it. His head didn't seem to be fixed in my direction. It turned this way and that. A few times, he even glanced over one shoulder or the other.

The full moon lit his hair and shoulders, but not his face. Most of his front was vague with shadow. I could make out his silhouette clearly, though. He was wearing shorts, but no shirt. When I caught a side view, he didn't seem to have breasts.

That was my big clue as to his gender.

The stranger still might've been a girl—maybe a thin and shapeless tomboy—but I doubted it.

This was a guy.

A guy who'd come sneaking out of the woods and was making his way closer and closer to the house.

Soon, the door bumped softly shut in front of me. I fastened its lock, then took one step backward and stopped.

I knew *exactly* what to do.

Hurry over to the telephone and call the police.

It's what I *intended* to do.

But the telephone was out of reach. To put my hands on it, I would need to abandon the glass door and make my way through the darkness to the other end of the couch.

That couldn't be done without losing sight of the intruder.

So I stood where I was, and watched him.

He still seemed unaware of my presence. Maybe that was an act, but I doubted it. Though he was stealthy about the way he approached the house, he didn't seem to be in any hurry.

Maybe he cut the phone line and knows I can't call for help.

Don't be ridiculous, I told myself. That's movie stuff, cutting phone lines. Nobody does it in real life.

Do they?

More than likely, he didn't even know I was in the house: I'd turned off the lights fifteen or twenty minutes before he put in his appearance. For all he knew, nobody was home.

But how long had he been watching?

What if he'd started watching *before* the lights went out?

Suppose he's been watching me all day?

When that thought shoved its way into my mind, I suddenly felt sick with fear.

What does he want?

Maybe nothing. Maybe he's just a guy who happens to enjoy wandering around in the middle of the night. Maybe just someone who got lost in the woods and only now has managed to find his way out.

Or a harmless nut of some kind.

Or . . .

A burglar. A rapist. A killer.

Trembling, I watched him step onto the concrete directly across the pool from where I stood.

He had no weapons or tools that I could see.

But his shorts had pockets.

Near the edge of the pool, he stopped. He seemed to stare straight at me.

He can't see me, I told myself. The room's completely dark. The moon is probably glaring on the door glass.

His head swiveled slowly from side to side. He turned around in a complete circle as if to make sure he wasn't being observed. Then he took off his shorts.

They appeared to be cut-off jeans. First he had to unbuckle his belt. After the belt was open, he unfastened a button or snap at his waist and lowered the zipper. Bending over, he drew the shorts down his legs. Then he stepped out of them and stood up straight.

The moon, high in the sky behind him, rimmed his body with white so I could see right away that he didn't have on a stitch of clothing.

Though his front was poorly lighted, I could see the general gray of his bare skin all the way from his face down to his feet. His eyes and mouth looked like dim smudges. His nipples were like an extra set of eyes spaced wide apart on his chest. His navel was just a small, dark dot. Down from there was more skin, then a nest of hair and his penis.

He stood there for a while as if he wanted me to take a good, long look at him—even though I *know* he couldn't see me standing on the other side of the glass door.

Then he looked around, turning his head and body. When he turned, I got a side view.

It made me feel a little sick.

And very frightened.

He wants to shove that into me.

No, he doesn't, I told myself. He doesn't even know I'm here.

He'd better not. If he knows, he won't quit till he nails me with that thing.

The prowler sat down on the concrete, swung his legs over the edge of the pool, scooted forward and slid down into the water.

3

IN THE WATER

You suddenly couldn't see him at all. He'd vanished. I stared at where he'd been, but he was gone as if he'd turned invisible.

Not invisible, but black.

The pool looked empty. I knew it wasn't, though.

I pictured him swimming underwater for a few more seconds, then bursting out, hurling himself onto the pool's edge and dashing at my door.

The door might slow him down, but it wouldn't stop him.

I mean, it was *glass*.

I tried to prepare myself for the shock of a sudden assault.

Don't scream, just turn around and run like hell.

Go for the kitchen.

Grab one of the butcher knives.

I saw him.

Out near the middle of the pool, the back of his head and then his buttocks slid across the moonlight's silver path. He seemed to be on his way to the shallow end, doing a leisurely breast stroke.

Not coming for me, after all.

Not yet.

But the pool had tile stairs underwater at a corner of the shallow end. When he came to them, he might climb out.

I stepped a little closer to the glass door.

He didn't swim toward the stairs. Instead, he kept to the center. At the end of the pool, he stood up. His wet skin gleamed in the moonlight, but only down to his waist. There, the black water cut him off. He looked as if he'd lost his lower body—legs, ass, and the all the rest—as if whacked apart by a terrible sword.

The saber.

I suddenly remembered Charlie's saber. It hung on hooks above the fireplace in the living room, along with a framed citation that had something to do with the Civil War service of his great-great-grandfather.

The saber was an actual relic of the war.

It hadn't belonged to Charlie's ancestor, though; Serena had bought it for him as a Christmas present.

We'd all fooled around with it, now and then.

It was about four feet long, and sharp.

Out in the pool, the stranger turned around. He eased down into the water, his body disappearing until nothing was left except his face. Then he started swimming again, apparently on his way to the deep end.

I stepped backward, turned away from the glass door and went to get the saber.

I'd forgotten that the foyer light was on. It was halfway down the long corridor, too far away for its brightness to reach the doorway of the den. But I saw it the moment I stepped out. Seeing the foyer light, I also remembered that the living room curtains were wide open.

The wall out there was mostly glass from one end to the other, from floor to ceiling. Like the wall of an aquarium.

From anywhere near the deep end of the pool, the stranger would have a fine view in.

I muttered a curse.

To be honest about it, I said "Shit."

I hated my stupidity for not remembering to shut the curtains before dark. Bad enough that I'd missed out on popcorn because they were open, but now I couldn't even go for the saber.

Obviously, I *could* go for it if I wanted to.

But I'm not that stupid.

Suppose, so far, the guy had no idea that anyone was in the house? He sees me sneaking through the living room, trying to get the saber, and he'll know I'm here.

He'll assume I'm alone.

Maybe he'll like the looks of me. Even though I'm no glamour queen, I've got a great figure and I *am* wearing a clingy, revealing robe.

And he is already naked and aroused.

Maybe, so far, he'd only been interested in a little midnight skinny-dipping. But seeing me . . .

No way.

I wasn't going to risk it.

I'll wait till he tries to break in.

And maybe he won't, I thought. Maybe he really did come here only to use the swimming pool. He might do a few laps, then walk back into the woods and that'll be the end of it.

He might be breaking in right now.

I stepped back into the den. This time, I shut the door behind me to make sure no light could possibly sneak in from the foyer.

It had already dimmed my night vision. Except for the outside glow coming through the glass door, everything in the den looked much darker than before.

From where I stood, I could only see a small section of the pool. The stranger wasn't in sight, and that worried me. So I hurried.

My bare left foot kicked a leg of the coffee table. From the sound, you'd think I'd struck the table with a hammer. My toes crumpled. Pain rushed up my leg. Tears flooded my eyes. My mouth flew open to let out a cry of agony, but I kept quiet and hobbled sideways and fell backward onto the couch. The couch scooted and bumped the wall. Flinging my leg up, I clutched my ruined foot.

From the feel of things, I figured two or three toes might be broken.

But the pain subsided after a couple of minutes.

Wet-faced and breathless, I fingered my toes. I wiggled them. They felt sore and kind of tired, but they seemed okay otherwise.

I wondered what the stranger was up to.

But I no longer wanted to look. I wanted to remain right where I was. The couch felt good under my back, even though my rear end was hanging off the cushion and I had to keep at least one foot planted on the floor to stop myself from sliding off.

Maybe I should swing my legs up, make myself comfortable, and stay put.

I wasn't *required* to stand at the door and watch the stranger swim his laps.

He would go away, sooner or later.

Go away, or break in.

If he tries to break in, I'll go for the saber. If he doesn't, I'll just . . .

What if I don't hear him?

Such a huge house, he could make almost any kind of noise at the other end and I'd be none the wiser. Especially now that I'd shut the den door.

Also, there was the air conditioner.

The house had central air.

I couldn't hear its machinery. The compressor, or whatever, was outside and pretty far away. But the den had a couple of vents and an air intake. They didn't make enough noise to notice, usually. Just soft, breezy, breathy sounds. But now they seemed as loud as a gale.

The stranger could hurl a brick through the living-room window and I probably wouldn't hear it.

Turn off the air.

The control box was mounted on the hallway wall, not far

from the den. Only minutes ago, I'd been standing within reach of it. Too bad I hadn't thought to reach out and flick it off. But my mind had been on the saber, not on the quiet noise of the air conditioner.

So, do it now.

I pushed myself off the couch and stood up. My toes ached, but not badly. I hardly limped at all on my way to the door. I wrapped my hand around its knob.

And suddenly wished, badly, that I hadn't shut it.

What if I open it and he's standing right there?

I pictured him on the other side of the door, naked and hard, dripping water onto the hallway carpet, grinning at me. He'd grabbed Charlie's saber on his way through the house, and held it overhead with both hands like a Samurai all eager to split me down the middle.

My imagination likes to torture me with stuff like that.

I figured he probably wasn't really there, or even in the house at all.

But my hand and arm felt frozen. I couldn't force myself to open the door.

Then all of a sudden I got to thinking the knob might start to turn in my hand and *he* might throw the door open, crashing it into me and rushing in.

This was just my imagination at work, and I knew it.

But it scared me.

I let go of the knob and backed away from the door, pretty much expecting it to fly open. But it stayed shut. So then I turned around and faced the sliding glass door.

From where I stood, I could see the pool. Not much of it, though.

And not the stranger.

Where is he?

This time, I was extra careful crossing the room. My feet hit nothing. As I neared the door, I put a hand forward. Soon, my fingers touched the cool glass.

I eased closer, peering out.

Still no sign of him.

When my breasts met the glass, I stopped. This was about as close to the door as I could get without bumping my nose or forehead.

I stared out.

Where'd he go?

He didn't seem to be in the pool, and he obviously wasn't standing nearby on the concrete or lawn.

Maybe he'd gone away.

Maybe he's already in the house.

The chill from the glass, seeping through my robe, was making my nipples ache. I eased back a little to get away from it.

The glass in front of my face had fogged up, so I wiped it with my hand.

And that's when I saw him.

He was in the pool, after all.

Maybe he'd been below the surface for a while. Or maybe he'd been floating somewhere that I couldn't see him.

Anyway, there he was.

He drifted on his back near the middle of the pool, his arms spread out, his legs apart. He didn't move a muscle. The water, calm and almost motionless itself, rippled around him, turned him slowly, eased him along as if it had a vague destination for him but wasn't in any hurry.

His wet skin shone like silver in the moonlight.

He looked asleep.

He was probably awake, though, feeling the lift of the water beneath him, enjoying its cool lick, relishing the warm breezes drifting over the regions of his skin that weren't below the surface.

He looked as if he might be waiting for a lover to come, drawn to him by his open naked body, lured by the invitation of the pillar of flesh that stood tall and ready, shiny in the moonlight.

What if it's me?

What if he's waiting for me?

He wants me, knows I'm watching, thinks he can lure me out of the house.

You've got another think coming, buster. You can wave that thing in the air till hell freezes over, or IT does. I'm not stepping one foot outside.

Just because he looked beautiful in the moonlight didn't mean he wasn't a rapist, a killer, a madman.

There *had* to be something wrong with him. A normal person doesn't sneak out of the woods in the middle of the night, strip naked and go for a dip in the swimming pool of a total stranger.

Maybe he knows Charlie or Serena and they told him it's okay.

That hadn't occurred to me before.

But it seemed highly unlikely. Virtually impossible. For one thing, they wouldn't give someone permission to use the pool in their absence without telling me about it. After all, I'd *be* here and take him for an intruder.

For another thing, I knew all their friends. The man in the pool wasn't one of them.

I didn't think so, anyway.

It was hard to tell exactly what his face looked like, but I was pretty sure that a body as fine as his didn't belong to anyone I'd ever seen around the house or pool.

Serena and Charlie were sociable people. They *did* like to invite friends over for pool parties. But I was the only one with permission to use it when they were away. That's another reason I knew this guy didn't belong here.

Nobody but me was allowed in the pool when they weren't home.

As far as I knew, anyway.

And I knew plenty. I'd been living over the garage for three years, and I could see the pool from my windows.

People just didn't show up and start using it. Whenever I'd seen anyone at the pool, Serena or Charlie or both of them had been there, too.

Of course, I hadn't spent all my time watching for pool activity. Things might've gone on, now and then, that I didn't know about.

But not much.

I've seen squirrels, raccoons, deer and other animals come out of the woods to drink at the pool. I've watched Charlie swim his laps at dawn when he probably assumed I was asleep. I've even observed the times, fairly often in the summer, when Serena and Charlie went skinny-dipping late at night. They kept the pool lights off, of course, and spoke in whispers or not at all. Whenever they used the pool that way, they always ended up making love. They did it right out in the open, so they must've figured I was asleep or blind. Whereas, actually, I happened to be looking out my window.

I was looking out my window more than anyone would've guessed, but I'd never found a *stranger* in the pool.

Not until tonight.

He'd hardly moved at all in the past few minutes. Just drifted this way and that on his back. I began to wonder if maybe he'd fallen asleep. If asleep, he must've been having a doozy of a dream.

The telephone rang.

After midnight, and it suddenly let out a loud jangle in the silence and darkness of the den.

I jumped and yelped.

Out on the pool, the stranger's head jerked sideways in the water. I couldn't see his eyes, but I knew he was staring straight at me.

4

THE PHONE CALL

Not that he could see me.

If you're in real darkness and someone else is out in the moonlight, he doesn't stand a chance of spotting you.

But I felt his eyes on me.

I flinched as the phone rang again.

A phone isn't meant to ring that late at night. It scares you. Even if you're *not* alone in the house and spying on a prowler, the ringing rips through your nerves.

Friends don't call after nine. Not unless there's an emergency.

It rang again, and I flinched again.

Out in the pool, the man rolled over, turned and started gliding toward me with his head up.

The phone rang again as I took slow backward steps away from the glass door.

Why did it have to be so loud?

I knew he could hear it. Maybe not this particular phone, but a general clamor. I'd been swimming in the pool myself, sometimes, when people called. Even with the doors and windows shut, you could hear rings and chirps and warbles and tweets from all over the house. I don't even know how many phones Serena had, but at least five—maybe seven or eight. It was a big house, and there were phones in nearly every room.

The only answering machine was in the den.

With me.

After the fourth ring came clicks that meant the machine was responding.

I kept creeping backward.

Outside, the stranger arrived at the side of the pool. He stood up, put his hands on the concrete edge, and seemed to stare straight at me.

I'm not big on distances. My guess, though—he was only twelve or fifteen feet away from the glass door. And I was on the other side of it, five or six feet back.

More clicks from the machine.

A man's voice said, "Ah, you finally got yourself an answering machine. Hope it's not because of me. But it probably is, huh? Who's the guy you got to record the greeting for you?" A pause. "Never mind. It's none of my business, I guess. Anyway, are you there? Judy? If you're there, would you pick up? Please? I know you probably don't want to talk to me, but . . . I don't want to lose you. I love you. Are you there? Please, talk to me."

He went silent.

The man in the pool jumped, planted a foot on the edge, and climbed out.

"The thing is, I'm not going to call again. I'm not going to beg you to change your mind. I'm not going to plead with you. I've got to hang on to a little of my dignity, you know?"

The man started walking slowly toward the glass door.

"So this'll be it. The ball's in your court. If you really want it to be over, fine. I'll accept that. I'll never bug you again. It'll be adios, Tony. Forever. I don't want that to happen, but hell . . . Are you there, Judy? It feels weird, talking to you this way. Would you please pick up, if you're there?"

The stranger arrived at the door and peered in.

Could he see me?

Could he hear the quick loud thudding of my heart?

I stood motionless, staring at him. He had his arms raised like a guy who's been ordered to "stick 'em up." His open hands were pressed against the glass. So was his forehead. But his nose didn't touch the glass. Neither did his chest or belly or legs. Nothing else touched except for the tip of his penis, which looked like a smooth and strange little face pushing against the glass to help him search for me.

"Okay," Tony said to the answering machine. "If that's how you want it. Anyway, I've moved to a new place. I couldn't stand being in the old apartment anymore, not after everything that'd happened there." He sounded as if he were trying not to cry. "I'll give you my number, and you can call me if you want to. If you don't call, I'll understand."

As Tony gave his new telephone number, the man outside took a step away from the door, reached down and grabbed the handle and jerked it.

Snatching up the phone with one hand, I blurted, "Tony!"

With my other hand, I slapped up the light switch.

A lamp came on by the couch.

The sudden brightness hurt my eyes, made me squint, obliterated my moonlit view of the stranger. The sliding door was now a mirror. It showed me a hollow, transparent version of the coffee table, the lamp, and me.

I saw myself with the phone against my left ear. I stood crooked, still bent sideways to the right as if frozen in my reach for the light switch. My belt had come loose. The open robe seemed to split me down the middle. It still covered my left side from shoulder to thigh, but my entire right side was bare to the gaze of the stranger.

If he was still there.

He must've leaped back when the light first came on.

Now he returned, looming out of the darkness just beyond the door and pressing his body against the glass.

Tony was talking into my ear. I didn't pay much attention, but he seemed to believe I was Judy.

The stranger gaped in at me. With his body pressed to the door, the lamplight reached him. He looked awful—grotesquely flattened and spread out—like an alien creature trying to ooze through the glass.

"HELLO!" I shouted into the phone. "POLICE! I WANT TO REPORT A PROWLER!"

"Huh?" Tony asked. "A prowler?"

The stranger writhed against the glass, licked it, rubbed it with his body and open hands as if making believe it was me.

From where I stood, it *looked* like me.

My reflection was superimposed over him.

He couldn't see that, though. And didn't need to, because he had a great view of the *real* me.

"YES! HE'S IN THE YARD! HE'S TRYING TO FORCE HIS WAY IN. THIS IS 3838 WOODSIDE LANE. YOU'VE GOT TO GET OVER HERE RIGHT AWAY!"

"Who is this? This isn't Judy?"

"HE'S A WHITE MALE, ABOUT TWENTY YEARS OLD, SIX FEET TALL, A HUNDRED AND EIGHTY POUNDS, WITH SHORT BLOND HAIR."

"Is this for real? Do you really have a prowler?"

"YES! AND HE'S NAKED, AND HE'S TRYING TO GET IN! YOU'VE GOT TO SEND A SQUAD CAR RIGHT AWAY!"

"Holy shit," Tony said.

"PLEASE HURRY!"

"Do you want me to hang up and call the police?"

Taking the phone away from my mouth, I yelled at the man, "THE COPS ARE ON THE WAY, YOU SICK BASTARD! THEY'LL BE HERE IN TWO MINUTES!"

I know he heard me, but he seemed to be lost in his own world of skin and glass and me.

Watching him, I saw myself. I looked like a ghost being molested by a mad, drooling mime. He writhed against me, caressed me, kissed me, then suddenly went rigid and started to jerk, shaking the door in its frame. For a moment, I thought he was having a seizure.

In a way, he was.

When I realized what was going on, I gasped and turned my head away.

My eyes met the light switch.

I shot my hand out and flipped it down. Darkness clamped down on the room.

The door stopped shaking.

I looked.

The stranger took a few steps backward, then whirled around. He ran to the edge of the pool, dived in, and swam for the other side.

While I watched him, I heard Tony's tiny, faint voice coming from the phone's earpiece down by my side.

The stranger boosted himself out of the pool, scurried over the concrete, swooped down and snatched up his shorts. He didn't put them on. Clutching them in one hand, he dashed onto the lawn and ran toward the woods.

I lifted the phone.

Tony sounded frantic. ". . . okay? Hello? What's happening?"

"I'm here," I said.

"What happened? What's going on?"

"I think it's all right now. He just ran away."

"You'd better call the cops."

"He thinks I just did. That's what scared him off."

"Maybe you'd better call them for real."

"I don't know. He's gone now."

"How do you know he won't come back?"

"Thanks a lot, Tony."

"Sorry. Are you okay?"

"Just a little shook up. I'm all by myself, and he came sneaking out of the woods behind the house."

"You said he was naked?"

"Yeah. Well, he took off his shorts and started swimming in the pool."

"Weird. You don't have any idea who he was?"

"Not a clue. Just some guy who came out of the woods."

"Miller's Woods?"

"Yeah."

"That's bad. A lot of real oddballs hang around in there."

"This is the first time anyone ever came sneaking out to use the pool. That I know about, anyway."

"You're lucky that's all he did."

"Yeah," I said. I thought about what he'd done on the door, but kept my mouth shut about it.

"You really should call the cops," Tony told me.

"I know. You're probably right."

"They keep finding bodies in those woods."

He wasn't telling me anything new. "Now and then," I said. "But most of them weren't *killed* there. They were just dropped off, you know? It's not like there's necessarily a homicidal maniac hanging around in the woods."

"*I* sure wouldn't want to live near them."

"Well, I don't mind. I like it, normally. It's nice and peaceful."

"You live there *alone?*"

"I'm alone tonight."

"Maybe you shouldn't be. I know you don't want to hear this, but you really *can't* be sure he won't come back."

"I wish you'd stop saying that."

"You sound like a nice person."

"Thanks."

"I'd hate to think you might end up . . . you know."

"I won't," I told him.

"Do you have a name?" he asked.

"No, actually I'm one of those people who isn't that lucky."

He laughed a little, and I smiled.

"My name's Alice," I said. (That isn't really what I told him. I told him my true name, which is a secret as far as this book is concerned . . . unless you're smart enough to find my hidden message.)

"Hello, Alice," he said.

"Hello, Tony." (Tony isn't his real name, either, by the way—in case you were daydreaming when you read the introduction. Tony, Serena, Charlie, Judy, etc.—all made up. The same goes for Miller's Woods, and so on. Just thought I'd remind you.)

"I guess I dialed a wrong number," Tony said.

"I guess you did."

"I was trying to call this gal . . ."

"I know. Judy. She must've dumped you, huh?"

"Something like that."

"You probably called her once too many times after midnight."

"Think so?"

"It scares people. You shouldn't do it."

"Maybe not."

"Besides which, it makes you sound desperate. If you want to get back on Judy's good side, you don't want her to think you're desperate about it."

"You're probably right."

"You bet I'm right."

"Good thing I dialed the wrong number," he said.

"I'm glad you did. My creepy visitor would probably *still* be here."

"So, what are you going to do?"

"Nothing. Go to bed, I guess."

"You shouldn't stay there. Not by yourself."

"I'll be fine."

"Is there a neighbor you could stay with for the rest of the night?"

"Not exactly. Nobody nearby."

"What about . . . ?"

"Anyway, I'll be fine. I really don't think he'll be coming back tonight. As far as he knows, the cops are on the way over."

"I hope you're right," Tony said.

"So do I."

"I'd hate to read about you in the paper."

"Me, too."

He laughed quietly. Then he said, "I'm serious about this, though. Is there a friend you can call? Someone who might be willing to come over? Maybe a relative?"

"None."

"What about heading over to a motel?"

"At this hour?"

"Most of them over by the highway are open all night. You might have to ring a bell, or something, but . . ."

"I'm not going to any motel. Are you kidding? I'm probably ten times safer staying right here than if I try to drive over to one of those places at this hour. Anyway, haven't you ever heard of Norman Bates?"

"You'll be fine if you don't take a shower."

"I'll just stay home and take one."

Tony was silent for a few moments. It made me wonder what he was thinking about. Then he said, "Look. Why don't I come over there? Just so you won't be alone in case this guy decides to try something."

His suggestion didn't come as a huge surprise. Still, it made me feel uneasy.

"I don't think so, Tony. Thanks for asking."

"I realize we don't know each other very well."

"We don't know each other period," I pointed out. "You called the wrong number and we've been talking for about five minutes. Now you want to come over?"

"I'm worried about you."

"Maybe you are and maybe you aren't. Maybe this whole thing's a set-up. It's pretty convenient, you just happening to call here when you did."

"I dialed the wrong number."

"Maybe you did and maybe you didn't."

"Jeez," he said.

For a few moments, he was silent.

Then he said, "Anyway, it's getting pretty late. I'd better hit the sack. Good luck with your intruder, Alice. It was nice talking to you. Pretty much. Bye."

He hung up.

5

EXIT

After that, I put down the phone and crept through the darkness to the sliding door.

The other side of the glass was smeared where the stranger had licked it, where he'd rubbed it with his wet face. It looked like a dirty car windshield after you've run wipers across it.

I found a clean place next to the mess his face had made, and peered out as if gazing over his shoulder.

The warnings from Tony made me nervous. Maybe the stranger *would* sneak back.

Maybe, next time, he wouldn't let a door stop him.

Not that it had actually *stopped* him, this time.

I could still picture him writhing against it.

Trying my best to ignore the image, I must've spent about ten minutes pressed to the glass. I had to make sure the coast was clear. But I couldn't get the awful picture out of my mind.

If he'd still been there—the glass gone—my right breast might've been pushing against his bare chest. He could've been squirming against me, rubbing me, spurting on me.

I finally stumbled backward to get away from the door.

The moonlight showed what he'd left on the glass.

It made me feel sick. Trembling, I turned away. I shut the curtains, then found my purse on the couch and made my way to the other door. I opened it and stepped into the hallway. This time, I was glad to see the foyer light.

This time, too, I wasn't afraid of being seen.

That's not quite true. The idea of being seen frightened me; it just didn't stop me. I walked swiftly down the hall and into the living room. Almost nothing showed on the other side of the glass wall. Just darkness. But the glass gave back an image of me.

Me, striding across the carpet, my purse swinging by my hip, the robe flowing around me, my legs flashing out long and bare as if the robe were an exotic gown with a slit up its front.

I looked like the heroine of a gothic romance.

Or a madwoman from a horror movie.

Especially when I reached up with both hands and lifted the saber off its hooks above the fireplace.

The saber felt good and heavy.

I stepped away from the fireplace, turned toward my dark image in the glass, and watched myself slash the air a few times.

Was *he* watching?

With the wall of glass in front of me and the foyer light behind my back, I could probably be seen clearly all the way from the edge of the woods.

I raised the saber high.

"You want me, pal?" I asked. "Come and get me."

I swung the blade a few more times.

I felt powerful and excited. I looked pretty cool, too.

But then I started to feel stupid and silly and even a little scared, so I turned away from the glass and hurried toward the foyer.

Normally, I would've left the house through the sliding door in the den. That was just my habit. It probably started because the den was where I spent most of my time, after dark. I'd be in it for hours watching the big-screen television, so I generally felt comfortable there and didn't want to wander through the huge, empty house to get out. So simple just to use the door that was there, slip outside, slide it shut and hurry over to the garage.

Not tonight.

I just couldn't. Not after what the stranger had done on the other side of it.

Somebody will have to clean that up, I thought.

Not me. Not tonight, anyhow.

Standing in the foyer, I wondered if there was anything I needed. I had my keys inside my purse. Since I planned to come back first thing in the morning, there was no reason to take my swimsuit, towel, oil, paperback, etc.

The doors were locked. I'd turned off all the lights except for those that were supposed to remain on all night.

I suddenly remembered the air conditioning.

Serena and Charlie usually turned it off before retiring— except when the weather was terribly hot.

When I was in command, I often forgot about the thing and left it going all night.

Since I'd just now thought of it, I rested the saber against my shoulder and marched up the hallway. At the thermostat, I flicked the switch to the Off position.

"What a good girl am I," I whispered.

Then I wondered which door to use.

Not the den door, that was for sure.

Serena and Charlie's bedroom had a sliding door. So did the living room, and the dining room beyond that. But all those doors could be seen from the back yard, the pool and the woods. If the stranger was watching, he might see me leave the house. He might even see me go to the garage.

And know where to find me.

I decided to leave by the front door.

First, though, I had to pee. The guest bathroom was just off the hall on my way back to the foyer, so I went in. I'd given little Debbie a Winnie the Pooh nightlight for her second birthday, and there it was, spreading a soft glow through the dark.

I didn't touch the switch for the overhead lights.

Late at night, it's always best to avoid turning on lights. At least if you're in a room with windows. The sudden brightness, where a moment earlier the windows had been patches of empty black, announces you to the world, gives away your exact location.

The bathroom had a pair of high, frosted windows that were clearly visible from nearly anywhere outside the front of the house.

So I settled for the light from Pooh bear.

With the door open and the lights off, I placed the saber and my purse on the rug just in front of the toilet. Then I took off the robe, draped it over a towel bar, and sat down.

Too bad I'd already shut off the air conditioning. Not because I suddenly felt hot, but because I was so noisy. Without the air going, the only sound in the house seemed to be me.

Talk about giving away your location!

Leaning forward, elbows on my knees, I could see out the open bathroom door. I kept watching. I half expected someone to drift by in the hallway, or come in.

The thoughts gave me gooseflesh. Prickly bumps sprouted all over me, the way they do sometimes when I try to squash a really awful spider in the corner of a ceiling and it gets away and falls on my bare arm.

I felt crawly all up and down my body.

Nobody showed up in the doorway, though.

Finally, I got finished. I was reluctant to flush, but did it anyway. In the silence, the noise of the flush was like a sudden roar.

So loud that *anything* might've happened somewhere else in the house: phones might've rung; somebody could have shouted out my name; the stranger might've smashed the glass of a window or door.

At last, the noise subsided.

I put the robe on, belted it shut, then crouched and picked up my purse and the saber. In the doorway, I stopped. I leaned forward, easing my head into the hall, and looked both ways.

Nobody.

Of course.

I stepped out and walked quickly to the front door.

Getting it unlocked and open would've been tricky with my left hand, since I'm a righty. So I switched the sword to my left hand. With the blade resting against my shoulder, I used my right hand to unfasten the deadbolt, turn the knob, and pull the door open.

It swept toward me.

For some reason, the porch light was off.

It shouldn't have been off.

And nobody should've been standing on the front stoop, but someone was.

A tall, dark figure reaching for me.

I shrieked.

Through the noise of my outcry, he said something. I couldn't hear it, though. Still shrieking, I swung the saber at him.

A left-handed, feeble try.

He staggered backward to avoid the blade.

It missed him, but he stumbled off the edge of the stoop and fell backward. He landed on the grass. A *whoomp* exploded out of him; the impact with the lawn must've knocked his wind out.

I leaped over the threshold, ran across the stoop and hopped down. Stradling his hips, I raised the saber high with both hands and swept it down as hard as I could.

It chopped his head down the middle, cleaving his face in half. It split his head open most of the way to his neck, but his jaw stopped the blade.

He thrashed and gurgled between my feet.

My saber was stuck, either between a couple of his lower front teeth or in the bone of his jaw. I shook it and tugged it. Instead of coming loose, it jerked his head this way and that.

At last, it came out.

I was all set to give him another chop, but he'd quit moving. He looked pretty dead.

Pretty isn't a great choice of words, under the circumstances. Anyway, there was no good reason to give him another whack.

I felt too shocked and worn out to do much of anything, so I just kept standing over him, his hips between my ankles. I had the sword clutched in my right hand, but held it off to the side so blood wouldn't rub off or drip on me.

I stood there for a long time.

Staring down at the body.

It was lit by the dim glow from a lamp near the driveway.

It wore a short-sleeved plaid shirt, blue jeans and loafers. No socks.

It sure wasn't my prowler.

I figured it was probably Tony.

6

DISCOVERIES

My guess was right.

When I finally recovered enough to move, I stepped away from him, put my saber down on the grass, then crouched beside him and searched the pockets of his jeans.

He had a comb and handkerchief in his left front pocket. A wallet in the left back pocket. In the right front, a leather key case and some coins. In the right back, a pistol.

A pistol!

Had he come here planning to stand guard and protect me?

Or to use the gun against me?

I put his things into the pockets of my robe, but the gun was too heavy. It felt like a hand tugging down on my pocket. Afraid it might ruin the robe, I took it out and carried it.

Back inside the house, I shut the door. I sat down on the cool marble floor of the foyer and inspected my findings.

The white handkerchief looked clean. I didn't study the comb very closely; combs can be gross. He had eighty-five cents in change. Six keys in his leather case. Thirty-eight dollars in the bill compartment of his wallet.

The wallet was *full* of stuff, but I won't bore you with a list. I'll cut to the chase, as they say. It contained two foil-wrapped condoms—meant for me?—and a driver's license that identified him as Anthony Joseph Romano.

His date of birth was two years earlier than mine, which made him twenty-eight. The photo must've been taken a few years ago, because he hardly looked old enough to be out of high school. He had short blond hair, freckles across his nose, and a friendly smile.

It made me feel bad, looking at him.

Knowing I'd killed him.

He'd probably driven over here to protect me. Nothing more sinister than that.

He thought he was being a good guy.

Like they say, "No good deed goes unpunished."

I felt rotten about killing him, but not particularly guilty. It wasn't *my* fault he paid me a surprise visit and got his head chopped open for the trouble. I hadn't *invited* him over.

He should've minded his own business.

Not only had he gotten himself killed, but he'd put *me* into a horrible situation.

What was I supposed to do now?

I stopped looking at his photo, and checked the address on his driver's license. 4468 Washington Avenue, Apt. 212. (Sounds like a real address, doesn't it? I made it up.) I knew the general area. It wasn't far from here. Less than ten minutes. After hanging up the phone, he must've grabbed his pistol and hurried right out to his car . . .

No.

He probably hadn't come here from the Washington Avenue address. He'd moved to a new place because of all the memories. That's one of the reasons he'd tried to phone Judy—to let her know his new phone number.

Unless he'd made the move a couple of months ago, the address on his driver's license almost had to be wrong.

I gave the wallet another search. Sure enough, tucked into the bill compartment was a folded slip of paper with an address scribbled on it in pencil: 645 Little Oak Lane, Apt. 12. (But not really.) This was probably his new address.

I put the paper back where I'd found it, set the wallet aside, and picked up the pistol.

It was a small, stainless steel .22 automatic with a black plastic handle. The fine print in the steel told me that it was a Smith & Wesson.

The safety wasn't on.

I dropped the loaded magazine into my hand, then pulled back the slide. Tony didn't have a bullet in the chamber. I shoved the magazine back up the handle until it clicked into place, then worked the slide, watching through the port to make sure it fed in a round. Then I thumbed the safety on.

After that, I just kept sitting there.

I didn't have the energy to get up.

Besides, get up and do *what?*

Deal is, I didn't know what to do next. So I just sat there, staring.

I've *gotta* do something, I kept telling myself.

What's the best course of action if you've just butchered an innocent man?

The answer probably seems obvious to you: call the cops and tell them the whole truth about everything.

Or fudge a little, maybe. Claim that he was holding the pistol when I opened the door. To make that version work, I would only have to take the gun outside and put it into his hand.

Which hand? That always trips up the criminals on TV. They stick the gun into the right hand of a lefty.

I'm a tad smarter than that.

Tony'd been carrying the weapon in his right rear pocket. Also, he'd reached for me with his right hand.

Reached for *me?* Maybe he'd been reaching for the door-bell button.

In either case, the evidence seemed to prove him a righty.

Not that it mattered. I had no intention of planting the pistol on him.

I had no intention of calling the cops, either.

Right now, you're probably thinking, *Oh, you stupid idiot! A guy you've never seen before in your life showed up in the middle of the night with a gun! It's a clear case of self-defense! Call the cops right now! Fess up! They probably won't even charge you with anything!*

Wrong.

Calling the police might be smart for *you* to do, but you're probably one of those people who's never gotten in trouble. A good, upstanding citizen.

If I were you, I probably *would* call the cops and admit everything. And I'm sure it'd turn out hunky-dory.

But I'm not you.

I'm me, alias Alice.

I could've gotten away with calling about the prowler. I might have actually done it, too, if the phone had been handy. It would've been safe. My troubles were several years earlier and in a different state. Cops coming over to save me from a prowler wouldn't even know about me or what I'd done.

But if they came to investigate Tony's death, they'd investigate me.

They'd run my prints.

Find out who I am.

After that, I wouldn't stand a chance.

So Tony had to go.

Tony *and* his car, if he'd driven one here.

Obviously, I had a long night ahead of me. But I stayed sitting on the marble floor for a while longer, wondering what to do first, where to start.

Finally, I decided to start by changing my clothes.

No matter what I might end up doing, I didn't want to do it wearing Charlie's robe. I liked the robe too much. It was bound to get bloody if I kept it on.

Whatever got bloody would have to be destroyed.

For that reason, I couldn't wear clothes belonging to Serena or Charlie. I wasn't eager to sacrifice any of my own clothes, either, but figured it had to be done.

Which meant a trip to my place above the garage.

Now that my mind was made up, I stuffed Tony's hanky and comb and everything else into the pockets of my robe. Everything except the pistol. I held on to that.

Then I went out the front door again.

I didn't plan to go back inside the house until everything was taken care of, so I locked the door and shut it after me.

Just for the hell of it, I went over to the porch light, reached up and gave the bulb a twist.

It turned easily.

The light came on, almost blinded me.

"Very interesting," I muttered.

Had Tony loosened it? Had someone else? Or had the bulb simply worked its way loose all on its own, with nobody's help? (Light bulbs do that, you know. Almost as if they're living creatures unscrewing themselves for sport or for reasons we'll never guess.)

I left it screwed in.

All the better to see by.

Here's the deal: I wasn't worried about anyone noticing Tony's body on the lawn. That could only happen if a person came down the driveway.

Not likely to happen at this hour of the night—or morning.

His body couldn't be seen from the street because a thick, tall hedge stood in the way. Hedges also ran along both sides of the lawn.

In addition to that, we had no neighbors.

None close enough to worry about, anyway.

There were vacant lots to the right and left, and a string of vacant lots across the road. The nearest house, a couple of lots to the left, was empty and up for sale. The nearest occupied house stood about a quarter of a mile to the right, and on the other side of the road.

We were pretty much alone out here.

It couldn't hurt to leave the light on. But then I thought, why take the risk? I wouldn't have any use for the porch light until I came back from the garage.

As I reached up for the bulb, though, my eyes strayed over to Tony.

I hadn't really seen him before. Not in halfway good light, anyway.

From the chin up, he was a horrible wreck.

You wouldn't recognize him as the guy in his driver's license photo.

He looked like a nightmare.

Considering the gory ruin of his head, I was surprised to notice how clean his clothes seemed to be.

With the light still on, I went over to him and checked more carefully. His shirt had a few spots of blood on it, but nothing obvious. His jeans seemed fine.

Why not?

First, I took the purse off my shoulder and removed my robe. I left them on the dry concrete of the front stoop.

Then I crouched over Tony and stripped him. It wasn't easy, especially because the night was so hot. Even though I'm in pretty good shape, I ended up out of breath and sweaty.

When I was done, I slipped into his loafers. They were a little too big for me, but I could walk in them okay. I carried his jeans and shirt over to the stoop and dropped them.

Then I stretched out naked on my back for a rest.

The concrete felt cool and nice.

Too nice. I could hardly force myself to get moving again.

Finally, though, I stood up to put his clothes on. I started with the shirt. It was very large, and hung halfway down my thighs. But it would do just fine. Next, I slipped his shoes off and climbed into the blue jeans.

They were way too big. When I had them all the way up around my waist, my feet were still inside the denim legs. Also, I had a huge amount of spare room inside the waistband. Looking down the gap, I could see all the way to my knees. I fastened the belt, anyway. It had enough holes to let me cinch it tight and keep the jeans from falling. With that taken care of, I bent over and rolled up the legs. The cuffs reached almost to my knees. I looked like I was wearing waders.

The jeans felt too hot and too heavy.

I needed them, though. I wanted the pockets; otherwise, I could've gotten rid of the jeans and just worn the shirt like a dress.

What I finally did was use the saber to cut the legs off. I took the legs off very high, then slit the sides almost up to the belt.

After that, the jeans felt light and airy.

What was left of them.

I returned all of Tony's belongings to the pockets where I'd found them. I also slipped my own key case into a pocket.

Then I unlocked the front door and went back inside the house, but only long enough to put my purse and Charlie's robe in the living room.

I left again.

Reaching up, I unscrewed the porch bulb. It was pretty hot by then, and made my fingertips smart.

7

CLEAN UP

Ever try to carry around a dead guy?

Let me tell you, it isn't easy.

So I left Tony sprawled on the lawn, right where he'd fallen, and went hiking up the driveway without him.

On the road, just to the right of the driveway entrance, a car was parked at the curb. It was the only car in sight.

The driver's door was locked, but one of Tony's keys did the trick. I climbed in and tried a key in the ignition. The engine started. Keeping the headlights off, I swung away from the curb, did a U-turn, and drove into the driveway.

When the trunk seemed to be even with Tony, I stopped the car. I got out and opened the trunk. It looked pretty empty except for the spare tire. Leaving it open, I went over to Tony.

I picked up his legs by the ankles, turned him, and started dragging him toward the driveway. The grass was still wet from the sprinklers. The wetness helped his body slide, but also made my footing tricky. A couple of times, my feet flew out from under me and I landed on my butt, which didn't feel too swift.

By the time we reached the edge of the driveway, I knew we had a problem. Not to be too graphic about it, his split head had left a trail across the grass. The stuff on the grass wasn't what worried me, though. Most of it would go away after the automatic sprinkling system had gone through a few cycles. Birds, ants, and so forth would take care of the rest. The problem, for me, was whatever might get on the driveway. I didn't want to wake up in the morning and find bloodstains on the concrete. They'd be hard to get rid of.

At first, the only possible solution seemed to be a plastic bag over Tony's head to catch whatever might want to slop out.

But I was in no mood to run around hunting for a bag.

Finally, I came up with a simple answer to the problem. All I had to do was turn the car sideways so its rear jutted out over the grass.

So that's what I did. The driveway was wide enough to make it fairly simple.

I lined the car up with Tony, backed up until the rear tires almost went off the edge of the driveway, then climbed out and looked at him.

Loading his body into the trunk was going to be a bear.

And messy, too.

But it couldn't be avoided.

Before getting started, I took off the shirt and cut-off jeans and tossed them onto the driver's seat. For one thing, I didn't want them to get gory. For another, the night was too hot for clothes, especially if you're doing hard work.

I stepped out of the shoes and left them on the driveway.

Then I walked onto the slippery wet grass, straddled Tony's hips, bent down, clutched his wrists and straightened up, pulling him. His back came off the ground. But then, instead of continuing to rise, he slid on his butt and went scooting between my legs. I scurried backward, trying to stay with him, and bumped into the rear of the car.

"Shit!"

He was up to his waist beneath the car like a grease monkey going under to make repairs.

Hanging on to his wrists, I waddled forward to drag him out. He just lay beneath me, staring at the show while I hobbled over him, my breasts lurching from side to side between my down-stretched arms.

By the time I'd left his head behind me, I was doubled over like a contortionist, my arms straining backward between my legs. At last, he started to slide.

I shuffled onward, pulling him.

He finally cleared the car. By then, I was huffing and sweaty again.

I sat down on the rear bumper.

"Should've minded your own business," I muttered. "You wouldn't be dead, for one thing. For another, you wouldn't be putting *me* through all this shit."

He didn't answer.

He probably figured, though, that I didn't have much room for complaining. I was still alive, after all, whereas he wasn't. I was inconvenienced, but he was toes up.

"This is more than a little inconvenience, buddy," I told him. "This is a major pain in the ass."

The night was way too hot for such work. Sweat was pouring down my body. It made my eyes sting. It tickled my sides and back.

How nice it would've been, just then, to go around back and jump in the pool.

Thinking about the pool, I remembered the prowler. A funny thing, though. The thought of him didn't frighten me, disgust me, thrill me—nothing. He'd lost all his powers to intimidate or fascinate me. Probably the moment I put the saber through Tony's head.

His fault.

All his fault.

True enough, I thought. That bastard got Tony killed as sure as if he'd been the one swinging the sword.

I oughta kill his ass for doing this to Tony and me.

If I went swimming, he might show up and give me the chance. I should take the pistol or saber with me, just in case.

But which?

I couldn't exactly *swim* with either weapon.

Forget it. Forget which weapon to take, forget having a swim. Time's a-wasting.

Tony had to be dealt with.

I tried again.

This time, I straddled his head instead of his hips. Bending down, I jammed my open hands underneath his shoulders and grabbed his armpits. When I lifted him, he started to slide away. Instead of letting him go, I hauled back on him, pulled him against me and hoisted him up.

His full weight shoved against my chest.

Instead of rushing forward and throwing him headlong into the trunk, the way I'd figured, I found myself suddenly staggering backward. I fell, and he came down on top of me. His split-open head mashed against my face.

I wanted to scream.

But you can't scream with your mouth shut. God knows, I kept it shut. If I hadn't, it might've ended up full of Tony's brains or whatever.

So the scream only happened in my mind.

Twisting and bucking, I threw him off me.

I crawled away from him. Still on my hands and knees, I lost my steak supper on the grass. The steak, and then some. I couldn't stop vomiting. After a while, nothing came out except slobber.

Finally, I did stop. I crawled away from the glop, stayed on all fours while I tried to catch my breath, then struggled to my feet. Bending over, I put my hands on my knees. I stayed that way for a few minutes.

I felt stuff sticking to my face.

When I had the strength to move again, I wiped my face with both hands, then squatted and rubbed my hands against the damp grass.

I wanted to take a shower.

I wanted to *scrub* Tony off me.

His blood and goo.

But that would have to wait. First I needed to deal with his body.

I wandered over to it, being careful where I stepped with my bare feet.

"What the hell am I gonna do with you?" I asked.

"That's *your* problem," he seemed to tell me. "You should've thought of that before you split my head open, you dumb bitch."

He was sprawled face down, the way he'd landed after I threw him off me.

I grabbed the elastic waistband of his skivvies, hoisted him to his knees and started dragging him backward. We made it about halfway to the trunk of the car before the elastic gave out. The shorts tore away, and he flopped.

I tossed the useless rag into the trunk, straddled his butt, grabbed him by the knobs of his hip bones and hauled him up.

It seemed to be working.

I reared back, bringing him higher and higher.

Then my hands slipped off his hips. I wasn't ready for that. Not at all. I flew backward, slammed the rear of the car and tumbled into the trunk with my feet kicking at the sky.

It hurt so much that my eyes filled with tears.

He was *dead*, but beating up on me.

And *defeating* me.

"Bastard!" I shouted at him.

I could almost hear him laughing at me.

Crying, I twisted my body around and crawled out of the trunk.

Tony was sprawled on the grass.

"Think you can beat me?" I asked him.

"Think it?" I could hear him taunt me. "I *know* it! You're too weak to get me in the trunk. I'm too big, and you're too weak. I'll still be lying here tomorrow when the sun comes up. I'll still be lying here *next week* when Serena and Charlie come home."

"Oh, no you won't," I said.

But he was right in a way.

Not about me being too weak. I was in great shape, and I probably *could've* lifted him if everything hadn't been so wet and slippery.

He was right about his size.

He was too *big*.

I took care of that with the saber.

He lost ten or eleven inches very quickly.

I figured his head wouldn't make that much difference, though. It probably didn't weigh more than ten or fifteen pounds. So after tossing it into the trunk, I removed both his arms. They didn't come off as easily as his head. I couldn't just whack them off with a couple of good blows, but had to really work at it. And the arms were easy compared to his legs.

This was very rough work for a hot night.

When I had Tony down to his torso, I stuck the sword in the ground, got down on my knees, wrapped my arm around his chest, and picked him up.

At that point, he was still pretty heavy.

But manageable.

His torso shook the car when I dumped it into the trunk on top of his other parts.

I slammed the trunk shut.

By then, I was *really* tuckered out.

Not to mention filthy.

So exhausted I could hardly walk, I stumbled away from the driveway, found a clean place on the lawn, and flopped. The cool, wet grass felt wonderful. I lay on my back, panting for air, sweat pouring off my body.

In my mind, I was floating on the cool water of the pool.

That's how I'll spend tomorrow, I told myself. This whole mess will be over by then, and I'll do nothing all day except float around in the pool and drink ice-cold cocktails and sunbathe.

Something in the grass under my back started to bother me. A stone or a twig, probably. It had been pushing against me from the start, but I'd been too worn out to care.

Now, I rolled over to get away from it.

Flat on my stomach, I crossed my arms under my face. They were sticky, though, and didn't smell very good, so I got them away from my face and spread them out. With nothing for a pillow, I lowered my head onto the lawn.

But I didn't like having my face in the grass.

The grass tickled. Especially where it brushed against my eyelid and lips. Also, I wondered what sort of bugs might be under me. I didn't want ants or spiders crawling on my face, getting into my nostrils, my mouth, my eyes.

For that matter, I didn't like the idea of bugs crawling on me *anywhere*.

I wondered what might be drawn to me by the smell of Tony's blood.

Before you know it, I felt tiny creatures scurrying all over my bare skin. Most of them were probably just in my mind, but they seemed real enough.

That ended my rest period.

I got to my feet and staggered across the lawn. At the front of the house, in the space between a couple of bushes, was a coiled garden hose. Charlie used it, every so often, to wash the car in the driveway.

I used it to wash me.

The first water to blast out of the nozzle was warm from cooking inside the hose all day. I aimed the hard stream at my hands and forearms. It hit me with such force that it hurt, but it sure knocked the blood and filth off me.

Even before I finished hosing off my arms, cold water was shooting out. I adjusted the nozzle. The rough, narrow rod of shooting water spread out and became a spray. I could've made it a gentle, light shower, but I kept it powerful enough to do the job.

Raising the nozzle, I aimed down at the top of my head. The water drummed my skull, froze my scalp, matted my hair, rushed all the way down my body. I flinched under the frigid attack. I cringed and shuddered. After the first shock, though, it didn't feel so horrible. The spray was no less cold, but I must've been getting used to it. Pretty soon, it seemed pleasantly cool.

I moved the nozzle around, spraying myself straight in the face, under my arms and down my sides, and so on. When the water hit certain areas—where I was still especially hot—it again felt ice cold.

Soon, I was as clean as I could get without soap and hot water.

I felt human again.

But thirsty. Afraid of choking if I shot the water straight into my mouth, I aimed the nozzle sideways in front of my lips, darted my head forward and took bites out of the spray. It worked pretty well. But sometimes I didn't get away quickly enough. Then, the water pelted the inside of my cheek, making quick hollow tapping sounds, and flooded my mouth. I ended up choking a couple of times, but nothing serious.

After taking care of my thirst, I went on spraying myself.

Why stop?

For one thing, it made me feel so much better after all that hot, dirty work.

For another, I deserved a treat. I'd gotten Tony safely stowed inside the trunk of his car, so the worst part of the job was over. Now, it was just a matter of driving him away.

But to where?

Until I could figure out a good place to leave his car, there was no reason to quit enjoying the hose.

Just take it somewhere far away, I thought. The farther away, the better.

Oh, really? How do you think you'll get home?

How far away is *his* place? I wondered. Not the old place, but the new one. Which street was it on?

I tried to picture the writing on the slip of paper in his wallet.

Little Oak Lane!

Not far away, at all.

Well, four or five miles, but I could walk a distance like that in about an hour.

What if I drop the car off—with him in it—right where he lives?

Perfect!

They might not find his body for days.

And when they do, they won't have a clue as to where he went to get himself killed.

That matter solved, I dragged the hose across the lawn, being careful not to step in anything nasty. Along the way, I stopped and gave the saber a long, hard squirt. It was planted half a foot deep in the earth, and vibrated as the water struck it.

When I got in range of Tony's car, I twisted the nozzle. The spray tightened into a stiff tube of water that reached all the way. My aim was too high, at first. The water slammed against the rear window and seemed to explode off the glass, sending a shower skyward while most of the water sluiced down the top of the trunk. I lowered the nozzle slightly and hit the edge of the trunk lid dead on, nailed it where I'd touched it the most and where it was most bloody. The water blasted it, rumbling and bursting away.

Then I did the rear bumper, then the back tires.

Done with the car, I adjusted the nozzle to make a soft spray. For a while, I watered the lawn. Along with the lawn, I watered whatever of Tony was spread around. Even in the lousy yellow light from the porch and nearby lamps, I could see rusty stains on the grass, and small bits of him. My vomit, too.

Soon, the grass looked green again.

I carried the hose back to its place near the front of the house, arranged it in a proper coil, gave my hands a final rinse, then reached in between the bushes and shut the water off.

Not much remained to be done.

I gathered the two denim legs that I'd cut from Tony's jeans. With one of them, I wiped the saber.

I thought about taking the saber into the house, but I was naked and dripping and didn't want to bother. I certainly couldn't take it with me. So I slid it inside the severed legs of the jeans and hid it in the bushes.

That was pretty much the end of the clean up.

8

TONY GOES HOME

I was still wet when I put on Tony's jeans and shirt. They stuck to me. I slipped my feet into his loafers, then climbed into the driver's seat.

The car started fine. With a couple of easy maneuvers, I straightened it out. It ended up with its front toward the road.

Before taking off, I gave the lawn a final glance.

Everything looked okay.

Daylight might be another story, but I intended to take a good, long look at the whole area after the sun came up and make sure nothing showed that shouldn't.

Feeling weary but good, the job nearly done—and the worst of it definitely over—I gave the car some gas and headed for the road.

At the top of the driveway, I turned left. There was no traffic in sight, so I kept the headlights off and drove along the two-lane country road by moonlight. With the windows wide open, the night air rushed in. It felt wonderful, blowing against me. And it smelled so fine, too. Sweet and moist and woodsy.

I almost turned on the radio. It would've been great to be

tooling along through the darkness with a summertime song in my ears. But I was on a stealth mission. I kept the radio off, so the only sounds came from the car's engine and the hiss of its tires on the pavement and the wind rushing by.

It was lovely, even without a song.

It made me want to go out every night—but not with a dismembered body in the trunk.

Just drive and drive along the empty country roads in the moonlight, smelling the smells of the night, feeling the soft rush of the wind. Just roam with nowhere to go. And with nothing to give me that tingly little scared feeling deep down inside.

Of course, maybe the scared feeling gave the trip a little extra flavor.

It's hard to tell the difference, sometimes, between fear and excitement.

Anyway, the good part of the trip only lasted a few minutes. Coming to the town limits, I had to slow down and put the headlights on. Then I headed for Little Oak Lane, which I figured was in the newer residential area on the other side of town.

If I hadn't been in Tony's car (with him in the trunk), I probably would've made a straight shot through the middle of downtown on Central Street. I like to call it "the scenic tour," because there's nothing worth seeing in downtown Chester. (Not the town's real name. I've dubbed it Chester in honor of Chester from *Gunsmoke*—because it's a really lame town that just limps along.)

Downtown Chester fills both sides of Central Street for five blocks. And that's about it. The street gets pretty crowded during the day, though I can't imagine why. Maybe it's people looking to buy discount lamps or old-lady shoes. For any serious shopping, you go elsewhere. Like to the Ralph's supermarket or the mall or the Wal-Mart or Home Depot—none of which is anywhere near Chester's business district.

When I came to Central, I slowed down and looked. The

street was well lighted, and almost empty. But not empty enough. A couple of drinking establishments must've still been open. I spotted about a dozen parked cars, two or three people roaming around, and even one car heading toward me.

So I got away from Central and drove an extra block before turning.

On this road, nothing was open. I saw nobody milling about. No cars were coming, either. I glimpsed some activity when I looked down sidestreets, but nothing to worry me.

I only had two real concerns about the drive. First, that somebody would recognize Tony's car and remember that it was on the move that night. Second, that *I* might be seen behind the wheel.

Neither problem was likely to arise unless somebody got pretty close to us.

Which never happened, as far as I could tell.

I did take detours, a couple of times, to avoid approaching vehicles. Once, I even pulled to the curb, shut off the engine and headlights, and ducked until a car'd gone by. Later, driving past a jogger, I turned my head aside so he wouldn't be able to see my face.

I also had to wait at an intersection for an old bum lady to push her shopping cart across the street in front of me. Normally, a person like that would've given me the creeps.

But she didn't spook me at all.

I just worried that she might get a good look at me. Hunched over her shopping cart, though, she never glanced in my direction.

Soon after she'd gone by, I came to Little Oak Lane. Stopping under a street light, I pulled the slip of paper out of Tony's wallet and checked the address.

645 Little Oak Lane, Apt. 12.

It was only a block away.

A two-story, stucco apartment house with a subterranean parking lot.

Near the entrance, a driveway swooped into the lot.

Rolling slowly past it, I glanced down the concrete ramp.

Awfully well-lighted down there.

The little tremor in my belly grew large.

I drove around the block to give myself time to think. On the one hand, the building's lot seemed like the perfect place to drop off Tony's car. He probably had an assigned parking space in there.

Where better to leave his car than precisely where it *should* be?

Seeing it there in the morning, who would ever guess he'd gone somewhere in the middle of the night and gotten himself killed?

And his body might not be discovered for days.

On the other hand, someone might enter the parking lot and see me.

Which would screw up everything.

What are the chances?

Slim, I told myself. Very slim. The danger would only last for a minute or two—long enough to drive in, locate Tony's space, park his car, jump out and run back up the ramp to get outside.

Worth the risk.

I came to that conclusion just in time to make the turn.

Oh, God, here we go!

I swung to the right and drove slowly down the ramp into the lot. Nobody seemed to be coming or going. The place looked deserted except for the parked cars. Lots of them. I began to worry about finding a space for Tony's car.

That turned out not to be the problem.

Among the twenty or so parked cars, I found three empty spaces. But they were labelled with letters, not numbers.

L, R and W.

That was the problem.

One of them had to be reserved for Tony's car.

But which one? He rented apartment 12, not apartment L, R or W.

After making one full loop through the lot, I stopped and tried to think.

I sure didn't want to leave Tony's car in the wrong slot. That would make it *really* conspicuous. Better to abandon it on a street than to leave it in someone else's space.

A one-in-three chance of getting it right made for lousy odds.

I needed a clue, and fast. At any moment, one of the two missing cars might return and I'd be seen.

Think!

If Tony had been worried about forgetting the letter of his parking space, wouldn't he have written it on the same paper as his address?

I hauled out the paper again and double-checked it.

645 Little Oak Lane, Apt. 12.

No L, no R, no W. Nothing except the address.

Forget it! Park and get out of here!

No, wait!

Could there be a correlation between Tony's apartment number and any of the letters?

With the help of my fingers, I counted to the twelfth letter of the alphabet.

12 was L!

Fabulous!

It didn't make anything certain, but at least it was a clue.

I swung his car into space L, shut off the headlights, killed the engine, put the keys in my pocket, and pulled out Tony's handkerchief. With that, I wiped the steering wheel, shift lever, interior door handle, and every other surface that I might've touched. Then I climbed out, locked the door, and shut it so gently that it hardly made a noise.

For the next minute or so, I used the hanky to wipe the outside. The rear of the car was still wet from getting hosed. That didn't worry me much. It was just water. It would dry soon enough.

I saw no traces of blood.

Tucking the hanky into my pocket, I headed for the driveway ramp. It seemed like an endless distance away. I listened for sounds of approaching cars. And for footfalls. The only sounds came from Tony's loafers on my feet, clumping along the concrete. They sounded loud and hollow.

Finally, I reached the ramp.

My legs felt shaky as I hurried to the top.

Suddenly, I was out!

In and out, slick as a whistle, unseen!

I almost clapped my hands, but didn't. Someone might glance out a window to see who'd made the noise.

Feeling light and free, I quickened my pace.

I'd be home in an hour.

Five, six miles.

Maybe a little longer than an hour. At a good pace, I can make four miles in an hour. But it might take an hour and a half for six miles.

Then I got to thinking.

Suddenly, I wasn't certain of the mileage.

The drive had *felt* like a lot more than six miles. I must've been in the car for half an hour.

Half an hour, averaging about thirty miles per hour . . .

Fifteen miles!

But I did make those detours, pull over once, drive around the block while I was trying to make up my mind, and sit in parking lot for a few minutes trying to figure out which slot to use.

So maybe the distance was more like ten or twelve miles.

It can't possibly be that far!

But I had no way of knowing for sure.

During the drive over, I hadn't paid any attention to the clock *or* to the odometer.

If only I'd checked the odometer before starting out from home . . .

Or set the tripometer.

Oh, my God!

I stopped walking.

Was Tony's car *equipped* with a tripometer?

I tried to call up an image of the dashboard. I pictured a dashboard, okay, and it had a tripometer, but I didn't know whether my picture was accurate. Maybe I was just imagining the device.

But if Tony *did* have one, and if he'd set it to zero before coming to my rescue . . .

I had to go back.

9

THE LOST DETAIL

So many little details to think about.

And if you don't think about them, too bad, tough toenails, you're done for.

Just don't kill anyone. That's my big advice to you, if you're reading this. I've heard that books are supposed to be meaningful and help a person gain insights into themselves, or life, or something. So maybe that's what you should get from my book—don't kill anyone or you'll be sorry.

Of course, I guess any person with half an ounce of sense knows that already.

The bad part is, even if you know better, you might end up doing it anyway.

Like me.

I sure never *set out* to split open Tony's head. It could have happened to anyone. It's all a matter of circumstances.

Just like we're all at the mercy of our genes—which pretty much decide everything about how we look and act and even what diseases we'll probably get—we're also at the mercy of circumstances.

All of a sudden, WHAM! and we've killed someone.

You might be pretty smug and sure you'll never do it, but just try popping out of your house in the middle of the night and finding a stranger on your doorstep about to grab you. See what happens then.

See what *you'd* do.

It's you or him, and you figure he's there to rape or kill you. If you don't get him fast, he'll get you.

I bet you'd whack him if you could.

And then what would you do, after he's splayed out on your lawn as dead as a carp?

I know, you'd call the cops.

And ruin your life.

The thing is—do you want the straight scoop?

Even if you're a goody-two-shoes who has never been in trouble in your life, you'll be walking into a nightmare if you bring the cops into the picture. For one thing, maybe the courts won't see the killing as self-defense. You might get convicted of murder or manslaughter and end up in jail. But suppose you make out fine with the legal system? They either don't hit you with criminal charges at all, or you get acquitted. Great. Congratulations. But what about the friends and relatives of the guy you killed?

Ever hear of a wrongful death lawsuit?

Ever hear of revenge?

I think about stuff like this.

I bet you'd think about it, too, if you ever killed somebody. Even by accident.

You'd sure *better* think about it. Do you *really* want to call the cops? Especially considering this: if you don't call them—and you're smart and lucky and have the guts to do whatever it takes—the whole situation might *go away*.

Just like it never happened.

Me, that's what I wanted.

I wanted it to go away.

I would've done *anything* to make it go away, and that included making a return trip to Tony's car in the parking lot.

I hated to go back, but I *had* to.

With a simple push of a button, the tripometer's wheels would spin to 000 and the cops would lose their best clue about where Tony got killed.

I was sure glad I'd thought of it.

On my way to the parking lot, I tried to think of any other details that needed my attention.

I came up with nothing else in connection with Tony's car or apartment. Just set back the tripometer, and leave.

But several details would need to be taken care of, back home.

I made a mental list of them.

1. Immediately retrieve the saber from where I hid it in the bushes.

2. First thing in the morning, check the lawn carefully and clean up any remaining blood or debris. Whatever little pieces of Tony I might find in the grass (and there shouldn't be much) could go down the garbage disposal in Serena's kitchen.

3. Make sure to clean off the glass door where the stranger made his mess. (This had nothing to do with covering up Tony's death, but was for my own peace of mind.)

4. Clean the saber and return it to its proper place on the living room wall.

5. Get rid of Tony's stuff. If suspicion somehow ended up falling on me, I'd better not get caught with his jeans, shirt, wallet, shoes, etc.

That was all I could think of.

But I felt as if I must be forgetting something.

I kept going over the list in my mind, wondering what I'd missed.

And came up with:

6. Check the street in front of the house, just in case. He'd parked there. Maybe he'd dropped something.

7. Check the driveway.

Hell, check everywhere. And double-check. Make sure there's absolutely nothing that might lead anyone to think Tony was there, or that anybody'd gotten killed.

That should cover it.

But I *still* had an uneasy sensation that I'd forgotten a very important piece of evidence.

What could it be?

Maybe nothing. Have you ever started off on a trip feeling *absolutely certain* you'd forgotten something? Maybe you'd neglected to turn off the coffee pot, or you'd left behind your swimsuit or toothbrush? But you can't think of *what* it is, so you don't go back? Then it turns out that you hadn't forgotten anything at all?

I've had that happen to me.

Just as often, though, it turns out that the feeling was right and you *did* forget something.

Anyway, I still hadn't thought of it by the time I arrived back at Tony's building.

Then I had bigger things to worry about, such as being seen in the parking lot. I'd been lucky, last time. Going back down would be pressing my luck. Tempting fate. I didn't like it.

But I did it.

Dripping sweat, breathing hard and trembling, I walked to the bottom of the driveway. Nobody seemed to be around, so I ran all the way to Tony's car. I stopped beside it, huffing, and dug the keys out of my pocket. Then I unlocked the door, opened it, leaned in and stared at the dashboard.

A tripometer!

He *did* have one, and it showed 14.2 miles.

Divide it in half, you get 7.1 miles.

Almost certainly, that was the distance to Serena and Charlie's house.

Tony *had* set his tripometer.

My God! I thought. What if I hadn't thought of it?

Reaching into the car, I stabbed the reset button with my forefinger. The numbers spun back to form a row of zeros.

The evidence was erased.

With the hanky, I wiped the front of the button.

Erased?

Something about that word.

I locked and shut the car door and wiped its handle.

Erased.

Backing away from the car, I looked around. So far, so good. I headed for the driveway ramp, walking fast.

Erased?

Why did that word stick in my head? Should I erase something? Was there an incriminating note that needed to be . . . ?

The tape!

I chugged my way up the driveway.

That's it! The audio tape on Serena and Charlie's answering machine!

How could I possibly have forgotten about *that?* It had Tony's message on it, all that stuff he was trying to tell Judy.

The dead man's voice on a tape in Serena's home.

My God, how could a detail like that slip my mind?

At the top of the driveway, I hurried over to the sidewalk. Once more, I'd made it away from the parking lot undetected. Plus, I'd erased the mileage from the tripometer *and* I'd remembered the lost detail—the message tape.

Simple enough to get rid of that.

I added it to my mental list of things to do at home.

Erase it right away, tonight, as soon as you get back. Bring in the saber, then erase the tape. Maybe destroy it entirely, just to be sure. Burn it.

Leaving Tony's apartment building behind me, I walked to the corner of the block. There was no traffic in sight. I jogged across the street, then slowed to a long, easy stride.

Pace yourself, I thought. It's more than seven miles. That's a pretty good hike.

Should take less than two hours, though.

What if Tony taped the call?

I felt a flutter deep inside.

If he did . . .

He didn't, I told myself. Nobody does that.

Most people don't, anyway. It would be a very strange, abnormal thing to do. Illegal, too, unless you tell the other person about it.

But if he did record it, he's got my address on tape. My voice and my name, too. The minute the cops search his room, they'll find out everything.

BUT PEOPLE DON'T TAPE THEIR CALLS!

Of course they don't. And only a fool would return to Tony's in order to destroy a tape that doesn't even exist.

But might.

I'd have to actually go inside the building, break into his room . . .

I've got his keys.

But the risk! For nothing! For a tape that doesn't exist.

I continued walking, determined not to go back for the non-existent tape.

And I wouldn't have gone back, either.

I would've kept on walking home, but all of a sudden, from thinking about tapes and answering machines and telephones, something popped into my mind that made my insides go cold and squirmy.

Redial.

10

THE THIRD KEY

SHIT!

I had to go back again.

Almost nobody tapes their own telephone conversations, but damn near *everyone* has a redial button.

After our talk, Tony'd had no time to make another call. He'd probably dropped everything, grabbed his gun, rushed out to his car and sped over to guard me.

So a touch of the redial button on his phone would place a call to Serena's phone.

Unless the cops were very stupid or careless, they'd pay me a visit within hours of finding Tony's body.

I had to take care of the redial.

I turned around and headed back.

This is crazy!

But what choice did I have?

When you kill someone, you've *got* to clean up afterward. Not just the body and gore, but the rest of the pieces, too. Tripometers, telephone messages, redials, the whole nine yards.

It sucks big.

If you don't take care of every detail, you go down.

Not me.

When I was about to cross the last intersection before Tony's building, a car turned onto the road a block to my right. I lurched backward fast, heart slamming. Before the car even got close, I found a good place to hide behind a clump of bushes. I crouched there, gasping for breath, sweat pouring down my face and trickling down the nape of my neck. Tony's shirt clung to my back and sides. The seat of his jeans felt damp against my butt.

Waiting for the car to pass, I picked up the front of the shirt and wiped my face.

And wished I were back home so I could jump into the swimming pool.

That suddenly made me picture the prowler in it, drifting on his back, and how the moonlight glinted on his body.

His gorgeous body.

Stop that! I told myself. He's a disgusting pervert! And this is all his fault. If he hadn't come along, Tony would still be alive. I wouldn't be here in the bushes, hot and miserable and hiding like a criminal. And I wouldn't need to break into Tony's apartment in the middle of the night.

The car passed me and kept on going.

I stayed hidden for a while.

Cars have rearview mirrors.

When it was out of sight, I stood up, plucked the clinging clothes away from my skin, and returned to the street corner.

I stared at Tony's building.

Talk about pressing your luck.

I felt like running away.

But the details had to be taken care of, or I'd be sunk.

I started to cross the street.

What'll I do when I'm inside?

1. Find Tony's telephones. (Remember, he might have more than one.)

2. Make a few random calls on any phones I find to make absolutely sure redial won't give away Serena's number.

(Also, if the cops manage to check Tony's phone records, there'll be calls originating from his place *after* the one to Serena. That should help.)

3. Check around to make sure there's no tape recording of his call. If there is, take it. But there won't be.

4. How about leaving his wallet and keys in his room? That way . . .

No, I'd better keep them. No telling where my fingerprints might be. And what if I should need his keys again, later on? Keep that stuff and get rid of it later.

Anything else while I'm in his room?

Just be careful about fingerprints and stuff.

And don't get caught.

What if he has a roommate?

That idea gave me a scare, but only for a few seconds. Tony was twenty-eight years old. Apparently, he'd just moved into the new place because of Judy. He'd loved her so badly. They'd spent so much time together at his old place that he just couldn't stand to be there without her.

A guy like that doesn't have a roommate.

Probably.

The danger would be from tenants of other apartments who might notice me in the building's entryway and corridors.

Nobody'll see me. Not at this hour of the night.

What about security cameras?

As I approached the front stairs, I spread the collar of my shirt and lifted it, pulling the shirt up to hide most of my face.

You didn't do this in the parking lot, stupid.

Fear slammed through me again.

Had there *been* security cameras in the parking lot?

I didn't know.

I hadn't noticed any, but I hadn't been looking, either.

Instead of climbing the stairs to the front doors, I made a third trip to the parking lot. This time, I searched high and low for video cameras.

I was awfully damn shaken up.

What the hell would I do if I *found* cameras?

I didn't have the slightest idea, but I'd probably be sunk. There I'd be on video tape somewhere, delivering Tony's car in the middle of the night—even wiping it for prints!

I felt sick inside just thinking about it.

Thank God, there didn't seem to be any video equipment down there.

As you might've already noticed, the parking lot didn't have a gated entrance, either. *Anyone* could've driven or walked in, as I proved. Frankly, the lot had no security whatsoever.

Nor did the rest of the building, as I soon found out.

This might surprise some of you. You might even think I'm lying. Because if you live in a place like Los Angeles or New York City, you probably think *every* apartment house in the world has security measures like a Wells Fargo bank.

But you're wrong.

In Chester, we did have plenty of buildings designed to foil criminals. But we also had some that were wide open— ungated, unguarded, uncameraed, and virtually unlocked. They were usually older places that didn't charge you a fortune in rent.

They aren't only in Chester, either.

I'd lived in a few of them, myself, before coming to town and moving in over Serena and Charlie's garage. They weren't so bad. You had to worry about prowlers, but at least you had your freedom. You weren't locked in a cage, and your every move wasn't caught on video tape. There's a lot to be said for that.

Even if you *aren't* doing something bad.

If you *are* up to no good, a lack of security is splendid.

After finishing my search for video cameras, I didn't even bother going back outside. I just trotted up a stairway near the front of the parking lot, came to an unlocked door, opened it and found myself inside the foyer.

The foyer and corridor were dimly lighted.

I saw no one.

Nor did I hear any sounds from the rooms as I sneaked down the corridor looking for apartment 12.

Everyone's asleep, I thought.

God, I hope so.

I felt like a wreck. My mouth was dry, my heart slamming, my whole body dripping with sweat. I was panting for air like a worn-out dog. And shaking like crazy.

The nasty green carpet silenced my footfalls.

But every so often, a board creaked.

What if somebody hears me?

What if a door suddenly opens?

A door wouldn't even have to open—each had a peep-hole. Someone might look out at me and I'd never even know.

I felt sick with fear.

If anybody sees me, it blows the whole deal.

What'll I do?

Pray it doesn't happen.

At last, I came to number 12. As quietly as possible, I reached into the right front pocket of my cut-offs and pulled out Tony's key case. I unsnapped it.

Of the six keys, two belonged to Tony's car.

Four to pick from, but one of them didn't really look like a room key. It might go to a padlock, or something.

So I selected a key from the remaining three.

You can't fool around with a bunch of keys and not make *some* noise. They clinked and jingled, sounding awfully loud in the silence.

When I finally had the key pinched between my thumb and forefinger, I couldn't hold it still. My hand shook so badly that the tip kept scraping around on the face of the lock, and wouldn't go in the hole.

At last, it went in.

But just the point of it. I tried to force it in the rest of the way, but it wouldn't go.

When that sort of thing happens, sometimes you've got the key upside down. So I turned it over and tried again.

No luck.

Wrong key.

With more clinking and jingling, I fumbled about for key number two.

By the time I had it ready, my hand was shaking worse than ever. The key bumped and scratched against the lock, and kept missing the hole. I used my left hand to hold my right hand steady. That didn't help a lot, but it helped some. Enough.

I made it to the hole.

This time, the key slid in all the way.

Yes!

But I couldn't turn it.

Shit!

No matter how hard I twisted the key, all it did was rattle deep inside the lock somewhere. It wouldn't turn. The damn thing seemed to be frozen in an upright position.

Letting the bunch of keys dangle, I looked at my hand. I had a red imprint on my thumb and forefinger.

I wiped my hand dry on the front of my shirt, then tried again. This time, I twisted the key so hard that I started to worry about breaking it.

So I quit and let go again.

What the hell is wrong? I wondered. The key fit. It had gone in all the way. Why wouldn't it turn?

Maybe it's the wrong damn key.

But it *fit!*

Sure. Okay. It's the right size to go in the hole, but not completely right.

Obviously not right enough to unlock the door.

I jerked it out, turned it over, then tried to stick it back in. This time, it would only go halfway in.

I muttered, "Shit," yanked it out, then fumbled for the third key. And dropped the whole case. It landed on the carpet in front of the door with a quiet thump and a loud jangle.

I crouched and grabbed it.

Then stood again, holding my breath and glancing up and down the corridor.

Nothing happened.

I took a deep breath, sighed with relief, and got back to work.

Having dropped the case, I'd lost track of the third key.

All three "door" keys—including the two failures—looked pretty much alike.

So I picked one at random.

As I aimed it for the lock hole, the door swung open in front of my face.

11

APARTMENT TWELVE

A young woman inside the room frowned out at me. Maybe "frown" isn't the right word, since she didn't seem angry. She looked concerned or confused.

God only knows how I must've looked.

I felt as if the floor had dropped out from under me.

What's she doing here?

Nobody's supposed to be here!

"Are you all right?" she asked.

"I . . . I must have the wrong apartment, or . . ."

"This is twelve," she said, then glanced at the number on the door as if to make sure of it.

She must've just gotten out of bed. She had a crease on her cheek, her short blond hair was mussed, and she wore wrinkled pajamas.

She was probably two or three years younger than me.

And beautiful.

Not exotic, glamorous beautiful.

Wholesome, girl-next-door beautiful, like an Iowa cheer-leader.

I would've given my left arm to look half as good as this gal.

"Where are you trying to go?" she asked.

"Maybe I'm in the wrong building."

She shrugged.

"Is this 645 Little Oak Lane?"

Why hadn't I said 465? She would've told me, "Oh, no, this is 645. I'm afraid you *do* have the wrong building." And that would've been the end of the situation.

But I was curious, for one thing. I wanted to find out what was going on.

For another thing, the damage was already done. She'd seen me.

And I didn't know what to do about it.

After hearing the address, she nodded and looked more confused than before. "You seem to be in the right place, but . . ."

"Doesn't Tony live here?" I asked.

"Tony?"

"Yeah, Tony." I tried to remember his last name. "Romano."

"What?" Now, she seemed confused *and* surprised. "Tony Romano?"

"Is this his apartment?"

"No. This is *my* apartment."

"But you know him, don't you?" I asked.

"Sure. Do you?"

"He gave me this address."

"What for?"

"He said he lived here. And that . . . I should come over tonight. He gave me his keys. See?" I held up the key case in front of her. "I was supposed to let myself in. And wait for him."

"Huh?"

I shrugged.

"But he doesn't live here," she said.

"What do you mean?"

"This isn't his *place*. It's mine. He lives over on Washington Avenue."

"Are you sure?"

"I'm sure, all right. I used to spend half my life over there. Why on earth did he give you *my* address?"

"I don't know."

But I suddenly had a pretty good idea how I'd gotten the wrong address—and who *she* was.

"Are you Judy?" I asked.

"Yeah?" She said it softly, like a question.

I put on a big smile. "You're Tony's girlfriend!"

"Not anymore. But yeah. We were . . ." She shrugged.

"It's nice to meet you. My name's Alice." I held out my hand, and she shook it.

"Hi, Alice," she said.

"So, why did he give me *your* address?" I asked.

"I have no idea. It's weird. But Tony can *be* weird, sometimes. Why don't you come on in? Maybe you should call him, or something." She opened the door wider and I stepped into her apartment.

Only a single lamp was on. It didn't do a very good job. It cast a yellowish light that left corners of the living room in shadows.

I looked around and didn't see anybody.

From the looks of the furniture, Judy wasn't exactly rich. She had an old armchair, a sofa with threadbare cushions, a few lamps and small tables, and bookshelves against most of the walls. The shelves were crammed with books, mostly paperbacks.

After shutting the door, she said, "Tony does oddball stuff, sometimes."

"Yeah, I've noticed."

"Isn't that one of his shirts you're wearing?"

I forced a smile.

Wearing his jeans and shoes, too.

She wasn't likely to recognize them, though. Most blue jeans and brown loafers look pretty much alike. Besides, I'd customized Tony's jeans.

"I'm just borrowing his shirt for the night," I told her. "Mine got spilled on."

"So you saw him tonight?" She didn't sound suspicious, just curious.

"Yeah, we had dinner together."

"How's he doing?"

"He really misses you."

She winced slightly. "I miss him, too. Sometimes. Not that I'll ever go back to him. Would you like something to drink? A Pepsi or a beer or something?"

"Okay, sure."

"How about a beer?"

"Great!"

Being careful not to touch anything, I followed her into the kitchen.

She turned on a light and went to the refrigerator. The top of her kitchen table was hidden under a computer and piles of books and papers.

"So, how do you know Tony?" she asked.

Without even pausing to think, I said, "We met at a bar. The Cactus Bar and Grill."

"Really?" She set a couple of beer bottles on the counter, then reached up and opened a cupboard. "I ate there with him once. I'm surprised he went back. He thought they had lousy margaritas."

"He sure put down a lot of them the night we met."

"No kidding." Shaking her head, she filled a pair of glass mugs with beer. Then she turned around and handed one to me.

"All he could talk about was you," I said. "And how much he loves you."

"Really?" Her smile seemed a little sad.

"Yeah. He's miserable."

We went into the living room. Judy sat in the armchair, and I took the sofa.

I still had no idea what I was doing.

That's not quite true.

I was stalling.

Playing things by ear.

Because I had no idea what to do.

Shoot her?

I was sitting on Tony's pistol. It made my butt hurt on the right side, and I would've been glad to take it out of my pocket.

But *shoot her?*

Gunshots in a place like this, at an hour like this, would probably wake up half the people in the building.

I'd be shafted.

"So you don't think you'll get back together with Tony?" I asked, then tried the beer. It was very cold and bitter and I liked it a lot.

"Not a chance," Judy said. "Did he tell you why we broke up?"

For a while, I couldn't answer because I was busy swallowing that wonderful beer. Then I said, "I think it was too painful for him to talk about."

"He was probably too embarrassed."

"Really?"

"Yeah. It's not the sort of thing you want to tell people about. Especially not a woman."

"Oh, well, you don't have to . . ."

"*I'll* tell you. Hey, I've *got* to tell you, if you're going with him now. He beat me up."

"He *beat you up?*"

"Yeah."

"My God! Why'd he do that?"

Judy's face suddenly changed from nicely tanned to bright red. "Well, he was drunk. It was a sex thing. He wanted to do something, and I wouldn't let him."

"So he *pounded* you?"

She nodded. Her face was scarlet.

"What did he want to do?" I asked.

"It doesn't matter."

An idea struck me. Frowning, I leaned forward and said, "Do you want to know why I'm *really* wearing Tony's shirt? Because he ripped mine off me. Tore it right off."

She looked shocked. "Tonight?"

"Yeah."

"Jeez. Was he drunk?"

"As a skunk," I said.

" 'Cause, I mean, he's not usually like that. How long have you known him?"

"Just a few days."

"He must be in really bad shape. I mean, we went together for months, and he never pulled anything like that. He drank too much a few times, but he never *attacked* me. He was always so sweet. You wouldn't have thought he had a mean bone in his body. Till that night he went berserk on me."

I nodded eagerly.

We've both been there, girl!

"Tonight," I said, "was the first time he ever got ugly with me. I couldn't believe it. He'd seemed so gentle, before. Like a really sensitive, sincere guy."

"Exactly," Judy said.

"But, boy . . ." I shook my head. "Not tonight. He scared me half to death."

"What did he do?"

I drank some more beer, sighed, then set the mug down on the table in front of the sofa and said, "Well, he came over to my place for dinner. After that we went and saw *Independence Day*. Everything was fine till after the movie. We went back to my place and had a few drinks. We were planning to fool around, but my roommate came home. She always shows up at exactly the worst possible time."

Judy smiled slightly. "That's what roommates are for."

"Do you have one?" I asked, suddenly worried.

"Not since college."

"They can be a real pain in the butt," I said.

"No kidding."

"Anyway, the three of us sat around and had a few drinks. And I could tell that Tony was starting to lose his patience. He wanted to . . . you know, mess around. But we couldn't do it in front of Jane. Finally, he said it was time for him to go home. And he asked me if I wanted to come with him. So I said, 'Sure,' and we left."

"Was he okay to drive?" Judy asked.

"No. Hardly. But neither was I. I mean, we were both pretty looped. We shouldn't have driven at all. But I wanted to get out of there, too, before something happened between him and Jane. She was starting to look at him a certain way, you know? Besides, I was interested in seeing where he lived. He'd been kind of funny about the place, like he didn't want me there for some reason."

"Strange. He had *me* there all the time."

"Well . . ." I shrugged. "Who knows? Maybe that had something to do with it. You know? The way he feels about you, maybe he thought I might—taint the place, or something."

"That'd be really strange."

"Anyway, he didn't take me there, after all. He drove us into the woods, instead."

12

TONY TALES

"Drove into *what* woods?" Judy asked.

"Miller's Woods."

"You're kidding. At night?"

"Yeah. Tonight."

"You *let* him?"

"Like I said, we were both a little smashed."

"My God."

"We went to that picnic area. With the fireplaces and tables?"

Judy nodded. "I've been there a few times. Never at night, though."

"Well, that's where we went."

"Was anybody around?"

"Just me and Tony. Which is what he wanted, I guess . . . to have me out there alone. Anyway, we went over and sat on one of those tables."

"You got out of the car? Weren't you frightened?"

"Yeah, sort of. As a matter of fact, that was the whole problem. It was so dark and spooky. I had this awful feeling like we were being watched. I wanted to get the hell out of there.

But Tony kept saying there was nothing to worry about. And he laughed at me for being scared."

"That wasn't very nice," Judy said.

"I didn't think so, either. I thought it was rotten. So I *really* wasn't in any mood to fool around with him. Anyway, we were sitting on top of a picnic table with our feet on the bench. Tony had a bottle of tequila. He drank from it with one hand and rubbed my back with the other. Before you know it, he snuck that hand under my blouse. Then he started trying to unhook the back of my bra, so I told him to stop it."

"Naturally, he didn't."

"Of course not. He went ahead and unhooked my bra, so I stood up on the bench and said, 'I mean it, Tony. Not here. This place gives me the creeps.'

"He said that's what he likes about it. So I said, 'Let's just go over to your apartment, okay?' Then I jumped off the bench and started walking away, but he suddenly leaps up and grabs me by the collar and jerks me off my feet. But he catches me, you know? So then I'm leaning against him and he reaches around in front and rips my blouse open. I mean, he was just vicious about it. It was a pullover, and he tore it apart right down the front and ruined it. Which is the *real* reason I'm wearing his shirt right now."

Judy nodded, a solemn look on her face. "Not because yours got spilled on."

"That was a little fib. I'm sorry. I never thought I'd end up telling you this stuff." I tried to smile, making it look like a strain. "You're really a good listener, Judy."

"Thanks. I've been through a few of these things, myself."

"Guys are such awful pigs."

"They can be."

"He completely ruined my blouse."

"He's ruined a couple of mine, too," Judy said. "And a good dress."

"Tore them?"

"Different things."

I could tell she didn't want to go into details, so I went on with my story. "The whole thing just scared the hell out of me," I said. "Him flipping out like that. And also, you know, being in those woods. I really panicked. I just wanted to get away. But he wouldn't let me. He jerked my shorts down and threw me onto the picnic table. I tried to get up, but he slugged me in the stomach."

Judy winced as if she could feel the blow, herself.

"That knocked my wind out. All I could do was squirm on the table. It felt like I was drowning. Then the next thing I know, he's on top of me. We're both naked and he's . . ." I made a face. "You know."

"Screwing you?"

"Yeah."

Her face suddenly went crimson again, and she said, "In the right place?"

"Huh?"

"Never mind." She was really flustered. "It's none of my business. Forget I asked, okay?"

"You mean, did he do it to me in the vagina?"

"Well. Yeah."

"Yeah, that's where."

Grimacing, she said, "And not with anything funny?"

"What do you mean, funny?"

"He obviously didn't, or you wouldn't have to ask."

"What'd he do to *you?*"

"Nothing. I wouldn't let him. That's why he beat me up." She smiled a little sadly. "You should've seen me afterward. I was a wreck. You look like you lucked out."

"This was my lucky night, okay."

"You got off without too much damage. That's all I meant."

"I guess that's true."

"How did it turn out?" she asked.

"Where were we?"

"On the picnic table."

"Oh, that's right. He was screwing me. In the vagina. With his penis. Without a condom."

"Well, at least you don't have to worry about AIDS or anything. I happen to know that he's perfectly healthy."

I laughed.

Couldn't help it.

Luckily, I didn't have a mouthful of beer. It would've spewed.

Judy raised her eyebrows as if she hoped I might let her in on the joke.

"As a matter of fact," I said, "he isn't."

"Isn't?"

"Perfectly healthy."

"What do you mean?"

"He probably has a major headache, right now. If he's awake yet."

"Awake?"

"I knocked him out cold with his tequila bottle. He'd left it on the table where I could reach it. So while he was busy humping me, I grabbed it and gave him a good one. Busted it against his head."

Judy's mouth dropped open. She gaped at me, an odd look in her eyes as if she might be tempted to laugh, herself.

"Knocked him out cold," I said. "But he was still on top of me, so I rolled over. He fell off me *and* the table, and whacked the bench, then rolled off *it* and landed on the ground. Took a pretty good fall."

"Was he all right?"

"Not really. He was out like a light and his head was bleeding. He wasn't dead, though."

"Where is he now?"

"I don't know. And I don't care. He's probably on a back road, somewhere, walking home. But he won't have an easy time of it. I was still really angry at him, you know? A bit *more* than angry. I was furious. I mean, he'd raped me. Wouldn't you call that a rape?"

"I'd call it a rape," Judy said.

"So would I."

"Are you going to press charges against him?"

"I don't think so. I think I've punished him pretty good *without* the cops. You know what I did? I left him there in the woods completely naked. Out cold, and naked as the day he was born. I kept his shirt, since he'd wrecked mine. All the rest of his clothes, I burned in one of the fireplaces. His underwear and everything. Except his shoes. I threw those into the woods. He'll never find them. Then I hopped into his car and drove off."

"You really left him there?"

I grinned. "Seemed like a good idea. Part of my revenge. But it didn't seem like *enough* revenge. So I thought I'd drive over to his apartment and trash the place. Just to teach him a lesson, you know? Teach him that he can't do that sort of thing to a girl."

"So why did you come *here?*"

"I thought *this* was his place. I'll show you." I drank the last of the beer, set the mug on the table again, then pulled Tony's wallet out of my rear pocket. Taking out the slip of paper, I walked over to Judy's chair. "See this?" I handed it to her.

She scowled at it. "That's *my* address. It's also my handwriting. I gave this to Tony . . . months ago. When we first met."

I sighed and shook my head.

She held the paper toward me.

"You might as well keep it," I told her. On my way back to the sofa, I stuffed Tony's wallet into my pocket.

"What made you think this was *his* address?"

"I found it in his wallet. I just assumed it was where he lived. Pretty stupid, huh?"

From the look in Judy's eyes, she seemed to agree. But she didn't make any sort of crack about it. All she said was, "You should've checked his driver's license."

"He didn't have it with him."

"He *didn't?*"

"He'd gotten it revoked."

She gasped. "You're *kidding!*"

"No. They took it away from him about a week ago. For drunk driving and leaving the scene of an accident."

"My God! An accident?"

"It wasn't anything serious. Nobody got hurt. But Tony sped off, afterward. He got caught about a mile away. He was lucky he didn't end up in jail."

"Poor Tony," Judy said.

"Yeah. He's been having a hard time of it, lately. He just can't get over losing you."

"Jeez."

"Anyway, that's why he didn't have a license. When I found the address in his wallet, I just automatically figured it must be where he lived. So here I am. Guess I would've figured out something was wrong when none of his keys fit the door."

"I heard you trying them," Judy explained.

Trying to look embarrassed, I asked, "Did I wake you up?"

"No. I wasn't asleep. I'd *been* asleep, but then I had this horrible nightmare that woke me up. Really freaked me out."

"I hate nightmares."

"Me, too. I think they're scarier than real life."

"Think so?"

"Sure," she said. "Nightmares just give you raw fear. If the same stuff happened in real life, you'd still be scared, but you'd also be thinking rationally and trying to figure things out. How to get away, that sort of stuff. In nightmares, all you have is the fear. Just fear, and nothing else. That's what makes them so terrible."

"But you wake up from nightmares," I pointed out.

"I sure woke up from this one tonight. And then I wasn't very eager to fall asleep again. If you go back to sleep too soon, you know, you can wind up back inside the same nightmare. So I got up and went to the bathroom."

"*That* gives me the creeps," I told her. "Going to the john in the middle of the night. I always think I hear things."

"I heard *you* trying to unlock the door."

"Oh, wow. That must've freaked you out."

"I didn't think it was *my* door. I thought it might be the one across the hall. But the sounds went on a lot longer than they should've, so I looked out the peephole."

"And there I was."

"There you were."

"You sure scared the hell out of me, opening the door like that."

"I didn't mean to scare you," Judy said. "I just thought you looked like you needed help."

"You were right about that."

She didn't say anything for a few seconds, just looked at me like maybe she was worried about hurting my feelings or making me mad. Then she said, "Now it's Tony who needs the help."

"What?"

"I don't blame you for what you did to him," she said. "I'm sure he deserved it. Maybe even worse. But . . . I owe him. If I hadn't dumped him, none of this bad stuff would've happened tonight."

Funny, but she was absolutely right about that.

Then she said, "It sounds as if he's . . . come apart at the seams."

"He really has," I said.

13

RINGING UP THE DEAD GUY

"I just can't leave him out there," Judy told me.

"He's probably on his way home, by now."

"But he was still unconscious when you drove off and left him, wasn't he?"

"Dead to the world."

"So for all we know, he might *still* be out cold."

"I guess it's possible," I admitted. "Look, I have an idea. Why don't you give him a call?"

It seemed like a fine idea. Judy didn't know that he'd moved to a new apartment. She would obviously dial his old number and get a recorded message explaining that Tony's phone was out of service.

"Maybe he's already home by now," I added.

"It's worth a try."

Judy leaned forward in the big, old chair and stood up. Her phone was on the lamp table near the end of the sofa. As she walked over and picked it up, she said, "I can't imagine he's home, though. Not if he had to walk." She picked up the handset and started to tap in a number. "It's an awfully long way from Miller's Woods to his place."

"Especially if you're bare-ass naked," I said.

Which made her laugh. "You're terrible," she said.

"Yep."

Listening at the earpiece, she suddenly frowned. "His number's been changed," she muttered. "They're going to . . ." She stopped to listen.

They're giving her the new number! I couldn't even *begin* to figure out the ramifications of that.

While I sat there, stunned, she tapped in a series of numbers.

A moment later, she met my eyes and said, "It's his machine."

"Maybe you'd better hang up."

"He might be monitoring."

Should I stop her?

Maybe not. This could be a good deal.

Or a disaster.

"Hi, Tony," she said. "It's me, Judy. Are you there?" She stopped talking. She waited.

Leave it at that! Don't say another word!

"I guess you're not home. Okay. Well, I just called to see how you're doing. Give me a call back if you want to. I'm still at the same number. So long."

She hung up.

"We'll probably get to him before he even hears it," she said.

"I imagine so," I said.

"It's funny that he changed his number. Do you know why he did that?"

I couldn't come up with a good lie right off the bat, so I just said, "No idea."

"Maybe it has to do with his accident."

"Could be."

"At any rate, he hasn't gotten home yet. I'm sure he would've picked up."

"You can bet on that. He's been dying to get a call from you. But you never know, maybe he's taking a shower or something. We probably ought to wait a few minutes and try him again."

Judy shook her head. "No. I don't want to wait any longer. I need to go out and find him."

"Want me to come with you?"

"You don't have to," she said, and turned away.

"Sure I do," I said. From my seat on the sofa, I watched her stride into a nearby room and switch on a light. At the other end of the room was a rumpled bed.

Judy stepped out of sight.

Raising my voice, I said, "I can't have you going out there all by yourself. Something might happen to you."

"I'll be all right," she called.

"Maybe. But what if you're not? I'm the one who left Tony stranded. I'd feel awful."

"You hardly even know me."

"I'd feel awful, anyway. You're a nice person."

A quiet laugh came from the bedroom. Then Judy said, "Well, I'm not sure how nice I am, but thanks."

"You *are* nice. And trusting. I mean, I'm a complete stranger, but you let me in here in the middle of the night. You even gave me a beer."

"Well, we've got a mutual friend, I guess. Or enemy."

"I want to help you look for him. Really."

"Fine with me. I might be a nice person with a lot of sterling qualities, but I am a chicken. It'll be great to have you along."

"You and me, Judy."

She came out of the bedroom. Her pajamas were gone, and she was no longer barefoot. She wore white socks and blue sneakers, a pale blue skirt, and a short-sleeved white blouse that looked crisp and cool. Most of the blouse's buttons weren't fastened yet. It wasn't tucked in, either, and hung down like a miniskirt. Only a few inches of her real skirt showed in front of her thighs.

"You're wearing a skirt?" I asked.

"It's a hot night."

"Tony'll like that."

"I guess so," she said.

"And no bra."

She laughed. "Hot night. Besides, look who's talking."

"I have an excuse. Tony wrecked mine."

"I don't *need* an excuse. You're not my mother." Grinning, she looked down and worked on fastening the rest of her buttons. "It's not like I'm trying to do Tony any favors," she said. "I just want to be comfortable."

"That's fine," I said. "Hell, you look great."

"Thanks. I feel great. This is kind of fun, in a way. It's like going out for an adventure."

I found myself grinning. "Yeah," I said. "It is."

Finished with her buttons, she hurried into the kitchen. She came back with her purse and slipped its strap onto her shoulder. "All set," she said. "You ready to go? Do you want to hit the bathroom first?"

"Ah. Maybe so. Good idea."

She pointed the way.

I went in, turned on the light and shut the door. The bathroom was small, but very clean. A wonderful, flowery aroma filled the air. It seemed to come from a bar of soap on the sink.

Not wasting any time, I took the .22 out of my back pocket, pulled my cut-offs down and sat on the toilet.

While I peed, I wondered what the hell I'd gotten myself into.

A complete disaster, that's what.

I'd actually brought Tony's car—and corpse—to Judy's building, not his.

Even if I could somehow learn the location of his new apartment—which seemed impossible—the plan was blown anyway because I'd come face to face with Judy.

Killing her wouldn't fix everything, but it had to be done.

The worst part of it was, I liked her.

Too bad I hadn't shot her right away. It would've been easier. Now that I knew her, it was going to be tough.

I kept staring at the pistol in my hand.

Maybe I should just do it. Go out there and shoot her right now.

With my thumb, I switched off the safety. It had been hiding a small red dot.

Wait till she turns around. Get up real close behind her, then put a couple in the back of her head.

Don't let her know what's coming. That way, she won't be scared.

And won't scream, either.

Maybe she'll scream because it hurts.

I imagined it all happening, and it made me feel sick.

Let it wait, I told myself. There's no big hurry. We'll be leaving in a few minutes. Wait till we're someplace where nobody will be likely to hear the gunshots.

Right away, I felt better.

I still had to kill her, but not until later.

I thumbed the safety back on, then reached over and set the pistol on the edge of the sink.

When I was done at the toilet, I pulled up my cut-offs and fastened the belt tight enough to keep them from falling down. Instead of putting the pistol into my back pocket, I slipped it into the right front pocket. That way, it would be easier to take out.

Then I washed my hands.

There was a mirror above the sink.

I hardly recognized myself. My hair looked strange—damp, ropey and coiled. My face was shiny with oils and sweat. The afternoon in the sun had turned it a dark, coppery color. My eyes looked all wrong—the whites too white, the gaze too intense.

I looked a little mad, a little wild.

Like someone well suited for bloody work.

I washed my hands with hot water, using the nice soap.

When I finished, my hands smelled like spring flowers. I rinsed my face with cold water. I cupped some water to my mouth, and had a few swallows.

After drying, I used the towel to wipe the faucet and toilet handles and the light switch. I put the towel back on its bar, then shut off the light with the edge of my hand. Standing in the dark, I slipped my hand under the front of my shirt and grabbed the doorknob to let myself out.

"Ready?" Judy asked.

"All set," I told her.

Our beer mugs were gone.

Along with my fingerprints!

Smiling, I said, "You cleaned up already?"

"Yeah. I hate coming back to a mess. Did you want your mug?"

"I just thought I might have a drink of water."

"It's already washed, but I'll get you a clean one."

Already washed!

"Never mind," I said, pleasantly relieved. "We'd better go."

"Are you sure? It wouldn't be any trouble."

"Yeah. Hey, I'd just end up having to pee again."

"Okay."

"Let's go."

Judy walked in front of me. I followed her toward the door, the pistol swinging in my pocket, rubbing against my thigh. She opened the door, then stepped aside.

I went out into the hallway. Nobody was there.

Judy came after me, using the outside knob to pull the door shut. Then she gave it a couple of twists and shoves to make sure the door was locked.

Which took care of any prints I might've left on the knob. Side by side, not saying a word, we walked down the silent hall to the foyer. There, she whispered, "Where'd you park Tony's car?"

"In the lot."

"*This* lot?"

"Yeah."

"You found an empty space for it?"

"I put it in L. Is that okay?"

"Fine. That's right next to mine."

As we hurried down the stairway, she said, "I've got an idea. Why don't we leave it there and take my car?"

"Are you sure you want to?" I asked.

What does this do to my plan?

Not that I actually *had* a plan anymore.

"This whole business is pretty hairy," she said. "Going to the woods at this time of night. I'd just rather be doing it in my own car. At least I can be pretty sure it won't break down on us."

"Fine by me," I said. "You drive."

"You point the way."

We came out of the stairwell into the parking lot.

Nobody else seemed to be around.

My loafers clopped loudly on the concrete floor. Judy's sneakers were nearly silent.

"If we find Tony," she said, "we'll bring him back here so he can drive himself home. Unless he needs emergency treatment."

"There's his car," I said, pointing at it.

"Yeah."

It looked just fine sitting there. A few shiny drops of water sparkled on the trunk and rear bumper, but I saw nothing to worry about.

"That's a good place for it," Judy said. "Nobody ever parks there but guests. It can stay right where it is for a few days, if he needs to be hospitalized or something."

"I don't really think he'll need to be hospitalized," I told her.

14

NIGHT RIDERS

"Exciting, isn't it?" Judy said as we reached the top of the driveway ramp.

"What is?" I asked.

"This. Going out like this." She swung her car onto the road and picked up speed. "I never go anywhere this late at night. I'm almost always asleep by now."

"Me, too," I said, but I wasn't really paying attention.

I was preoccupied, just then, with my feelings of relief. Now that we'd left the apartment building behind us, I was finally free of Tony.

I mean *free!*

He and his car were *gone!*

Adios, toot-toot, bye-bye!

I would never go near them again, and nobody would ever find out what I'd done.

Not even Judy.

I looked over at her. She kept turning her head, glancing around like an eager tourist. There wasn't much to see, though, unless you're fascinated by empty streets, porch lights and darkness.

"It *is* exciting to be out like this," I told her.

"Sort of spooky, too," she said.

"If you think it's spooky now, wait till we get to the woods."

"I can hardly wait."

"Do you know how to get there?" I asked.

"I can find Miller's Woods all right, but I'm not sure about the turn-off to the picnic area. How about you?"

"I'm pretty sure where it is."

We were nearing the business district, so I said, "You'd better not take Central. When I came through, there were some unsavory characters hanging around."

"We can do without unsavory characters," she said.

A block short of Central, she turned onto the same street I'd used earlier. It looked deserted.

"The fewer people see us," I said, "the better."

"You're probably right."

"Two gals by themselves."

"Are you trying to scare me?"

"We just have to be careful, that's all. You never know who might be out there."

"Most people are all right," Judy said.

"Not the sort who are cruising the roads at this hour."

"We are."

"We're the exception. Anyway, it only takes one lunatic to spoil the night."

"You're a regular cockeyed optimist," she said.

"That's me."

"Maybe instead of a lunatic, we'll run into a wonderful, charming stranger."

"Run over one?"

"*Into*." She turned her head and smiled at me. "You're a trouble maker."

"Yep."

"I know 'em when I see 'em. I'm one, too."

"You? A trouble maker? You seem like such a *nice* girl."

"I'm that, too."

"How can you be nice *and* a trouble maker?"

"I make benign mischief."

Normally, I might've laughed at that. It was a pretty cute thing to say, *benign mischief*. But it almost made me cry.

Here Judy was, out in the middle of the night on a mission of mercy. Having herself an *adventure*. She's nervous but excited and having fun, saying cute stuff, and she doesn't have the slightest inkling that I'm going to leave her dead in the woods.

It was awfully sad if you think about it.

And I couldn't *help* but think about it, riding along in the car with her.

On her last ride.

Too bad she wasn't an ugly, snotty, miserable bitch. Then I wouldn't have felt so bad.

"Are you okay?" she asked after a while.

"I guess so."

"You're kind of quiet. Worrying about lunatics?"

"Sure am."

"Well, I think we'll be perfectly safe as long as we stay in the car. We really shouldn't need to get out, I don't think."

"Maybe not," I agreed. "Depending on Tony."

"With any luck, we'll find him walking along the roadside before we even have to go into the woods."

"I sure hope so," I said.

But I didn't really think it stood much chance of happening.

We were nearly to the town limits when Judy said, "Uh-oh."

"What?"

"Here comes your lunatic, now."

"Very funny." Twisting sideways, I looked out the rear window and saw a pair of headlights in the distance.

"Man," Judy said, "he's really barreling down on us."

"Just drive normal," I told her. "Don't speed up or anything. It might be a cop."

"That'd be fine by me."

The car bore down on us, full speed.

"What the hell is he *doing?*" Judy blurted.

The headbeams surged in through the windows and glared off our rearview mirror.

"God!" Judy cried out. "He's going to ram us!"

But he didn't.

At the last instant, the car swerved to our left.

It started to roar past us, then slowed enough to match our speed.

It wasn't a cop car.

Cops don't drive Cadillacs. Not in Chester, they don't. Not in any town I've ever heard of. This thing looked like a giant old gas-gulping monster that belonged in a junk yard, not on the road. A real old clunker, but its engine sounded *hot*.

As it tooled along beside us, the guys checked us out.

Two of them.

Judy gave them a glance, then turned her face straight forward.

I was leaning toward the dashboard so I could look past her. I had a lousy view of the driver, but the one in the passenger seat looked like a tough guy. He stared back at us. He looked all of about eighteen years old and had a crew cut. A cig dangled off his lips. He wasn't wearing a shirt.

"Real charming," Judy said quietly, as if addressing the windshield.

"Don't do anything. Don't even look at them." As I gave that advice, I settled back into my seat and stopped looking at them myself.

A few seconds later, the car sped past us and swerved into our lane, barely missing our front bumper. Judy hit the brakes. As I was thrown forward, she flung an arm across my chest. Her arm didn't stop me, but my hands did. I slammed them against the dashboard.

The Cadillac pulled away from us.

"You okay?" Judy asked.

"Yeah. Thanks."

"Bastards," she muttered.

We were moving along at a crawl.

The Cadillac kept going, gaining speed, and soon vanished around a bend in the road.

Judy gave us a little gas. As we picked up speed, she took a deep breath. Then she said, "Maybe you'd better put on your seatbelt."

"Not me."

"Huh?"

"I don't use them. I'll take my chances with the windshield."

"Yeah?" She gave me a look, but there wasn't enough light in the car to see whether she was smiling, smirking, frowning, or something else. "I'll keep mine on," she said. "Safety first."

"No faith in your own driving?" I asked.

She laughed.

We glided around the bend. Ahead of us, the road was dark except for the moonlight. No sign of the Cadillac.

"You think they're gone?" Judy asked.

"Looks that way," I said. "But things aren't always how they look."

"I guess they were just fooling around."

"Looks that way."

"Could've gotten ugly. Maybe this wasn't such a hot idea, after all."

"What?" I asked.

"Coming out to look for Tony. I mean, what if those two guys had gotten *serious*?"

"Do you want to call it off and go back?"

She didn't answer for a few seconds. Then she said, "I guess if they'd meant to nail us, they would've done it."

"Probably."

"Probably just wanted to give us a thrill."

"As long as they don't show up again," I said, "we might as well keep going. We're more than halfway there."

"Gone past the point of no return?"

"Yep."

"Gotta keep going, then."

"You and me, babe."

She turned her head toward me. Again, I couldn't see her expression. She said, "Can you imagine what a couple of guys like that might do if they got their hands on Tony?"

"On *Tony?*"

"Yeah."

"Wouldn't be pretty."

"I'd like to be there to see it," Judy said.

"Whoa! What kind of talk is that? We're on a mission to rescue the guy!"

"That doesn't mean I wish him a full and rewarding life of health and happiness. Not after what he did to me. And to *you*, for that matter. It'd be sort of neat to see him really get creamed by a couple of punks."

"I did a pretty good job on him," I said.

"But just think what a couple of punks like that might do."

"You shock me, Judy. I am truly shocked."

"Sure you are."

"Now, give me a clue. Why exactly *are* we driving out here to rescue him?"

"Good question."

"Maybe we *should* turn back."

"Nah," she said. "Can't."

"Why not?"

"It's my fault he's out here tonight. I'm the one who made him nuts. He wasn't a bad guy before I made him crazy. It's my fault he beat *me* up, and it's my fault he attacked *you*."

"That's ridiculous."

"No, it's true. I got him into this mess, so I've now gotta help him get out."

"Whether you want to or not."

"Yeah, sort of. No, I want to. I mean, we had a lot of great times together. Before he went off the deep end."

"You just feel sorry for him."

"Maybe. I don't know. I was in love with him. That sort of thing . . . I can't just pretend it never happened. He was the most important thing in my life for a while. The things we did . . . they're all part of me, and always will be . . . in spite of everything else."

"You're nuts," I said.

She laughed softly. "Think so?"

"Yeah. You sound like you're *still* in love with him."

"Maybe with the way he used to be."

"Well, that guy's gone forever."

"I know. It can never be the same. But still, I owe him. For the good times, and because this crazy stuff happened because of me."

"You gonna kiss and make up with him?"

She let out a sharp laugh. "No way!"

"Yep. And you'll take him back to your place . . . supposedly so he can pick up his car. But before you know it, you'll be asking him in for a beer. Maybe a coffee. Then wham! You're all over each other."

"Not a chance."

"Next thing you know, it's Humpty Dumpty time."

"No!" she blurted, laughing, and slapped my leg. "That's not going to happen. No way! Not in a zillion years."

I happened to know she was right.

"It's what *he'd* like to have happen," I said. "He wants you back."

"Well, I don't want *him* back."

"He kept pretending *I* was you."

"He what?"

"Yeah. He'd shut his eyes whenever we were making love, and call me Judy."

"Oh, my God." She sounded appalled. "Really?"

"Yeah. He even did it tonight when he had me on the picnic table."

"While he was *raping* you?"

"Yeah. He kept saying stuff like, 'How do you like it, Judy? Huh? Big enough for you, Judy? Oh, Judy, you're so tight and wet. I love your tight, wet pussy.'"

"*Tony* said that?"

"Not exactly. I cleaned it up a little. He didn't say pussy."

"Oh." She stared straight out the windshield. Her face looked gray in the moonlight, but I bet its true color was bright red.

"That's when I hit him with the bottle," I explained.

"Good going."

"Like I told you, guys are pigs."

"I'm willing to concede that *he* is."

"Trust me, they all are."

"I wouldn't go along with that," she said. "Not a hundred percent."

"Ninety percent?" I asked.

She said, "Ninety-nine."

So then I *had* to laugh.

"I tell you what," she said. "When we *do* find Tony, I'll run him over."

"All *right!*"

15

INTO THE WOODS

But she was joking, of course. About running him over. She wanted to rescue Tony, not kill him.

More's the pity.

If she'd been sincere in her desire to murder the guy, I might've changed my mind about killing her.

No, not really.

Here's the deal. No matter how much I might like Judy (and I liked her plenty), no matter how much she might despise Tony (though I frankly believe she still loved him in spite of everything), no matter *ANYTHING*—she had to die.

Didn't she?

Because if she lived, she could tell on me. I'm not saying she *would*. But she might. And then where would I be?

Up the infamous Creek of Shit without a paddle, that's where.

Kill her, and I'm home free.

Well, not completely. There was still the little problem of the redial button on Tony's phone. If he even *had* a redial button. Wherever his phone might be. In his mystery apartment, wherever that might be.

I wished I could get to it, but I didn't know how.

What could it show the cops, anyway? Only that Tony's last call had been to Serena and Charlie's phone.

It didn't prove that anyone had answered it.

Serena and Charlie were away on a trip. I, of course, never heard the phone ring because I never left my room over the garage.

There was only one problem with that.

Phone records would show that the call had lasted a while. Four or five minutes? Which would lead the cops to figure he either talked to someone, or left a message on the answering machine.

My insides shriveled.

They'll want to hear Tony's message.

But I couldn't *let* them hear it.

One little button on a telephone was going to destroy me if I couldn't come up with a way to find Tony's new apartment.

"We're almost there, aren't we?" Judy asked.

For a second or two, I didn't know what she was talking about. Then I saw the woods on both sides of the road. "It'll be pretty soon," I said. "The turnoff. It'll be on the right. Shady Creek Picnic Area."

"I hope he's okay."

"But not *too* okay?"

"Medium okay, medium hurt. Maybe in great pain, but with no permanent damage."

"You're so caring, Judy."

"I just hope he's there. I thought we'd find him before now. You know, on his way home."

"Don't forget, he's naked. He probably hides when a car comes along."

"Yeah. We might've gone right by him."

"Or he could've taken a different route."

"What other route? There's *only* one way to get back to town from out here."

"If you stick to the roads," I said. "But maybe he took a

shortcut through the woods." I spotted the sign up ahead and said, "Here it comes."

Judy slowed down.

"I bet we'll find him here," I said as she made the turn.

"You hit him that hard?" she asked.

"No. He's probably conscious by now. But if *I* were in his shoes . . . or shoeless and bare-ass naked, as the case may be . . ."

Judy laughed softly.

"I might just decide to stay put. At least I'd be in the middle of nowhere and surrounded by trees, so I wouldn't need to worry about everyone *seeing* me."

"You'd have to go home eventually."

When she said that, I immediately thought of my prowler. Maybe he was a guy who *hadn't* gone home eventually.

"I might just decide to stay in the woods," I said, "and live like Tarzan."

"Yeah. I can just see Tony swinging through the trees."

"I said grab the VINE!"

Judy laughed, shaking her head. Then she said, "Ouch."

"How would you know?" I asked.

"It's *gotta* hurt."

"I guess so."

I *knew* so. I bit one, once. Chomped it right off, in fact. You should've seen the guy! It hurt, all right.

Don't go feeling sorry for him, though. And don't think I'm some kind of evil person or nut. He shouldn't have gone and stuck it someplace where it didn't belong. Especially not after I'd begged him not to.

He got no worse than he deserved.

But you should've heard him scream! It hurt, all right! And then he went crazy trying to get it out of my mouth. He yelled, "Give it back! Give it back, you fucking bitch!" I guess he figured they could sew it back on for him at a hospital. But I wouldn't let him have it. He kept yelling and hitting me, but I went ahead and chewed it up. After I swallowed it, he *really* went berserk and almost killed me.

Anyway, enough about that. Like I said near the front, this book isn't an autobiography. I just had to tell you about that incident because of how it fit in with what Judy and I were saying on the road to the Shady Creek Picnic Area.

I didn't tell Judy about it, though.

I never told *anyone* about it, until now. Not even my mom or the people in the hospital where they took care of me afterwards. I made up a story about getting beaten up by a mugger, and the guy never told.

I don't know what ever happened to him.

Well, I can vouch for two or three inches. Not the rest, though. When I got better and went back to school, we had a new principal. He got hired because the one before him had suddenly and mysteriously left town.

Anyway, that's *really* more than I intended to tell. I guess I'll leave it in, though. Why not? It's the truth. And it also goes to show you what pigs men are—even school principals.

I only have one regret about what I did to him.

No mustard!

That's a little joke.

Anyway, I've strayed away from the real story.

When I left off, I'd just told Judy the old Tarzan joke about grabbing the vine, and we were having some laughs about that. She was driving us along the road to the picnic area. She thought we might find Tony there. I was sitting in the passenger seat, and had Tony's pistol in the front pocket of my cut-offs. I'd be using it on her pretty soon.

The next thing you know, we came to the end of the road. The pavement spread out into a clearing with logs laid out to show you where to park. There were places for six or eight cars, but no other cars were there. Judy drove up to one of the logs and stopped.

The beams of our headlights reached out into the picnic area, lighting a couple of the green wooden tables.

"I don't see him," Judy said. "Do you?"

"No. But we weren't up here. We were down by the creek. If you want, I'll run down and see if he's there."

"No, don't do that. We'd better stay in the car."

"What if he's still unconscious?" I asked.

"I don't know."

"I'll just run down and take a quick look."

"No, don't."

"It'll only take a minute."

"I'll go with you," Judy said, and shut off the headlights. The night dropped down on us.

"My God," she said. "It's dark out here."

"Do you have a flashlight?"

"Sure. Back in my bedroom. Maybe I should go get it." But she was kidding. Instead of turning the car around, she shut off its engine and unfastened her seatbelt.

"Ready?" I asked.

"Not hardly. I don't want to go out there."

"Then stay here. That's fine. I'll just go . . ."

"No way. If you're going, I'm coming with you."

"Then we might as well get it over with," I said, and opened the passenger door. The car's overhead light came on.

"Much better," Judy said.

I climbed out. My legs were trembling. I was shaking all over, and sweating. My heart was pounding like mad. I was a genuine wreck.

For one thing, the place gave me the creeps. As a general rule, I don't like to be in forests at night. Plus, a lot of bad stuff had gone on in Miller's Woods, and I was a little nervous about the prowler. He might be nearby. After his visit to Serena and Charlie's house, he'd gone back into the woods only about a mile from here.

My other reason for being a wreck is that I had to kill Judy. It stank, but there was no way out of it. And this was the perfect place for it.

Dark as death, secluded, and within reasonable walking distance of home if I took the shortcut through the woods.

When we shut our doors, the light in the car went out.

We met in front, but didn't say anything. As if we were afraid to speak. Afraid of who might hear us.

Side by side, we walked up the gentle slope toward the place where we'd seen the picnic tables. We could still see them, but now they looked so dark and vague that they hardly seemed real.

Here and there, tiny dabs of moonlight made it down through the trees. A soft, warm breeze was blowing. It might've felt good, if things had been different. Just then, there *was* no such thing as good. Good, for a while, seemed to be gone from the face of the earth.

We walked past the picnic tables, and went on to the crest of the hill. There, we stopped and gazed down toward the creek. I saw a few places that looked like moonlight glinting off water. And I saw a flat shape that might've been a picnic table. But nothing looked very clear or very real. Mostly, there was only darkness.

"I've got a bad feeling about this," Judy whispered.

What are you, psychic?

"What kind of bad feeling?" I asked. I didn't really want to know, but I had to ask.

"Like we're really going to regret going down there."

"You don't have to go down."

"Yeah. I do."

Brave, innocent, stupid Judy.

16

KILLING JUDY

As we made our way down the slope, I reached into the front pocket of my cut-offs and took hold of the pistol. With my thumb, I flicked its safety off.

"Tony?" Judy called softly. "Are you there?"

I slipped the .22 out of my pocket, but kept it by my side, out of sight.

"Tony?" she called again. "It's Judy. Are you down there?"

I didn't want her to know what was coming, so I slowed down a little. She was about one stride downhill from me and two feet to my left when I brought the pistol up and fired point blank at the side of her head.

That should've done it.

But on the way up, the muzzle of the pistol snagged her ear.

I must've been standing too close. Probably because of the darkness.

She yelped, "Ow!"

The pistol spat out a bright, quick flash. In that instant, I saw the tilt of Judy's head and the angle of my pistol.

And I couldn't tell if I'd gotten her.

But she cried out, grabbed her head above the ear and fell, tumbling crookedly.

On her way down, I took aim but decided not to fire again.

For one thing, I didn't want the noise. If you haven't been around a .22, you might think it just makes a tiny bang like a cap gun, or something. But it's more like a strong firecracker.

BAM! My ears were ringing from the shot, and the sound of the blast must've carried for a mile.

I probably could've heard it from my room above the garage, if I'd been there.

My prowler *must've* heard it, unless he'd left the woods entirely.

He's the other reason I didn't put a few more rounds into Judy. The fewer I used on her, the more I'd still have in the pistol in case I met *him* on my way back home through the woods.

Him, or some other creep.

(What about the guys in the Cadillac? Were they gone for good?)

So instead of using Judy for target practice as she tumbled down the slope, I thumbed the safety on and hurried after her. She rolled all the way to the bottom, her arms and legs flopping around. When the ground leveled out, she rolled over a couple more times and stopped.

She came to rest in a patch of moonlight.

Her white blouse had come unbuttoned. It was wide open, leaving her bare to the waistband of her skirt. The skirt had gotten pushed up around her hips.

Except for the patch of white fabric between her legs, she looked like somebody who'd just gotten herself raped and murdered.

Raped and murdered.

An idea suddenly leaped into my head.

A brilliant idea.

I slipped the pistol into my pocket, then picked Judy up

by the ankles and dragged her toward the picnic table. Along the way, she groaned a couple of times.

Still alive.

But she didn't struggle at all, just remained limp.

I stopped dragging her when the backs of my knees met the edge of the picnic table's wooden bench. I lowered her feet to the grass.

With such deep darkness, I couldn't see any blood on her. But her head *had* to be bloody. So I took off my shirt—Tony's shirt—and put it near the end of the bench, out of harm's way.

After that, I straddled Judy, squatted down, grabbed her sides just below her armpits, and pulled her up to a sitting position. Then I hugged her against me and stood up.

A good thing I'd taken off the shirt. Her face was so slippery against my shoulder and breast, it must've been covered with blood.

Though Judy felt awfully heavy, she didn't weigh nearly as much as Tony. I managed to seat her on the bench and lean her backward against the edge of the table. Then, keeping a hand on her shoulder so she wouldn't tip over, I climbed on top of the table. I crouched down, grabbed her, and hauled her up.

Then I stretched her out so she was lying lengthwise on her back.

By that time, I was sweating like a hog. I wanted to get it done, though, so I didn't waste any time resting.

First, I pulled the blouse off her shoulders and about halfway down her arms. Which made her bare all the way down to the top of her skirt. It also pinned her arms against her sides, in case she might wake up and try to struggle.

Second, I rucked her skirt up around her waist. I was tempted to take it off her entirely. Some guys do that, preferring their victim naked. But most of them, when it gets to a certain stage, are in an awfully big hurry to *get in*. They'll just shove the skirt up and go for it. Some guys even *like* you to be wearing clothes when they screw you. It turns them on.

I know all about this sort of stuff.

When you're built "like a brick shithouse," you learn plenty.

I'm what you might call an expert.

Anyway, never mind.

After I'd shoved up Judy's skirt, I spread open her legs about as wide as they would go, so her feet hung over the sides of the table.

Next, I had to rip her panties off. A guy who wants to rape you will hardly ever just pull them down. He has to do it with violence. If he has a knife, he'll cut them off you and maybe cut you a little bit in the process. Some guys will tear them off with their teeth. That can hurt, too. Accidently on purpose, they'll bite more than your panties. Usually, though, they rip them off you with their hands. That's how I decided to do it.

On my knees between Judy's legs, I slipped a hand inside the crotch of her panties. The flimsy fabric was moist. I jerked it sideways hard and fast. Half the crotch panel ripped away from her waistband. One more tug, and it tore completely off. I let go, and the tattered flap fell against the table top. She still wore the narrow strip of elastic low across her belly, but there was nothing in the way.

Then I went to work on her.

Coming to my senses afterward, I found myself sprawled on top of her. I was completely naked. She was slippery underneath me, and still alive. I felt the slight rise and fall of her chest, the thump of her heartbeat.

Suddenly, a hot sickness rushed through me.

What have I done?

Blown everything.

All I'd wanted to do from the start was clean up after myself, make it impossible for anyone to suspect me of killing Tony—destroy every link to me, wipe out every trace.

What'll I do?

For starters, I pushed myself up. Our bodies came apart with quiet, wet sounds. I climbed off her, got down from the top of the table, and sat on the bench. Leaning forward, I put my elbows on my knees and tried to figure a solution.

I must've looked like that statue, *The Thinker*.

The famous one by the sculptor, Godzilla.

Just kidding. Rodin, right?

The Thinker, but a female version and built like a brick shithouse.

Thinking, *How the hell do I get out of this?*

What a mess.

If only I'd kept things simple! But no! I had to get clever and tricky. Make them think she was murdered by a rapist. Brilliant idea!

In the process, I'd turned her into a petri dish of Alice samples.

So clean her up!

Sure thing, I thought. What about the *marks*. I'd put on her body?

The Thinker returned to thought.

Suddenly, I sat up straight and blurted, "Yes!"

First, I had to find my clothes. I slipped into my shoes—Tony's loafers. Then I hunted for my cut-offs. I found them on the ground where I'd thrown them during the frenzy with Judy. I put them on the bench so they wouldn't get lost again.

Carrying Tony's shirt, I went to the creek. Though I could hear the quiet gurgle and see bits of moonlight glinting on the water, the embankment took me by surprise. It was like stepping off a stair in the darkness. I gasped and fell and hoped like hell I wouldn't go down on a sharp rock.

Luckily, I hit nothing but water. It was about a foot deep. It splashed up cool against my face and underside as my hands and knees punched through the surface. The rocky bottom hurt my knees a little, but not much. The shirt protected my hands.

I eased myself all the way down into the water so it covered me and glided gently over me. It felt wonderful. It probably wasn't very clean, though. Not like the swimming pool.

Thinking of the pool, I couldn't help but remember the prowler. I pictured him floating on his back, and how he'd gleamed with moonlight. So beautiful and dangerous. Then he was out of the pool and squirming against the glass door, throbbing and spurting.

If they find some of that stuff on Judy . . .

That'll cinch it for sure.

My brilliant idea was suddenly more brilliant than ever.

But it would require a trip to Serena and Charlie's house.

It'll be worth it.

Not wasting another moment, I pushed myself out of the water. With the sodden shirt in my hands, I climbed the bank and hurried to the table.

Judy was sprawled on top, the same way I'd left her.

Sitting on the bench, I dumped the water out of my shoes. Then I put them on again, climbed the bench and bent over her. Starting at her face, I washed her with the shirt. Water spilled off her, running onto the table, dribbling through the cracks between its boards and hitting the ground under the table with quiet splattery sounds.

I thought the water might wake her up, but it didn't. She stayed limp.

I mopped her neck, her shoulders and breasts, then decided I needed more water. So I hurried back to the creek. This time, I didn't fall in. With the shirt sopping again, I returned to Judy and worked my way lower down her body.

I made two more trips to the creek for water.

By the time I was done cleaning Judy, I'd drenched her from head to ankles and scrubbed every inch of her with the shirt.

Every inch of her front, anyway.

I didn't turn her over, or see any reason to.

She gave me no trouble at all, just stayed limp except for a few times when she squirmed. Now and then, she made soft moaning sounds.

I washed the shirt out a final time and put it on the bench with my cut-offs.

It took a while, in the darkness, to find a good stick. There were plenty to choose from, though. I finally came up with a piece of branch about four feet long. At one end, it was just about the right thickness to wrap my fingers around. From there, it tapered down to about half that size. It had a few small limbs along the way, but I snapped them off.

Then I knelt on the table and went back to work on Judy.

Right away, she flinched and cried out and tried to sit up.

I clubbed her down with the heavy end of the stick. Four or five blows to the head and face, and she was limp again. After that, I focused on the places where I might've left bruises with my teeth and hands.

Really laid into her.

The heavy end made thunking sounds when it struck her. The other end whistled each time I swung it down, and whapped her skin like a switch.

She never flinched or cried out. Those early blows to the head had done her in.

At least for now.

Exhausted and drenched with sweat, I went down to the creek. I rolled in the cool water, then lay on my back for a while with only my face in the air. It felt great. But work still needed to be done.

Not quite ready to get going, I stayed in the water and made a list in my head:

1. *Make sure Judy is dead.*
2. *Wipe my fingerprints off her car.*
3. *Run back to Serena and Charlie's house.*
4. *Collect the sample off the glass door.*
5. *Run back here.*
6. *Add the sample to Judy's body.*
7. *Go home.*

It all had to be finished before sunrise. How much time did that give me? Two or three hours, probably.

Plenty of time.

But not if I spent the rest of the night relaxing in the creek. So I climbed out and returned to the table. Kneeling on the bench, I put my ear close to Judy's mouth. She didn't seem to be breathing. Nor could I find a pulse at her neck or wrist.

She seemed to be dead.

But I'm no expert on that sort of thing.

I had to be completely sure.

The best way, I decided, was to cave in her head with a rock. Why use a rock? Because I didn't want to fire my pistol again, I had no knife or saber, strangling or suffocating her seemed iffy, and drowning her in the creek would've been too much work. With a good, heavy rock, I could crack open her skull and spill her brains out and *know* she was dead.

To get one, I returned to the creek.

Standing in the water, I reached down between my feet and plucked out a rough-edged rock the size of a baseball.

It should do the job fine.

With the rock clutched in my right hand, I climbed onto the bank and took a couple of strides toward the picnic table.

And stopped.

The top of the table was speckled with moonlight.

A flat, empty surface.

Judy was gone.

17

GONE

No!

She wasn't on the table, but she couldn't be *gone*. Maybe she'd rolled off and fallen.

I ran to the table.

Without enough light to see if she was on the ground, I searched for her with my feet. I circled the entire table, sweeping my feet this way and that, hoping to kick her.

No Judy.

I tossed the rock away, dropped to my hands and knees, and crawled under the table. The ground was soggy.

No Judy.

I crawled backward. Clear of the table, I scrambled on my knees to the bench where I'd left my clothes. My shirt and cut-offs were still there.

So was the pistol.

My panic faded a little.

I stood up, quickly put on the shorts, and pulled the pistol out of my pocket. Turning slowly, I scanned the area. Judy couldn't have gone far. In her shape, she was lucky she'd been able to move at all, much less get down from the table and sneak into the trees.

Unless she had help.

The prowler, for instance.

The idea sickened me with dread, but only for a moment.

Nobody had come to Judy's rescue. I was almost certain of that. I can't explain exactly why, but I'd sensed from the start that we were alone in our clearing by the creek. I'd felt the solitude, the privacy. I'd never doubted it.

"Judy?" I asked. I didn't call it out, but spoke in a normal voice. And knew she was near enough to hear me.

Probably hiding in the bushes or trees just beyond the table, not daring to move because she knows I'll hear her.

"Where are you, Judy? It's me. Alice. Are you all right? I'm sorry I ran off and left you, but . . . I thought you were dead. Somebody ambushed us. Do you remember that?" (I figured her memory might be fuzzy about a lot of stuff, because of being shot in the head, etc.) "You got shot and went down, and I ran for my life."

I saw no movement in the darkness of the woods. I didn't hear anyone, either.

"Then I came sneaking back and saw this awful woman. She had you on top of the table. She was beating you with something. I wanted to help you, but . . . I wouldn't have stood a chance, you know? I mean, she had a gun. She would've shot me, just like she shot you."

I stopped telling the story, and listened.

Nothing.

"She finally quit beating you and went away," I said. "She ran into the woods. I followed her for a couple of minutes to make sure she was really leaving, then I came back to help you, but . . . Where are you?"

No answer.

I wondered whether she was already out of earshot, or unconscious again—or just didn't believe me.

"It's safe for now," I told her. "But that woman might come

back pretty soon. You'd better come out. I know you must be scared and confused—and in terrible pain—but if she comes back . . . Please, Judy! I'm scared. Let's get out of here! I'll drive you to the emergency room."

Drive?

What if Judy *wasn't* cowering in the darkness beyond the table or unconscious or sneaking deeper into the woods?

What if she was circling around me?

Going for her car!

I snatched my shirt off the bench, then whirled around and raced to the slope. I chugged my way up it, pumping hard with my arms, the pistol in one hand, the shirt in the other. The wet shirt slapped my side. My breasts leaped about wildly. Halfway up the slope, one of my loafers flew off. I didn't dare stop for it.

At any moment, Judy might reach her car, climb in and drive away.

I knew it would happen.

It WON'T happen! Look what I did to her! How can she make it to the car? She can't.

But she will.

I was doomed. I'd been doomed from the start of all this, and I'd known it, but I'd resisted.

In my mind, I heard the engine start. I heard it kick over again and again, roaring defeat at me.

But I didn't hear it for real.

Not yet.

Dashing over the crest of the hill, I saw the vague shape of the car in the darkness ahead.

No sign of Judy.

Of course not. She was already behind the wheel, concealed in darkness behind the windshield, reaching for the ignition.

I dodged a picnic table and sprinted toward the car.

With every stride, I expected the headbeams to shoot out and blind me.

But they didn't.

The engine didn't turn over.

The headlights stayed dark.

Nothing happened.

Staggering to a halt, I ducked down a little and peered through the open window of the driver's door.

Nobody there.

Nobody in the back seat, either.

With the last of my energy, I jogged in a circle around the car to make sure it was safe. Then I slipped the .22 into my pocket and pulled open the driver's door. The car filled with light. Squinting, I dropped into the seat. The key was in the ignition. Judy must've left it there when we set out to search for Tony. I jerked the door shut and the light went out.

For a while, I just sat there streaming sweat and gasping for breath.

I could barely put my thoughts together, I was so pooped.

But I knew I'd lucked out. I'd gotten to the car first. Judy had lost her chance to drive away.

My skin itched from the heat and sweat. When I couldn't stand it any longer, I rubbed myself with the shirt. It was still wet. It felt cool and wonderful.

I started feeling better about things.

Nobody ever said it would be easy, I told myself. It's a tricky business, trying to get away with this sort of thing. There are bound to be setbacks.

By and large, I'd handled matters fairly well so far. I would've met with complete success if I hadn't gone to Judy's apartment by mistake.

Pretty big damn mistake.

Bigger for her than me. She'd be dying because of it.

I rubbed my face and chest again, then leaned sideways and used the shirt to wipe off the interior handle of the passenger door. I also did the window sill and dashboard. Then I sat up straight and wiped the steering wheel.

As I did that, I realized that one of my shoes was gone.

Gotta go find it.

Time's a-wasting.

I pulled out the ignition key. With the key case in one hand and my shirt in the other, I climbed out of the car. Again, the light came on. In its glow, I saw the strap of Judy's purse on the floor. She'd apparently shoved her purse underneath the driver's seat.

I started to reach for the strap, then stopped myself.

What do I need her purse for? Just have to get rid of it later, like Tony's wallet.

I would've been better off if I'd never touched Tony's wallet. That's what got me into this.

Finding that paper with the wrong address.

So I decided to leave Judy's purse untouched.

Standing in the V of the open door, I did some more mop-up with my shirt. Then I shut the door and wiped its outside handle.

I dropped Judy's keys into a pocket of my cut-offs, then went around the car to take care of fingerprints I might've left on the outside of the passenger door.

The surface of the parking area was pavement littered by old leaves and twigs. I doubted that my bare foot was leaving any tracks. To make sure, though, I opened the passenger door. The interior light came back on, and spilled a yellow glow onto the pavement. I did a couple of tests with my bare foot. Nothing showed, so I shut the door and wiped it again and took off.

I headed back to the scene of Judy's escape.

She'll be down there, somewhere. Maybe trying to crawl away, or hiding in the bushes.

Maybe watching me.

About halfway down the slope, I found my shoe. I slid my foot into it. Then I put the shirt on. It stuck to my skin. I left it unbuttoned so air could get in.

About the next step I took, my shoe slipped on the wet grass. I started to drop backward, but caught my balance in time and stayed on my feet.

Close call, I thought. What if I'd fallen and really hurt myself? Bumped my head on a rock, or something, and got knocked out cold? Then *I'd* be the one in big trouble. Judy could come up here and finish me off. Or take her car keys and escape. Lucky thing . . .

Would she?

What if she saw me fall, tumble down the slope, and not get up? Would she come out of hiding?

She might.

Or she might figure it's a trick.

I took a few more strides, then pretended to trip over a rock or something. Yelling, "AHHH!" as loud as I could, I windmilled my arms, stumbled a couple of times as if trying to regain my footing, then plunged headlong.

I wanted it to look real.

It suddenly was real.

I slammed against the ground. It knocked my wind out and seemed to kick me into the air. I flipped over. The ground kept battering me, shoving me along. I twisted and rolled and flopped, arms and legs flying, all the way to the bottom.

Like Judy after her fall down the same slope, I came to rest on my back.

History repeats itself.

At least I hadn't been shot in the head.

I felt plenty bruised and scratched and battered, though. And I'd lost *both* shoes.

Plus the pistol.

I should've been able to feel its weight against my right thigh, but the pocket had an awful lightness.

So much, I thought, for another brilliant idea.

Now what?

I had two choices. Either forget the trick and go looking for the pistol, or stay on my back and pretend to be unconscious.

I felt vulnerable without the gun. But I could get along without it for a while. I didn't need artillery for handling Judy.

Just stick with the plan for ten or fifteen minutes, I told myself. See what happens.

It might be a waste of time.

On the other hand, searching for her in the dark woods would probably be a waste of time, too. If she'd found herself a good hiding place, and didn't make any noise, I'd hardly stand a chance of finding her. Unless I tripped over her, or something.

This way, at least, was restful.

Just don't fall asleep, I warned myself.

There probably wasn't much danger of that. Though I was worn out, I didn't feel sleepy. I was too tense for that. And too uncomfortable. The tumble down the slope had bruised and scratched me. I felt small pains in a dozen places, and I itched in about a dozen more.

I ached to rub my injuries, scratch my itches.

But I couldn't do it.

Judy might be watching.

Or so I thought, anyway, until she shrieked, *"No!"* into the night somewhere far away.

18

CRIES IN THE NIGHT

Either Judy, or someone else.

It had to be Judy, though. A woman's voice, and coming from the right direction. Who else *could* it be?

If it was Judy, she'd missed my tumble down the slope and she wasn't watching me now. My fall had roughed me up, but accomplished nothing. I got to my feet, wincing a couple of times.

Standing there, I searched my pockets. Tony's wallet was still in my back pocket. I still had all the keys, too. Apparently, nothing had fallen out except the gun.

I wiped the sweat off my face and rubbed my hurts and itches and stared into the woods.

Nothing to see.

I heard the trees whispering quietly with the breeze. Birds and crickets and other forest sounds. But not another outcry.

Okay, I thought. What's going on?

She'd shrieked like someone scared witless, or hurt, or both.

So, was it real or fake?

If fake, she must be trying to lure me into a trap. A gutsy

move. A crazy move. Hell, I was bigger and tougher than Judy. I'd already beaten the snot out of her. And I had a gun. Her only real chance of survival was to *avoid* me.

But you never know with people. They do weird, stupid stuff sometimes. Especially when they're scared. Maybe Judy thought she could out-smart me.

Maybe she'd figured out a great, flawless trap.

On the other hand, she might be in real trouble.

Either way, I didn't have a choice. I had to go looking for her. And finish her off, unless somebody'd already saved me the trouble.

I wasn't going anywhere, though, without the pistol.

I wanted to find my shoes, too, but they didn't matter much. The .22 mattered plenty.

Turning away from the woods, I searched the grassy area around my feet, looking for the gun. I'd been aware of losing my shoes early in the fall, but didn't have a clue as to when the gun had slipped out of my pocket.

It didn't seem to be nearby, so I began to study the route of my fall. For the most part, the slope was clear of trees. A lot of moonlight got through. Before even starting to climb, I picked out half a dozen chunks of darkness. A couple of them would probably turn out to be my shoes. I saw nothing that might be the pistol, though.

I started trudging up the slope, taking it slowly, hunched over, my knees bent and my arms swaying. I must've looked like a kid playing elephant. It was a nice, relaxing posture. But I was too tired and hot to be comfortable. My shirt stuck to my back with sweat. My eyes stung. My face and chest itched with trickles of sweat.

I started out thinking the pistol would be the real problem. Because it was flat and so much smaller than the shoes, it might disappear in the grass. I even worried that I might not be able to find it at all.

But I found it first, only about fifteen feet up the slope. The way I was bent over with my arms swaying, I almost brushed it with my fingertips before seeing it. The pistol lay nestled in the thick grass. In the moonlight, its stainless steel finish looked gray like dirty snow.

I snatched it up.

Then I rubbed it against the front of my cut-offs to wipe off the dew from the grass.

Afraid of losing it again, I kept it in my hand.

A few minutes later, I came across one of the loafers. I slipped my foot into it and went looking for the other.

One shoe off and one shoe on . . .

"*Help!*"

This time, I recognized Judy's voice. Or thought so, anyway. It's how she might've sounded, squealing out a plea to be saved.

She's gotta be in deep shit.

Or else a great actress.

But my guts told me this wasn't faked.

So did my skin. Though burning hot and slick with sweat, I felt goosebumps spreading up my thighs and belly and breasts. The hairs on my arms stiffened. Prickles scurried up my back and the nape of my neck. My nipples tingled and got hard. Goosebumps crawled over my cheeks, my forehead. My scalp crawled.

It's pretty much what happens every time I get a strong case of the creeps, the willies, the heebie-jeebies.

And I had them now.

Something about the sound of Judy's cry for help, maybe. Or what it triggered in my imagination.

Something awful had happened to her.

Or someONE.

Something or someone worse than me.

Turning around slowly, being careful not to slip on the wet slope, I stared at the woods. There was nothing to see.

Judy's cries had come from deeper in. The first had sounded nearer than the second. Was she running away from a pursuer? Or was she already caught, and being carried?

If he kills her, I'm in business.

But killing her was *my* job. It gave me a queer feeling to think of it being done by someone else.

Who? My prowler?

I hurried to find the other shoe. No more cries came from the woods while I hunted for it.

Is she already dead?

Did she get away?

This might sound odd, but I didn't want either to be true.

Finally, I found the loafer. I slid my foot into it, then turned around and started making my way down the slope again—carefully. I'd found out the hard way that the slope was tricky and not as gentle as it seemed.

Safe at the bottom, I broke into a run. And ran like crazy until I came to the picnic table. There, I stopped and listened. Mostly, all I heard were my heartbeats and my hard breathing.

What's he doing to her?

The sick bastard.

I thought about what he'd done to the glass door.

Might not even be him.

I stepped past the end of the table, took my usual route to the creek, and knelt in the water. Then I twisted around and sat down on the bottom. A tricky thing to pull off, one-handed. But I managed to do it and keep the pistol high and dry.

No, not because I was afraid of getting my ammo wet.

As a fan of mysteries and thrillers, I've read enough to figure out that most people who write them don't know squat about firearms. (That goes double for the people who make movies and television shows.) One thing I know, and some of them don't, is that ammo won't get hurt by a little dip in the creek.

The reason I kept the pistol high was in case I needed it fast. I didn't want to shoot it and find out, too late, that I had a barrel full of water. I wasn't sure about a .22, but some guns can blow up if you pull a stunt like that.

(Anyway, I just wanted to make that clear. I don't want you to read my book and think I'm one of those idiots who worries about a little water wrecking my ammunition.)

Okay.

So there I was, sitting in the creek and holding my pistol overhead while I rested and cooled off. The water sure felt good. Cool and smooth. With my left hand, I cupped some of it into my mouth.

And there I sat.

Not really wanting to move.

The water felt great, rushing against me. And it tasted great, too. Fresh and woodsy.

But I was wasting time.

Scared to move.

On my right, the woods loomed high, hiding the moonlight. A kingdom of darkness. It was where I needed to go. Judy was over in that direction.

But so was whatever horrible creature or person had made her shriek.

I didn't want to go there.

I felt safe in the creek. And the area to my left seemed even safer. That's where the picnic table was. The one I'd had Judy on. I could see a bit of it through the trees. In that same direction was the slope to the parking lot. And Judy's parked car. And the roads out of the woods.

In that direction, nothing bad would happen to me.

I could even drive away in Judy's car, leave it somewhere in town, and walk home.

I *wanted* to do it.

To put an end to all this. To stop being scared and tired and hurt. To go home and lock myself in my good, safe room above the garage and maybe never come out again.

I *longed* to do that, and forget all about Judy.

And save myself.

Whatever got her might get me.

Leaning forward, I lowered my shoulders and head into the creek.

I would've looked very odd to anyone watching me.

All they'd see was my arm sticking up, holding the pistol high. Like the Lady of the Lake with better weaponry.

I've got a gun, gang. What the hell am I scared of?

I stayed under for a while longer. Then my lungs started to ache, so I came up for air. And struggled to my feet. And trudged through the knee-deep water, my shirt clinging like someone else's sodden skin, my shorts so wet and heavy that they hung low on my hips, ready to fall.

I climbed the bank on the side of the creek where the forest began. With the pistol clamped under my left armpit, I tugged my cut-offs up and tightened the belt. Then I took off my loafers, emptied them, and put them on again.

I was shivering slightly. No matter how hot the air is, it always feels chilly when you first come out of water. Also, I hadn't gotten over being scared.

The pistol gave me enough courage to go on, but it didn't make me fearless.

I was still vulnerable.

After all, a .22 doesn't pack much punch.

And I'd never counted the rounds in the magazine, so I didn't know how many cartridges were left. They were single-stacked, I knew that. Fully loaded, a magazine that size might hold about eight or ten.

I'd already fired one.

And maybe it hadn't been fully loaded to start with.

I could find out how many rounds were in the gun. But not without unloading it. Which didn't seem like a great thing to try. In the dark, I might drop a couple of cartridges and lose them on the ground. Or what if somebody came along while I stood there with a handful of loose ammo?

Doesn't matter, anyway. When I run out, I run out.

Let it be a surprise.

I started walking into the dark woods, keeping the pistol down close to my side, raising my left arm in front of me for protection against crashing into tree trunks or low branches. I walked slowly, unsure of where my feet might land. Very soon, the chill from the water went away. The air again felt hot and heavy. Here, surrounded by trees, I felt no breeze at all.

I walked without knowing where to find Judy.

Just that her cries had come from deeper in the woods, somewhere east of the creek.

I walked slowly in that direction and tried not to make much noise.

19

THE SEARCH

Soon, I began to think it was a waste of time. I might search till dawn and never find Judy.

How *could* I find her? Miller's Woods went on for miles, and she might be almost anywhere. Maybe I'd already missed her. I might've walked on past her and left her behind. With any step I took, she could've been a hundred yards away to the north or south. Or sprawled unseen in the darkness five feet away.

It would take a huge stroke of luck for me to find her.

And maybe that wouldn't be so lucky.

Maybe I'd be luckier *not* finding her.

If she'd faked the outcries, a trap was waiting for me. If she *hadn't* faked them, I might have to face whatever had torn those shrieks out of her.

Even if I couldn't find Judy, *it* might find me.

It or he.

Probably a he.

Most monsters are.

At any moment, he might jump me from behind. Take me

down and drag me away. Do things to me so I would cry out in terror and pain just like Judy.

The pistol might not do much good if he caught me by surprise. Or if there turned out to be more than one guy.

I knew what it was like. All of it. To be jumped from behind. To be outnumbered. To be beaten and tortured. To be raped, gang-banged, sodomized and all the rest.

No, not *all* the rest.

I hadn't been killed.

Not yet.

I'd been *left* for dead, but not killed.

I'll tell you about it. I hadn't planned on getting into stuff like this, but what the hell. Why should I keep it a secret?

It happened when I was eighteen, and got a flat tire on a highway outside Tucson. I was alone. Alone, I tried to change the flat. But three guys in a pickup truck stopped to "help." They helped me, all right. Drove me off into the desert and spent all night "doing" me, doing everything that popped into their sick ugly heads. By the time they were done with the fun, I apparently seemed to be dead. So they dug a grave for me, rolled me into it and covered me up. Then they drove off and left me. I would've ended up dead for real, but I'd landed at the bottom of the grave with an air pocket under my face. I also would've ended up dead if they hadn't been such lazy bastards. They'd dug the grave too shallow, hadn't bothered to pile some heavy rocks on top, and so I managed to crawl out. Then I was picked up by a family of off-roaders who happened to come along in a Jeep.

You might think nothing would scare me, after being through a deal like that.

But guess what.

It's the opposite. *Everything* scares me.

You've probably heard the saying, "What doesn't kill me makes me stronger." It might be true, as far as it goes. I have gotten stronger and stronger from all the bad stuff. But I've also gotten more and more afraid.

So even as I crept through the dark woods hoping to find Judy, I shivered with fear and felt ready to scream and wanted to run for home.

If the fear wasn't bad enough—and it was plenty—I also had accidents. I was trudging through rough wilderness, not hiking on a path through a park. All I could see were a few bits and pieces of moonlight, dim gray blurs that might be anything, and blackness that might be *nothing*.

I hated walking into the black places. I might drop into a pit or step on a body or get leaped on by a madman. And the gray places weren't much better.

Three or four times, I tripped and fell down.

Twice, I scraped the top of my head against low limbs.

Countless times, I was whipped across the face by unseen branches or bushes.

Only once did I get the *real* shaft. Striding through a black place, I walked straight into the end of a large, broken limb. I never saw it coming and didn't even slow down. Just plowed into it. It slammed into me above my belly button. It probably would've plunged all the way through and killed me if it hadn't been so thick. Instead of skewering me, though, the branch gouged me, caved me in, punched my breath out and knocked me backward. I fell sprawling.

For a while, I twisted and squirmed and couldn't breathe.

When I was able to catch a breath, I curled onto my side and clutched my belly. The wound felt raw and seering hot. Not very deep, but awfully painful. I held it with both hands and cried.

Finally, I was ready to get up. I found the pistol on the ground beside me, then struggled to my feet.

Judy no longer mattered much.

I really had no hope of finding her, anyway.

And so what? With or without me, she probably wouldn't leave the woods alive. Not unless she'd faked those cries, which I doubted.

n if she gets away, I told myself, she doesn't know who r where I live.

She knows my face.

So what? Unless she bumps into me at the supermarket . . .

What if she describes me to a police artist?

That could be bad. Sometimes, those drawings turn out to look exactly like the suspect. I might be watching the TV news in a few days and end up staring at my own face. Most of the people in Chester would see it, too. Even though I pretty much kept to myself, I wasn't a total recluse. I'd be recognized, for sure.

On the other hand, maybe Judy wouldn't be able to describe me. Though we'd spent time together in her well-lighted apartment, she hadn't gotten a good look at me *after* I shot her in the head and pounded the daylights out of her with a stick. It's very common for head injuries to screw up your short-term memory.

That's what I've read, anyway.

In my own experience, I've always been able to remember every detail no matter *where* I got injured, in the head or otherwise.

I wouldn't have minded a little memory loss, here and there. Especially if I got to pick which memories to dump.

Memories can be a real pain.

While I was thinking about all this, I kept on sneaking through the woods. I'm not sure, though, whether I was looking for Judy or for a way out. I just kept moving along, trying not to get hurt again. I still couldn't stand up straight or take a deep breath because of ramming into the branch.

Every now and then, I imagined how it would feel to catch a branch that way in the middle of my face. That was almost enough to make me sit down and wait for dawn. But I kept moving, anyway.

I needed to finish with Judy and get back to Serena and Charlie's house before daylight.

The lawn might have some Tony on it. The saber was still hidden in the bushes. I needed to do a whole slew of other chores, too, like make sure nobody would ever hear Tony's voice on the answering machine, and burn his wallet and . . .

Firelight!

In the distance ahead of me and off to my left, I saw bushes and low-hanging tree branches that trembled with yellow-orange light.

This is it! Has to be!

I made my way slowly toward the glow, trying to be quiet.

Let this be it! Let it be Judy!

I walked as close as I dared to the firelit clearing, then crawled even closer and peered through a gap in the bushes.

And found her.

Found a tent, a campfire, and Judy.

The green tent was pitched a few yards to the right of the fire. The fire, burning brightly, cast its glow far enough to shine on Judy.

Nobody else seemed to be there.

But *someone* belonged to the campsite. Someone had pitched the tent, built the fire, and captured Judy. Someone had *put* her this way.

She stood under a tree limb, her arms high, her wrists tied together. The rope went over the top of the limb. I couldn't see where it came down, but the other end must've been tied to a tree somewhere behind her. She wasn't dangling, or standing on tiptoes, but she didn't have enough rope to let her slouch. She looked as if she were *stretching* for the ground. Her back was arched. Her skin was pulled so taut that all her ribs showed. Her breasts were drawn high. Her belly looked flat and long. She stood with her legs pressed tightly together. Her feet, flat against the ground, weren't tied.

When I'd left her on the picnic table, she'd been wearing her shoes and socks, her skirt, and her blouse. The skirt had been rucked up around her belly and her blouse had been pulled half off, but she'd still had them on. Now, they were gone.

All she wore now was a hat and a gag.

An old, felt hat covered her head all the way down to the eyebrows. Her upraised arms pinned the brim up against its sides. The strange hat must've belonged to her attacker. Maybe he'd jammed it on her head to hold a bandage against her gunshot wound. Or maybe he liked how she looked in it.

The hat made her look like some sort of beautiful hillbilly girl. Maybe the Feds had stripped and tortured her, trying to make her give up the location of her moonshine still.

Of course, she couldn't tell any secrets with the gag in her mouth. It looked like a red bandana. The sort of thing you might see tied around the forehead of Willy Nelson or around the neck of a too-cute-for-words dog. In this case, it was stuck in Judy's mouth and tied somewhere behind her neck.

A gag like that could suffocate someone. But Judy seemed to be okay. From where I watched, I could see her ribcage expanding and contracting. She was able to breathe, if only through her nose.

Her eyes were shut. She couldn't be unconscious, though, and still stand that straight and rigid and hold her head up.

Probably just resting.

She'd had a hard night.

Mostly because of me. Well, *all* because of me, in the sense that I'd dragged her into the whole mess.

Just goes to show what a wrong address can do.

But I'd also been the one who shot her and beat her with a stick. From my hiding place behind the bush, I could see plenty of bruises and scratches and swollen places on her body. Most of them had been put there by me.

Maybe all of them.

Some bastard had grabbed her, brought her here, stripped her, tied her under the tree, shoved that silly hat onto her head and gagged her mouth, but I wasn't sure he'd hurt her.

Don't forget the shrieks.

He'd probably raped her. He *must've* raped her. You don't grab a gal and strip her naked and hang her by a rope that way, and *not* rape her. Logic tells you that.

I couldn't tell by looking, though.

This may sound funny, but I *hoped* he hadn't done it.

Judy didn't deserve that kind of treatment. She was a beautiful, fine, sweet girl, and I liked her. I never saw her as my enemy. Only as my problem.

She could "finger" me.

So she had to go.

But not like this?

I hated it to be like this.

But in part of my mind, I knew it was perfect! This was like a best-case scenario. *I* wouldn't be murdering her at all. And therefore, nobody could ever pin it on me. They'd nail *this* bastard for it, or nobody. And they'd likely figure he's the one who chopped Tony into little pieces, too.

Because of this guy, whoever he might be, suspicion would never fall on me. I ought to be cheering him on.

But I couldn't.

I didn't *want* him to rape her, kill her, touch her.

Weird, huh?

I'm not sure how to explain it. Maybe I'm not even sure *why* I felt that way. It wasn't that I wanted to save her, or spare her the pain, or anything like that.

I mean, I did and I didn't.

I would've *loved* to spare her, but she had to go.

The thing is, I had to be the one to do it.

Not this guy, whoever he might be.

Not this stranger, this interloper, this *thief*.

She was mine, not his.

20

CHOICES

Opening her eyes, Judy stared straight at me. I caught my breath. My heart pounded faster.

Can she see me?

I didn't think so. I was well hidden in the bushes.

If I can see her, she can see me.

Maybe so, I thought. But I still doubted that she'd spotted me. She didn't react, just stood there the same as before, stretched tall, her skin agleam in the firelight.

I raised the pistol and took aim.

Judy still didn't react, so she was obviously unaware of me and the gun.

I aimed for her heart.

She was about twenty-five or thirty feet away. That's farther than it sounds, when it comes to hitting a target with such a small handgun.

I could certainly hit her. But *where* wasn't certain at all.

Shooting for her heart, I might just as easily hit her in the neck or shoulder or breast or stomach. I might only nick her in one side or the other.

The chances of killing her with the first shot were slim.

It might take three or four rounds to do the job.

Then what would I have left for the guy who'd brought her here?

And where the hell was he, anyway?

Asleep in the tent? Maybe. Or maybe wandering the woods to gather firewood.

Or sneaking up on me.

When that little idea popped into my head, I got goose-bumps again. They went scurrying everywhere. I brought the gun back close to my body and dropped onto one knee. Twisting from side to side, I checked behind me.

Nothing but darkness.

And I couldn't even see the darkness very well. The camp-fire had ruined my night vision.

My hearing was okay, though. I heard nobody trying to sneak up on me.

Doesn't mean he isn't.

I turned forward again and studied the campsite. Judy's head was now bowed and her eyes seemed to be shut. Maybe she'd fallen asleep or passed out.

Other than that, everything looked the same.

I stared at the tent. It was about as high as my chest (if I'd been standing up) and maybe seven or eight feet long. Big enough for one or two guys sleeping lengthwise. No light seemed to be on inside it. With that kind of material— nylon, I guess—the light would've seeped right through. From where I stood, I couldn't see whether or not the front was open.

The longer I watched the tent, the more certain I felt that Judy's attacker must be inside. Cozy in his sleeping bag, and fast asleep. After all, he'd had a long and busy night. And that's what guys do after they've screwed you—they sleep.

If he *was* asleep in the tent, I could do whatever I pleased.

But what *should* I do?

1. *Kill them both?*
2. *Kill him and rescue Judy?*
3. *Avoid him and rescue Judy?*
4. *Avoid him and kill Judy?*
5. *Avoid them both, go home, and hope for the best?*

Other possibilities entered my mind. Most of them involved trying to capture the guy, and what I might do with him afterward. Or what Judy and I might do to him. Or what the three of us might do together.

That stuff didn't seem practical, though.

Too risky.

Basically, I had only the five realistic choices. I gave them a lot of thought. Each had merits and disadvantages. After a while, though, I managed to rule out the plans that involved killing the man.

You don't want to kill your fall guy.

That whittled the choices down to three. Should I kill Judy, rescue her, or go home?

If I went home, the guy would still have her as a prisoner to torture, rape and murder as he wished. From a purely logical standpoint, I couldn't ask for anything better. But I hated the idea. He had no right to her. She was mine, not his.

Which didn't seem like a very good argument.

I mean, this was supposed to be about my survival. If the guy kills her, I'm home free. I'd be a fool to interfere just because of some bizarre emotional thing about Judy.

The logic nearly convinced me to leave her.

But then I found a fairly good argument against it.

What if he doesn't kill her?

It seemed ridiculous, at first. A guy in his position *had* to finish Judy off. You can't let a girl live after this sort of thing. She'll tell on you.

But something might go wrong.

Maybe he doesn't have what it takes to finish her off. Or what if she escapes? Or maybe somebody comes along and scares him away or arrests him or . . . who knows? I could think up plenty of scenarios.

Hell, I'd gotten away a few times myself. I'd gotten out of tougher jams than this one Judy was in.

If I could do it, she could, too. She might not be as tough as me, but she was likely smarter.

Anyway, I just couldn't count on the guy killing her. And that gave me the excuse I'd been looking for. The option of walking away was no good.

That left me with two choices. Do I kill her or rescue her?

Judy obviously needed to be killed. And I should do it quietly, with a rock. But should I do it here, or "rescue" her and take her somewhere else to do it?

If I did it here, the guy would still have her body. I didn't like certain aspects of that, but I *really* liked the aspect that he might get caught with it.

On the other hand, if I "rescued" her, we could go somewhere else and have plenty of privacy. I liked the idea of that. I liked it a lot. But disliked the possibility that she might escape from *me*.

Whereas she wouldn't stand a chance of escape if I walked over and bashed her head in while she dangled there.

It was a hard decision.

I kept going back and forth.

I couldn't make up my mind.

So finally I decided not to decide. I would play it by ear.

In the clearing, Judy still hung with her head down and her eyes shut. But the campfire had dwindled. Her skin no longer shimmered so brightly with the golden light. She looked darker now, and less distinct.

If I waited a while longer, the fire might dwindle down to nothing and I would have darkness on my side.

Then again, I might be running out of night.

I'd lost track of time, but figured it had to be after three o'-clock in the morning. Maybe even after four. Waiting any longer would be foolish.

Carefully, I stood up. My body felt stiff and sore, but I managed to rise without groaning or making any other sound. With the pistol in my right hand, I crept away from the clearing. Then I slowly circled around to the other side, staying in the darkness. Finally, I approached the campsite from behind Judy.

The fire had dwindled even lower. Judy was little more than a dark shape hanging below the limb, a silhouette against the fire's dim glow.

There was still no sign of the man who had put her there.

From my new position, I could see the front of the tent. Its flaps were shut. I figured he must be inside.

Fast asleep.

Standing motionless for a while, I watched and listened. Then I moved in with slow, gentle steps. Though I tried to be silent, a little noise couldn't be helped. The ground was covered with old leaves and twigs. The leaves sounded like wads of paper crinkling and crunching under my shoes. Some twigs broke like toothpicks. Others snapped like pencils.

I kept my eyes on Judy. She never flinched or raised her head, never reacted in any way to the sounds of my approach.

When I was only a few strides away from her, I realized that I didn't have a rock yet.

Stopping, I squatted and studied the ground. There were old, dead branches scattered around, but no rocks. None nearby, anyway.

Too bad I didn't have the one from the creek.

It's not that there were no rocks in sight. I saw a whole bunch of them. But they were out in the middle of the campsite. Three or four boulders, large enough to sit on, were arranged near the fire. I couldn't really use one of those. But dozens of smaller rocks, stacked about a foot high, formed a low wall around the fire.

Most of them looked to be the right size for pounding out Judy's brains.

Most of them would probably be hot, too. But there had to be some that wouldn't burn my fingers, and I only needed one.

To get it, of course, I would need to abandon the darkness and enter the clearing. Stride out past Judy. Search for my rock out in the open, directly in front of the tent.

Why not?

Judy's head was down and the tent flaps were shut.

Besides, her mouth was gagged. Even if she saw me, she couldn't cry out.

Also, I had the pistol. If things went sour, I could start shooting people.

Before going anywhere, I made sure the safety was off.

The gun shook like crazy in my hand. I was plenty scared. But this wasn't the creepy sort of fear that gives you goosebumps. This was the kind that makes your heart pound like a club, makes you shake like a lunatic and sweat like a glass full of ice in a heat wave. It makes your legs feel so weak you think they've decided, on their own, to keep you from walking into trouble.

But I *made* mine walk.

There's this thing about me. Maybe you've already noticed it. I'm the sort of gal who gets things done. I'll do almost anything, no matter how dangerous or messy or awful it might be, if I figure it's a thing that needs doing.

I wanted a rock, so I made myself go for it.

Staying about five feet away from Judy's left side, I walked softly past her. She just stood there, arms high, head down. Except for her breathing, she didn't seem to move at all.

When I was in front of her, I looked back. I'd expected a better view, but the flames had sunk very low. She was bathed in a murky glow that trembled with shadows as if I were looking at her under water.

I couldn't even tell whether her eyes were shut.

But she didn't act as if she saw me.

I kept walking.

I glanced at the tent, scanned the clearing ahead of me, checked over each shoulder, eyed the tent again, and several times twisted around for a brief look at Judy.

And wished I could see her better.

Darkness was good for sneaking around, and I should've been grateful for it. But I'd expected more firelight. I wanted to be able to see what I was doing—and see Judy.

So when I reached the fire, I crept around to the other side, crouched down by a small pile of wood, and started adding sticks to the shaky remains of the flames.

21

A HELL OF A GAL

Within a few seconds, the fire grew brighter. I added more sticks, and larger ones. They crackled and snapped, crawling with flames.

As I built up the fire, I kept watch on the front of the tent. It stayed shut. No light or sounds came from inside.

I added larger sticks and chunks of branches.

It seemed crazy, even to me. Had I lost my mind? Did I want to get caught?

Who knows?

I kept telling myself that nobody wakes up just because a fire outside the tent is getting larger.

But it was getting louder, too. A lot more snapping and crackling. And every so often, a burning stick would go off with a *bam*!

I refused to stop adding wood, though, until the fire was large and bright.

Bright enough for its light to spread over Judy.

When her skin gleamed like molten gold, I stood up. I started to step around the fire, then realized I'd forgotten to grab a rock.

Bending over, I patted a few of the rocks along the top of the fire circle. They all felt hot enough to scorch my fingers.

Neat play.

If I'd been taking care of business, I would've found one *before* building up the fire.

Too late, now.

But the far side of the wall wasn't being lapped by flames, so I hurried over there. Sure enough, several of the rocks were only mildly warm.

After switching the pistol to my left hand, I used my right to pick up one I liked. It was shaped like a large wedge of pie, and must've weighed three or four pounds. Perfect.

On my way over to Judy, I turned around completely a couple of times. The clearing, now alive with firelight, looked deserted. Nobody seemed to be peering out at us from the woods. The tent was dark, its flaps still shut.

Judy's head still hung down. She didn't seem to know I was there.

I slipped the pistol into my pocket, held the rock behind my rump so she wouldn't be able to see it, and walked up to her.

Where my shadow fell on Judy, her shine vanished. I stepped sideways enough to let the firelight reach her.

Her skin was so sweaty she looked as if she'd been rubbed with oil.

"Judy?" I whispered.

She didn't stir.

I slid my left hand gently up her side. She was slick and smooth and hot.

"Judy?" I asked, a little louder.

She still didn't respond. My hand was just below her armpit, so that's where I patted her a few times.

"Judy. Wake up. It's me."

Nothing. So I gave her a good, solid smack in the same place. Her breasts lurched. With a gasp, she jerked her head up. She looked into my eyes.

"It's okay," I said. "I'm here to save you."

Her eyes flicked from side to side, studying me. She moaned into her gag.

I glanced over my shoulder to make sure nobody was coming. Then I faced Judy again and went into my routine. "I thought you were dead," I told her. "Somebody ambushed us and you went down. Do you remember?"

She shook her head slightly from side to side.

"I ran away. But you were gone when I came back. So I've been looking for you. I've been searching all over. I had no idea . . . Then I saw the firelight. Just hang on, I'll get you out of here."

She nodded, moaning again.

"I'll take the gag off, but you've gotta be quiet."

Keeping the rock out of sight, I reached up with my left hand and tried to work the bandana loose. It was too tight. So I stepped around behind her, set the rock down on the ground, and used both hands to work on the knot.

Why was I even bothering?

Why not just bash her head open and be done with it?

Maybe for the same reason I'd wasted time building up the fire. Whatever reason that might've been.

Just to delay things? To put off the moment when I would have to kill her?

Maybe.

How should I know? I'm not a shrink.

All I know is that I needed to take her gag off. After a minute or two, the knot came loose. I untied it and slipped the bandana out of her mouth. I stuffed it into my pocket, then picked up the rock and stepped around to her front.

She was taking deep breaths through her open mouth like someone who'd been held underwater way too long.

"Are you okay?" I whispered.

She nodded, and kept on taking huge breaths.

"Who did this to you?" I asked.

"Don't . . . know."

"You don't *know?*"

"It's all . . . dark. Blank."

"Do you remember how you got here?"

Her head shook slightly.

"Or who beat you up?"

"No."

"Or tied you like this?"

"Just . . . we were walking. You and me. Looking for Tony. And then . . . I don't know. Somebody must've . . . brought me here."

"But you don't have any idea who?"

"Did Tony?" she asked.

"I don't know," I told her. "I never saw who did it, either. But somebody shot you and then must've carried you here. Maybe it *was* Tony. Do you think he would shoot you?"

"I don't know. Yeah. Maybe. He was awfully . . . crazy about me."

"Does he own a gun?"

"Yeah.

"Maybe it *was* Tony," I said. "Do you think he's in the tent over there?"

"Don't know."

"He might be," I told her. "I'm pretty sure *someone's* in it."

"Oh, God."

She sounded frightened.

"Don't worry. I'll get you out of here."

"Hurry, okay? Please?"

"Tell me if he comes out."

She nodded.

"Tell me if *anyone* comes out. We don't know for sure it's Tony."

"Okay."

"I'll have to untie you."

"Okay."

Not wanting to set the rock down again, I slipped it underneath my shirttail and shoved a corner of it down inside the right rear pocket of my shorts.

Then I reached high with both arms. As I stepped in against Judy, the front brim of her hat shoved me in the face.

"Let's get rid of this," I whispered, and gently lifted the hat off her head.

She winced.

"Sorry."

"It's okay."

Her hair looked wet. Shiny golden curls were matted flat against her scalp. If there was blood, I couldn't see any. But another red bandana, folded into a pad, was clinging to the side of her head above her ear. Her ear had a crusty nick on top. The pistol sight must've done that.

Turning away, I gave the hat a fling. It sailed across the firelit darkness and landed in some nearby bushes.

Just as I faced Judy again, the makeshift bandage lost its grip and fell. It dropped softly onto her shoulder. I stuffed it into a pocket, then looked closely at her gunshot wound.

The bullet had taken an upward course, gouging a path through her hair and scalp. The furrow looked shallow and about half an inch high. The hair around it was stained a rusty color, but the wound didn't seem to be bleeding anymore.

"You were really lucky," I whispered.

"I don't feel so lucky."

"It just nicked you."

"It hurts like crazy."

"You're lucky you aren't dead."

"I feel like I've got the worst hangover in history."

"Must've been the beer."

"Sure," she said. And a corner of her mouth tilted upward, trembling. I guess it was supposed to be a smile. The other corner of her mouth, red and swollen from when I'd worked her over with the stick, didn't move at all.

"We'll get you some aspirin," I told her. "But first we have to get you out of here." Reaching for the rope around her wrists, I leaned forward. Our bodies met. I couldn't help that. It was necessary if I wanted to work on the rope. My shirt was open. We were bare against each other except for my shorts.

"Sorry about this," I whispered.

"It's fine." When she said that, I felt her breath against my lips. I was slightly taller than Judy, but her head was tipped back. Every time she exhaled or spoke, soft air brushed my lips and entered my mouth.

Our difference in size made her breasts level with mine. Our nipples met. Hers were hard, too.

"Scared?" I asked.

"Yeah."

"Same here. But don't worry. I'll get you out of this."

"Hurry, okay?"

"I'm trying. Where are your clothes?"

"I don't know."

"Maybe they're in the tent."

"Yeah."

"Unless he burnt them. Or maybe he left them in the woods somewhere."

"I . . . they're just gone. I don't know where. I was like this when I came to."

"This is a tough knot," I told her. Which was sort of a lie. I was only fiddling with the thing, not really trying to undo it.

"You can get it, can't you?" Judy asked. She sounded worried.

"I'll get it."

"What if he comes out?"

"Just give me a warning. I'll take care of him."

"But he has a gun."

"He does?" I asked, forgetting.

Judy hesitated a moment. Then she said, "He *must* have one. He shot me, didn't he?"

"Yeah. I forgot about that for a second. My God, if he comes out with a gun, we've had it."

"Maybe you oughta run and try to get help."

"And leave you here? No way. We're in this together. You and me, honey."

Murmuring, "Thanks," she eased her head forward. Her

cheek brushed against my jaw. Then she rested her face against the side of my neck. "You're risking your life for me," she whispered.

"I'm a hell of a gal," I told her.

"Yeah," she said. "You are."

A few moments later, I told her, "This knot's *really* giving me trouble. I can hardly hold my arms up." With that, I lowered them and put them around her. "Don't worry, I'm not quitting. I just need to rest for a minute." I gave her a gentle hug. She winced and stiffened. "Sorry. Did that hurt?"

"Yeah, a little."

"He must've really done a number on you."

"I guess so. I don't even know what he did. But I'm . . . awfully sore. All over. Inside, too."

"The dirty bastard."

"He'd better not've made me pregnant."

"Don't worry about it. If we don't get you out of here, it won't matter."

"Trying to cheer me up?"

"How am I doing?" I asked.

"A lousy job."

I gave her rump a pat, then said, "I'd better get back to work." Reaching high again, I started to fool with the knot.

"If you get me out of this," she whispered, "I'll owe you my life."

"Forget about it," I said.

"I'll do *anything* for you."

"Anything?"

"Anything."

22

HERE COMES TROUBLE

"Okay," I said. But was she serious? She sure sounded serious, all right. Not only about doing "anything" for me, but about her memories of what had happened to her.

Her *lack* of memories.

But what if she was lying?

What if she remembered *everything?*

"What's wrong?" Judy whispered.

"Huh?"

"You're suddenly . . . all tense. I can feel it."

"It's the knot," I said. "It's too tight." Shaking my head, I let go of the rope. I put my arms around her.

"Are you quitting?" she asked. She sounded scared like a little kid in the dark.

"No. No way. I'll never quit on you. I just have to figure out another way."

"What about the other end of the rope?" she asked. "He tied it to a tree behind me." She went rigid. I suddenly knew exactly what she'd meant about *me* going all tense. She felt as if a live current had zipped through her body. But hardly missing a beat, she said, "Maybe it'll be easier. Why don't you go over and give it a try?"

"You *did* see him," I said, letting go of her and taking a step backward.

She shook her head. "I didn't see *anyone*. All I know is that it's tied to a tree back there. I didn't see who did it, or when, or *anything*. I turned around and saw it there, that's all."

"What are you so nervous about?"

"What do you think? Jeez, Alice. If we don't get out of here, that guy's gonna come out of his tent and kill *both* of us."

"Is he?"

"*Yes! What do you think is going on?*"

I put my hands on her sides and said, "Why don't you tell me?"

She stared into my eyes. She was breathing hard again, her ribs rising and falling under my open hands. I could feel tremors running through her.

"Do you think I did this to *myself?*" she whispered.

"No, of course not. But I think you know more than you're telling me."

"Look, just get me down. Please. I don't care about anything else. I don't care what you did. I just want down from here before he . . ."

"Tell me the truth," I said. "The truth shall set thee free."

"You shot me. Okay? Then you put me up on the picnic table and . . . I don't know what. You were *doing* stuff to me. And then you went at me with a stick or something. I think you knocked me out with it. When I woke up, you were gone. So I climbed off the table and hid in the bushes. And then later I ran for my life. I kept running till *he* caught me. *Now* will you get me down from here? Please? I don't know why you did any of that stuff, and I don't care. I'll never tell anyone. I promise. It's just between you and me, okay? Just get me out of here."

"You lied about everything," I muttered. My fingers ached from digging into her ribcage, but I didn't let go.

"I meant it about owing you," she said. "I meant that. Get

me out of here and I'll do *anything* for you. I'll give you all my money, everything I own. I'll go with you. I'll live with you. I'll be your slave. I'll be your lover. Whatever you want. *Anything*. Just get me out of here."

"What makes you think I want any of that?" I asked.

"Don't you?" It sounded more like a challenge than a question.

"I'd like to have the truth," I said. "How's that? How about the truth right now?"

"Like what?"

"What about this guy?" I asked. "Who is he?"

"I don't know. I don't *want* to know. He's *horrible*."

"More horrible than me?"

"You're not so bad. When you're not trying to kill me."

"Haven't lost your sense of humor."

"Just get me away from him. Please. I'll never tell on you. I promise. Cross my heart and hope to die."

"Nobody keeps their word anymore."

"I do."

"That's a good one, coming from a liar."

"I'm telling the truth now," she said. "If you get me away from this guy, you'll never regret it. I'll never do anything to hurt you. Never. I'll never say a word against you. I'll *lie* for you. I'll take blame. I'll do whatever it takes. I swear to God."

"What'd he *do* to you?"

"We don't have time. Come on, Alice. If he wakes up . . ."

"*Does* he have a gun?"

"I don't know."

"How did he get you?"

"He jumped me from behind. I'll tell you everything later, okay? We haven't got time for this. You've gotta untie me. Please!"

"Shhh. Raise your voice, and you'll wake him up."

"Maybe I *should*," she blurted. "Maybe I *will!* Stop screwing around and get me down from here!"

"Shut up!"

"Get me *down!*"

I clamped her left nipple between my thumb and forefinger and twisted it. She flinched and writhed. Breath hissed out around her teeth. "Just shut up," I told her.

She jerked her head up and down.

"Now, tell me about our friend in the tent. I take it he's not Tony."

"No," she said, and panted for air.

"Who is he?"

"I don't know."

"What does he look like?"

"Big."

"Big? What's big?"

"*He* is."

"How big?"

"I don't know. Don't just keep . . . Do you *want* him to catch us?"

"He doesn't scare me," I said.

"Then you're dumber than you look."

I gave her a very hard pinch and twist. She cried out and squirmed. Then, gasping for air, she blurted, "You stupid bitch, now you've done it. He's gonna come out!"

"I'm trembling."

"You oughta be! We'll be next."

"Huh?"

"He's got a body in the tent with him. Some dead woman. He *eats* her."

"*What?*"

"*He eats a dead woman in his tent!*"

I didn't like the sound of that.

But I didn't have time to give it much thought, because I heard the tent flaps whap open behind me.

Letting go of Judy, I spun around. The weight of the pistol slapped my left thigh. A good thing, since it reminded me that I had it in the wrong pocket.

I went for it left-handed as this *guy* crawled out of the tent.

In spite of Judy's description, I still expected him to be my prowler.

But he wasn't.

My prowler was sleek and handsome.

Not a fat, bald, drooling slob.

He really *was* drooling, too. Slobbering all over the place as he struggled to his feet.

Grunting.

Naked.

Filthy with old blood that looked brown and crusty.

Coated with curly, filthy hair all the way down from his shoulders to his feet.

Only one part wasn't hairy. It jutted out in front of him, so big he was getting drool on it.

He lumbered toward me, hunched over, his arms outspread as if he wanted to give me a bear hug. But he had a knife in one hand, a hatchet in the other.

No kidding.

They didn't look any too clean, either.

He grunted and laughed as he picked up some speed and charged at me.

You've gotta be kidding!

I had this urge to laugh. But what came out was a scream. Behind me, Judy screamed, too.

This might've been hilarious in a movie.

I mean, the guy was such a monstrosity! It crossed my mind that all this was some sort of a gag. But I figured it must be real.

I forced my eyes away from him just long enough to glimpse a shadowy body inside his tent. I couldn't be sure, but it looked like a woman. And it looked dead, to me.

I started firing.

Better late than never. The deal is, I'd had a little trouble with the pistol. I began to go for it when the guy first came crawling out of the tent. But it was down at the bottom of my pocket, and I had to drag it out with my left hand. I'm a righty. So after I got the pistol out, I spent a few moments switching it to my right hand. Only after that did I start pumping bullets into him.

I pulled the trigger fast.

BAM-BAM-BAM-BAM-BAM!

But he didn't go down.

He was backlit by the fire, so I couldn't see where I was hitting him. I *had* to be hitting him, though. I'm an okay shot and this was close range and he was a large target charging straight at me. How could I miss a thing like that?

I couldn't, that's how.

I was hitting him, all right. But the little .22s weren't doing the job.

In another second, he'd be on me. I had Judy at my back, so I dodged sideways, holding fire. He tried to follow me, but he was too big and clumsy. He couldn't change course in time.

Judy kicked out at him. She was probably trying for his nuts. I heard the *smack* sound of her bare foot meeting his skin, but he didn't cry out or drop.

He plowed into her.

His body slammed against Judy and crashed through her, knocking a grunt out of her as he sent her flying backward and upward, twisting at the end of her rope. Stumbling past where she'd been, he managed to turn around and start coming after me again.

Judy came swinging toward his back like Tarzan on the attack. But I don't think she meant to do it. She was at the mercy of the rope and the whims of motion.

She meant what came next, though.

As the guy staggered toward me, Judy raised a slim bare leg and kicked him in the back of his head. She rebounded away from him, spinning wildly.

He grunted, stumbled forward and fell to his knees.

I ran up to him, fired a shot into the top of his shiny head, then pranced backward out of reach, not sure what to expect.

What I *hoped* was that he'd drop like a sledge-hammered bull.

But instead, he squealed and started crawling forward, trying to get up.

I glanced at the pistol. If I'd been out of ammo, the slide would've been locked back. It was forward. Which meant I had at least one more round.

There might be a couple, but I could only count on one.

So I wasn't eager to use it.

As he stumbled to his feet, I hurried around behind the campfire. He lurched toward me, hunched over, arms out like before as if he wanted to give me a big, friendly hug. He still had the knife in one hand and the hatchet in the other.

By now, he had a face of blood from my shot to his head. The rest of his body was a mess, too. A worse mess than before. Now, it wasn't just the woman's old, dry blood. It was *his* blood, too, and plenty of it. It was pouring out of four or five holes in his chest and belly.

Have you ever seen those cartoons where a character gets all shot up, then drinks a glass of water and suddenly he's squirting out of every hole?

It was like that.

Except these holes weren't really squirting. They were flowing like garden hoses when the water is just barely turned on.

A guy shot up like that shouldn't have still been coming at me. And he certainly shouldn't still have a hard-on. What kind of a freak *was* he?

"You're dead!" I shouted as he lumbered closer. "Fall down, you motherfucking idiot! Don't you know when you're dead?"

He raised his head slowly and grinned at me.

What a nice thing. What lovely teeth. Brown and crooked. Maybe it was just my mind playing tricks, but I thought I could see shreds of flesh caught between some of them.

I gagged.

He stopped just on the other side of the fire. Still grinning, he drew back his right arm. He was getting ready to throw the hatchet at me.

I stuck my own right arm straight out over the fire, shouted, "Eat this!" and fired.

Instead of going into his open mouth the way I wanted, my bullet slashed his right cheek open and punched a hole through his earlobe.

My slide locked back.

I gasped, "Shit!"

He hurled the hatchet. It flew at me over the fire, tumbling, coming straight for my face.

I dodged it. The damn thing came so close that I felt a gust of air against my left cheek. And I'd lurched sideways too fast. I stumbled, trying to stay on my feet. Then I fell.

The bastard cried out, "Ah-*ha!*"

He thought he had me.

As he staggered his way around the fire, I rolled over, got to my hands and knees, and tried to scurry up. My feet slipped on the dewy grass. I fell and banged my knees, and he gained on me.

"Get *away* from me!" I yelled.

He grunted and kept coming.

He was almost on me by the time I made it up and launched myself out of reach.

"Thata girl!" Judy cried out.

Cheering me on from the sidelines.

"Get his ax!" she yelled.

I'd already thought of that.

I'd already spotted it, too. The hatchet lay flat on the ground about fifteen feet beyond where I'd been standing before my fall.

I could get to it, but I needed a lead. I'd have to swoop down and snatch it up. Without a good lead, he might end up on my back.

"Die, you bastard!" I yelled as I ran.

He giggled. *Giggled!* Do you believe it?

Maybe he had a right to giggle. He'd taken all the bullets I could throw at him. Now, he was only a few strides behind me. He'd be on top of me if I slowed down to pick up the hatchet. And he'd probably plunge his knife into my back.

So I didn't slow down, I dived. Slamming the dewy grass, I slid on my chest and belly, my arms reaching out ahead of me. In mid-slide, I grabbed the hatchet with my right hand. As I skidded to a stop, I flipped onto my back.

Grinning, the big boy sank to his knees in the grass just beyond my feet.

He clamped the knife between his teeth, then leaned forward and clutched my ankles. Grunting, he jerked them apart. He started pulling me toward him.

I don't know what the hell he thought he was doing.

Well, maybe he wanted to pull me closer in order to work some sort of mischief on me. If you can call rape and murder mischief, which I'm not sure would be proper.

Anyway, he obviously wasn't thinking straight.

How *could* he, with all those bullets in him?

I slid toward him on the seat of my cut-offs. He kept forcing my legs farther apart as if he wanted to dive between them. Judy dangled in silence from her limb.

When he dragged me close enough, I raised the hatchet high and swung it down with all my might. It got him in the back of the head.

WHUNK!

Chopped him deep, the hatchet busting through his skull and into the mush underneath. Blood and stuff flew up, glistening in the firelight.

He grunted.

He farted.

Then he plunged forward.

Like he had it all planned to land on top of me and pin me down, crush me, suffocate me, kill me with his corpse.

I jerked the hatchet, trying to turn him away. With a slurp, it jumped out of his head and I was left holding it. Before I could scoot out of the way, he bumped me in the stomach. Then his head slid lower as if he wanted to shove it down the front of my cut-offs. It was too big to fit in, though. So it stayed outside. The next thing I knew, it was shoving at my crotch. As he kept on falling, his head acted like a plow and pushed me ahead of him.

By the time he'd finished, I was in the clear.

23

SURVIVOR

Utterly worn out, I lay on my back and figured I might stay that way for an hour or two. But the top of the guy's head was jammed between my legs, big and leaking blood through my cut-offs and making me all sticky down there.

So I squirmed to get away from it.

When nothing of me was touching him anymore, I sprawled and shut my eyes and took deep breaths.

Vaguely, I knew that I had to get up. A lot needed to be done. But I had no interest in moving.

"Alice!" Judy called.

"Yeah?" I answered, not even bothering to lift my head.

"Are you okay?"

"I guess."

"Is he dead?"

"Pretty sure."

"That's great. You really did great. You saved our lives."

"Yeah."

"Can you come over here and cut me down?"

I didn't answer, just sighed and stayed on my back.

After a minute or two, Judy said, "Please?"

"What's your hurry?" I called to her.

"This isn't very comfortable."

No kidding, I thought.

Even though the ground felt good under my back, I wasn't very comfortable, either. I ached just about everywhere. I was sweaty and itchy. And I didn't like how my cut-offs were soaked with the dead guy's blood. I needed a bath and a bed.

"Alice?"

"Yeah?"

"Come on, okay? Please?"

"Yeah, yeah. I'm coming." I picked up the hatchet, got to my feet, and stood over the body. It wasn't a pretty sight, I can tell you that. You should've seen the butt on this guy. It would've ruined your appetite for a week.

Anyway, I thought about going for his knife. It had fallen out of his mouth when I chopped him. It was probably on the ground underneath him, somewhere in the region of his waist.

Only one problem about getting it.

I didn't want to touch him.

"What're you doing?" Judy asked.

"Nothing."

I'd managed to keep Tony's loafers on, so I sat down on the grass near the side of Fatso the Friendly Corpse. Drawing in my legs, I swiveled around so my feet were aimed his way. Then I leaned back, braced myself up with my arms, placed the bottoms of my shoes against his hip and buttock, and *punched out*.

His body lurched and shook, but didn't go much of any-place. So I kept ramming it with both feet, shoving it and kicking it until finally he rolled onto his side as if he wanted to take a look at this gal who was making his life so difficult.

The knife was a little lower than where I'd expected to find it. Good thing I hadn't tried to grab it by reaching under him. I might've gotten a handful of something that wasn't a knife.

Anyway, I picked it up.

The fire had dwindled quite a bit, by then. On my way over to it, I found the .22 on the ground. I couldn't remember dropping it, but there it was. When I put the pistol into the right rear pocket of my cut-offs, I noticed that I'd lost the rock I'd tucked back there.

I kept losing stuff.

It was turning into a trend.

Near the campfire, I set down the hatchet and knife on one of the larger rocks. Then I went to the small pile of firewood and started adding pieces to the flames. Soon, a pretty good blaze was going.

I emptied my pockets to find out what I still had.

The pistol. Two red bandanas and one white handkerchief. Judy's keys, Tony's keys, my keys. And Tony's wallet.

Inspiration striking me, I dropped Tony's wallet and keys into the fire.

"What're you doing?" Judy asked.

"A little house-cleaning."

I put everything else back into my pockets. Down in the fire, flames wrapped the black leather wallet and key case.

So much for my fingerprints.

I realized, of course, that the keys wouldn't burn. I'm not stupid. Maybe some of the things in Tony's wallet would survive the fire, too. But that was fine. His stuff, being found here in the campsite with everything else, would probably make the cops think Tony was just another victim of Fatso.

I stood there, added more wood, and even turned the wallet over with a stick to make sure it was burning okay.

Then I retrieved the knife and hatchet. I dropped the hatchet into the fire, but kept the knife. After watching for a while to make sure the handle was catching fire, I started toward the tent.

But changed my mind. For one thing, I'd seen more than enough nasty stuff for one night. The remains of Fatso's last victim, last lover, last meal—whatever—were in there. I didn't need to see her close up and personal.

For another thing, why risk leaving evidence of myself inside or near the tent? I happen to know that people *always* leave stuff behind at crime scenes: a telltale hair or fingerprint; samples of their own blood, saliva, semen, etc.; maybe a hat, maybe a glove. This one serial killer in L.A. actually got caught because he lost his *wallet* at the scene of a crime and it had his driver's license in it. Talk about morons!

But here's the deal. I couldn't possibly leave any evidence of myself in or around the tent if I stayed a safe distance away from it.

So I avoided the tent and headed for Judy.

She was all golden and gleaming in the firelight, standing there straight and rigid with her arms high, like before. The gag was gone, but she was breathing hard, anyway.

Gasping for air and staring at me.

"You saved my life," she said. Her voice sounded rough and shaky.

"I know."

"I'm not your enemy."

"Who said you are?"

"Nobody. But look . . . I know you think I'll tell on you, but I won't."

"Tell about what?"

Looking me straight in the eyes, she said, "You killed Tony."

"Really?"

She nodded. "That was his wallet you threw in the fire, wasn't it? His wallet and keys."

"Who's to say?"

"Me. You killed Tony. Then you were trying to cover it up, but you came over to my place by mistake. So then you figured you had to kill me, too. Because I'd be able to recognize you. And you *still* want to kill me, don't you?"

"That's right, Sherlock."

"Well, don't. Okay? You don't have to."

"Afraid I do."

"No, look. Like I said, you saved my life. I'm not going to do anything that'll hurt you or get you thrown in jail or anything."

"It doesn't bother you that I killed your old lover-boy?"

She didn't answer right away.

"Come up with a good one," I suggested.

"It bothers me," she said. "Sure it does. We *were* in love. But maybe he deserved what he got."

"And maybe he didn't," I said.

"Either way, he became my enemy when he attacked me. And you *became* my friend when you killed Milo."

"Fatso? You know his name?"

She nodded. "Milo. That's all I know. And I know that you saved me from him. I would've ended up in the tent." She shuddered, and I actually saw her chin tremble. She said, "*You're* my friend now. And forever. I won't betray you."

"There's only one way I can be sure of that," I told her.

She glanced at the knife in my hand. Then, very quickly, she said, "No, look, I've got a plan."

"Let me guess," I said. "The plan is for me *not* to kill you."

"Will you *listen?*"

"I've got places to go . . ."

"I'm Milo's *victim!*" Judy blurted. "I've got his sperm in me to prove it!"

"You do?"

"What do you think? The first thing he did was rape me. He got me about ten minutes after I ran away from you."

The idea of it sickened me. That filthy, bloody slob, grunting and drooling on top of Judy while he shoved his vile cock into her.

"I'll tell the cops *I* killed him," she said.

"Sure."

"No, listen. I'll say that Tony and I came over to park and mess around. We were going at it on the picnic table when all of a sudden this *stranger* jumps us and kills Tony. See? That gets you off the hook for Tony."

"I'll be off the hook for Tony the second I kill you."

"I wouldn't know about that. Maybe, maybe not. But I don't think you really *want* to kill me. You don't, do you?"

"Just go on with your story."

"Okay. So Milo kills Tony, and I make a break for it. But he catches up to me. I can show the cops right where it happened. My clothes'll be there. Most of them, anyway."

"Yeah. Your panties are over by the picnic table somewhere. In pieces."

"I'll say Tony did that. He *has* done it."

"Yeah."

"But they'll find everything else in the place where Milo got me. They'll find other stuff there, too, if they really look for it."

"Like what?"

"You know."

"Your blood and his semen?"

Nodding slightly, she said, "And I guess our footprints. Anyway, it'll all back up my story. And then I'll explain about him bringing me to the camp, here, and hanging me up like this."

"Which he did," I threw in.

"Right! And the cops'll find that poor woman in the tent, and they'll know I would've been next. They'll figure Milo was some kind of Dahmer. I'll be a hero for killing him. And you'll never enter the picture."

"How do you plan to explain killing him?"

"Easy. While Milo was asleep in the tent, I got my hands loose and found his gun."

I switched the knife to my other hand, then reached into my pocket and pulled out the pistol. I raised it in front of her. "This one, right?"

"Right."

"It's Tony's gun," I explained. "How do *you* get hold of it?"

"Easy." A smile twitched at the unhurt corner of Judy's mouth. "Tony took it with him when we were making out on the picnic table. He would've *done* that, too. We came here sometimes, did I tell you that? We hardly ever stepped a foot out of the car, but Tony knew this was sort of a dangerous area, so he always brought his .22 along, just in case."

"Why didn't he use it when Milo attacked?"

"It was in the pocket of his jeans, and his jeans were down around his ankles. He couldn't reach it in time. Then, after he was dead, Milo took the pistol. And kept it."

"Where?"

"In a pocket."

"A pocket of what?" I asked.

"He was wearing overalls most of the time. You know, *bib* overalls?"

"Cute. The pig dressed up like a farmer."

"Yeah. And he kept the gun in his pocket. So when I finally got my hands free, I snuck into his tent and found it. But he woke up and came after me. That's when I start shooting him. Just like you did. From there on, my whole story can be almost exactly the same as how it really happened, but it'll be me instead of you."

"I could leave you the loafers to wear," I suggested. "That way, you'd match the footprints."

"Good idea."

I nodded, frowning, wondering. "It's not a bad plan," I admitted. "Almost sounds like something *I* might've come up with."

"It'll work."

"That's what *you* think."

"What's wrong with it?"

"Lots of stuff."

24

FRIENDLY PERSUASION

"Like what?" Judy asked. "What's wrong with my plan? Tell me. Maybe we can work it out."

"I'm running out of time, here."

"Alice, look. I'm giving you a chance to walk away from everything. If we can work this out, the cops will think nobody was involved but me, Tony and Milo."

"Here's one little problem," I told her. "Tony's body is in the trunk of his car. Which is parked in the garage of *your* apartment building."

She gaped at me. For a few seconds, she looked stunned and lost. But she recovered fast. "Easy," she said. "Take my car. Drive to my place, put my car back where we got it, and come back here in Tony's car. Park it where mine is, now. Then just leave his body in the trunk and be on your way. I'll say Milo put him in the trunk. Hey, that'll be perfect! He knocked me out and left me on the picnic table. That way, I'm out cold while he hauls Tony's body over to the car. But before he can make it back, I come to and run into the woods. Then he hunts me down and, you know . . . the rest."

"That sounds okay. But where are you while I'm driving the cars back and forth?"

"I'll stay right here in camp."

"Like a good little girl," I muttered.

"Okay. Well, leave me tied up. But if you do, you'll have to come back and cut me loose after you've dropped off Tony's car. I mean, I can't exactly be found like this or it'll blow the whole story."

"It'll blow the story if I help you. They'll wanta know who cut the rope."

"Then just untie the knot."

I shook my head.

She stared into my eyes and said nothing for a few moments. Then, in a softer voice, she said, "You don't have to do it now. It can wait till you come back."

"When I come back?"

"From switching the cars."

"Oh. Right." I pulled one of the bandanas out of my pocket, wiped the knife clean, and tossed the knife to the ground. Then I stepped behind Judy.

"What're you doing?" she asked.

"I don't want you yelling for help."

"I won't. I promise. Don't put that on me. Please."

"There are other ways to shut you up," I said.

She didn't argue after that, but just stood motionless while I put the gag into her mouth and tied it behind her neck.

Then I stepped around to the front.

She stared into my eyes. She was breathing hard again, air hissing through her nostrils.

"I'm not switching the cars," I explained. "It's a stupid idea. Somebody'd probably see me. Anyway, I'm too tired to play any more games. What I'm going to do, Judy, is leave you here just as you are."

She nodded slightly.

"I'm not going to kill you. Okay?"

Her nod grew a little more enthusiastic.

"I mean, you helped me out with Fatso. If you hadn't kicked him in the head . . . I don't know, maybe he would've gotten me. So I owe you for that. Besides, none of this is your fault. I just bumped into you by mistake. Wrong address. I was afraid Tony might have a redial button . . . Whoa!"

Judy's eyebrows lifted.

We needed to talk.

Instead of bothering to untie the gag, I hooked a forefinger underneath it at each corner of her mouth, pulled roughly, and dragged it down over her chin. The bandana hung around her neck like a dog scarf.

And like a dog, she panted for air.

"What about redial?" I asked. "Did Tony have it?"

"Just . . . wait."

"Come on. Did he? I know he moved to a new apartment and you've never been there, but what sort of phone did he have at his old place? He might've taken it with him. Did it have redial?"

"If I tell . . ."

"You'd *better* tell, unless you wanta die right now!"

"No gag, okay? Please?"

I punched her in the belly. A good hard one. Her breath gushed against my face. She couldn't fold over because of the way she was hanging; instead, the blow made her knees jump up and sent her swinging backward.

When she swung forward, I caught her by the sides. I stopped her, held her steady for a moment, then took a couple of steps backward so I could see her better.

Mouth agape, she wheezed for breath. Her eyes were shut tightly. She kept her knees high, so all that held her up was the rope around her wrists.

She *really* looked as if she were being stretched. Her arms and torso actually seemed longer and skinnier than before. Her belly was sunken in. Her ribcage was high and bulging. Her breasts were pulled almost flat against her chest.

"It's okay," I said. "Put your feet down."

She just kept hanging there, gasping.

"Put them down and stand up."

She didn't.

Instead, she blurted, "I just . . . I just . . . You didn't have to . . ."

"Shut up and tell me about his redial!"

"Okay. Okay."

"Stand up!"

She lowered her legs until her feet met the ground. Though she still had to stand tall, she no longer looked as if she were being pulled apart on the rack.

"Now," I said, "what about it?"

"He doesn't. Have it."

"Have you been to his new place?

She shook her head.

"Then how do you know what kind of phone he has?"

"I . . . gave it to him."

"What?"

"His phone. I gave it to him. When we were . . . going together. He . . . I don't think he'd . . . get rid of it."

"I'm sure he wouldn't," I said. "Not if it came from you. And it didn't have redial?"

"No. Huh-uh."

"Are you sure?"

"I'm sure."

"You've told me a lot of lies tonight," I pointed out. "How do I know this isn't another one?"

"I swear. Honest to God."

"Why'd you buy him a phone that didn't have redial?"

Her face contorted with confusion or pain or disgust—hard to tell which, since it was sort of battered. She said, "Huh?"

"If you're buying your boyfriend a new telephone, why do you get him one that doesn't have a redial button?"

"I don't know. It didn't . . . I didn't *buy* it for him. It was my *old* phone. I got a new one . . . I was going to throw it away, but . . . he asked me for it. So I gave it to him."

"Why do you want to lie about a thing like this?" I asked her.

"I'm not lying."

"Did you forget about Tony's *answering machine*?"

"No. That's what it was . . . an answering machine. The one I gave him."

"I don't think so. Tony told me that you never *had* an answering machine."

"But . . . That's not so."

"Oh, yes it is. Why did you lie about it?"

"I didn't. Honest."

"You lie like a rug, Judy."

"So do you."

"But I'm *running* this show," I said, and started to unbuckle my belt.

"What're you doing?"

I pulled the belt out of its loops, and my cut-offs fell down. I stepped out of them.

"Hey," Judy said. She sounded like a kid again. "Come on, Alice. Don't."

"Admit you lied."

"Haven't you hurt me enough?"

"I saved your life. Remember? You said I can do anything I want."

"Why do you want to *hurt* me?"

"Because you lied. Admit you lied."

"Okay. I lied. Okay?"

"You didn't give him his phone?"

"No."

"You wanted me to leave here thinking he *didn't* have redial. Why?"

"I don't know."

I swung the belt. My sidestroke, at a slightly downward angle, caught her just above the hip then curled around and lashed her across the buttocks. She jerked and gasped.

"Why?" I asked again.

"I don't *know* what he's got!" she blurted.

"Then why did you lie?"

"You won't . . ."

"Won't what?"

"Believe me."

"Try me."

"It was just . . . just because . . . I didn't want you to worry."

"What?"

"Your . . . You must figure . . . redial's got your number. If he *has* it. You're scared."

"Does he have it? Do you know?"

"He's got it."

"Shit!"

"It's . . . I know his answering machine. It's got . . . every-thing."

"Fuck!"

So then I sort of lost it.

I whipped the hell out of her with Tony's belt, lashing her with all my strength, circling her as I swung.

Finally, my arm fell to my side, spent. The belt swaying by my leg, I stumbled around to Judy's front.

She was limp, her feet on the ground but her knees bent, all her weight on the rope again.

The fire had burnt down low, so I couldn't see her very well.

I staggered over to it, squatted, and added some twigs and branches. I could hardly catch my breath. Sweat poured off me. The shirt was clinging to my back and my loafers felt slimy inside. I didn't like being this close to the fire. It was too damn hot. But I wanted the fire bright, so I kept adding fuel for a while.

Finally, the light reached Judy and turned her to polished gold. Along with her other injuries, she now had stripes. In some places, the stripes bled. All down her body, her skin was shiny with blood and sweat.

I rose from my squat and hobbled over to her.

She was panting for breath and crying. It made her shake a lot.

I picked up my cut-offs, then stood to the side and watched her.

She was *really* shaking. It made me wonder if she had a fever.

"Sorry you made me do that to you," I said.

She raised her head and looked at me.

"Now, I suppose you'll tell on me."

Her head moved slowly from side to side.

"No?" I asked.

When she spoke, her lips made some small bubbles. Red bubbles of spit and blood.

She said, "You . . . saved . . . me."

"You're not gonna tell?"

"Milo . . . did . . . it."

As I worked Tony's belt into the loops of my cut-offs, I said to Judy, "How do I know you're not lying again?"

She didn't answer.

I fastened the belt, then looked down at the knife on the ground.

I knew that I ought to finish her off.

I'd told her that I wouldn't, though. And besides, you should've seen her. She looked so vulnerable and hurt, hanging there in the firelight. And so beautiful. And she had that bandana hanging around her neck.

I bet you couldn't have killed her, either.

"You'd better not tell on me," I said to her. "If the cops ever come looking for me, I'll hunt you down. And what I'll do to you . . . you'll wish I'd left you for Milo."

She moved her head slowly up and down.

"Hang in there, honey," I said. And then I left.

25

ON THE WAY OUT

Dumb, I know.

Just call me Miss Sentimental. I knew better than to walk off and leave her alive, but that's exactly what I did. My heart got in the way of my brain.

I'd gotten to like her. That was the problem. It isn't easy to kill someone you like. Let that be a warning to you.

Of course, as I wrote early on, it's better not to kill anyone at all. Hell, look what happened to me all because I got carried away and whacked Tony with my saber. An *accident*, and look at all the shit that's already flown because of it. And we've still got plenty of book to go, so you don't even know the half of it yet.

You give some poor jerk a chop in the head and you're in for a world of troubles. So try not to do it.

Anyway, I left Judy behind, hanging by the rope and pretty beaten up—but alive—and hurried out of the clearing.

After so much time with the firelight, the woods seemed blacker than a pit. I walked slowly, feeling my way with both hands, trying not to crash into anything or fall down again.

Before long, I'd lost all sense of direction and didn't know *where* I was.

Somewhere in Miller's Woods, that's all I knew for sure.

But I still had high hopes of finding my way home before dawn.

As I trudged through the woods, my night vision returned. No longer completely blind, I could make out the shapes in the darkness.

I kept thinking about how stupid I'd been about Judy. If only I'd finished her off, I would now be completely in the clear. The cops would never in a million years connect me with anything.

Now, I was in Judy's hands.

She probably *would* finger me. Why not?

Because I'd saved her from the clutches of Milo?

I'd also spared her from myself.

I mean, I'd hurt her, but I hadn't killed her. So, really, I'd saved her life *twice*.

She *owed* me, and she knew it, but she would probably spill everything to the cops anyway. As you may have noticed, she's a goody-two-shoes. A regular Girl Scout. A gal like her might be grateful to me and she might lie sometimes—for instance, if she's trying to pull a trick on someone planning to kill her—but she'll have this compulsion to be truthful to the cops.

She'll rat me out.

Which wasn't exactly a sudden revelation. I'd known it all along. Sort of. Even while she'd been telling me about her big plan to leave me out of the picture, I'd never quite believed she would carry out her end of it.

Maybe she'd *thought* she would.

Or maybe the whole business had been a lie to save her ass.

Well, *something* had saved her ass. I'm not sure what. Maybe a combination of things.

Such as a ton of luck. Plus the facts that she was beautiful and friendly and all that. And I knew it was only by a mistake of mine that she got dragged into this whole mess in the first place. Then I had to feel sorry for her because she'd gotten herself raped by Milo. Then I had to feel grateful because she kicked him in the head. Then she confused me with promises about never telling on me.

Those are probably some of the things that saved her, but maybe not all of them.

Who knows why stuff happens?

Not me, that's for sure.

I'm *interested*, and I like to look for answers, but the answers don't seem to be very simple and I've got a feeling that there're secret forces at work. Genes, for instance. Or Fate. Or God. Or gremlins. Or certain stuff you don't want to admit, not even to yourself. I mean, who the hell knows? Maybe we aren't even *supposed* to know the real answers.

Maybe "the truth *is* out there," like they say on the TV show, but that doesn't mean we can ever find it out.

All I knew for sure was that I *didn't* kill Judy, so now my life was in her hands.

It made me feel like a patsy. A softie. A dope.

But it made me feel good, too, somehow. I liked knowing that she was still alive back there at the camp. And that she was only alive because of me.

In a few hours, she would probably be back in her apartment.

Even if she couldn't get out of the rope, somebody would be sure to find her soon.

Maybe not.

Though I knew Miller's Woods pretty well (at least in daylight), I wasn't exactly sure where the campsite was located. It might've been in a remote part of the woods, not close to any trails. I mean, if you're going to do what Milo'd been doing to people, you'd make sure to set up camp where a bunch of nature lovers won't stumble into it.

He must've had plenty of confidence in its remoteness, or he wouldn't have built a fire. He'd not only built the fire, but he'd left it burning—and Judy dangling—while he went to bed in his tent.

That's confidence.

Or stupidity.

He must've been awfully sure, too, that he'd tied Judy so well she didn't stand a chance of getting loose.

What if she can't get loose and she doesn't get found?

She could die at the end of that rope.

That'd be fine, I told myself. If she dies that way, it won't be my fault. Milo put her there, not me. But she'll be just as dead, so she won't be able to tell on me.

I wondered how long it would take her to die that way.

A few days?

Hell, somebody would probably find her before that. Or she'd work her way out of the rope.

I could go back and save her.

Yeah, right. In my condition, I'd be lucky to make it home. I sure couldn't turn back, now, and go hunting for the camp.

Maybe tomorrow. Get some rest, and go looking in daylight.

1. Why would I want to?
2. I probably couldn't find the campsite again, even if I tried.
3. If I *did* find it, the cops might be there waiting for me.

Maybe I'm a sentimental fool, but I'm not crazy.

Eventually, after trekking through the woods for at least an hour, I made my way into familiar territory. I'd really hoped that I might come out in Serena and Charlie's back yard, but it didn't work out that way. The familiar territory was only the creek.

But I sure was glad to find it.

I worked my way out to the middle of the creek (without falling!), sat down, leaned back, and let the wonderful, chilly water rush all over me. It felt so good it hurt.

I was in awful shape. I'd never been so worn out in my life, and I still had a long hike home. At least a mile through the woods. It made me almost cry, just thinking about it.

The night was still dark, though. I still had time. So I lay in the water with just my face out, and rested for a while. Soon, the water didn't feel so cold. It seemed cozy and almost warm.

A nice bath. Gotta have a nice, long bath when I get home.

Then I thought about how to get there. I'd made the hike between home and the picnic area many times during my three years living above Serena and Charlie's garage. Never in the dark, though. I'd always been afraid of the woods at night.

They even frightened me a little in daylight. Though I loved the solitude and quiet, I'd always been aware that someone might be lurking nearby, watching me, stalking me. Not that I'd ever discovered anyone doing that sort of thing. But I'd felt the potential. I'd even felt the urge, myself, to sneak around and spy on other people I found in the woods.

A few times, I'd surrendered to the urge.

But that's another story.

The deal is, I knew how to get home from the picnic area by hiking through the woods. But I wasn't too sure about doing it at night. The trails got tricky in places. I might miss a turn-off and end up lost. There were slopes and ditches to contend with. I might take a bad fall. Or walk into a broken limb and skewer myself.

What about taking Judy's car?

At first, the idea seemed incredibly idiotic. For one thing, somebody might see me driving it. For another, what would I *do* with her car afterward? Where would I leave it?

I'd be asking for trouble.

On the other hand, I had Judy's keys in my pocket. Her car was waiting for me just up the slope from the creek and it could get me home in less than ten minutes.

Fantastic!

I'd park it in the garage, directly under my room, where it would be safely hidden. I could dispose of it later—tomorrow night, for instance.

I was awfully tempted.

It'd be so easy!

But it'd be so *incriminating*, too. What if I got caught with Judy's car?

Then came a thought that changed everything.

If I leave it here, somebody might get suspicious and go looking for her.

That settled the matter.

With her car gone, no park personnel or random visitor or cop would start wondering who it belonged to. And if a friend or relative should report Judy missing tomorrow or the next day, her car wouldn't be found in Miller's Woods to give searchers a starting place.

I *had* to take it home.

Feeling fairly rested and revived and eager to get started, I stood up in the creek and waded ashore. Then I crouched in the bushes for a couple of minutes to make sure the coast was clear. I didn't see or hear anyone. So I walked over to the picnic table, my shoes squelching with every step. At the table, I sat on the bench, took off my loafers, and dumped the water out of them.

I put one of them back on, then changed my mind.

They were Tony's shoes. Evidence. I really didn't need them anymore, since I planned to be driving home instead of walking. Also, disposing of them here and now would save me from having to deal with them later.

I still had one bandana, and used it to wipe the shoes clean. Then I threw them into the bushes behind the picnic table.

For a while, I thought about getting rid of the rest of Tony's stuff. But that would mean driving home naked. I might get away with it, but the risk was too big. If I happened to drive past a cop . . .

Besides, everything except the belt would be easy enough to burn.

And *none* of it could be traced back to Tony, I was pretty sure of that.

Barefoot, dressed in nothing but the cut-offs and shirt, I walked away from the picnic table and headed for the slope below the parking area. I couldn't see Judy's car. It had to be up there, though.

It better be!

I trudged slowly up the slope. The dew made the grass slippery.

I remembered the big, fake tumble I'd taken on this very hillside in hopes of tricking Judy. And how the pistol had fallen out of my pocket.

Suddenly alarmed, I slapped my pockets.

No pistol!

For a moment, I thought I'd lost it again. Panic hit me. But then I remembered that I wasn't *supposed* to have it. I'd gotten rid of Tony's pistol on purpose, back at the camp.

What a relief!

But then, still in a fret, I checked the soggy pockets of my cut-offs to make sure I hadn't lost the keys.

I felt only two sets.

Which scared me all over again until I recalled that I'd thrown Tony's keys into the fire and I only *wanted* to have two sets: mine and Judy's.

What if I tossed in the wrong keys?

With a groan, I stopped climbing the slope and pulled both key cases out of my sodden pocket and studied them. I recognized my tan leather case right away. But I wasn't too sure about Judy's.

Find out soon enough.

I hurried the rest of the way up the slope, trying to ignore the nasty cold feeling in my stomach. At the top, I spotted Judy's car.

It was still the only car there.

Breathless from the climb, I walked slowly over to it.

After checking inside and underneath the car to make sure I was alone, I opened the door. The overhead light came on inside. I climbed in and shut the door.

And hoped I hadn't thrown the wrong keys into the fire.

It wouldn't have surprised me much, the way things had been going so far.

The first key I tried didn't fit.

But the second did. I twisted it, and the engine started.

"All *right!*" I blurted.

Keeping the headlights off, I backed up and turned around. I drove out of the parking area. Enough dim light came down through the trees to let me see the pavement of the road out. I didn't put the headlights on until I came to the main road north of the woods.

26

HOME AT LAST

You might find this hard to believe, but I made it back to Serena and Charlie's house without any trouble at all. I saw nobody. Every road I traveled was empty. I could hardly believe my luck, especially figuring how lousy most things had gone that night.

The night was still dark, but starting to get pale in the east by the time I swung into the driveway.

I checked the front lawn on the way by, but couldn't see much. So I drove ahead, stopped in front of the garage, and climbed out of the car. Standing there, I scanned the rear of the house, the pool area and lawn, and the dark border of the woods.

Everything looked fine.

No sign of my prowler.

The truth is, he didn't worry me.

For one thing, I figured he was probably long gone by then. I'd made him think I was on the phone with the cops, so this was probably the last place where he wanted to be.

For another thing, I was too worn out to care.

Also, I'd killed Milo the Monster, so what did I have to fear from a nice, clean-cut pervert like my prowler?

Just *let* him come, I thought.

Over by the side of the garage door, I tapped the code number into the key pad of the remote control box. The motor hummed and the door started its noisy rise.

I returned to Judy's car. When the garage door was all the way up, I drove inside and parked in the empty space beside my own car.

The space was where Serena and Charlie sometimes parked their Land Rover. Not often, though. They rarely bothered to put it in the garage. Usually, they parked on the driveway so they'd be close to the house.

But they were gone for a week, and so was their Land Rover.

Nobody would have any reason to open the garage door and find a stranger's car inside.

I killed the headlights and engine, removed the key from the ignition and shoved the key case into my pocket. Leaving the windows down and the doors unlocked, I climbed out. I glimpsed Judy's purse on the floor, but didn't touch it.

The garage door was still open. Nervous about that, I hurried over and thumbed the button to start it shutting. As it rumbled down, I returned to Judy's car and closed the driver's door. Then I went to the side door of the garage and let myself out.

With that door locked behind me, I gazed up the stairway to my room.

And wanted to climb it.

Go in and clean myself up and fall in bed and not get up for hours and hours.

But I had a few matters to take care of, first.

Such as the saber.

I found it in front of the house, hidden in the bushes. Leaving it encased in the denim legs of Tony's jeans, I carried it to the front door. The door was locked, of course. In my key case, though, I kept a full set of house keys. It took me a minute to find the right one, but then I unlocked the door, let myself in, and set the sword down on the foyer floor.

Then I went out again to look around. The sky was slightly lighter than before. It looked like dusk—the way things are in the evening a while after sundown and just before night takes over. Not the greatest for trying to see. I would need to inspect the area again in daylight. But I had to do it right away, even in such mediocre light, just in case there might be something nasty in plain sight.

A finger, for instance.

An ear.

Whatever.

First, I inspected the driveway between the house and the road. Then I walked back and forth a couple of times on the road in front of the house.

Everything looked fine.

So I returned to the front lawn and started traipsing over it, head down, studying the grass. This search paid off. I found a few small pieces of Tony. Some skin and muscle, I guess. Nothing anyone would be likely to recognize as human, but I picked them up, anyway. You can't be too careful about such things.

The left front pocket of my cut-offs had nothing important in it—just a bandana and hanky, so I stuffed the pieces in. Better than carrying them around in my hand, I figured. But they didn't feel very pleasant. There was nothing between them and me except a thin, wet layer of cloth. They sort of rested against my thigh, soft and gooshy. I tried to tell myself this was no worse than wandering around with some raw chicken in my pocket. It didn't help much, though. For one thing, I've never roamed around with raw chicken in my pocket. I mean, who does? I really couldn't trick myself into thinking it wasn't Tony.

I felt pretty disgusted and crummy.

This was the sort of thing you'd find *Milo* doing.

With the stuff in my pocket, I couldn't concentrate too

well on my search anymore. So I decided to quit and try again later.

Before going back into the house, I sat on the stoop and checked the bottoms of my bare feet. They were wet. Bits of grass and leaves clung to them. I didn't see any blood, though.

I took off my shirt and used it to clean my feet. Then I went inside, carrying it.

In the kitchen, I turned on the light and made sure the curtains were all shut. Then I draped the shirt over the back of a chair. Stepping up to the sink, I dug into my pocket and pulled out the Tony parts. They were slimy. They also had some ants crawling on them, which didn't make me feel too great about hauling them around in my pocket. I stuffed them down the garbage disposal. With water running, I switched on the disposal to grind them up.

Then I washed my hands very quickly, snatched my shirt off the chair and rushed over to the laundry room, which was just off the kitchen.

I tossed the shirt into the washing machine, then whipped off my belt. My cut-offs dropped to the floor. I stepped out of them. Standing there bare naked, I checked myself for ants. I was feeling itchy, but couldn't find any critters. So I picked up the cut-offs and emptied the pockets. The shorts, hanky and bandana went in with the shirt.

I set the keys aside, added detergent to the wash, and started the machine. While it was filling, I hurried to the foyer and slipped the saber out of the denim legs. Sword in one hand, legs swinging in the other, I returned to the laundry room. I tossed the legs into the machine with the other stuff.

Back in the kitchen, I stood at the sink and washed the saber. It *looked* clean even before I started. I must've done a pretty good job on it with the hose. But I scoured the thing with a rag and liquid soap, being especially careful to get at the crevices where the blade joined the handle.

You can never get rid of *all* the blood. That's what I'd read, anyway. Police investigators would take the sword apart and find traces, no matter what I might do.

I wasn't doing this for the police.

I was cleaning it so Charlie or little Debbie wouldn't notice blood on the saber next time they took it down to play "charge" or "Peter Pan" or something.

With a dish towel, I wiped every bit of water off the sword. Then I dried my own bare front, which had gotten splashed.

On my way into the living room, I changed my mind about hanging up the weapon right away. What if some water or blood was trapped inside the handle, and leaked on the wall?

Besides, I sort of liked having it handy.

So I took it with me.

In the den, I set it down and turned on a lamp. Right away, I looked toward the sliding glass door where my prowler had been. I couldn't see it, though. The curtains were shut.

Thank God.

What I *didn't* need to see, on top of everything else, was the mess my prowler had left behind.

With a feeling of relief—and a touch of nausea just from thinking about what he'd done—I turned my attention to the answering machine. It blinked a tiny red light to let me know we had a message.

I poked the "new message" button.

The quiet hiss of rewinding tape seemed to last a long time. When it stopped, Tony said, "Ah, you finally got yourself an answering machine. Hope it's not because of me. But it probably is, huh?"

Listening to him, I felt strange.

So much had happened in the hours since he'd made that call. Especially to him.

But my own life would never be the same, either. Nor would Judy's.

Or Milo's, for that matter.

All because Tony had dialed a wrong number.

He'd probably only been one digit off, or reversed something.

And *WHAM!*

Just goes to show what can happen because of a little mistake.

"The thing is," he was saying, "I'm not going to call again."

How right you are, I thought.

But I didn't laugh, I wrinkled my nose.

And kept listening.

He sounded like a pretty nice guy.

When he started in about moving to a new place, I pulled open a drawer of the telephone stand and hunted for something to write with. There were plenty of ballpoints and pads of paper. And some miniature tape cassettes. I snatched up a pen and note pad just as he started to give his new phone number.

While I was busy writing, his call ended.

That's because I had picked up and blurted, "Tony!"

My voice wasn't there. Nothing else was there. The tape stopped, and the machine made a few beeps to let me know there were no more messages.

I frowned at Tony's phone number for a few moments, not sure why I'd bothered to copy it down.

Maybe it would come in handy for something.

But probably not.

It was only on paper, though. I could burn it easily enough, later on—along with the rest of the note pad, so nobody would ever be able to discover the *imprint* of Tony's number.

For now, though, I had another matter to deal with.

I opened the answering machine, pulled out the tape, and replaced it with a spare cassette from the drawer.

Then I stood there, staring at the machine and wondering what to do next.

Get everything together.

Seemed like a good idea. With the note pad and cassette in one hand, I picked up the saber. Then I headed for the laundry room. Along the way, I noticed my favorite blue silk robe draped over a chair in the living room, where I'd put it such a long time ago. It had pockets and I needed pockets.

But I was awfully hot and sweaty and dirty, so I decided to save the robe for later.

I walked on through the kitchen and entered the laundry room. The washing machine was still going, of course. My belt lay on the floor, and the two sets of keys were on a shelf beside the washer.

Except for Judy's car and the odds and ends in the washer, that was everything.

I wanted to keep it all with me.

But I left it in the laundry room for a couple of minutes while I rushed into the kitchen. Serena keeps a drawer full of small bags. I grabbed one, returned with it, and loaded it up with the two sets of keys, the tape cassette and note pad. I wound up the belt and stuffed it inside, too.

Leaving the washer to finish its business, I carried the saber and bag into the living room. There, I grabbed Charlie's robe.

In the hallway, I stopped just long enough to flick the air conditioner on. Then I went to the end of the hall and entered Serena and Charlie's bedroom. It was dark with the curtains shut. I didn't turn any lights on, though. I just walked straight through to the master bathroom.

I swung the door shut with my elbow, bumped it with my rump to make it latch, then elbowed the light switch. I needed a hand, though, to lock the door. So I held the sword between my legs and thumbed down the lock button.

After that, I hung the robe on a hook. I set my bag on a counter near the sink and took the saber with me to the sunken bath tub.

I set it down on the tile floor beside the tub.

Not that I'm paranoid, or anything. I just wanted to be safe. And what good is a weapon if it's out of reach when you need it?

While the tub was filling, I used the toilet. Then I stood in front of a full-length mirror and looked at myself.

What a wreck.

My hair, dark and clinging to my scalp, looked as if I hadn't shampooed it in a month. Everywhere, my skin looked greasy. I must've had about two dozen scratches on my front and back. Several of them had bled. I didn't have much blood on me, probably thanks to spending time in the creek. But some of the scratches looked like bright red threads across my skin. I had plenty of welts and bruises, too.

The grand-daddy of all my injuries was my stomach, where I'd walked into that broken branch. It had rammed me and gouged me raw. Skin was ruffled up around the edges of the wound, and I had a bruise the size of a grapefruit.

Nothing looked bad enough to require medical attention, though.

I'd gotten off lucky.

At least compared to a few other people I could think of, such as Tony, Milo, the gal in Milo's tent, and even Judy.

Three out of four needed a coroner, not a doctor.

I wondered how Judy was doing.

Probably still hanging there. Her wrists had been tied together *very* well. She might not be able to get loose at all. Not without help, anyway.

Watching myself in the mirror, I raised my arms high and crossed my wrists. I stood as Judy had been standing, probably *still was*. It made my breasts lift and my belly sink in. I've got a terrific build, but I looked even better that way.

Anybody would, I guess.

Maybe that's why guys like to string up their victims by the wrists.

No. It might be one of the reasons, but not the main one. I'd spent enough time with Judy to know the truth about that. I sure did like how she looked so stretched and taut, but more important was that her whole body was right there dangling in the open. Nothing was hidden.

You had total access.

You could swing her. You could spin her. You could wander around her, look at any part of her. You could pick up her legs and spread them apart. Touch any part of her. Hurt any part of her.

I turned around slowly, staring at my reflection in the mirror.

And wished I could see Judy again.

27

Splish-splash

Over at the tub, I shut off the faucets and eased myself down into the deep, hot water. It made my scratches sting a little, and felt like burning oil on the raw gouge from the branch. None of the really bad pain lasted more than a few seconds, though.

I leaned backward, easing myself down. Soon, my whole body was submerged except my face. The back of my head lightly rested against the rear of the tub. My buttocks lightly rested on the slippery tiles of the bottom. Nothing else of me touched the tub. I felt cool air on my face. Everywhere else was water. Its liquid heat surrounded me, wrapping me, caressing me softly all over, whispering in my ears, licking me between the toes and sliding into every crease and crevice.

It was luscious.

Heavenly.

After so many rough hours of fear and pain and strenuous labor, I'd come to a place of peace. My arms drifted beneath the surface, weightless and limp by my sides. My legs, open and bent at the knees, lingered at mid-depth as if held off the bottom by ribbons of silk. I heard little more than the quiet lapping of water. My muffled heartbeat sounded calm. Breathing slowly, I felt hot currents rub against my chest and breasts.

I supposed it would be a good idea to sit up, soap myself and shampoo my hair. But I couldn't force myself to abandon the luxury of lounging motionless.

Suspended in the lazy heat.

After a while, my mind seemed to slide off into the air and drift out over the woods. I wasn't searching for anything, just drifting. But when I saw the glow of a campfire, I went down for a closer look.

I found Judy suspended from the limb like before, shiny as oil and glowing with firelight. She still wore the red bandana loose around her neck.

But all her injuries were gone.

She looked beautiful.

As I walked up to her, she said, "I knew you'd come back, Alice."

"Then you knew more than me."

"I've *always* known more than you," she said, and gave me a sly grin.

"I didn't even know how to find this place," I told her.

"How *did* you find it?"

"Just luck. It's been my lucky night."

"Mine, too," Judy said.

"How do you figure that?"

"You came back for me, didn't you?"

"Yeah. I did. I couldn't just leave you here."

"You're such a softie."

"That's me," I said, and smiled.

"Give me a kiss, you softie."

Her words shocked me, thrilled me. I laughed and shook my head. "No, I don't think so. Thanks anyway, but . . ."

"You don't have to be afraid of me," she said.

"I'm not afraid of you."

"You love me, don't you?"

"No!"

"You came back because you love me."

"That isn't why."

"Then why?"

"Only because it was wrong to leave you here. And because I don't want you to die like this. I wouldn't be able to stand it if you died like this. You never did anything to hurt me. And you helped me with Milo."

"You love me, don't you?"

"Stop saying that."

"Kiss me, and I'll stop saying it."

"I don't want to kiss you."

"Yes, you do." She slid her tongue slowly across her lips, moistening them so they glistened. "Don't worry. It won't hurt a bit."

"I know it won't hurt," I said. "That's not why."

"Then why?"

"Just because."

"I'll never tell," she said. "I promise. Nobody will ever find out about this. It'll be our secret, just between you and me."

"I don't know."

"Yes, you do. You've wanted to kiss me from the start."

"No."

"Everywhere. You've wanted to kiss me everywhere. My mouth, my breasts . . ."

"Shut up."

"Everywhere."

"No."

"Do it, Alice. Now. I want you. And I want you more than anything."

I nodded, trembling. Then, I leaned in until our bodies met, and kissed Judy lightly on her open lips.

Her arms and legs clamped around me.

"Now I've got ya, bitch!"

But it wasn't Judy saying that.

It was a man, his voice low and scratchy and *gleeful*.

This wasn't Judy at all, not anymore. It was Milo, face

bloody and eyes bulging, squeezing me so hard with his arms and legs that I was sinking deep into the soft bulges of his body, being enveloped by him. As I tried to scream, his mouth covered mine. His writhing lips felt slimy. He stuck his tongue into my mouth. Only it wasn't his tongue. It was hard and thick, and he shoved it in deep. Thrust it down my throat.

I'll bite it off, you . . . !

I suddenly came wide awake and found myself staring up through the water.

Shit!

I rammed my elbows against the bottom of the tub and burst through the surface fast, choking. I sat there, wracked with coughs. Some water had found its way into the wrong place, that was for sure. Probably not much, but enough to keep me coughing for a while.

After I finished, my chest ached every time I took a deep breath.

I was okay, but didn't feel much like trying to relax in the water again. For one thing, I might catch another snootful. For another, I didn't want any more dreams.

Dreams are so damn weird. If you ask me, the point of every single dream and nightmare is just to torment you. That's all any of them ever do. They scare the crap out of you or they humiliate you. Or else they tantalize you with a situation that is really fabulous, wonderful beyond belief—only to jerk it away from you.

They twist things.

They really suck.

And they seem to be ten times worse—more real and more twisted—when you're really tired.

I was hugely tired, so I didn't dare relax again. I opened the bathtub drain and got to my feet. The water almost came up to my knees. The tub was so large, though, that I didn't need to worry about it overflowing. As the water gurgled out, I slid the plastic curtain shut, turned the faucets on, and lifted the gizmo to start the shower.

The hot, stiff spray hissed down, pelting my scalp and face and shoulders. It felt great.

But two things were wrong.

First, the water made too much noise coming out, splashing my skin, pattering against the plastic curtain, raining against the water pooled in the tub. It made me worry about all the things I *couldn't* hear. In other rooms, phones might be ringing. A window might be breaking. Someone could even kick open a door and I wouldn't be able to hear it.

Second, the frosted white shower curtain hung between me and my saber.

What if I *needed* it?

After worrying for a while, I slid open the shower curtain, bent over and picked up the saber. I brought it in with me. Then I shut the curtain again and set the sword on the bottom of the tub.

I couldn't hear any better, of course, but now I had a weapon. That made things all right.

I went ahead with my shower, sudsing myself all over with a bar of soap, then shampooing my hair, always being careful where I put my feet.

Naturally, nobody came along and tried to attack me.

They never attack you when you're ready for them.

How about if old Mother Bates had swept open the shower curtain and found Janet Leigh facing her with a *cavalry saber!* Would've changed the course of movie history.

Anyway, *I* was ready. But nobody came.

Just as well. I'd had a long night.

When I was done with the shower, I turned off the water and opened the curtain. Squatting down, I picked up the sword. Then I climbed out of the tub, set the sword aside and stepped over to the towel rod.

Two matching bath towels hung there. They both looked clean, but I could tell that they weren't fresh from the laundry. I didn't know which had been used by Serena, which by Charlie, so I just grabbed one and started drying myself with it. The towel was enormous, thick and soft. As I buried my face in it, I wondered who it had rubbed, and where. Not that it mattered much. I was just curious, that's all. Either of them using it on any parts of themselves was fine with me, and nice to think about.

After drying myself, I dried the sword. I was very careful doing that, because I didn't want to cut the towel.

Then I applied some of Serena's roll-on deodorant to my underarms. I knew this was hers, not Charlie's, because I recognized the scent.

I used Serena's hairbrush. The mirror was fogged up, except near the bottom, so I had to squat very low in order to see my head in it. I gave my hair a quick brushing, then stood up again.

Finally, I put on Charlie's silk robe and left the bathroom. Of course, I took along my sword and bag of goodies.

While I'd been in the tub, the sun had come up. Even with most of the curtains shut, the house was filled with grayish light.

In the laundry room, I took all my things out of the washing machine. I loaded them into the drier and started it. Then I went to the front door.

I opened it and walked to the edge of the stoop.

Morning was here, all right. The sun was still very low in the east. It spread brilliant, golden light across the lawn, making the dew sparkle. There didn't seem to be any breeze at all. The warm, moist air smelled of flowers and grass. Birds twittered in the distance. I heard a woodpecker somewhere. Insects were humming and buzzing. It was as quiet and peaceful all around me as a forest glen.

It was lovely.

When I stepped down, the grass felt warm and wet under my bare feet. I wandered slowly, looking for bloodstains and pieces of Tony. I saw a few butterflies. And some bees. But nothing bad.

The lawn seemed fine.

I was about to take a closer look at the driveway, but heard the far off sound of a car engine. It sent a tremor through my stomach. I figured the car must be coming here. Quickly, I turned around and walked toward the front door.

The car sound grew louder.

Cops?

No way, I told myself. They couldn't be after me. Not yet, anyway, and probably never.

What if it's Serena and Charlie?

Maybe something had gone wrong with their trip. It hardly seemed likely. Anything was possible, though. People *do* return home unexpectedly.

I felt cold and sick inside with the idea that it might be them. I could probably hang up the sword and clear out the clothes drier in time, but what about Judy's car in the garage?

I leaped onto the stoop, planting wet footprints on the concrete, and rushed to the front door.

The car sounded as if it had almost reached the driveway.

Brakes squeaked a bit.

I shoved open the door and ducked inside.

Before I had a chance to shut the door, though, I heard a familiar sound.

THWAP!

I'd rarely been outside at this time of the morning, but I'd sometimes heard such a sound coming through my windows above the garage.

It was the *Chester Tribune* smacking the pavement near the end of the driveway.

Standing in the doorway, I shook my head and smiled. I felt like a dope for being so scared.

After the sound of the car engine faded, I went to get the paper. On my way up the driveway, I looked again for evidence of Tony.

There was nothing.

The paper had landed on the pavement a few yards down from the top, so I didn't need to go all the way to the road. I went the rest of the way to the top, anyhow, just to take a look around.

Everything seemed fine.

I walked back and forth on the road in front of the house, searching.

Satisfied that there was nothing to find, I returned to the driveway. On the way down, I picked up the newspaper. I peeled off its rubber band and unrolled it.

The headline read:

ALICE SOUGHT IN MURDER SPREE!

Just kidding.

I half *expected* it to say that, but it didn't.

I don't remember what the hell the headline was. It had nothing to do with me.

As I carried the *Tribune* down toward the house, though, it gave me an idea.

28

YVONNE

Until I've had a cup of hot, black coffee, I'm useless in the morning. And this qualified as morning, even though I'd never gone to bed.

Back inside the house, I tossed the *Tribune* onto the kitchen table and set to work making a pot of coffee. I knew right where to find everything. Before long, the cozy aroma of coffee filled the kitchen.

I had to wait for the pot to fill, though, so I sat at the table and looked through the newspaper. It didn't contain a single story about anything I'd been involved with last night.

Nothing in the Obituary section, either.

None of which came as much of a surprise.

When the coffee was ready, I poured myself a mugful. I almost took it outside to drink it by the pool. That would've been nice on such an early, lovely morning. On my way to one of the back doors, though, I remembered what the prowler'd done. That changed my mind. So I returned to the kitchen table and looked at the newspaper again while I enjoyed my first mug of coffee.

I went straight to the movie ads. I like movies. Chester had a cineplex with six theaters. Not bad for such a worthless little town. Some good stuff was playing. I checked the times on a couple of them, and wondered about going to a movie today.

Why not? I deserved a treat, the way I'd toughed it out and taken care of so many problems.

One problem still needed to be dealt with, though.

Tony's redial.

I now had a plan.

If it works, I thought, I'll take in a movie afterward to celebrate.

When I went for a refill on my coffee, I checked the clock on the kitchen wall.

6:20.

I should probably wait until after 8:00 to try out my idea.

To help pass the time, I decided to make myself a huge breakfast. Normally, I don't have any breakfast at all—just coffee. But I'd had a long, hard night. I'd gotten enough exercise to kill off a high-school football team, picked up scads of minor injuries (food heals), and must've burnt off one or two zillion calories. I deserved a *feast*.

While a skillet full of bacon was sizzling on a burner, I made myself a Bloody Mary. I prepared it my special way— half tomato juice and half vodka, double the usual amount of Worcestershire Sauce and Tabasco to give it a real bite. After stirring it around with ice cubes, I squeezed a slice of lime into it. Then I sprinkled ground pepper over the top.

It tasted so fine.

I sipped it while I finished tending to the bacon, made some toast and fried a couple of eggs. After buttering the toast, I topped each slice with an egg. Then I sat at the table and devoured it all.

One of the best things you can put in your mouth is a piece of buttered toast that's dripping with egg yellow. Try it by itself, or with a chunk of egg white and a bite of bacon. Wash it down with coffee or a Bloody Mary. Mmmmm.

I hated to see the last of it go.

After breakfast, I did the dishes and skillet by hand and put everything away. I was tempted to have another Bloody Mary, but resisted the urge. One had been enough to make me feel pleasant. A second might knock me off my feet.

I needed to have my wits about me—and my feet under me—for taking care of the redial problem.

Before leaving the house, I hung the saber on the wall where it belonged. I also hung Charlie's robe in the bedroom closet and put on my swimsuit from yesterday. The swimsuit was all I had to wear, because I didn't want to use Tony's clothes again now that they'd been washed. In the laundry room, I emptied the drier and stuffed everything into a grocery bag.

Carrying my bags, my purse, and the *Chester Tribune*, I left the house and went up to my room over the garage.

It was nice to be in my own place again. It felt so safe and cozy. I wished I could stay—climb into bed and bury myself under the covers and sleep for ages.

Maybe later.

A lot later.

First, I needed to hide Tony's things. I hung up his shirt in my closet, just as if it were my own. I folded the cut-offs and slipped them into a dresser drawer where I kept other pairs of shorts. The handkerchief and bandana also went into drawers. I put the note pad and both sets of keys in my purse. I hid the cassette tape in a chest pocket of an old flannel shirt near the back of my closet.

That left nothing except the severed denim legs of Tony's jeans. They certainly weren't incriminating, so there was no reason to hide or destroy them. I decided to take them out to the car with me. They might make good rags. So I folded them and set them near my purse.

Next, I took off my swimsuit. I put on thong panties and a bra, then stood like a dope and wondered what else to wear.

Making the decision wasn't easy. Mostly because I didn't really know what I'd be doing. Also, maybe, because I needed sleep. And the Bloody Mary might've had a little to do with it.

Finally, I made up my mind and got dressed.

With my purse, the morning newspaper and the denim legs, I hurried downstairs and let myself into the lower part of the garage.

I took Judy's car.

I didn't like the idea of driving it around. I wanted to dump it somewhere and be done with it, but using my own car for a mission like this would've been idiotic.

Judy's car, at least, couldn't be traced to me.

And I doubted that anyone would recognize me. Not in my sunglasses and red wig.

Yeah, I had a wig on.

I kept a small collection of them, just in case. A gal never knows when she might want to alter her appearance a bit. Or a lot.

The curly red hair looked pretty damn gawdy, but that was the idea. Gawdy all the way. My lipstick was too bright, too red. My gold hoop earrings were the size of bracelets. If people saw me, *that's* what they would see. They'd never stand a chance of recognizing—or identifying—me, Alice.

I drove to the busy area near the highway. Some of the locals call it "motel row." But it had a lot more than just motels. Along both sides of the highway were tons of restaurants and gas stations, and even some fruit stands and gift shops.

There were also scads of public telephones.

You hardly ever find phones in enclosed booths, anymore. I didn't want to deal with highway noise, so I parked the car and went into a restaurant called Pokey's. The hostess was busy seating a family, so I went straight for the restrooms. Near the end of the corridor, I found two public phones between the doors marked Guys and Dolls.

Nobody was using them.

I took the note pad and a pen out of my purse. After checking the newspaper, I jotted down a number I'd found on the masthead.

Then I dropped a quarter into the phone and made the call.

"*Tribune* circulation," a woman's voice told me. "This is Yvonne. May I help you, please?"

"I hope so," I said. "This is Mrs. Tony Romano. I'm afraid we didn't receive our newspaper this morning."

"May I have your phone number, please?"

I read her Tony's number off the pad, and figured she was probably tapping it into a computer.

"Yes. You *should've* gotten it by now, Mrs. Romano. I'll . . ."

"The thing is," I said quickly, "we haven't been getting it since our move. We just recently moved to a new place. I was wondering if there might be a mix-up and maybe it's still being delivered to our old address on Washington."

"Hmm. No. We have it here as being delivered to 8448 Adams."

I wrote the address on my note pad.

"Is that your correct address for delivery?" Yvonne asked.

"Yeah, it is." Laughing softly, I said, "So much for my theory."

"Well, I'll make sure we get this straightened out for you, Mrs. Romano. We'll have this morning's paper to you within the hour."

"Thank you very much."

"Thank *you* for being a subscriber, and we do apologize for your inconvenience."

"No problem. Thanks again. Bye-bye."

I hung up and grinned.

After glancing around to make sure nobody had an eye on me, I wiped the handset and number pad with a tissue. Then I walked out of Pokey's and climbed into Judy's car.

Next stop, Tony's place!

I felt brilliant.

Of course, the trick would've fallen flat if Tony hadn't been a *Tribune* subscriber. Lucky me, he was. And lucky me, he'd been prompt about giving the paper his change of address.

If my luck held, I would walk up to Tony's front door and find it unlocked.

Which was *sure* to happen.

Sure.

In my dreams.

Too bad I'd gotten rid of Tony's keys. I could've stepped right up to his door, unlocked it and walked in easy as pie. But last night, I'd been sure there was no possibility of learning his new address. I'd been *positive*. There just wasn't any way to do it, not without drastic steps such as questioning people in his old building.

Besides, I'd already thrown his keys in the fire before Judy told me that she knew for a fact he had redial.

If only I'd kept them!

Thought I was so smart, throwing all that stuff in the fire.

Yeah, yeah, burn the evidence! Great idea!

Shit!

Of course, the keys would probably still work fine. All I had to do was drive over to Miller's Woods, hunt around until I find the campsite, dig the keys out of the cold campfire, hike back to the car and drive all the way over to Tony's . . .

That's all.

And in the meantime, maybe the cops might find Tony's body.

If they haven't already.

And they get to his place ahead of me.

What if they're already there?

Tony's address on Adams was only a few blocks away from Judy's apartment building. Just for the sake of caution, I made a slight detour and drove to her place, first. The neighborhood probably would've been crawling with cops and curious neighbors if Tony's body had been discovered. But it was quiet, so I drove on.

As I drove, I wondered how to get inside his apartment.

I had no idea.

I planned to play it by ear.

Now, you might be asking yourself, *All this over a redial button? Is she nuts?*

Maybe.

I wondered about that myself.

But I kept picturing a cop in Tony's apartment. He notices the redial feature and thinks, *This'll have the last number Tony ever called! It might even belong to the murderer! Check it out!* So he gives it a try. Next thing you know, Charlie's voice is in his ear, saying, "Thank you for calling. Nobody is available to answer the phone, right now, but if you'd like to leave a message . . ."

This'll *really* get the cop going. Especially if he ever lays his hands on the phone company records and finds out what *time* Tony made the call—and how long it lasted.

He'll be very eager to pay Charlie a visit.

But Charlie and Serena are out of town for the week.

And the only person with access to the house and phone is me.

Not a pretty picture.

But I now had a chance to make it go away.

All I had to do was get inside Tony's apartment and make one telephone call.

Worth a little risk, don't you think?

I thought so.

But then, I'd been through a lot, so maybe I wasn't thinking very straight at the time.

29

MURPHY

Leaving Judy's car parked around the corner, I walked back to 8448 Adams.

It was an old, single-level building with eight small units and an open, grassy courtyard in the middle. I didn't know Tony's apartment number. So instead of entering, I just looked the place over and kept walking.

Each front door had a mailbox nearby. Too bad. If you're in a complex with a bank of mailboxes, the post office requires names on all the boxes. But when you've got your own box, like at this place, you don't need to put your name on it. And nobody does.

Three of the units had newspapers in front of them.

One of those was probably Tony's.

But which?

Had the *Tribune* delivery person shown up yet with the replacement? If not, I could simply wait for him and see what he does.

But there was a slim chance that he'd already been here and gone. (He certainly wouldn't have left a *second* paper on the doorstep.) If he'd already shown up, I would have an awfully long wait.

There was just no way to know for sure.

Anyway, I didn't have time to waste. I had to get this done and get going.

Maybe the car ports or garages would give me a clue as to Tony's apartment number. So I headed for the end of the block to look for an alley entrance.

And heard a distant siren.

Oh, my God!

The sound froze me.

My mind went nuts. The cops had found Tony's body, knew I'd killed him, knew where to find me, and were swooping in for the arrest. In a matter of seconds, squad cars would roar around the corners and shriek to a halt. Cops would leap out and come at me with their guns drawn.

I had an urge to break into a run.

The siren's cry grew louder.

They can't know it's me! How can they know it's me?

Just play innocent, I warned myself. Admit nothing. Stay calm.

What can they really prove?

As the siren noise bore down on me from behind, I turned my head and looked over my shoulder.

Siren blaring, lights aflash, an ambulance sped by me and kept going.

I laughed at myself. But my heart was thumping like mad, and I was suddenly out of breath.

Even after the ambulance was out of sight, I stood there gasping, trying to calm down.

Not enough sleep, that was the problem.

That, and a little too much stress.

Maybe I should've had that extra Bloody Mary with breakfast, after all.

I've gotta get out of here!

But I couldn't just give up on Tony's place without at least trying to get in. It was almost a miracle that I'd been able to find out his address. I was *meant* to come here, get inside somehow, and take us off his redial.

Just go for it!

I turned around and walked back to his building. I wasn't sure what to do. Go door to door, maybe, saying my car broke down and I need to use a phone . . .

MANAGER

It was a sign near the door of apartment one.

The building manager would *have* to know Tony's apartment number. And he or she would have keys for it.

I hurried over and rang the doorbell.

I did it with a knuckle.

Knuckles don't leave fingerprints.

Nothing happened, so I rang it again. This time, a man's voice called, "Hang on, there! I'm on my way!"

A few seconds later, the front door swung open. The screen door still stood in the way. Through the gray mesh, I could barely make out the man on the other side.

"Well, hello there," he said.

"Good morning," I said.

"Take a step backward, and I'll open the screen. Don't wanta knock you on your keester, do I?"

I took a step backward, and he swung the screen door open. He held it wide with an outstretched arm. He was maybe about thirty years old. He had messy brown hair and wore glasses. He also wore a Bear Whizz Beer T-shirt that showed a grizzly bear peeing in a woodland stream. His shorts appeared to be swimming trunks, even though the apartment building didn't seem to have a swimming pool. He was barefoot.

Not much to look at, but he had a nice smile and I sort of liked the glint in his eyes.

"My name's Fran Johnson," I told him, and held out my hand.

"Murphy Scott." He gave my hand a hearty shake as if we

were old pals. "Pleased to make your acquaintance, Fran. And what brings you here, this fine morning?"

"I'm looking for my boyfriend, Tony. Tony Romano."

"Ah, Tony!"

"He lives here, doesn't he?"

"He does indeed. I helped him move in last Saturday. Apartment six, directly across the way."

Nodding, I muttered, "Six, I know," and glanced over my shoulder at the unit on the other side of the lawn. It was one of the three with a *Tribune* on the stoop.

I faced Murphy again and said, "The thing is, he isn't . . . I'm afraid something might be wrong. We were supposed to meet for breakfast this morning, but he didn't show up. I waited over an hour for him."

Frowning, Murphy shook his head.

"Have you seen him at all this morning?" I asked.

"Nope. I just got up."

"I phoned him a few minutes ago, but all I got was his answering machine."

"Maybe he screens his calls."

"But I told him it was me, and he still didn't pick up."

"He might've been indisposed at the time. That sort of thing happens. He could've been taking a shower, for instance."

"Maybe, but . . ."

"A lot of possibilities." With a sheepish look on his face, Murphy said, "Sometimes, guy's just . . ." He shrugged. "Were you getting along all right?"

"Sure. I mean, as far as I know. Nothing *seemed* to be wrong. And we had this date for breakfast."

Frowning past my shoulder, Murphy said, "He hasn't picked up his paper yet. Maybe he just overslept or something."

"But he didn't answer his phone."

"Why don't you go over and give his doorbell a ring or two?" Murphy suggested.

"I already tried, but . . . okay."

While Murphy watched, I walked across the grass to unit

six and pushed the doorbell with my knuckle. The sound of the ringing gave me flutters in the stomach.

What if he comes to the door?

Yeah, right. In his condition?

But somebody else might open it.

A cop. A friend. A twin.

Be ready for anything. Stay cool.

The door stayed shut.

I rang the bell a few more times, then turned around and headed back for Murphy. As I walked toward him, he checked me out.

Normally, I don't like it when guys do that.

Most guys are pigs.

Anyway, I didn't mind Murphy looking me over. I'd only just met him, but I already knew he wasn't some kind of asshole. Also, I could tell that he liked what he was seeing, and I can't say I blamed him.

Along with my red wig, bright lipstick and enormous earrings, I wore a yellow blouse the color of a lemon. I would've preferred a halter top, but had to keep my midriff covered because of the injury. To make things interesting, I'd left a few of my upper buttons undone. Plenty of cleavage showed.

My legs were scratched and bruised, too, so I couldn't wear my really short, snug shorts. I'd chosen a skirt, instead. A light, full skirt of forest green. It drifted against my legs and had a slit up one side. In a certain light, you could see through it.

The whole outfit was intended to draw men's eyes. To attract them and *dis*tract them. They would see the flamboyant redhead, the stacked and leggy broad—not me.

My shoes, actually, weren't part of the outfit. The costume screamed out for something like gold lamé slippers or snake-skin boots. But I wore white sneakers for comfort and speed.

Murphy, watching me, shook his head and smiled.

"What?" I asked.

"Tony's gotta be either nuts or dead to miss a breakfast with *you*."

I must've blushed. I sure felt very hot all of a sudden.

"The thing is," I said, "he's diabetic. Did he tell you about that?"

Murphy lost his smile. "Oh, man," he said. "No, he didn't say anything about that. Diabetic? Maybe we'd better have a look. I'll go get the keys."

He vanished inside, but his screen door barely had time to swing shut before he pushed it open and came out. As I followed him across the courtyard, I scanned the rest of the apartments. I saw nobody.

He pulled open Tony's screen door and knocked a couple of times on the wooden door. But he didn't wait for a response. He stuck a key into the lock, turned it, and pushed the door open. Then he called out, "Tony?"

We both listened, but heard nothing.

"Tony? It's Murphy, the manager. Are you here?"

Still no answer, so Murphy stepped inside. I crouched, picked up the *Tribune* by the rubber band around its middle, and entered behind him. We were in a small, tidy living room.

I saw Tony's answering machine on a lamp table beside his couch. "Maybe I'd better wait here," I whispered. "In case he's . . . indecent or something."

"No problem," Murphy said, and hurried away to search the apartment.

The moment he stepped into the bedroom, I rushed forward, tossed the newspaper onto Tony's couch, swung my purse behind my back to get it out of the way, and picked up the telephone.

At the sound of a dial tone, I started to tap numbers into the keyboard.

The three-digit local prefix.

Then four random numbers.

In the earpiece, I heard quiet, ringing sounds.

YES!!!

Murphy, coming out of the bedroom, looked at me and shook his head.

I gave him a smile, then spoke into the mouthpiece. "Barb? It's me, Fran."

Murphy hurried on, apparently to check the kitchen.

"I got the manager to let me into his apartment, but he doesn't seem to be here." Then I called out, "Murphy, any sign of him?"

"Nope."

To the ringing phone, I said, "I guess it's good news. I was really afraid he might've had another seizure."

Murphy came back into the living room, his eyebrows raised, his head shaking.

"Any sign of him?" I asked.

"Nothing. He's not here."

I gave Murphy a grateful smile, then told the phone, "He's definitely not here . . . No, I don't know if his car's here."

"I'll go look," Murphy said.

A moment later, he was gone. The screen door clapped shut behind him.

I hung up.

Then I flipped up the plastic cover of the answering machine, took out Tony's tape cassette, shut the cover and gave it a quick wipe with my skirt. I tucked the tiny cassette down the front of my panties.

After that, I picked up the phone and tapped in another set of random numbers.

This time, somebody picked up after the first ring. A man's voice said, "Hello?"

I didn't say a thing.

"Hello? Who is this?"

"This is Margaret," I said, "from Westside Marketing Research . . ."

"Not interested," he said and hung up.

I still had the apartment to myself. As I tried a new number,

I noticed a calendar beside the answering machine. It was the kind that has a small, separate page for each day of the year. The number showing on the right was yesterday's date.

The thick stack of pages on the left side of the center rings told me that Tony was in the habit of turning them over, not ripping them out.

From the other end of the line came a busy signal.

With the edge of a fingertip, I flipped the calendar page over so today's date showed.

Then, hearing a quick approach of footsteps on the outside walkway, I said into the phone, "Maybe so. I sure hope so, anyway."

As the screen door opened, I turned around and smiled at Murphy.

He came in, shaking his head. "Car's gone," he whispered.

"Thanks, Murphy." Into the phone, I said, "Tony's car is gone . . . I have no idea . . . Well, I'd much rather be stood up for a breakfast date than have Tony in a coma, or something. I'm *glad* we didn't find him, you know? . . . Right, I'll let you know if I find out anything. Bye-bye."

I hung up, then said to Murphy, "That was Tony's sister. She's even more worried than I am. I made the mistake of calling her from the restaurant . . . They're really close. I thought she might know where he was. But I only ended up scaring her half to death."

"He's probably fine," Murphy said.

"I sure hope so."

"Ready to go?"

No! My fingerprints were all over the phone.

"Yeah," I murmured. "I guess."

He frowned slightly, but turned around and started toward the door.

"I don't . . ."

He looked back. "What?"

". . . feel so good."

30

MDS

I let out a moan and tried to look nauseated. Bending over, I put my hands on my knees.

"Are you sick?" Murphy asked.

"No, no. I'll . . . be fine. Just . . . I'm a little dizzy, that's all. I'd better just . . . I'll be fine in a minute. I'm sorry."

"Hey, no problem."

"I'd better sit down," I said, and sank to the floor.

Murphy squatted in front of me, looking appalled. "What's the matter? Do you need an ambulance, or . . . ?"

"No. No. I'm . . . I get this way. It's my . . . condition kicking up."

"Condition?"

"MDS."

"I don't know what that is."

As far as I knew, neither did anyone else. I'd just then made it up. "Morning Dehydration Syndrome," I explained.

"Huh?"

"It's because I missed breakfast, and . . ." I trailed off and hung my head.

"Dehydration?" he asked.

"Water. I need . . . water."

"Okay. Hang on." Murphy sprang up, dodged past me, and went rushing for the kitchen.

The answering machine was next to my shoulder and slightly behind me. I stood up quickly and turned around. As I listened to cupboards squeak and water run, I picked up the telephone's handset, wiped it all over with my skirt and returned it to its cradle. Then I gave the phone's keypad a quick rub. When the kitchen faucet shut off, I sank to one knee. I was struggling to rise as Murphy trotted in with a glass of water.

"Be careful," he said.

Wobbling, I made it to my feet. But as I reached for the glass, I lost my balance accidentally on purpose and fell toward Murphy, bumping the glass. The whole load of water caught me in the chest. It drenched the top of my blouse, doused my exposed cleavage, soaked through my bra, and poured down between my breasts.

As I sagged and grabbed Murphy by the shoulders, some of the water underneath my blouse even raced down my belly and soaked the top of my skirt.

He wrapped his arms around me and pulled me against him.

"My God," he gasped. "Are you okay?"

"I . . . yeah. Just . . . a little dizzy. Just . . . I'll be . . . fine . . . In a minute."

"Are you sure?"

"You won't let me fall, will you?"

"I don't think so," he said, and I felt his arms tighten against my back. He still seemed to be clutching the glass in one hand. His other hand was open and pressing firmly against me.

"I'm not too heavy, am I?" I asked.

"No. No, not at all."

"I'm starting to feel better."

He didn't say anything, but his open hand began to move up and down a little, caressing my back.

"Good thing you're so strong," I told him. "I would've fallen flat on my face."

"Sure glad that didn't happen."

"I'm really sorry about all this."

"No need to be sorry about anything."

"It's so embarrassing."

"Nothing to be embarrassed about."

"Stumbling around like a drunk."

"These things happen. But we'd better get some water into you."

"Instead of 'onto' me?"

He laughed quietly, his chest shaking against my breasts.

"What I really need is a towel," I said.

He laughed again. Then he said, "I think you *are* feeling better."

"You don't feel so bad yourself."

He didn't laugh at that one. He just made a sound like, "Mm?" and seemed to tighten up slightly. "I'd better get you that water," he said. "If I let go of you . . . ?"

"I'll be okay."

He loosened his hold. Easing backward, he stared at my face. He looked worried. "Okay?"

"So far, so good."

He backed away from me. The front of his pale blue T-shirt looked wet from where he'd been pressed against me. "You steady?" he asked, looking from my face to my blouse and up to my face again.

"Fine," I said.

"I'll just be gone a second."

"Why don't you see if Tony has some beer?"

"*Beer?*"

"Yeah. A good, cold beer. That'd be a lot better than water."

He grinned. He glanced at my blouse again, and said, "Beer's *always* better than water."

"Especially on a hot day like this."

"I don't know about borrowing Tony's beer, though—if he has any. I hardly know him, and . . ."

"Yeah, you're right. And maybe he wouldn't want *me* drinking it. Maybe he wouldn't even want me to *be* here." I shrugged. "I mean, the way he stood me up this morning, no telling what's going on. Maybe he's decided to hate me, or something."

"I can't imagine that."

"*I* can. Guys are such . . . Maybe we'd better get out of here before he shows up and starts trouble."

Murphy frowned and nodded, then said, "If you'd like a beer, I've got plenty of cold ones over at my place."

BINGO! His place. Exactly where I wanted to go. I planned to seduce him, then act as if I hadn't really wanted him to do *that*. Afraid I might charge him with sexual assault, he would make damn sure he never told the cops about me. Brilliant, huh?

"Are you sure?" I asked. "I don't want to . . . you know, make a nuisance out of myself."

"Be glad to have you."

"That'd be great."

"Let me put this away," he said, and headed for the kitchen with the glass.

When Murphy was out of sight, I looked down to check my blouse. The water had drenched me in the middle, but more on the left side than the right. The pink of my skin showed through the yellow fabric. On the left, I could also see the outline and pattern and red color of my bra. And my nipple. Not the *color* of my nipple, but the way it was sticking out as if it wanted to poke a hole through the thin, wet layers of my bra and blouse.

No wonder Murphy'd had such trouble keeping his eyes away.

As water started running in the kitchen, I bent over and looked at Tony's floor. There were just a few damp places on the carpet. Most of the water had ended up on me.

Soon after the kitchen faucet shut off, a cupboard squeaked open and I heard the quiet thump of the glass being set on a shelf. Then the cupboard bumped shut.

I took another look at my left breast. My blouse still clung to it, and my nipple still jutted out. My right one was erect, too. I could feel it that way, but it didn't show so much because that side was fairly dry.

"Still on your feet," Murphy said. He looked both happy and nervous as he came toward me.

"I'll be fine now."

"You still want the beer, don't you?"

"You bet."

I walked out ahead of him, going slowly and trying to look a little shaky on my feet. Then I waited in the sunlight while he locked Tony's main door and eased the screen door shut. Coming over to where I stood, he took hold of my arm and led me carefully across the courtyard.

"My place is sort of a mess," he warned.

"Is your wife out of town, or something?"

"Who's married?"

"You're not?" I tried to sound surprised, but I wasn't. After all, he didn't wear a wedding ring.

"Not me," he said.

"That's a surprise. I thought all the good guys were taken."

He shook his head and laughed softly. "I'm not taken. And what makes you think I'm a 'good guy?'"

"I can tell."

He held the screen door open for me. His main door wasn't completely shut, so I pushed it out of my way and stepped into his apartment.

As Murphy came in, he asked, "Want the air conditioning on?"

"It's up to you."

"I usually like to leave it off in the mornings. You know, keep the place wide open so the air can get in."

"That's fine."

"But if you're hot . . ."

"This is nice."

"Okay." Leaving the main door wide open, he stepped around me and spread his arms. "Home, sweet home. Make yourself comfortable and I'll get us a couple of cold ones."

"Great."

Over his shoulder, he said, "I don't usually drink in the morning."

"What do you usually do?"

"Read and write."

"Ah," I said.

Murphy disappeared into the kitchen.

Unlike Tony's living room, this one had bookshelves standing against every available wall. They were loaded with hardbounds and paperbacks in a fabulous disarray.

The whole room was in disarray.

Cluttered with books, mostly.

But a lot of other stuff, too.

You couldn't even see the top of the coffee table. Along with all sorts of mail and magazines and a few pens and pencils, it was cluttered with three Pepsi cans, a couple of wadded napkins, and a paper plate littered with an empty Brie wrapper, a used knife smeared with white cheese, and cracker crumbs.

I moved a couple of pillows aside. As I sat down, I slipped the strap of my purse off my shoulder. I put the purse down between my hip and the end of the couch, where it wouldn't be in the way.

"What do you write?" I called.

"Crap that nobody wants to publish."

"That sounds lucrative."

I heard him laugh.

Then he came walking in with two beer bottles in one hand, two large glass mugs in the other, and a plastic bag of pretzels hanging from his teeth.

He set it all down on the coffee table without moving anything out of the way.

"There we go," he said. After tossing the pillows aside, he sat on the couch.

Not far away from me, but not very close, either.

He poured beer into the mugs, and handed one of them

to me. Then he opened the pretzels and placed the bag on the couch between us.

Turning toward me, he hoisted his mug and said, "Down the hatch."

We bumped our mugs together.

I took a drink. The beer tasted great.

Murphy drank, too. When he came up for air, he said, "There goes my writing for the day."

"Not much of a loss, if it's crap."

He laughed. "You're right."

"*Have* you had stuff published?"

"Oh, sure. I do all right. Not as well as I'd like, but not too badly."

"What do you write?"

"Crime novels."

"*Murder* mysteries?"

"Sort of."

"Cool."

"*TRIBUNE!*"

The sudden shout made me jump. Beer slopped out of my mug and splashed the middle of my chest—like the water, but not as much. And colder!

A moment later, I heard the slap of a newspaper smacking concrete outside.

Turning my head, I looked out the screen door and across the courtyard. A rolled *Tribune* lay on the stoop in front of Tony's door.

Murphy, frowning, leaned forward to see past me. "Well," he said. "That's odd."

31

THE OFFER

"Kind of," I said, and shrugged and changed the subject. "I'm sure klutzy this morning." I reached out and took a wadded napkin off the coffee table.

Murphy watched me blot the beer off my chest, but he said, "Tony already *had* a paper. Why would they bring him another one?"

"Some sort of mix-up?" I suggested, and slid the damp ball of paper down between my breasts. "They usually just do that if you call."

"But he *got* his. And he's not even *home*."

I grinned and pulled out the napkin. "It's a *mystery*, isn't it? You're a mystery writer. What do *you* think?"

He made a face, narrowing one eye and turning down a corner of his mouth. "Well, let me think. Obviously, someone called the *Tribune* and asked for a new paper to be delivered. Since Tony is gone, it'd be stretching things to assume that *he* made the call."

"Wouldn't make any sense at all," I agreed.

"So somebody *else* must've asked for the paper."

"But why would anyone want another paper delivered to Tony's place?" I asked.

"Elementary, my dear Fran."

"Oh?"

"Sure. It was some sort of a mix-up."

I laughed and drank some more beer.

"It was delivered to Tony's *by mistake!*" he pronounced.

"Sent to the wrong address?"

"Exactly!"

"You're a genius!"

"You bet," he said, and laughed. "Somewhere along the way, somebody misunderstood the address, or wrote it down wrong, or hit a wrong computer key . . . something like that."

"You're a regular Travis McGee," I told him.

He beamed. "You know McGee?"

"Sure."

"Well, now. I'd give you a beer, but you've already got one."

"Well, I'll take another when this one's done. Maybe I've read some of *your* stuff. What name do you write under?"

"My own."

"Murphy Scott?"

Looking pleased that I'd remembered, he said, "That's it."

"What are some of your books?"

"There've only been two so far. That have gotten published, anyway. *Deep Dead Eyes* and *The Dark Pit.*"

"Neat titles," I said.

"Thanks."

"How are the books?"

"Brilliant."

"I thought you said they're crap."

"That was before I found out you're a reader."

"That makes a difference?"

"Sure. To someone who isn't a reader, I might as *well* be writing crap."

I laughed. "You're weird, you know that?"

"Maybe a little. How about you?" he asked. "Are *you* weird?"

"What do you think?" Reaching out, I grabbed a few pretzels out of the bag between us. "You're the mystery writer. What do *you* make of me?" I chomped a pretzel and grinned at him.

Taking a long drink, he gazed at me over the upper rim of his mug. Then he set down the mug, turned sideways on the couch so he faced me, and said, "I'll say this about you. You're not what you seem."

It made me feel a little sick to hear him say that.

And it probably showed on my face.

Suddenly, the pretzel in my mouth went so dry I had a hard time swallowing it. I had to wash it down with some beer. Then I asked, "What do you mean?"

"Well," he said, "you're not really a redhead. That's either a dye job or a very good wig, I'm not sure which."

"What makes you think it isn't natural?"

"A couple of things. Redheads usually have light skin and freckles, whereas you've got a nice dark tan. Also, you have brown eyes and eyebrows."

"Ah. Okay. You're right. It's a wig. Anything else?"

"I guess that's about it," he said.

Alarms went off inside me.

I could tell by the look in his eyes that there was something else.

Something a lot bigger than my hair color.

"What is it?" I asked.

He shrugged. "This and that. Why don't you tell me?"

"Tell you what?"

"Who you really are."

"I'm just me."

"And what's really going on."

"Nothing's going on."

"Hang on," he said. "I want to show you something."

"Okay."

I sat there with my beer while he got up and walked over

to a corner of the living room. There, he crouched over a cardboard box and opened its lid.

I thought about bolting.

I also thought about attacking him.

But I had no idea what he knew—or what he thought he knew.

Besides, I sort of liked him.

He took a book out of the box, then came back to the couch and handed it to me. A hardbound copy of *Deep Dead Eyes* by Murphy Scott.

The front picture showed a dead woman under water. You seemed to be looking down at her from the surface of a lake or river as if you were in a rowboat or something. She was a few feet below the surface, and sort of blurry. She seemed to be naked, but you couldn't make out the details very well. What you could *really* make out was the way her eyes were gazing up at you.

"That's for you," Murphy said.

"Really? Thanks. Will you autograph it for me?"

"Sure thing. But first, take a look at the back cover."

I flipped the book over. On the back of the dust jacket was a black-and-white photograph of Murphy standing in front of a tree. In jeans and a plaid shirt, he looked like a hunter or fisherman. The picture, taken at an odd upward angle, looked as if the photographer had been more interested in the tree than in Murphy. The tree sure looked a lot more menacing than the author.

"Do you recognize me?" he asked.

"Sure. Nice picture."

"Thanks. And it shows that I *am* who I say I am, right?"

"A writer, you mean?"

"Yeah."

"That's either you, or you've got a twin."

"It's me," he said.

"I believe you."

"Want the autograph now?"

"Sure." I handed the book to him.

Holding it, he bent over and searched the cluttered table until he found a pen. Then he stepped around the table, sat on the couch and opened the book on his lap. He turned to the title page. At the top right corner, he scribbled the date. Then he smiled at me and asked, "Do you want it personally inscribed?"

"Sure."

"To . . . ?"

"Me."

"Fran?"

"Sure."

"*Are* you sure? Is Fran the name you want on here? Is Fran your *real* name?"

"Why shouldn't it be?"

He made a little shrug, then lowered his head and wrote a brief message in the book. Below the message, he scratched his autograph. Then he passed the book to me.

The inscription said:

To Fran,
My mysterious and beautiful guest—
Tell me your story.
Who knows? Maybe my next book will be about you.
            Warmest Regards,
                Murphy Scott

I lifted my eyes to his. "Thanks," I said, and shut the book.

"How about it?"

"Tell you my story? What makes you think I *have* a story?"

"Your red hair."

"And what else?"

"Your telephone call to Tony's sister."

"What about it?"

"It was a fake. You were still on the phone with her when I came back from checking for Tony's car. Remember?"

"Yeah."

"And you told her that Tony's car was gone?"

I nodded.

"Well, I could hear the busy signal."

"No, you couldn't."

"Yes, I could. I was standing right next to you. I heard it coming out of the earpiece. It was very quiet, but . . ."

"There *wasn't* any busy signal. I was talking to Tony's sister."

"The question is, why?"

"She was worried about him."

"You weren't talking to her. You were talking to a busy signal. But that's all right. Okay? I just want to know what's going on. I'm curious. Maybe it *is* something I can write about. And maybe I can help you."

"Who says I need any help?"

"You've gotta be awfully desperate to put on a disguise and come over here the way you did—make up a story about being stood up for *breakfast.*"

I shook my head and tried to look stupid.

"And *Morning Dehydration Syndrome?* You've got to be kidding."

"Just because *you've* never heard of it . . ."

He smiled and shook his head. "And the second *Tribune*? You must've called in the request for it. My guess is, you needed to get into Tony's apartment for some reason, but you didn't know which one it was. So you called for a replacement paper. You wanted to see where it got delivered."

"You *oughta* be a writer," I told him, smiling and shaking my head. "With an imagination like that . . ."

"Am I wrong?"

"Dead wrong."

"Oooh. Don't say things like that, okay? To a writer, that sounds like some sort of ironic foreshadowing. I'm not at all interested in getting myself killed. I'm fascinated by your situation, that's all."

"You don't even know my situation."

"Tell me about it."

"What do you *think* is going on?" I asked him.

"Tony had something in his apartment, and you wanted

it. You *had* to get it. Maybe you figured you just couldn't wait for the *Tribune* guy, so you thought up the breakfast story and came to my door, hoping you could trick me into letting you into his place. While I was searching for him, you tried to take care of your problem, whatever it was. And you made the fake call to his sister to add a touch of verisimilitude to your story."

Laughing, I said, "What a crock."

"Was he blackmailing you? What?"

"He stood me up for breakfast."

Murphy raised his right hand and said, "No matter what, I'll never tell a soul."

"Nothing to tell."

"I'll give you a thousand dollars for your story."

"Haw!"

"And if it's something usable, we can work out a deal so you get a percentage of everything."

"You really *are* curious."

"Nothing like this has ever happened to me before," he said.

"Nothing like what?"

"I'm minding my own business when a gorgeous mystery woman comes to my door and drags me into her intrigue."

Gorgeous?

"It's a first," he said. "This sort of thing just doesn't happen in real life. Not to me, anyway. At least it never did until this morning."

"Maybe I'd better leave."

"No, don't. Please. You've got no idea how great this is. For me. Do you want another beer? Something else? Just name it, I *have* to know what's going on. Was Tony blackmailing you? Did he have pictures of you, or . . . ?"

I shook my head.

"What'll it take for you to tell?" he asked.

"I guess I'll take another beer," I told him.

Nodding, he stood up. "You won't run off, will you?"

"Not a chance."

He raised his eyebrows as if he wanted to know why.

"I *can't* run off," I explained. "I might have to kill you."

Which was a joke. I didn't intend to kill him. There'd be no need for it. Like I already mentioned, I planned to ensure his silence by getting him to screw me.

32

LEVERAGE

Entering from the kitchen with two fresh bottles of beer, Murphy looked eager and excited and not at all worried. He sat down on the couch and filled our mugs with beer.

I took a drink, then said, "Before you get too comfortable, you'd better shut the front door. And get your checkbook."

"Sure. Okay."

He got up again, closed the main door, disappeared into another room and came back with it.

I held out my hand.

"You want to *see* it?"

"You're curious about *my* story, I'm curious about yours."

"Well . . ." He shrugged, then handed the checkbook to me.

I flipped through his check stubs. He hadn't been very diligent about keeping track of his balance, but I performed some simple math along the way. By the time I came to the final stub, he seemed to have about twelve thousand dollars, give or take a few hundred. I looked up at him and said, "Not bad."

"Well, I just got an advance."

I felt a little giddy. When you don't have a job and your

bank balance is less than two hundred bucks, twelve thousand looks like a fortune.

I gave Murphy a frown. "You could've offered me a little more than a thousand."

"Well . . . How much *do* you want?"

"How about ten?"

"*Ten* thousand? I wouldn't have anything left to live on. Whatever I've got now, it'll have to last me for *months*."

"How many months?"

"I don't know. It all depends. Six or eight, maybe. And I have an estimated income tax payment coming up in September. That'll clean me out if I don't get something else by then. And I probably won't. The taxes always clean me out."

"Suppose you give me five thousand?" I suggested.

He grimaced.

"Five thousand in cash, up front, and you can have my story. I'll sign a paper, giving you all the rights to it. You won't have to cut me in for a percentage or anything, even if it's a bestseller or blockbuster movie. How does that sound?"

"I don't know," he said.

"If you get low, just don't pay your estimated tax on time."

"Easy for you to say."

"My story could make you a lot of money."

"I don't even know if I can *use* your story. I don't know, what it is."

"And you never will unless you cough up the five grand."

He scowled at me, but with a glint in his eye. He almost seemed to be smiling as he sat down on the couch and reached for his beer. He drank some. Then he said, "Just give me a hint."

"A hint?"

"Something to whet my appetite. Enough to make me take the risk. I mean, five thousand dollars . . . That's a load of money."

"Suppose I tell you that I killed two people last night—in self-defense—and one of them was probably a serial killer?"

He gaped at me.

"What do you say to that?" I asked.

"If it's true . . ."

"It's true."

"Do the police know about it?"

"I don't think so. *I* sure didn't tell them. But they'll find out eventually. Today, probably. But maybe not till tomorrow or the next day. It all depends on when certain things turn up."

"Bodies?"

"Basically."

"*You* should tell the cops. Especially if . . . you said you killed them in self-defense, right?"

"That's what I said."

"Is it true?"

"Pretty much."

"*Pretty much?* You mean it *wasn't* self-defense?"

"No, it was. Yeah. It's just . . . all sort of complicated."

"You've *gotta* tell the cops."

"Bullshit. Don't give me that."

"Is Tony one of the people you killed?"

"I'm not saying. I'm not telling you anything else. Not till I've got the money."

Scowling, he took off his glasses. He rubbed his eyes as if he were suddenly feeling very tired. Then he muttered, "Man, oh man."

"How about it?"

He shook his head. "This is a real mess. I had no idea you'd *killed* anyone."

"Wouldn't be much of a story for you if I hadn't."

"But how can I write it?"

"You're a *fiction* writer. Turn it into fiction. Change all the names—not that you know *my* real name, anyway."

"I guess I could do that. But if anyone finds out . . ."

"*I'll* never tell, you can bet on that."

"What if they catch you?"

"They won't. I've covered my tracks. There's absolutely no evidence connecting me to anything."

"There's me," he said.

"I know."

He gave me a weary smile.

"Don't worry," I said. "You don't know enough to do me any harm. What could you tell the cops?"

He shrugged slightly. "Not much."

"At this point, you don't know who I killed, or how, or where. For all you know, I've been lying about everything. Also, you don't know who I am. You don't even really know what I look like."

With a smile, he said, "So, you don't think you'll have to kill me?"

I smiled back. "Only if you don't pay up."

"I don't suppose you'll take a check?"

"Cash only."

"I'll have to pay a visit to the bank."

"I'll have to go with you."

"Sounds good to me," he said. "But you might want to think twice about going in. They have those security cameras."

I grimaced. He was right about the cameras. Even with the wig on, I didn't like the idea of being caught on video tape. But if I didn't go inside with him . . .

"How do I know you won't snitch on me?" I asked.

"I won't. But I don't expect you to believe it." He shook his head. He drank some beer. "There must be a way."

I drank some beer and frowned and tried to think of something, too.

After a while, he said, "I don't know."

"Come on. You're the writer. Think of something."

"Well, I've got no intention of turning you in. You might just try a flying leap of faith."

"Yeah, right. You seem like a good guy, Murphy, but I'm not ready to trust you with my life."

"Suppose you *had* something on me? If I turn you in, you turn me in."

That seemed like a pretty good idea. I should've thought of it myself. But I saw a big problem with it. "What are you going to do," I asked. "*Kill* somebody?"

"Maybe nothing quite that drastic."

"It'd have to be drastic. Something you'd at least go to prison for. And something that nobody could know about except me, so you'd be completely in my hands."

He shrugged.

I felt a sudden rush of heat that must've turned my face bright red.

Murphy saw.

"What?" he asked.

Feeling all squirmy inside, I said, "Nothing."

"Come on. Have you got an idea?"

"Well . . . yeah, but it's pretty far out."

"That's not always a bad thing. Sometimes, far out's the only way to go. Let's hear your idea."

"How would you like to rape me?"

It was his turn to get red. His mouth drooped open. He said, "Uh. What?"

"Told you it was far out."

"Rape you?"

"Right. Well, more like *pretend* to rape me." I tried to smile, but didn't do a very good job of it. I felt awfully embarrassed and excited. I was trembling like mad. Streams of sweat were dribbling down my sides.

"Geez," Murphy said. "I don't know."

"You'd have to really go through with it, though. We can't just *say* you did it. I'd need the physical evidence to prove my case against you."

Looking flushed and disoriented and a little amused, he said, "And this would be so you'd have leverage to keep me from tipping off the bank teller, or someone, that I've got a killer in my car?"

"Basically."

"Which I have no intention of doing, anyway."

"So you say."

"It's the truth."

"This'll be my insurance. I won't even go with you to the

bank. I'll stay here and wait. If the cops come to arrest me, they'll find a rape victim in your bed."

"You're nuts," he said, looking terribly nervous but amused.

"Think so?"

"Definitely."

"How about it?"

"It's not rape if you consent, so it wouldn't really be a crime."

"Nobody'll ever know I consented. And we'll make sure it looks like a rape. I'm already pretty banged up from last night, so. . . ."

"I suppose you'd need to bang *me* up, just to make it look good."

"Some. Yeah. Good idea."

"You're very big on tricky stuff," he said.

"It seems like a great solution to me. I mean . . . *I'm* willing to go through with it if you are. What about you?"

"I've got a suggestion."

"Yeah?"

"Why don't we hold off on the so-called 'rape' till after I get back from the bank? You'll already have your money, then. There won't be anything hanging over our heads, so we'll be able to relax and take our time and . . ."

"And *I* won't have anything to hang over *your* head when you go into the bank."

"You've gotta have that leverage, huh?"

"Yep."

"But if we wait till afterwards . . ."

"I'm starting to think maybe you don't want to do it at all."

When I said that, he smirked and set down his beer mug and moved the bag of pretzels out of the way. I put down my mug, too.

He reached over and clutched the front of my blouse with both hands.

"Do you want me to rip it off you?" he asked.

"Gotta make it look good."

"What'll you wear later?"

"We'll think of something."

"Do you want me to do it right here?"

"We were sitting here having a couple of beers. You invited me in after we came back from Tony's apartment."

"And what were we doing there?" Murphy asked, still clutching my blouse.

"He'd stood me up for breakfast."

"You're going to stick with that story?"

"Sure. After we'd looked for Tony, I wanted to wait for him in his apartment. But you wouldn't let me."

"But you'd killed him."

"Who, me? For all you know, he isn't even dead. Anyway, you wouldn't let me stay in Tony's place, but you said I could come over here to wait for him. You said we could have a couple of beers and wait for him together."

"Very good. Maybe *you* should be the writer."

"Maybe so," I said. "Anyway, so I just innocently sat here and had a couple of beers with you while I was waiting for my boyfriend to get home, and all of a sudden you grabbed the front of my blouse and *ripped* it open."

As I said, "*ripped*," he did it.

33

GETTING DOWN TO BUSINESS

Tore my blouse wide open.

My buttons went *pup-pup-pup*. The tail came jerking up out of my skirt's waistband.

Murphy shoved the blouse off my shoulders, then stopped and held it there. "How's that so far?" he asked. His voice sounded pretty shaky.

"Not bad at all," I said.

"Thanks."

"Now, hit me in the face."

"I can't hit you."

"Go ahead."

"No way."

So I slapped him, knocking his head sideways and putting a handprint on his face. He looked startled. "Like that," I told him.

"Maybe this isn't such a good idea," he said.

"You don't think so?"

"Why don't I just go to the bank and . . ."

Hooking a finger under the right cup of my bra, I stretched aside the flimsy red fabric, freeing my breast.

Murphy stared at my naked breast and moaned.

"Go ahead and feel," I said.

"I don't think . . ."

"Don't think, just do," I said. With that, I took hold of his wrist, pulled his hand away from my blouse and pressed it against my breast.

His hand felt smooth and cool.

He had a look on his face like a teenage kid who'd never done anything like this before. Embarrassed, confused, astonished, thrilled, grateful.

I was giving the guy a real treat.

Maybe giving myself a treat, too.

"Now what're you gonna do?" I asked. I had a little tremble in my voice that wasn't supposed to be there.

Staring into my eyes, he squeezed my breast gently and then let go and put his arms around me. He pulled me toward him and touched his lips softly against mine. With one hand, he took off his glasses. He set them on the back of the couch, then kissed me again, this time pushing firmly against my open lips, his mouth open slightly, his breath going into me.

I started feeling soft and lazy inside. As if the kiss was sapping my strength away. And my worries. And my plans. I felt all vague and peaceful. I almost could've drifted down into sleep, but I felt a curious eagerness about what Murphy was doing to me and what he might do next.

His phone rang.

We both flinched.

It rang again.

He took his mouth away from me and whispered, "I'd better get it."

I nodded.

Murphy grabbed his glasses, then got up from the couch.

I untwisted myself and leaned back against the cushion. I felt as if I'd been dragged roughly from a wonderful place and abandoned.

I felt a little better, though, when he sidestepped past my knees and I saw the front of his shorts.

Arriving at the lamp table, he picked up his phone just after the fourth ring.

"Hello? . . . Oh, hi, Harold . . . No, it's fine. What's up?"

He turned toward me, made a face that made me smile, and ogled my exposed breast. Then his eyes lowered to my belly as if drawn by my injury down there. I knew how awful it looked, but I didn't try to cover it. He frowned at the bruised and gouged skin, then met my eyes with a look of concern.

I wiggled my eyebrows at him.

Brightening up slightly, he said into the phone, "Yeah. Sure I've heard of him . . . Yeah, I saw those movies . . . He does? . . ." Looking me in the eyes, he suddenly grinned. "The most exciting book he's read all year? Cool . . . Uh-huh . . . Sure . . . Yeah, maybe we'll at least get an option out of it . . . Right, can't hurt . . . *Five* copies? Geez. I guess they think I get 'em free . . . Yeah, I know . . . Today? They *can't* get them today. Don't they know I'm out here in the boonies? Where are they, in L.A.? . . . Oh. Same difference. Anyway, I don't care who they are, I'm not driving to Culver City. Not today. It's about a six-hour drive, and I've already got plans."

He gave me a smile.

I flexed a muscle to make my breast hop, and his eyes got very wide.

"I don't care," he said into the phone. "The best I can do is send them overnight express, and I'm not too sure about that . . . Well, they're always like that. They want everything yesterday, and then you drop everything to get the books off and you end up never hearing from them again anyway . . . I know . . . Well, let me have the address. I'll get the books to them as soon as I can."

He couldn't seem to find a pen or paper on the lamp table.

Leaning forward, I snatched a ballpoint and the *TV Guide* off the cluttered table in front of me. Then I twisted around and reached them over to him.

"Thanks," he whispered.

He dropped the *TV Guide* onto the lamp table and started to write on its back cover.

"Got it," he said, and read the address back to Harold. Then he listened and nodded and said, "Okay. No problem. And thanks. You never know, maybe this'll turn into something . . . Right. Take it easy. Bye."

He hung up the phone and said, "My agent."

"Sounds like he had some good news for you."

He shrugged. "Yeah. Well, sort of. Some bigwig movie producer's all hot for *The Dark Pit*. I'm supposed to drop everything and . . ."

"I heard."

"It's no big deal."

"They want to make a *movie* out of your book? Sounds like a big deal to me."

"These things usually don't go much of anywhere. These movie people . . . They'll tell you it's the greatest book in the history of the world, then they'll offer you about three hundred dollars for an option."

"Three *hundred*? You're kidding."

"That'd just be for rights to fool around with the book for six months or something. And then you'd get maybe a hundred thousand if it goes into production."

"*That's* a lot."

"But you never get it, because nothing ever gets that far."

"Some stuff must."

"Yeah. But not much. It's mostly a big waste of time. I don't jump through hoops for those guys anymore."

"*I* would, if I were you."

He smiled and said, "You being *you*, you might."

"What's that supposed to mean?"

"You're not *me* standing here looking at *you* right now."

"I'll keep," I told him, and drew my blouse shut to hide my breast. "You shouldn't pass up a fabulous opportunity like this."

"I know," he said, and leered.

"I don't mean *me*."

"I do," he said.

He held out a hand. I took it, and he pulled me to my feet. I stepped around the end of the coffee table. When I was standing in front of him, he let go of my hand. With both his hands, he slipped my blouse off my shoulders and down my arms. It drifted to the floor behind me.

"What'll you do about the books?" I asked.

He shrugged. "Maybe call Federal Express."

"You don't want to deliver them today?"

"I've got better things to do," he said, and slid his gaze down my body.

Blushing, I said, "I could go with you."

"It's an awfully long drive."

"I don't mind. I could tell you my story on the way."

"We'll see."

"If I can stay awake."

"Maybe you can take a nap while I go to the bank. You do still want your money, don't you?"

"Darn right," I said.

"And I can't go get that till after I've raped you?"

"Darn right again. So you'd better get to it."

"Are you sure you feel up to it?"

"You bet."

"You're awfully banged up. What happened to you? All these bruises and everything?"

"Rough night."

"Were you in *fights?*"

"Sure. Fights, falls, collisions. You name it, it happened. But don't worry. I'm fine." Bending down, I raised a foot and started to pull off my shoe.

Murphy put a hand on my shoulder to hold me steady.

"Thanks," I said. I tossed the shoe toward the couch. It landed on the floor with a thump. "They've gotta be artfully arranged," I explained.

He shook his head. "Of course."

I shifted to my other leg, pulled off my other shoe, and tossed it across the room. Then I stood up straight and smiled at him.

"Anything else?" he asked.

"Just be a little careful around my stomach."

"What happened there?"

"Nailed by a tree branch. Walked right into it in the dark. But maybe I'll tell you all about it in the car. If we ever get there."

"I guess you want me to get on with it."

"Good guess, Sherlock."

"Where do you want me to start?"

"Surprise me."

With a silly smile on his face, he put his arms around me and drew me forward. His mouth came at mine. I slapped him. The blow sent his glasses flying off his face. He looked startled and hurt.

"None of that kissy stuff," I said. "Get rough. This has to look good."

"Why does it have to *look* good? Nobody'll ever know it happened."

"They will if you double-cross me."

"I'd never . . ."

"You're a guy. Guys do stuff like that."

"Not me."

"Guys'll stab you in the back, lie . . ."

"Not me."

"But I don't know that for sure, do I?"

"Guess not," he admitted. Then he started to unhook the back of my bra.

And I suddenly realized that I still had the miniature cassette tape from Tony's answering machine hidden inside my panties. If this went much further . . .

"Rough!" I snapped and shoved him away.

As he came back at me, I tore the bra off, myself, and threw it to the floor. "Take me to your bedroom," I gasped.

He grabbed my arm, but I pulled free.

He looked confused.

"My God, do I have to draw you a picture?"

"I don't want to hurt you," he said.

"Pretend it's a game."

"But . . ."

I whirled around and ran from him.

Instead of coming after me, he went hunting for his glasses. So I stopped. With my back to him, I quickly slipped a hand down my skirt and plucked the cassette out of my panties. It was wet and slippery.

What'll I do with it?

My purse was on the couch, all the way across the room. No way of getting there without Murphy seeing me and wondering what I was up to.

I had no idea where to hide the cassette, so I kept it in my hand. I wiped it against the back of my skirt as I turned to face Murphy again.

He didn't seem to know where his glasses had landed after I'd knocked them off his face.

"There on the table," I said, pointing.

"Ah." He found them, picked them up, checked them out, and put them on his face. "Thanks," he said.

"Now come and get it," I blurted, and ran.

This time, he chased me.

All right!

He probably could've caught me if he'd tried, but he stayed a stride or two back. I made straight for the doorway of his bedroom and lunged through it.

Murphy close on my heels, I raced across the floor and leaped onto his bed.

Luckily, his curtains were shut.

I stopped in the middle of his springy mattress. Bouncing, I turned around to face him.

He stopped at the foot of the bed and gaped up at me, his face strange with perplexity and delight.

"What're you staring at, big guy?"

He didn't answer, just watched.

Even though I wasn't bouncing very hard, my breasts were flying around like crazy. And he was gazing at them as if mezmerized by how they jumped and lurched.

"What're you gonna do now, hotshot?" I asked. "Just gonna stand there gaping at my boobs?"

Bending over, he reached out and grabbed my ankles and pulled.

I let out a squeal and landed on my back.

He jerked my ankles wide apart. My left leg came out of the slit in my skirt, and was bare all the way up to my hip. "How's that?" he gasped.

"Shut up and fuck me," I said.

34

THE ART OF SEDUCTION

Off came his Bear Whizz Beer T-shirt. He pulled it up his torso and over his head. While his eyes were behind the T-shirt, I stuffed the cassette tape underneath the pillow.

As he tossed the shirt aside, I braced myself up on my elbows so I could see him better.

He was slim and nicely built, and had a good tan.

Still in his shorts, he planted a knee on the mattress and got ready to climb up.

"Why don't you get rid of the shorts?" I said.

"Huh?" he asked.

"And how come you're wearing *swimming trunks?* You don't even have a pool."

"They're comfortable."

"Well, take them off."

More flustered than usual, he said, "I don't . . . I'm not wearing any . . . you know, underwear."

"Good. Take off the trunks and get up here."

"You gonna look?"

"Of course I'm gonna look."

"Do you *have* to?" he asked.

"You're some rapist."

"I'm not a rapist."

"Are you a virgin?"

"No," he said. "It's just that . . . we hardly even know each other."

"You've already seen plenty of me," I informed him. "And you're about to see the rest. So let's have a look at you."

"Well . . ."

"When do you plan to stop blushing?"

"Sometime next year, I should imagine." Bending over, he pulled down his trunks. When he stood up straight, they were out of sight. "There," he said.

"Wow," I said.

He gave me a twitchy, embarrassed smile.

"Get up here," I said.

"Just a second, I'd better grab a condom."

"No, don't. You're raping me. I need your semen for evidence. You can't use a rubber."

"I don't know if that's such a good idea."

"It's the whole point."

He looked hurt.

So I said, "Well, it *was* the whole point, anyway. Before you got me all worked up like this." Squirming a little and staring him in the eyes, I undid both the buttons that held my skirt together at the hip. I spread the skirt open. I still had my panties on, but nothing else. There was about as much to my panties as a pirate's eyepatch. The band and patch were red like my bra. "I've still gotta have the *evidence*," I explained.

He gaped at me for a while, his mouth hanging open. Then he said, "We really need to use protection."

"I won't get pregnant. You don't have to worry about that. I just finished my period." A fib, but so what?

You should've seen him go red. Guys really hate to hear about your period. Normal guys, anyway. Perverts are a different story. I knew this pervert named Jack, and he used to keep track of my time of the month so he could . . . Never mind. I can't tell every story I know, or you'd never find out what happened between me and Murphy. Anyway, believe me, you don't *want* to know about Jack. He was mental.

Murphy, still on the subject of condoms, said, "It's not just about you getting pregnant."

"I know. You're worried about diseases."

"Yeah."

"Do you have any?" I asked.

"No."

"Neither do I."

"I still think we'd better . . ."

"Don't you believe me?" I asked. "You think I'm *lying?*"

"You might be. Hell, *you're* afraid I'll turn you in the minute I get alone. Why can't *I* be afraid you'll give me AIDS and kill me?"

"I haven't been with a guy in about five years," I told him. "I don't shoot up drugs. I haven't had any blood transfusions. And I've had annual check-ups. I'm not gonna give you any disease."

"Five years?" he asked.

"I've been saving myself for you."

He smiled and said, "Right."

"By the look of things, it was well worth the wait."

"Thanks, but I still want to use a condom." He turned away and walked toward his dresser.

"Come on, no. I want to feel *you* in me."

As he pulled open a drawer, he looked over his shoulder at me.

"You wear one of those," I said, "it's like getting fucked by a balloon."

He laughed softly and shook his head. "It's not much better from this end, believe me." Then he started searching through the drawer. "Maybe after we've known each other longer . . ."

"Next time, I'll bring a note from my doctor. If there is a next time."

"I hope there will be," Murphy said.

I said, "Me, too."

Then I pulled the skirt out from under me and pushed it aside until it fell to the floor. On my back, I brought my knees up to my chest and peeled my panties off.

Murphy found what he was looking for, turned around and came back toward the bed with a foil packet pinched between his thumb and forefinger.

"Would you like me to do the honors?" I asked.

"Like what?"

"If you *have* to wear it, I might as well get the fun of putting it on you."

"Okay. If you want to."

Sitting up, I swung myself around. I sat on the edge of the bed, my feet on the floor. "Right here." I spread my knees and patted the side of the mattress.

Murphy stepped in between my legs.

"Man, look at that thing."

He glanced at it and shrugged.

"Looks like a cannon."

Blushing deep red, he muttered, "No it doesn't."

"Hope it doesn't go off by accident."

"Hey."

"Might blow out my eye."

"Jeez."

I grinned up at him. "What?"

"Do you have to talk about it?"

"Just admiring the equipment."

"Do you *have* to?"

"I don't *have* to."

"It's just . . . sort of embarrassing."

"Okay. I'll stop talking about it."

"Thanks," he said.

"Me and my big mouth," I said.

"That's all right."

"But are you *sure* you want to cover this baby up with a nasty old rubber?"

"That's the only way I'll . . . yeah. I'm afraid so. Sorry."

"Okay. It's a shame, but if you insist . . ."

"I do."

"Okay. Well, give me that thing."

He handed the packet to me. I tore it open and pulled out the condom. It felt warm and slimy. "Yuck," I said. "I *really* want this in me. What is it, *used?*"

"Just pre-lubricated."

"I know, I know. I was kidding. But yuck. I mean, really."

"We don't have to do this," he said, and placed his hands gently on my shoulders.

"Don't have to use the rubber?"

"Not if we call the whole thing off."

I looked up at him. "Do you *want* to call it off?" I asked.

"Do I look like it?"

"Hardly."

He started to rub my shoulders. And kept rubbing them as I leaned forward.

But it wasn't the condom I put on him.

It was my mouth.

He gasped and arched his back and squeezed my shoulders. But he didn't complain or try to pull back.

Dropping the condom, I clutched his buttocks. I dug my fingernails in, drew him closer to me and slid my lips down his thick shaft, taking him into my mouth until no more could fit in.

He stood rigid and moaned.

I pulled slowly back, sucking as I went.

He shuddered.

I squeezed his buttocks and went down again, my lips a tight, sliding ring.

"Don't. Uh. Y'better stop."

Up again, pulling at him, sucking.

"Ahhh!"

Down, taking him in deeper and deeper.

"No, y'gotta . . . I'm gonna . . . !"

I jerked my head up suddenly and he popped out of my mouth with a wet slurp. I tugged his ass. As he stumbled toward me, I shoved at the floor with my feet, springing up from the mattress and wrapping my arms around his back.

He fell forward, trapped between my thighs. I fell backward, pulling him down on top of me.

On the way down, he prodded my right thigh so I shifted a bit to take care of the aim.

My back hit the mattress.

And in he went.

He was awfully big, but I was juicy.

Pre-lubricated.

He went sliding in all the way. It felt huge, but I liked how it filled me and stretched me. I hugged him tightly and clamped my legs around him.

Grunting, he tried to push himself off me.

For about two seconds.

Then, with a moan, he kissed me and shoved his tongue into my mouth and jammed a hand in between us and grabbed one of my breasts and thrust at me with his hips and throbbed deep inside me, spurting.

"So much for condoms," I whispered.

I held him hard against me.

The moment he finished pumping, though, he started to struggle so I let him go. He didn't have any mattress under his knees. As he squirmed backward, he no sooner got out of me than he slid off the edge of the bed.

Raising my head, I found Murphy on his knees. He was red and gasping, and had a dazed look in his eyes.

He still had his glasses on and they'd gotten knocked crooked.

I gave him a cheerful smile.

"That was a . . . lousy trick," he said.

"I thought it was a *good* trick. Hell, so did you. You loved it. You went nuts."

He shook his head, glanced between my legs, then turned his head away and straightened his glasses.

"There's nothing to worry about," I told him. "I didn't *give* you anything—expect maybe the quickest, hottest fuck of your life."

"I wanted to use a condom."

"I didn't. And you didn't *need* one."

"I sure hope not," he said, and stood up.

He was sticking straight out as if pointing at something across the room.

"Wanta do it again?" I asked.

"No."

"Are you sure?"

He glanced at me, looked away, then turned to me again and stared at my sprawled, naked body.

"How about it, big fella?"

Though he frowned as if angry at me, he was rising. "You're a real piece of work," he said.

"Yep." Writhing, I rubbed my breasts and licked my lips. "How about another piece?"

His smile broke out. "Don't you think I'd better get to the bank?"

"Don't you want to rape me again?"

"Who raped who?"

I laughed. "You loved it. And you'd love to do it again, wouldn't you?"

"Don't you want me to get the money?"

"Yeah. Sure. I want the money, but . . ."

"Then I'd better go."

"Okay. But first you have to tie me up."

"Tie you up?"

"Of course. I'm your prisoner."

"That's crazy."

"If you call the cops on me, I want them to find me naked and tied to your bed."

"I'm not going to call the cops."

"This'll be my insurance. Now, go find some ropes or something, okay?"

35

TIED

"How's that?" he asked.

Stretched out spread-eagled on his bed, I strained at the ropes. They creaked a little, but held. "Excellent," I said.

He stood near the end of the bed and stared down at me. He was a little out of breath. And hard. "Anything else I can do for you?" he asked.

"Climb on."

"Don't you want the money?"

"Yeah, I want it."

"Then you'd better let me leave, don't you think?"

"You'd better put some clothes on first."

"Thanks for the reminder."

I watched him go to the closet and take out a pair of jeans and a short-sleeved shirt. When he had them on, he sat at the end of the bed to put on his socks and shoes. "Any last minute instructions?" he asked.

"Small bills."

"How small?"

"I don't know," I said. "But that's what the gangsters always want. Small bills."

He looked over his shoulder at me and smiled. "My gal, the crime wave."

My gal?

He'd said it in a kidding way, but I liked it.

"Anyhow," I said, "big stuff is hard to spend."

"Let's at least get most of it in hundreds and fifties," he suggested. "Otherwise, you'll have an awful lot of cash to lug around."

"I guess that'll be okay."

He turned away and finished putting on his shoes. Then he stood up and faced me. He looked good. "Any other orders, Vito?" he asked.

"One more. You'd better gag me so I can't cry out for help."

"Why on earth would you want to cry out for help?"

"Because you're holding me prisoner."

"But I'm *not* holding you prisoner."

"I know that, you know that, but the cops won't know that, will they?"

"The cops again."

"Just find a handkerchief or something and tie it around my mouth."

"You might suffocate."

"Tie it loose."

He smirked and shook his head, then turned away and went to his dresser. I heard a drawer open. A minute later, he said, "I don't think my handkerchiefs are big enough."

"Well, find something."

He left the room. I heard his quick footsteps, a drawer sliding open and shut, then more footsteps. He came back with a white dish rag.

"How's this?" he asked.

"Perfect."

Kneeling beside me on the mattress, he wound the towel into a thick strip. I lifted my head off the pillow and opened my mouth. He stuffed the towel in. Then he knotted it behind my neck.

"Okay?" he asked.

I said, "Uhhh," into the rag.

Grinning, Murphy said, "I should've done this to you a long time ago."

I said, "Haw haw."

"Will you be okay like this?" he asked.

If I don't get a stuffed-up nose.

I nodded.

"I'll get back as fast as I can," he said. Bending down, he kissed me on the forehead.

Then he hurried away. I heard his footsteps as he wandered around the apartment. I didn't know what he was doing, but figured he was probably getting his keys, wallet, checkbook, that sort of thing. Then he took a leak. He flushed the toilet. He washed his hands. Finally, the front door thudded shut.

I was alone.

Tied up and gagged.

And I liked it.

The mattress felt good underneath me.

I could breathe okay through the dish towel.

The room was hot, and everything had a yellow hue because of the sunlight seeping through the curtains. A breeze was gently lifting the curtains. It smelled of flowers and mowed grass. Every so often, I felt the air sneak softly over my body.

It may sound strange, but I actually liked the feel of being pulled by the ropes. My whole body felt lean and taut.

I thought of Judy hanging by her wrists in the firelight, and how fine she'd looked.

Is she still there? I wondered.

Maybe she'd already managed to work her way loose. Or maybe someone had found her and set her free.

Maybe she's still there, just the way I left her.

She's there and I'm here. We're both naked. We're both tied and helpless. We have our wounds, but we're beautiful—stretched taut and lean.

While thinking about her, I must've slipped off into sleep.

Soon, she came walking over to the foot of the bed. The red bandana hung loose around her neck, and that's all she wore. She held a knife in her right hand. "Well, well, well," she said. "Look at you."

"I'm sure glad to see you," I said, and wondered vaguely how I was able to talk through my gag. Then I realized that the gag was gone. "I've really missed you, Judy," I said. "I've missed you so much."

"I've missed you, too," she said.

"How did you manage to get free?"

She raised her left arm and showed me the rough, bloody stump at her wrist. "Had to gnaw my hand off," she said.

"My God."

She smiled sweetly and shrugged. "Ah, it wasn't so bad. You do what you've gotta do. Looks like you're in a predicament, yourself."

"Not really."

"You don't think so?"

"No. This is just to look good in case Murphy gets the cops on me."

"He won't do that."

"You never know," I said. "Guys'll stab you in the back."

"Not this one. He loves you."

"He *loves* me? Do you think so?"

"Sure. He's head over heels."

"I don't know."

"Trust me," Judy said.

"I sure hope you're right."

I hoped so badly that she might be right. It made me feel excited and sad and warm to think that Murphy might actually love me.

It made me feel a little like crying.

"I *know* he loves you," Judy assured me. "But that doesn't mean he'll come back and untie you."

"Oh, he will."

"Maybe he will and maybe he won't. Do you want me to cut you loose, just in case?"

It didn't seem necessary. After all, I was sure that Murphy would soon be back. But I liked having Judy in the room with me, and wanted her to come closer.

So I said, "Yeah, maybe you'd better."

Smiling, she strolled over to the bed. She climbed onto the mattress, swung a leg over me, and sat on my belly. Then she leaned forward. Her left breast looming over my face, she started to saw at the rope around my right wrist. Her breast shook with the quick movements of her arm.

Then it stopped.

She'd quit trying to cut through the rope.

I pulled, but my arm was still tied down.

"Why are you stopping?" I asked.

"I changed my mind. I don't think I'll cut you loose, after all."

"Why not?"

"Just remembered something."

"What?" I asked, with a bad feeling starting to chill my stomach.

"*You* didn't cut *me* down."

"I know, but . . ."

"Why should I cut you down, when you left me hanging in the woods?"

"I had to," I said.

"And I had to chew my hand off, or I'd still *be* there. You know what? It hurt."

"I'm sorry."

"You oughta be."

"I am."

"Prove it," Judy said.

"How?"

"Kiss me."

Her breast hovered low over my face, swaying slightly, looking golden in the soft sunlight coming in through the curtains. Her nipple was just above my mouth.

Opening my mouth, I raised my head off the pillow.

I flicked her nipple with my tongue.

"Not there," she said, and thrust the gory stump of her wrist into my mouth.

"*Eat it!*" she yelled.

Shocked awake, I cried out—into my dish rag—and tried to sit up.

The ropes held me down.

I struggled to fill my lungs, but couldn't get enough air. Not with the gag in my mouth. Murphy had left some slack in it, though. Rubbing my cheek against my shoulder and shoving at the rag with my tongue, I quickly got my mouth clear and took deep, quick breaths.

As I calmed down, I started thinking.

First, I'd caught a mouthful of water in the bathtub.

Now this.

Both times, I'd fallen asleep dreaming of Judy, then gotten startled awake, only to find myself suffocating.

Maybe she's trying to tell me something.

What am I supposed to do, go back and cut her down before she has to gnaw her hand off?

Maybe she's already done it!

Hell, she couldn't chew her hand off even if she wanted to. It was too high above her head.

I realized that I wouldn't be able to chew mine off, either.

What if we're both stuck?

Don't worry about it, I told myself. For one thing, I can probably get free if I really have to. For another, I won't have to. Murphy should be getting back pretty soon.

How soon?

I had no idea how long he'd been gone. I'd fallen asleep almost right away, but how long had I been under? It didn't seem like very long. Ten or twenty minutes?

He'll be back any time now, I told myself.

How do you know?

Where's his bank?

He hadn't told me, but it had to be somewhere in town, probably no more than a ten-minute drive from here.

Ten minutes each way. That makes a total of twenty. And

there might be a line inside the bank. So give him another ten minutes for the line.

That adds up to half an hour.

But maybe the line is really long.

Or they give him trouble about making such a large withdrawal.

Or he decides to take care of another errand or two before coming back.

Or his car breaks down.

Or he has an accident.

Or the bank gets robbed while he's there.

And the bank robbers take him hostage.

Or shoot him.

Or he drops dead of a heart attack.

Or an aneurism.

HE'S NOT DEAD, DAMN IT! HE CAN'T BE! HE LOVES ME!

Calm down, I told myself. For one thing, he's *not* dead. For another, he doesn't *love* me. That was Judy saying that. In a dream. Has nothing to do with reality.

Like I said before, dreams stink. They're no good for anything. They only exist to torture you any way they can.

He doesn't love me, I told myself.

But he *will* be back.

The bank *didn't* get robbed while he was there. That's nonsense. Paranoia.

He'll be back any minute.

Sure he will.

But maybe with cops in tow.

Maybe he's been lying to me from the start and right now he's telling the cops all about me.

No, he wouldn't dare.

No matter what story he might tell the cops, he'd be in a world of trouble the moment they found me tied to the bed. A naked woman, roped down, with numerous minor injuries and his semen inside.

Before you know it, they'll be thinking *he* killed Tony and abducted Judy and me.

For a while, I tried to come up with a good story to explain how it all worked. Maybe the four of us went to the park together on a double-date. I was Tony's date and Judy was Murphy's date. But then Murphy decided he wanted *both of us*, so he killed Tony, chopped him up and put him in the trunk . . .

How does Milo the Killer Slob fit in?

Maybe Judy escaped from Murphy, only to be grabbed by Milo—a thrill-killer lurking around in the woods in search of victims. He jumps her and takes her to his camp . . .

Awfully far-fetched.

Keep it nice and simple.

I could just say Judy ran off into the woods and I don't know what happened to her after that.

But what about Tony's car? I'd have to explain how it ended up back at Judy's apartment building—with his body in it.

That'd be a good trick.

It's probably not the only problem, either.

What about the tape from Tony's answering machine? If the cops showed up and cut me free, they would be sure to find it under the pillow.

Murphy put it there.

Simple.

But how could I possibly come up with a sensible story that explained everything?

Claim amnesia.

Good idea.

Tell the cops I don't know how *anything* happened. Last I remember, I was walking back to my garage after watching the television in Serena and Charlie's den.

That should work.

At least until Judy spills the beans.

If she talks, I'm screwed.

I should've killed her when I had the chance.

Maybe it's not too late.

I suddenly had an urge to get free, run out to Judy's car

and speed over to Miller's Woods, find the camp and finish her off.

Do it now. Get out of here before Murphy comes back.

But the ropes held me down.

I strained at them with my arms and legs. They were nothing but pieces of old clothesline, and seemed to stretch as I pulled. They also tightened around my wrists and ankles. I kept pulling, anyway. For all I knew, Murphy might've done a lousy job tying the other ends around the legs of the bed. Maybe something would give, down there. Or maybe I could break the ropes by sheer strength.

They held, but I didn't give up.

I pulled, jerked, kicked, squirmed and bucked. Soon, I was out of breath and pouring sweat.

I quit struggling, and rested.

The ropes had tightened so much that they'd cut off my circulation. My hands and feet were numb. The pillow case and sheet underneath me felt soaked.

Gasping for air, I blinked sweat out of my eyes.

And thought, Maybe I *can't* get loose.

I can! I will!

Just give me a minute to catch my breath.

While I was waiting to make my next try, someone rang the doorbell.

36

INVADER

At any time of the day or night, I hate the sound of a doorbell. It almost always means someone has shown up uninvited.

An intruder is barging into your life.

Invading.

No matter what, it's annoying and a little scary.

But just try having the doorbell ring when you're naked in the bedroom of a guy you hardly know, you're tied down, and your legs are spread apart about as far as they'll go.

When I heard that doorbell, I felt as if someone had shot a hose full of ice water up my bowels.

I froze.

The bell rang again.

Nobody's home! Go away!

What if it's the cops?

So what if it is? I told myself. Cops can't come into a place without being invited. Not unless they have a search warrant.

They can't possibly have a search warrant.

Can they?

The bell rang again.

GO AWAY!

Calm down, I told myself. Whoever it is, they can't get in. Sooner or later, they'll give up and go away.

Again, the bell rang.

Persistent . . .

What if it's burglars?

They do that. They pick a place that looks deserted. But before they break in, they ring the doorbell to make sure nobody is home. If someone comes to the door, they have a little story to tell. "Is Doug there? No? Oh, I must have the wrong address." But if nobody answers the doorbell, they figure the place is empty and safe to rob.

In they come . . .

And find me like this.

Should I call out?

And say what? *I'm here, but I can't come to the door right now!* Like I'm on the john, or something. *Could you come back in a few minutes?*

No, I thought. Don't do it. Keep your mouth shut.

The little town of Chester has its share of crime. I mean, what place doesn't? But the odds had to be slim that the doorbell was being rung by a burglar. *Especially* when you consider that, since just after last midnight, I'd run into a weirdo flasher *and* a serial killer. On top of all that, a *burglar*? Not likely.

Not impossible, either. But . . .

Someone used a key on the front door. I heard its quiet ratchety sound as it slid into a lock, heard the latch click back, heard the knob rattle, heard a sigh of hinges as the door swung open.

Shit! Now what?

A man's voice called out, "Murphy? Yo, Murph? You home? Helllllo? It's only me from across the sea!" He waited a few seconds, then said, "Yo ho ho, guess you're not home."

I heard the door shut, but I didn't know whether he was inside or out.

Until I heard his footsteps on the carpet.

Great! I'm gonna get found!

Some creep I don't even know is gonna see me like this.

He must be Murphy's best friend or brother or something. You don't give a spare key to just anyone.

This guy is about to have the surprise of his life.

I heard the television come on. It sounded like CNN's Headline News.

That's right, I thought. Sit down in the living room and watch some TV news. Just stay put. Don't move. Murphy'll be home pretty soon. He'll figure a way to steer you out of the place, and you'll never be the wiser.

From the TV came a nifty British voice talking about tribal massacres in some African country. Zaire or Rwanda or some damn place.

Suddenly, during a pause in the broadcast, I heard footsteps again. These were quiet, as if the intruder had taken off his shoes.

What's he doing?

Going into the kitchen for a beer?

The only route to the kitchen—or just about anywhere else in the apartment—would take him past the open bedroom door.

Maybe he won't look in.

Fat chance.

I shut my eyes and went limp.

The footsteps suddenly stopped. The intruder said, "Whoa!"

I kept my eyes shut and tried to keep my breathing shallow and slow.

Let him think I'm out cold or dead or something. I sure didn't want to strike up a conversation with the guy.

"What the hell's going on here?" he muttered, and came walking slowly into the room. "Lady?" he asked.

I didn't stir.

He said, "My God, what's Murphy *done?*"

He sounded as if he were standing at the foot of the bed. I tried not to think about the view he had. But I could feel myself blushing.

I was blushing, sweating, and my heart was pounding fast. Couldn't he see any of that?

Not where he's probably looking.

"Wow," he said. "Oh, Murphy, Murphy. How'd you land a babe like this?"

Down between my legs, the mattress sank in.

The mattress shook, making me wobble.

What's he doing?

A hand patted me on the thigh. Very high up on my thigh.

"Hello?" he asked. "Young lady? Can you hear me?"

I didn't respond.

"Must be out cold," he muttered.

Moments later, a light fabric fell across my face.

Then two hands were gently caressing my thighs. "What a piece," he muttered. "Man, oh man. Murph, you lucky dog. No wonder you tied her down. Couldn't let something like this get away from you."

His tongue got me. I gasped and flinched with the sudden shock of it, and knew the game was up. With no more need to play possum, I writhed as his mouth stayed where it was and his hands roamed up my body and found my breasts. He caressed them, gently massaged them, squeezed my nipples and pulled while his tongue flicked and delved. Soon, I was panting, thrashing against the ropes.

His mouth lifted off me. "Looks like I've awakened Sleeping Beauty. Does this mean I'm a prince?"

It was the same, fake voice.

But this time, I recognized the mind behind it.

"You bastard!" I gasped out.

Opening my eyes, I found a pale blue shirt on top of my face.

Murphy swept it aside and smiled down at me. He was kneeling between my legs, totally naked and erect.

"What do you think you're doing?" I asked.

"What do you think?"

"You scared the hell out of me."

"Good," he said. Then he came down and planted his

mouth on my mouth and pushed himself slowly into me until I had all of him. Then he pulled most of the way out, and thrust in so hard that the ropes bit into my ankles and I yelped into his mouth.

He murmured, "Sorry."

Then he clutched me by the shoulders to hold me still so the ropes wouldn't hurt me again.

And went at it.

He went crazy on me, plunging and ramming as if he needed to get someplace where nobody'd ever gone before.

By damn, I think he succeeded.

He blew the roof off the joint, so to speak.

I'd never gone through anything like it. My guess is, neither had he.

When he was done, he stayed inside and settled down heavily on top of me, gasping for air. When he could talk, he said, "Are you okay?"

I answered by flexing some muscles down there.

He said, "Ooooh."

After a while, I said, "That was a rotten trick, you know."

"Huh?"

"Faking me out. Pretending you were somebody else."

"Oh. That. Yeah. Figured I owed you one."

"Very nice."

"I enjoyed it," he said.

"You've got a real mean streak," I told him.

"That makes two of us."

"So, did you get the money okay?"

"Yep. Everything went smooth as silk."

I gave him a couple more flexes, and felt him starting to grow.

"How come no condom?" I asked.

"Didn't see much point. Not after the way you got me before."

"For which you decided to pay me back by impersonating a stranger and scaring me shitless."

"Not exactly."

"No?"

"That's just . . . the way it turned out. What I'd planned to do was come straight in, strip naked and jump on you. No tricks. But when I showed up, there was a bunch of Jehovah's Witnesses at the front door."

"You're kidding. That was a Jehovah's Witness ringing the doorbell?"

"Yep."

"Never figured that."

"I figured you were probably freaking."

"I wasn't *freaking*."

He laughed. It felt strange and great, the way he shook on top of me and deep inside me while he laughed.

"I might've been mildly concerned," I admitted.

He laughed some more.

"What freaked me," I explained, "was when some sneaky, rotten son-of-a-bitch unlocked the door and came in."

"That was me," he said.

I said, "Duh."

He laughed again.

"Bastard."

"You loved it."

"Not the trick, I didn't. That really stank."

"Who did you think I was?"

"One of your horny buddies. Or maybe a brother."

"Whoever you thought I was, you must've liked him. I didn't hear any complaints."

"That's only because I was trying to play possum."

"If you *hadn't* been playing possum, you would've seen right away that it was only me. The moment I walked into the bedroom. I didn't throw the shirt over your face until pretty far along."

"What if I *hadn't* figured it was you?" I asked. "Were you just going to screw me and leave, so I'd go on thinking it was someone else?"

"I knew you'd recognize me. I'm surprised it took you as long as it did."

"It was the prince crack," I explained, and had to smile.

"Ah, well."

"When I heard that, I knew it was you."

"Not only beautiful, but smart."

"That's me," I said. Turning my head, I kissed the side of his face. Then I asked, "You gonna let me up, now?"

"Maybe I will and maybe I won't."

"My hands and feet are numb."

"Oh. Uh-oh." He pushed himself up and slid out of me. Frowning, he said, "I should've untied you first thing. I didn't realize the ropes were that tight. I'm sorry."

"Hey, it's fine."

Kneeling over my chest, he leaned forward, reached out with both hands, and started trying to untie my left wrist.

It reminded me a lot of my Judy dream.

Except that Judy'd had breasts and a knife.

Soon, Murphy managed to pluck open the knot. He loosened the rope around my wrist, and I pulled my hand free. It really was numb. I shook it, trying to get some feeling back, while he worked on the knot at my other wrist.

"I shouldn't have made these so tight," he muttered.

"Had to make it look good."

"Not really," he said. "I came back without any cops."

"See? It worked."

He laughed, and kept on struggling with the knot.

With circulation coming back, my left hand began to feel hot and get pins and needles. I kept flapping it around and wiggling my fingers.

"This one's sure tight," he said.

"Maybe you should get a knife."

"Yeah. That might save a lot of trouble."

He tried for another few seconds, then climbed off me and the bed.

"Back in a second," he said.

I raised my head off the pillow and watched him stride toward the doorway. His tan stopped just above his rear end, and started again at the tops of his legs. His ass looked pale as cream, and smooth. The firm, round buttocks took turns flexing as he walked.

In the doorway, he turned around.

I liked the front view better.

Leaning sideways, he rested a shoulder against the door frame and smiled at me. "Can I get you anything else while I'm in the kitchen? A glass of water for your Morning Dehydration Syndrome? A Pepsi? A beer?"

"Just hurry, okay? If I'm tied up much longer, something may have to get amputated."

He raised his eyebrows. "If anything has to come off, may I have it?"

37

IDENTITY CRISIS

"Very funny," I muttered.

"I'll take anything. I'm not picky."

"Every piece of me is precious?"

"You got it."

"Go!"

He laughed and hurried away.

With my free left hand, I reached under the pillow and grabbed the miniature cassette. I thought about hiding it on my person, so to speak. But what if Murphy decided to have another go at me while it was in there?

So I just slid it between my back and the mattress, where it would be easy to reach.

I no sooner had it out of sight than Murphy came hurrying in with a knife. He carried it in his right hand, down low by his side. Its blade, at least eight inches long, was straight out and pointing at me.

The blade wasn't all that was pointing at me.

They were level with each other, both tilting at the same slightly upward angle, and one about as long as the other.

While the knife swung back and forth at the end of Murphy's arm, the thick shaft bounced and swayed with each step he took.

"You come well armed," I said.

He smirked and shook his head, but didn't say anything.

Stopping beside my right hand, he bent over and eased the blade down onto the rope. He wouldn't be going for the knot, but for the clothesline itself where it was tight around my wrist. Only the thickness of the rope—less than half an inch—stood between the blade's edge and my skin. "Don't move," he muttered. "I don't want to cut you."

The way he was hunkered over with his head down, his hair fell across his brow and hid his eyes. He looked like a big kid with a messy mop of hair.

As he gently sawed the rope, his hair hardly moved at all, but the motions of his arm were enough to shake his rigid penis from side to side.

Finally, he cut me.

"Ow!"

"Sorry," he said, quickly stepping back. "Are you all right?"

"Yeah. Probably. What's one more cut?"

"I think that'll do it, though. Try giving a hard pull."

I jerked my arm downward. The rope held it for a moment, then made a quiet *puh!* and let me go.

"I'll get your feet," Murphy said and stepped toward the other end of the bed.

I brought my right hand down. It was surrounded by a deep red indentation from the rope. The knife had made a shallow, half-inch slice. Bright red blood was sliding out, streaking my wrist and forearm. I quickly licked the streaks away, then covered the wound with my mouth.

Murphy was watching. "Maybe I'd better get you a bandage," he said.

"It's no big deal. Why don't you go ahead and cut me loose? We can worry about a bandage later. Anyway, we may need several by the time you're done."

"I'll be a lot more careful," he said. "And this time, I'll go for the knots."

"Good idea."

Bending over my left foot, he started to work the knife back and forth. Its edge made soft, rubbing sounds against the rope.

"I haven't really had much practice at this sort of thing," he said. "Not since I was a kid." He lifted his head and smiled. "In my neighborhood, we were *always* tying people up."

"Sounds like you lived in an interesting neighborhood," I told him.

"I never tied up anyone like you, that's for sure. But I *wished* I could. I've always wanted to. This was like . . ." He shook his head and sighed. "Unbelievable," he said.

"Any time," I told him.

He grinned, then lowered his head and resumed cutting.

He managed to slice the ropes off both my ankles without drawing any more blood.

When he was done, he asked, "How's that?"

"Great. Thanks. But I don't think I can move."

He picked up my legs and eased them together. Then he sat on the end of the bed, turned sideways, and raised my feet onto his lap. He massaged them with both hands. "Let me know when they're better," he said. "I'll help you into the bathroom and we'll take care of your cut."

"Okay. Thanks."

"And I don't think we should make that drive to Culver City."

"You don't?"

"Screw them," he said. "I'll FedEx the books. It won't kill them to wait a day longer."

"I don't want to be responsible . . ."

"Oh, don't worry about it."

"What if I hadn't been here?"

He shrugged. "Who knows? But that's not how it went down."

"So, if we're not going to Culver City, what'll we do?"

"Whatever we want."

"I want my five grand," I told him.

He grinned. "I want to hear your story."

I said, "Okay." Though I smiled, I suddenly had a bad feeling inside—which must've showed.

"Something wrong?" Murphy asked.

Something was wrong, all right.

So far, he and I . . . we'd been getting along awfully well. I liked him better than any guy I'd ever known. A lot better.

Maybe I was even falling in love with him.

And maybe he had similar feelings about me.

But if I told him my story—the truth—it would probably ruin everything.

I mean, the truth might make me look pretty bad in his eyes. Might even disgust him. Especially when he hears about the way I chopped Tony into pieces, and about some of the things I did to Judy.

I can't tell him!

We kept looking at each other.

Frowning, Murphy asked, "Are you feeling okay?"

"It's just . . . I've got a little headache. Do you have any aspirin, or . . . ?"

"Sure. I'll get it for you." He slid a hand up the bottom of my leg, gave my calf a friendly pat, then lifted my feet off his lap, stood up and lowered them to the mattress. "Would you rather have Excedrin, Tylenol or Bufferin?" he asked.

"You must get a lot of headaches."

"I get my share. What'll it be?"

"How about Excedrin?"

Nodding, he took a few steps away from the bed, crouched and picked up his trunks.

"You're getting dressed?"

"You've got a headache."

"What does one have to do with the other?"

"You mean it wasn't a hint?" he asked, looking flustered.

"I'm not much for hinting. But if you want to go ahead and get dressed . . ."

"Well . . ." He shrugged and smiled. "Maybe we should

give you some time to get over your headache before we, uh, do anything too strenuous."

"Maybe so."

He stepped into his trunks, pulled them up, then left the room without putting on a shirt.

I reached under my back and grabbed the cassette. Shoving it into my mouth, I climbed off the bed. Then I swooped down and snatched my skirt off the floor. On my way to the door, I swept the skirt around my waist and fastened its buttons. Then I took the cassette out of my mouth. Clutching it in my right hand, I stepped through the doorway.

No sign of Murphy.

From the television came the voice of a man praising the courage of Paula Jones.

From the bathroom came a sound of rushing water.

Walking fast, I crossed the living room. Went straight to my purse near the end of the couch. Bent over it and spread it open.

All I meant to do was drop the cassette inside.

But I gaped at what was in there.

The usual stuff: lipstick, my compact, some tissues, a couple of tampons, my sunglasses, and so on.

Plus two sets of keys—mine and Judy's.

And the note pad with Tony's new telephone number.

And my wallet.

My wallet!

With my own driver's license inside.

With my photo on it.

And my true name.

And real address.

"Oh, my Christ," I murmured.

My hand trembling, I shoved the cassette down deep into the purse.

I felt sick.

Had Murphy looked?

He could've. He'd been out here alone before going to the bank, and then again after returning.

But did he?

Maybe he'd turned on the television so the voices would cover any sounds he might make while searching my purse.

But he'd been busy taking off his clothes.

And probably excited by his plans for me.

His blue jeans were draped over the cushion at the other end of the couch. His socks and shoes were on the floor over there.

"Oh, you're out," he said.

I turned around to face him. "Dressed, too."

"Well, sort of." He glanced at my chest, then quickly raised his eyes to my face.

"I thought maybe I had some chewing gum in my purse, but I guess not."

"I'm afraid I don't have any," he said, "or I'd get you some." He came toward me holding a glass of water in one hand, a plastic container of Excedrin in the other. "You don't seem like the chewing gum type," he said.

"What type is that?"

"Airhead."

"Keeps my breath minty fresh," I chirped, and stepped around to the front of the coffee table.

"Nothing wrong with your breath."

A couple of strides away from me, he stopped.

I reached out for the glass of water, but he pulled it back slightly. "Now, be careful," he said. "Let's not spill, this time."

"If I do, I won't be getting my blouse wet."

"Guess not." Blushing deep crimson, he gave the glass to me.

While I held it, he opened the Excedrin. I put out my left hand. He shook a couple of tablets into my palm. I tossed them into my mouth and washed them down with the water.

He waited until I'd lowered the glass, then asked, "How's the cut?"

I glanced at it. "Not so bad. See? The bleeding's stopped."

"Does it hurt?"

"Nah. It's just a nick. I'm fine."

"We'd better put something on it, anyway."

"How about your lips?"

He laughed and blushed. A real blusher, that Murphy.

"I was thinking of an antiseptic," he said. He took the glass from me and set it on the table. He put down the Excedrin bottle, too. Then, holding my hand, he led me across the room. "We'll touch up the rest of you, too, while we're at it."

"I can use a little touching up."

In the bathroom, he poured some hydrogen peroxide onto a cotton ball and patted the cut on my wrist. It felt cold. It fuzzed a little on the slit.

After bandaging my little cut, he took out a fresh ball of cotton. He soaked it with hydrogen peroxide and started dabbing at my other injuries—the scratches and nicks and gouges from last night's accidents. The liquid touched me with coldness. Here and there, it dribbled down my skin.

When it stung the wound on my belly, I gasped and stiffened.

"Sorry," he said.

"That's okay. A little pain is good for the soul."

"I'm not so sure about that."

"It feels so good when it stops."

"Can't argue with that one," he said.

"I like how this stuff feels, though. It's so nice and cool."

He said, "Hmm." With a fresh, dripping ball, he gently swabbed my right nipple.

Unaware of any injury there, I looked down. My nipple appeared to be fine. The chilly fluid made it pucker and jut out. "Now you're treating places that aren't hurt," I pointed out.

"Yep," he said, and moved the cotton ball to my other nipple.

I shivered a little with the good feel of it.

Then I undid my buttons, and my skirt fell to the bathroom floor. "Anywhere else need a touch-up?" I asked.

He squatted down in front of me. "I should say so," he said. "You've gotten yourself banged up pretty good."

"Do what you can. I'm in your hands."

Each time he touched me with a wet ball of cotton, I flinched a bit. Not because it hurt, but because it felt so cold on my hot skin.

Down low in front of me, he found a scratch here, a scrape there. He dabbed them. And he dabbed places where I had no injuries at all.

I turned around. He touched chilly balls of cotton to the backs of my thighs and to my buttocks. Then I felt his lips, his tongue. He kissed and licked his way up my back until he was standing.

When he pressed himself against my body, I found out that his trunks were gone. He was smooth and bare all the way down. And I could feel the hard length of him pressing against my lower back.

Nibbling the side of my neck, he reached around me with both hands and took gentle hold of my breasts.

The cotton balls and the bottle of hydrogen peroxide must've been down on the bathroom floor with his trunks.

He writhed against my back, sucked my neck and squeezed my breasts. Then one of his hands roamed down my front and slipped between my legs. Moaning, I squirmed against him.

After a while, I managed to turn around so we were facing each other. By then, I was in such a frantic delirium that I hardly knew what was happening.

He slammed me against the door frame.

As he pulled at my buttocks, I climbed his body and wrapped my legs around him.

He thrust into me.

I hugged him with my arms and legs.

He pounded me against the frame as he tried to ram up higher and deeper.

Then suddenly he was throbbing and pumping.

I clung to him, shuddering with my own release.

As our frenzy subsided, we remained clutching each other, my back against the door frame, my feet off the floor, my legs and arms around him. He stayed in me. We both panted for air.

I gasped, "My God, Murphy."

He gasped, "My God, Alice."

38

THE SLIP

Every time I remember it, I get the same awful, sick feeling in the pit of my guts.

Murphy saying my name.

My real name.

(Not Alice, by the way. But my real name was on my driver's license and on a dozen other items in my wallet, and that's the name that came out of Murphy's mouth as we clutched each other in the bathroom doorway.)

Alice, not Fran.

He *had* searched my purse.

He knew who I was and where I lived.

Letting go of his back, I clutched his hair with both hands and jerked his head back, tilting his face toward mine.

"What'd you say?" I asked.

"Huh? When?"

"Just now."

"Huh?"

"You called me Alice."

"Huh?"

"Why'd you call me Alice?"

"Did I?"

"You looked in my purse!" I blurted into his face. Then my right hand let go of his hair and I hit him with my fist. Punched him in the cheek so hard it jolted his head sideways.

And then he staggered backward.

Lurched backward, turning as if he wanted to set me down in the middle of the bathroom floor. But he didn't really have his balance anymore.

He couldn't stop.

Couldn't set me down.

It might've turned out all right, but too many things went wrong.

For one, Murphy kicked over the bottle of hydrogen peroxide. I heard it go over and roll, and heard its liquid gurgling out, slicking the tiles.

For another, Murphy had me clinging to him. Had me spitted on his cock so I couldn't jump down, couldn't get free, couldn't do anything to stop his sudden backward voyage across the bathroom.

Perched high and able to see over the top of his head, I saw what was coming.

"Watch out!" I yelled.

But he couldn't.

A moment later, the bathtub kicked his legs out from under him.

I flew face-first toward the tile wall on the other side of the tub. Throwing out my hands, I slapped the wall. My arms folded. I turned my face and my cheek struck one of my forearms.

From lower down came an awful thud like a coconut dropped on a concrete sidewalk. I not only heard it, but I *felt* it. Felt Murphy jolt between my legs and in me.

Suddenly, I felt a quick, sucking pull inside, and heard a slurp, and he was out.

And I was falling.

I threw my legs apart so Murphy wouldn't land on them.

My bare feet slapped against the bottom of the tub. For a

moment, I seemed to be standing, hunched low over Murphy as if looking for a good way to sit on him. It seemed like a *long* moment. I saw him down there, looking limp and odd. I sure didn't want to sit on him. But I probably would've done it, anyway, if I'd had a choice.

I didn't.

Because it *was* only a moment, and I might've *seemed* to be standing, but I wasn't.

I was just pausing in mid-fall.

Waving my arms, I tumbled backward. My butt slapped against the edge of the tub—between Murphy's knees. Then my legs flew up and I dropped to the floor.

My back *smacked* the tile floor.

Then my head thumped it.

And that, as they say, was "all she wrote."

At least for a pretty long while.

I don't know what I dreamed about. Probably something bad. Whatever it might've been, though, at least I didn't wake up choking.

Just with a horrid headache.

I was lying on my back with my legs up, calves resting on the edge of the tub. The way Murphy's feet were sticking out, I figured he was probably in the reverse of my position, and inside the tub.

"Murph?" I asked.

He didn't answer.

Then I remembered the sound and feel of his head striking the wall—and my glimpse of him as I fell.

"Murph?" I asked again. "Are you okay?"

Nothing.

"Are you dead?"

Nothing.

"God," I muttered.

Then I started to cry.

A word of advice: don't ever cry when you've got a splitting headache. The crying does something to the pressure inside your head. Pretty soon, I felt like I had a team of maniacs chewing and clawing through my brain.

It seemed to get worse and worse. I tore off my wig of red hair and flung it aside. I felt a little better without it, but not much.

The pain still raging, I clutched both sides of my head.

Finally, I figured my position on the floor wasn't helping matters. I needed to get up. So I drew in my legs. They were pretty numb from the calves down because of how they'd been resting on the tub's edge. But I brought them to my side of the tub, anyway, and shoved with my feet.

My back slid over the tile floor. As I scooted, the top of my head ran into Murphy's trunks and pushed them along in front of me. I ended up in the puddle of hydrogen peroxide with the plastic bottle against my shoulder.

For a while, I just lay there on my back, sobbing and holding my head, my legs straight out on the floor.

I knew I should be trying to get away.

But I couldn't.

And didn't really care.

I felt too miserable to care about anything.

I'd killed Murphy.

I'd damn near busted my own head open.

Maybe I did!

Raising my head slightly, I explored it with my fingers. My hair was wet—maybe with blood. But I found no gaping fissures, no spilling brains. Just a bump high on the back of my head, as if half a golf ball had been stuffed underneath my scalp.

I looked at my fingers. They were wet, but not bloody.

Pretty soon, I rolled over. I crawled out of the bathroom. Off the tiles and onto the carpet of the living room.

As I crawled toward the coffee table, CNN blared at me about some damn ferry boat sinking in some Godforsaken corner of the world.

Like I could give a shit. I had problems of my own.

The voices made my head throb.

So I took a detour to the television. Kneeling in front of it, I had to squint because of the picture's brightness. But I found the power button and hit it with a knuckle. The TV suddenly went dark and silent.

Much better.

Turning around, I crawled the rest of the way to the table. I grabbed its edge and pushed myself up. On my knees, I studied the clutter for a few seconds.

I was looking for the Excedrin and the water glass, but the first thing I saw was Murphy's book. The one that he'd autographed for me. *Deep Dead Eyes.*

It wasn't something I wanted to be seeing just then.

I looked away from it fast.

When I spotted the plastic bottle of Excedrin, I reached out and grabbed it. I pulled it over to me, then got hold of the glass.

It was half full of water.

I tossed four Excedrin tablets into my mouth. Then, with a shuddering hand, I picked up the glass. I gulped the water and swallowed the tablets.

They went down fine.

I was still awfully thirsty, though. Holding on to the glass, I struggled to my feet. I staggered into the kitchen, turned on the faucet, and filled the glass with cold water. I drank it all. Then I refilled the glass. This time, I sipped it slowly and looked around.

Murphy's kitchen seemed to double for an office. Its breakfast table held a computer, piles of paper and stacks of books. I could almost see him sitting at the table, rubbing his hair and frowning with thought.

No more books for him.

Starting to feel worse, I turned away and saw a clock above the kitchen's entryway.

1:25

Early afternoon. A lot earlier than I would've thought.

What'll I do?

I wanted to lie down on a nice bed and sleep. Make my headache go away. Make *all this* go away. At least for a while.

Lie down in my own bed . . .

But I couldn't do that, couldn't leave, not without taking care of the evidence.

A major clean-up to get rid of every trace of me.

It seemed like a huge, impossible job.

The way I felt . . .

I filled the glass once more with water, then carried it out of the kitchen and into Murphy's bedroom.

As I made my way toward the bed, I saw three of the ropes he'd used on me. They lay on the carpet like pale, dead snakes. Each was still tied to a leg of the bed.

I'll have to take those . . .

I saw the condom, too. On the floor where I'd dropped it when I took Murphy into my mouth.

The pale white disk looked like a sea creature you might find washed up on a beach, dead.

I'll have to get rid of it.

But I could do nothing, now.

I set the glass of water on the nightstand, then crawled onto the bed, sprawled myself out on its rumpled sheet, and buried my face in the pillow.

39

SO LONG, MY SWEET

Most of my headache was gone when I woke up.

I was still facedown on Murphy's bed, as if I hadn't moved at all during my nap.

I'd drooled all over his pillow.

The sheet underneath me was sodden with my sweat.

I thought how nice it might be to take a shower, but then I remembered that Murphy was in the tub.

Dead.

I'd killed him.

I hadn't *meant* to, but that didn't count for much: he was just as dead, either way.

And here I was, sprawled on his bed like Goldilocks.

What if somebody shows up?

I've gotta get out of here.

So I rolled over, twisted sideways until my legs fell off the edge of the mattress, and sat up. I groaned. My body felt ruined. I was sore and stiff and achy almost everywhere. But at least my head no longer burned with pain.

I could think again.

I could function.

I *could*, but *didn't*.

Not for a while, anyway.

For a while, I just sat on the edge of the bed, my head hanging, my back bent, my elbows on my thighs, my feet on the floor.

Almost like that statue, *The Thinker*.

But if anyone did a statue of how I looked then, he'd have to name it, *The Wasted*.

I knew that I needed to get off my butt and destroy every trace of my presence in Murphy's apartment and go home. But I couldn't bring myself to get started.

What's the point?

I felt as if nothing mattered anymore.

Why not just stay here?

Sooner or later, somebody would show up and find me, find Murphy, call the cops.

Who cares?

Why not go to the phone and call the cops, myself? Tell them everything. Put an end to all this.

But doing even that would've taken too much effort.

So I just kept sitting there.

Finally, I *had* to get up. It was either that, or flood the bedroom. Gritting my teeth, I made it to my feet. But I couldn't stand up straight. Hunched over slightly, I hurried to the bathroom. I slipped on the wet tile floor, but didn't fall. With my eyes fixed on the floor just in front of my feet, I found my way to the toilet and sat down without looking at Murphy.

I kept my head low while I went.

Stared at the floor.

But I could see him, anyway. That peripheral vision thing. The tub was a short distance over to my right. Even with my eyes down, I could see its long, white side. And Murphy's legs sticking out over the edge. And his face. He seemed to be peeking at me from around the side of his left knee.

Finally, I looked at him.

His eyes were open, but he wasn't seeing me.

He wasn't exactly Murphy, anymore. Whatever'd been

Murphy was gone. The thing in the tub was just a fair likeness, that's all. Somebody might've dropped by while I was asleep, snatched his body and replaced it with a dummy from a wax museum.

A dummy that didn't quite get it right.

Which was a good thing, I guess. I couldn't have stood it if *my* Murphy'd been in the tub.

But he wasn't.

When I finished on the toilet, I flushed and stood up and walked across the wet tiles to the side of the tub.

I stared down at the body.

And wondered what to do with it.

Leave it just as it is.

Sure. Why not? I didn't have the strength or desire to take it anywhere.

Besides, what could be accomplished by moving it?

I might try, if I had a good reason.

In spite of the difficulties and risks, I could probably haul Murphy's body to the parking lot of Judy's apartment building, or into Tony's apartment, or even over to Miller's Woods. But why? How could his body fit into the rest of it in any logical way?

I didn't see how.

No matter where they find him, it'll just add to the confusion.

If they find him just as he is, I thought, it'll look like an accident. While getting ready to take a shower, he somehow slipped and fell backward and bashed his head on the wall beside the tub.

Which had the advantage of being almost true.

Unless I did some major clean-up, however, they would also figure out that he'd been having sex with a woman just before his accident. And they might suspect she'd had a hand in his death.

If they got that far, they would look for samples of her hair, fluids, etc.

I'd *have* to make the clean-up effort.

I started with the bathroom. Taking care of the worst part first, I climbed into the tub, straddled Murphy's body and wiped the wall where I'd hit it with my hands. I didn't like standing there. Not one bit. I knew that *he* wasn't under me, but *something* was. Not a wax dummy, either—a naked stiff. It made me nervous. Like I half expected a spook of some sort to take over the body and make a grab for me. Or lurch up between my legs and give me a bite.

Me and my imagination.

I got a good case of goosebumps, but I was okay as soon as I'd climbed out of the tub.

Next, I put away the package of cotton balls and the hydrogen peroxide—which wasn't completely empty. (Naturally, I wiped the plastic bottle to take care of my prints.) Then I found all the used cotton balls on the floor and in the waste basket. I flushed them down the toilet.

Then I mopped the bathroom floor.

I wiped the toilet seat and the flush handle.

That was about it for the bathroom. For now. I'd be back again, but not until just before time to leave.

After putting away the mop and bucket, I went into the living room for my purse. As I headed for the couch, though, I saw a brown leather attaché case standing beside the front door. Though it must've been there before, this was the first time I'd noticed it.

Right away, I knew what must be inside.

I crouched beside it, set it down flat on the floor, snapped open its latches, and raised the lid.

The case was *loaded* with money.

Neat packets of one-dollar bills, fives, tens, and twenties. *He'd gotten it for me in small bills, just as I'd asked.*

Murphy's idea of a joke, I guess.

I would've thought it was pretty funny if he'd been there to enjoy the gag with me.

But he wasn't.

I smiled for about a second, then fell apart.

This was the worst yet. You'd think I'd never seen anything as heartbreaking as those five thousand dollars in small bills. I *bawled*. Tears poured down my face and spasms wracked my body. I ended up stretched out on the carpet by the door, crying onto my crossed arms.

When I finally ran out of tears, I felt empty and lazy. I was dangerously close to falling asleep, so I pushed myself up. Leaving the attaché case by the door, I hurried into the kitchen. I jerked a couple of paper towels off a roll by the sink, and used them to cover my hands while I pulled open a few cupboards.

I found Murphy's stash of grocery bags. The paper bags were folded neatly in a row inside a cupboard. I took out two, stuffed one inside another for double thickness, then returned to the living room.

Squatting over the attaché case, I double-bagged my cash.

Then I carried Murphy's empty case into the kitchen, set it down by the table where he used to work, and wiped it carefully with a paper towel.

I'd planned to do the bedroom next, but suddenly had an urge to take care of my kitchen chores. So I made a couple of trips into the living room to gather the beer mugs, bottles and water glass. I washed and put away the mugs and glass. I wiped the bottles and dropped them into Murphy's recycling bin.

Back in the living room, I saw the bag of pretzels on the coffee table. I had not only touched its cellophane bag, but I'd reached into it. My fingerprints might actually be *inside* the bag. So instead of trying to clean it, I decided to take it with me. It went into the grocery sack along with the money.

Well, I'm beginning to see that it might take me all day to describe every single step in detail. And who really wants to read about all that stuff, anyway? So I'll just summarize the rest of it, if that's okay with you.

Here's what I did—pretty much in order—before leaving Murphy's apartment.

1. *Placed my autographed copy of* Deep Dead Eyes *in grocery bag.*
2. *Put bottle of Excedrin in my purse.*
3. *Untied ropes from all four bed legs and tossed them into grocery bag.*
4. *Found knife Murphy had used to cut the ropes (and me), washed it in the kitchen, and put it away.*
5. *Flushed condom and condom wrapper down toilet (and again wiped handle).*
6. *Removed pillow case and sheets from bed, stuffed them into grocery sack.*
7. *Put clean sheets on bed, fresh pillow case on pillow.*
8. *Artfully arranged Murphy's trunks and Bear Whizz Beer T-shirt on bed mattress as if flung there in haphazard manner.*
9. *Took five copies of* The Dark Pit *from box, wrapped them for mailing, and labeled package with address Murphy'd copied onto the back cover of* TV Guide *(and his return address).*
10. *In bathroom, turned on shower so it sprayed down on Murphy.*
11. *Left shower curtain open and shower running.*
12. *Gathered my clothes and shoes, got dressed.*
13. *Put wig on.*
14. *Rearranged contents of grocery bag so that package of books went in on top of money.*
15. *Set grocery bags and purse near front door.*

That's pretty much all I did. It took a while—especially getting the books ready for mailing. I had to find tape and scissors, cut up a grocery bag, and be careful not to leave prints on any of the books or wrapping materials. A major chore.

I felt pretty good about doing it, though. I'd killed the poor guy, but at least he might get his chance at a movie deal.

Finally, all dressed and ready to go, I made the rounds

one more time. I picked up a few odds and ends that shouldn't be left behind, and gave a quick wipe to whatever I might've touched but couldn't take with me.

I didn't go into the bathroom, though. The floor was too wet from the shower, and the air was so thick with steam that I couldn't even see Murphy in the tub.

Returning to the front door, I tossed a few things into the grocery bag with the money, books, etc. I didn't think I'd be able to manage two bags, so I mashed down the one holding the dirty sheets and pillow case, and stuffed it into the other bag. Then I slipped my purse strap onto my shoulder. I put on my sunglasses and picked up the full bag.

It was pretty heavy. With my right arm, I hugged it against my chest. I used my left hand—wrapped in my skirt—to open the door.

For a few seconds, I stood there and looked out through the screen door. Nothing seemed to be going on outside.

From one of the nearby units came the noisy whine of a vacuum cleaner. I also heard television voices coming from somewhere.

But I saw nobody.

So I stepped out, pulled the main door shut, and walked briskly toward the sidewalk. I was several paces away from Murphy's unit by the time its screen door bammed shut.

40

LAST TASKS

Eyes turned toward me as I entered the post office. Mostly belonging to guys, of course. Scoping out this flashy red-haired babe with the body to die for, the slit up her skirt and her blouse half open.

I recognized nobody.

I don't think anyone looked high enough to see my face.

But I had my sunglasses on, just in case.

Holding the wrapped books low in front of me to keep the view of my cleavage clear, I walked straight over to the waiting line. There were ten or twelve people ahead of me.

I planned to send the books First Class.

I'd considered Overnight Express Mail, but it was after four o'clock by the time I reached the post office. I thought that might be too late in the afternoon for guaranteed next-day delivery, so why go to the extra expense?

Besides, if I sent the books Overnight, I would have to stand around and fill out a special label. I didn't want to fool with that.

First Class would get the books to the producers soon enough.

If not tomorrow, the day after tomorrow.

While I stood in the line, I set the package down on the floor in front of my feet. Then I took a twenty-dollar bill out of my purse. I also took out a couple of tissues.

Squatting down, I casually used the tissues to wipe the outside of the parcel where I'd touched it. (Cops *can* lift fingerprints off paper, you know.) I didn't pay attention to who might be watching, and didn't really care. A person's got every right to clean off a package before mailing it, right? It's nobody's business why, and who would ever guess I was doing it to ruin possible fingerprint evidence? Nobody, that's who.

Keeping a tissue in one hand and my twenty in the other so that my fingertips didn't touch the package, I picked it up again.

Then I just waited in line for my turn at one of the windows.

I kept my head down. Nobody talked to me, and I spoke to no one. It was a pretty long wait, though.

People are amazing. They'll go to a place like the post office, and half of them don't seem to have a clue. They'll step up to the window with a box that's still open, for instance, and ask to borrow some tape. Or when it comes time to pay, they'll have to spend five minutes hunting for their checkbook. Amazing.

Not to mention, the postal workers were in no hurry to set any speed records.

Finally, my turn came anyway.

I set my package on the counter, smiled, and said, "Good afternoon," to the clerk.

She gave me back a friendly smile, and said, "What can I do for you, honey?"

"I'd like to mail these books," I told her. My parcel was too large to fit through the slot under the panel of bullet-proof glass (or acrylic, or whatever), so she opened the panel like a door. I slid the package toward her, leaving the twenty on top, and said, "I'd like it to go First Class, please."

Nodding, she shut the panel. When she set the parcel on a scale, its weight and cost appeared on a computer screen. After slapping on some stickers, she pushed my change under the window and asked if I would like to have a receipt.

"No," I said. "I don't think I'll be needing one. Thanks."

"You have a nice day," she said.

"Thanks. You, too."

I turned away from her window.

"Next in line," she called.

The line had dwindled. Only three customers were waiting. Two women—one in her twenties and the other at least seventy—and a young guy probably no older than eighteen. Guess which one was looking at me.

He gaped at me, his jaw drooping.

But I doubt that he saw my face at all.

I walked on past him and out the door.

Just so the flashy redhead who mailed Murphy Scott's books would not be connected directly to Judy's car (on the slim chance that an investigator might actually look into the situation), I had parked her car a block away from the post office and around a corner.

Nobody followed me around the corner.

I climbed in and drove away.

I had no more chores to run. Only one thing still needed to be done: ditch Judy's car.

Abandon it somewhere, and walk home.

Walk home carrying the grocery sack loaded with my pretzels, my personally inscribed and autographed copy of *Deep Dead Eyes*, my souvenir pieces of rope, a pair of used bedsheets and a pillow case, and my five thousand dollars in small bills.

It wasn't terribly heavy, now that I'd gotten rid of the five hardcover books.

But heavy enough. I didn't care to trudge five or ten miles with it.

There was, of course, a simple solution to the problem.

Why not drive straight home, park in the garage and haul the sack up to my room, *then* take off again to find a distant dumping-spot for the car?

Simple, but not for me.

I just didn't have the guts to go driving Judy's car brazenly all over creation. Even the trip from Murphy's neighborhood to the post office had nearly undone me. Too much time had gone by since leaving Judy, Milo and Tony. Too much might've happened. What if Judy had already been reported missing? What if somebody had stumbled upon Milo's camp? Suppose Judy had escaped from the woods and told the cops all about me? What if Tony's body had already been discovered in the parking lot of her apartment building?

If anything of the sort had happened, every cop in Chester might be on the lookout for her car.

I wanted to be far away from it.

The sooner, the better.

Even if it meant a tough hike home.

But I couldn't just leave it *anywhere*. For one thing, I didn't want people to notice me getting out. For another, it really should, if possible, be abandoned in a place where nobody would pay attention to it for a while.

I came up with one idea after another, but found flaws in all of them.

Until I thought of the perfect place.

The mall!

The vast, indoor shopping plaza over by the highway was surrounded by acres of parking lots with probably more than a dozen entances and exits.

There was no parking fee, which meant no gates or cashiers.

With a steady flow of cars coming and going, one more would hardly be noticed.

I would hardly be noticed, entering, parking, walking away with my bag.

To top it all off, the lots were never completely empty. Even after the mall's closing time, plenty of vehicles remained because of people parking there, then walking over to nearby establishments. Scattered all around were mini-marts, restaurants, bars, and fast-food joints. There was even a supermarket. Some stayed open late, while others (including the supermarket) stayed open *always*.

In short, the mall's parking lots offered *anonymity*.

I could anonymously drop off Judy's car and walk away.

Her car might anonymously sit there, day after day, night after night, lost among the others.

Delighted, I headed for the mall.

About halfway there, I swung onto a little sidestreet. I pulled over and stopped the car in front of a house that had a For Sale sign on the front lawn. The house looked empty. Across the street was a vacant lot. Looking all around, I saw nobody.

So I grabbed one of the legs that I'd cut off Tony's jeans last night and climbed out of the car. With the denim leg, I wiped the exterior door handles and everywhere else that I might've touched.

Then I climbed in and did the interior.

Then I double-checked the whole car, inside and out, to make sure I hadn't missed anything. Judy's purse was still on the floor, partly hidden under the driver's seat. Fine. It could stay there.

Satisfied that I'd removed every trace of myself (to the extent that it can be done in a few minutes with a rag), I tossed both the legs into my grocery bag, started up the car again, and drove the rest of the way to the mall.

Plenty of other cars were coming and going.

I entered a parking lot over on the Macy's side of the complex, found an empty space, pulled in and shut off the engine.

Just for the heck of it, I left Judy's key in the ignition.

I wiped off the keys and key case, the shift handle and the steering wheel.

My purse and grocery bag were on the front passenger seat. Leaning sideways, I grabbed them.

I climbed out of Judy's car. Purse hanging by my side, I set down the bag. Then I looked around. Several people were in sight, some heading toward mall entrances, others returning to their cars. None paid any attention to me.

With one of the denim legs, I cleaned the interior door handle.

Then I flopped the leg back into the sack, hoisted the sack off the pavement, stepped out of the way, and flung the door shut with my knee.

Even as the door thunked, I realized that I'd forgotten to lock it.

I'd *meant* to lock it.

But this is better.

Leave it unlocked, key in the ignition.

With any luck, some creep might come along and steal the thing.

Walking away from Judy's car, I couldn't help but smile.

41

GOING HOME

Freedom's just another word for nothing left to fear.

As soon as I walked away from Judy's car, I felt hugely, enormously, wonderfully free.

I was done!

I'd severed my last major connection with the series of accidents and/or crimes that had started last night when I killed Tony. Sure, I still had possession of a few items such as the money and autographed book, but nothing that could draw me in as a suspect.

I was, as they say, "home free."

But several miles from home.

I started to hike across the parking lot, the grocery sack clutched to my chest. It was heavy enough that I needed to hold it with both hands.

Gonna be a long hike.

I hadn't walked very far, though, before I noticed that many of the kids roaming across the lot were carrying book bags on their backs.

Just what I needed!

Instead of striking out for home, I made a detour into the mall.

It was good to be in such a familiar place. Rarely a week ever went by that I didn't visit the mall at least once. I would spend a couple of hours there, just wandering, browsing through the stores, having a nice lunch at the food court. It was a quiet, pleasant place—and just about the *only* place in town worth going to, except for the cineplex.

Wandering the mall, a person can pretty much stay anonymous.

Pretty much but not completely.

If you visit the same shops or food stands time after time, certain employees will start to recognize you. They have no way to learn your name unless you introduce yourself or pay with a credit card or check, but some are bound to know your face.

Some might even know it well enough to wonder how come, today, I was wearing a bright red wig.

So my first stop, after entering the mall, was the ladies' restroom.

As I understand it, California has a law against security cameras in toilet cubicles. You can't blow your nose in this state without breaking the criminal code, but this is one law I really go for. I mean, you don't want some horny degenerate of a security guard watching you on TV while you're doing your stuff, if you get my meaning.

They're allowed to spy on you with hidden cameras just about everywhere else, but not when you're in a stall.

So that's where I went.

First, I availed myself of the toilet since it happened to be there anyway and it didn't look hideous. Unbelievable as this may seem, the last person using this public toilet had actually flushed it. Not only that, but (hold on to your hat), she hadn't left a puddle—or worse—on the seat! I was impressed and grateful.

Shit, I wanted to *meet* her!

Never mind.

With my purse hanging from a hook on the door and my grocery sack down on the floor, I hoisted my skirt, pulled my panties down around my ankles, and hovered a couple of inches above the seat. (Even if the seat looks clean, you sure don't want to sit on it. You don't even want to *think* about what's been on it.)

The toilet paper dispenser, of course, turned out to be empty. Always prepared, I used some tissues from my purse.

Then I flushed the toilet.

I've possibly done some lousy things in my life, but I've always flushed after myself.

Anybody who doesn't is nothing short of a pig.

After flushing, I pulled up my panties, stood in front of the toilet, and let my skirt drift down around my legs. Then I took off my gaudy red wig and stuffed it into the grocery sack.

Anything else I should do while I've got some privacy?

Of course!

It wasn't easy to do in the confines of the toilet stall, but I bent over, reached down deep into my sack, and pulled out a few packets of cash. I transferred some denominations back and forth. Finally, I ended up with about three hundred dollars, mostly in twenties and tens. I put that money into my purse.

Then I crumpled down the top of my sack so nobody would be able to see inside. I picked it up, took my purse off the hook, unlatched the door, and stepped out of the stall.

I stopped in front of a mirror. The redhead was gone. I looked like myself again. Almost.

Nobody else was using the restroom, just then, so I set down the bag, took a brush out of my purse, and spent a couple of minutes working my hair into shape. When I was done, it still wouldn't win any prizes. It no longer looked frightful, though.

Now that I was resuming my own identity, I fastened the upper buttons of my blouse. I also took off my big, hoop earrings and tucked them away in my purse.

All set, I picked up my grocery sack and walked out of the

restroom. I strolled the length of the mall, entered J.C. Penney's, found myself a nice green book bag (or backpack, as the case may be), and bought it with cash.

Right in front of the clerk, I removed its tags and stickers, stuffed my grocery sack inside, then swung the pack onto my back and slipped my arms through its straps.

On my way out, I wondered if I needed anything else before leaving the mall.

How about supper?

Wong's Kitchen in the food court had great orange chicken, barbecued pork, fried wonton, etc. I was tempted. But on the other hand, remaining at the mall would increase my chances of running into someone who knew me.

Get out now.

Go home.

I went straight to the nearest exit and walked out into the heat and glare of late afternoon. My sunglasses helped against the glare. After putting them on, I paused long enough to stuff my purse into the backpack.

Then I was off.

I started with a brisk pace, but couldn't keep it up for long. Though a breeze sometimes stirred against me, the day was too hot for hurrying. And I was in lousy shape from too little sleep, too many injuries, too much prolonged stress, and the ungodly amount of stenuous physical activity I'd gone through since the start of my problems last night.

Soon, I was short of breath, my heart was racing, and sweat was pouring out of me.

I slowed down.

Slow and steady gets the job done.

Before long, I was feeling a lot better.

I knew from my many trips to the mall, however, that it was six miles from home. At my usual pace, I could walk more than four miles per hour. This was probably half that speed.

Six miles at two miles per hour.

I did some tricky math.

A three-hour hike?

Dismayed by the idea of not making it home until about eight o'clock, I decided to pick up my pace as much as possible.

I must've been an interesting sight for the motorists as I hurried down the sidewalk. Even without the wig, I was conspicuous in my bright yellow blouse and flowing green skirt. Not to mention, as we all know, I'm built like a brick shithouse. Plus, my bra hadn't exactly been designed for maximum support, so my quick and bouncy strides made for a lot of bust action—which was exaggerated still more by the backpack. The pack's weight thrust my chest forward, while its straps drew my shoulders back and pulled at the front of my blouse as if trying to rip it open. If that weren't enough, every stride sent my bare leg swinging out through the slit in my skirt.

Every now and then, guys in passing cars tooted at me, whistled at me, or called out. Because of traffic noise, I couldn't really hear what they were yelling. Probably a combination of compliments, critical remarks, suggestions and offers—all crude.

When guys shout at you from car windows, they never say anything that *isn't* crude.

Before too long, the inevitable happened.

A car passed me, then slowed down, pulled over to the side of the road and stopped.

I felt only a slight sinking sensation. This was no cause for alarm—just a nuisance. Probably some jerk hoping to get lucky.

I kept walking, but picked up my speed as I neared the car.

When I came up alongside it, the passenger door swung open. Not even glancing in, I started to step around the door.

"Alice?"

A man, and he knew my name.

Instead of my name, it might've been the squeak and

crackle of ice beginning to break under my feet—if I were standing on a frozen lake a mile from any shore.

This can't be good!

I lurched to a halt, ducked, and peered in through the open door. Nobody in the passenger seat.

The driver looked familiar, but . . . I suddenly recognized him, and the ice froze solid again.

I felt so relieved that I was almost *glad* to see him.

"Elroy?" I asked.

"That's my name, don't wear it out."

The same old Elroy.

"I've got room for two in my buggy," he said.

"Are you offering me a ride?"

"Hop right in."

So I took off my pack. Holding it in front of me with both hands, I climbed into Elroy's car. Then I leaned out and pulled the door shut. "This is really nice of you," I said.

"Just call me Mr. Nice Guy."

In the past, I had generally called him Dork-head, but not to his face.

A couple of years earlier, he and I had worked in the same law office for about six months. We were both employed as secretaries. I couldn't stand him, but I'd always treated him okay, and he'd apparently liked me quite a lot.

"Buckle up for safety," he said.

Realizing that he probably wouldn't start driving until I'd complied with the rules, I brought the seatbelt down across my chest and latched it.

"I just couldn't believe my eyes when I saw it was you," he said, and checked the side mirror. "I said to myself, 'Elroy, that woman bears a striking resemblance to our Alice. Is it possible?' Well, then I kept watching you and saw that it was not only possible, but factual." He found an opening in the traffic and steered us onto the road. "I'm *so* glad to see you again. You're looking utterly splendid."

"Thanks," I said. "You're looking great, yourself."

So I'm a liar.

The one way Elroy did not look, and never would, was "great." A skinny little guy with slicked-down black hair, big ears and a pointy nose, he looked mostly like a rat. A dapper rat, he nearly always wore a white shirt and blue bow-tie. He didn't seem to have changed much—including his outfit— since I'd last seen him.

"I must say," he said, "we've missed you at the office."

"They can't be missing me much. Hell, they fired me."

"*I* miss you."

"Well, thanks."

"You always . . . cheered the place up."

"My manic charm."

"The other girls . . . they're all such snotty bitches. You were always nice to me."

"Well . . . thanks."

"It's *so* good to see you again. I just can't believe we've run into each other this way. I thought you'd left town."

"No such luck," I said.

"I'm sure someone told me you'd moved to El Paso."

"Someone's wishful thinking," I said.

"Are you still living above that garage?"

"Still there. But you don't need to spread the word around at the office."

Giving me a sly glance, he said, "Mum's the word."

"Thanks. Let them keep on thinking I'm in El Paso."

"It'll be our little secret."

"How *is* my old friend, Mr. Heflin, by the way?"

"Oh, Mr. Heflin. Polite. He is very polite to all the ladies. And he keeps his hands entirely to himself."

"Glad to hear it. And how is he around stairways?"

"Careful. Very careful."

"Has he made a complete recovery?"

"I shouldn't say 'complete.' No. Hardly complete. He limps. I suspect he'll *always* limp."

"Sorry to hear that," I said.

Which brought a squeaky laugh out of Elroy. He said, "Oh, Alice, I love it. You haven't changed a *bit*. Not one *smidgen*. You're such a terror."

"That's me."

"So, where can I take you?"

"Where would you *like* to take me?" I asked.

42

THE INVITATION

"Oh, my," Elroy said.

I gave him the eye and asked, "You didn't go and get married, did you?"

Fat chance.

But you never know. It's amazing, some of the losers who end up getting married. All they need to do is find someone who's an *even bigger* loser.

"Nope," Elroy said. "No ball and chain for yours truly. I've gotta have my freedom."

"Going with anyone?"

"Aren't *we* inquisitive?"

"I wouldn't want to get you into hot water with your sweetie."

"Hot water? How?"

"By having you over for dinner tonight. I happen to be house-sitting for my friends, this week. I've got their whole house all to myself. We could have cocktails by the swimming pool, and I'll barbecue some steaks on the outdoor grill. How about it?"

I'd been watching his face go through changes. The way I

read it, he was shocked and delighted by the invitation, but afraid I might be trying to embarrass him with a phony offer.

Casting me a smirk, he said, "Surely you jest."

I tried to look hurt. "I thought you said you were glad to see me."

"I *am*," he insisted. "It's just that . . . You aren't serious about . . . what you just said about dinner. Are you?"

"Of course I'm serious."

"Well, it sounds lovely, but . . ."

"Turn right at the next light."

"Why?"

"It's how we get there," I explained, smiling.

"No, I mean . . . I'd be happy to just drop you off. You don't have to make dinner for me."

"I don't have to, I want to."

"That's the part I don't get."

To be frank, I didn't quite get it, myself.

Until running into Elroy, I'd only wanted to get home as soon as possible and be alone. Have a drink, have a meal, take a nice long bath, and go to bed. And sleep and sleep and sleep.

However. Being given the car ride would save me at least two hours of hard walking. I owed Elroy for that. Besides, I could spend an hour or so treating him to dinner, and still be ahead of the game timewise.

Another thing. I needed a chance to figure out whether or not Elroy was a threat to me. If asked, he could testify as to the time and place he'd picked me up. But did it matter? If it *did* matter, I needed to figure out how to prevent him from talking.

And. This may seem odd, considering. For one thing, I'm pretty much of a loner. For another, I'd always figured Elroy for a dork. But I actually liked the idea of having him around when I got home.

Life is strange.

I don't know why anything happens. Why did I *really* ask Elroy to have dinner with me?

Maybe it was in my genes to invite him. Or in the cards. Or in the stars. Maybe I was programmed to do it by the Great Computer. Or moved by the Master of Games. Maybe God made me do it. Or the Devil.

If you want the truth, though, I guess the main reason must've had to do with Murphy.

It was Murphy, more than anything, that made me reluctant to be alone.

Too bad it couldn't be him instead of Elroy keeping me company.

But Elroy would be better than nobody.

I supposed.

"What are you scared of?" I asked him in a teasing way.

"Me?" Elroy asked. "I'm not scared."

"You seem awfully nervous."

"Do I? I'm just . . . surprised, that's all. We haven't seen each other in *ages*, and all of a sudden you're inviting me over to your place for dinner."

"My friend's place. Anyway, it seems like a fine idea to me. I always felt that we should've gotten to know each other better."

"I asked you out, remember? You turned me down."

I remembered, all right. He'd asked me out three different times, and I had always politely refused, claiming to have prior commitments.

"I had a rule against dating anyone at work," I explained. "But now that I don't work there anymore, I don't see any reason for us to stay away from each other. Do you?"

"Me? No. I never did."

"Then you'll have dinner with me?"

"I'd be most honored."

"Good deal."

After that, I gave him directions now and then, while he filled me in on doings at the office, gave me a summary of his own recent activities (dull as mud), and asked about mine. I didn't want to admit much of the truth, so I told him that I was now a mystery writer.

"Oh, how exciting! Have you had anything published?"

"Just one book, so far."

"But that's *spectacular!* I'm so excited for you."

"Thanks."

"The big bad girl makes good!"

I smiled at him. "Watch it, buddy."

"So, what's the title of your book?"

"Depths of Darkness."

"Excellent! It's so . . . evocative! And is it published under your own name? I do hope so. You've such an absolutely *luscious* name for a mystery writer."

"Think so?"

"Oh, indeed," he said. "But did you? Use your own name?"

"Absolutely."

"Oh, good for you!" He spoke my name slowly and dramatically, so it almost sounded like poetry. (My *actual* name, not Alice.) "It's so perfect, I just bet everyone must *think* it's a pen name."

"Maybe so," I said, starting to regret the fabrication.

" '*She writes with a poison pen.*' "

"Good one," I said.

"I can't wait to read it. It isn't about intrigue in a law office, is it?"

"Not exactly."

"Am *I* in it?"

Throwing him a mysterious smile, I said, "You'll have to read it and find out."

"Oooh. This is *so* exciting."

"I'll give you a copy if I can ever manage to get my hands on some."

"You don't have any?" He sounded shocked and appalled.

"Not at the moment. I only had twenty to start with. By the time I gave copies to my relatives and a few friends . . . and sent half a dozen to this film producer in Culver City . . . I'm trying to get more, but it isn't easy."

"That's awful."

"Well, it's ridiculous. Seems like everybody has the book but me."

"You don't even have a copy for *yourself*?"

"Not at the moment. I loaned my last copy to a friend. But don't worry about it, I'll send you one the moment I get a new shipment."

"I can hardly wait. Now, tell me about the movie version."

This is the sort of crapola one gets into, on occasion, when one lies.

So I kept making up more lies, sometimes telling him to make turns, until finally we reached Serena and Charlie's house.

"And here we are! Just go ahead and pull into the driveway."

He slowed his car, made the turn, and the house came into sight.

I nearly panicked.

What if I missed something?

I'd done my best to clean up the place and get rid of every trace of Tony, but I suddenly wasn't at all sure that I hadn't overlooked something.

A gob of brain on the front stoop . . .

I should've kept my mouth shut, let Elroy drop me off at the curb, told him thanks and goodbye—*not invite him in!*

Better yet, I never should've gotten into his car in the first place.

Thanks for the offer, Elroy, but I'm not allowed to ride with strangers—and I don't know anyone stranger than you.

"This is an absolutely lovely house," he said, and stopped his car. "I can't *wait* to feast my eyes on the interior."

"It's pretty nice," I admitted.

Gosh, Elroy, you know what? I'm not feeling so well all of a sudden.

It wouldn't be a lie.

Would you mind terribly if we didn't do this tonight? Why don't I give you a rain check? Better yet, why don't you give me your phone number, and I'll call you?

Very cute.

Only two problems with it. First, I would look like a creep. Second, I didn't really *want* to get rid of him.

I did a fine job of cleaning up. He won't find anything.

And if he does?

"Are you having second thoughts?" he asked.

"No. Are you kidding? This'll be great." With that, I opened the car door.

"Wait," Elroy said, opening his door. "I'll come around to your side and give you a hand."

"No, that's . . ."

He leaped out.

Clutching the backpack against my chest, I burst from the car. I made it to my feet about two seconds before Elroy arrived.

"Here," he said. "Allow me to take that."

"I'm fine."

He reached for my pack, anyway.

"No!" I snapped, and whirled around to put my back in the way. "I'm perfectly capable of carrying it myself."

"Whoa! Jeezle-peezle! Okay! Sorry."

"That's all right," I said, and turned around to face him.

"What do you have in there, the Crown Jewels?"

Terrific. Now I've made him curious.

Grinning, I said, "Curiosity killed the Elroy."

He laughed. "You are such a stitch, Alice. You haven't changed a single whit."

"I've changed my underwear once or twice."

His face went crimson.

"Sorry," I said. "I didn't mean to embarrass you."

"Of *course* you meant to embarrass me. It's part of your charm."

"Really?"

"Such a naughty girl."

"That's me," I said, and stepped around him. "Let's go this way."

He stayed by my side as I walked down the driveway.

When we came to the rear corner of the house, I quickly scanned the pool area, the back yard and the edge of the forest. I saw no one. Everything looked fine.

"Why don't you make yourself comfortable over by the pool?" I suggested. "I need to trot upstairs and take care of a few things, then I'll be right down and make us some drinks."

"Fine and dandy," he said.

But as I headed for the garage, he kept walking beside me.

"Is this *your* garage?" he asked.

"It's where I live. I just rent the upstairs."

"I'd be curious to see what it looks like."

I was beginning to remember *why* I'd formed such a strong dislike for Elroy.

"Maybe some other time," I told him.

"I'll stay out of your way."

"Why don't you just wait over there by the pool?"

"Are you sure you wouldn't like me to carry your pack up the stairs for you? You could go up first and unlock the door."

"No, that's fine. I can take care of it."

"I'd be more than happy to help."

"I'll be down in a few minutes," I said, hurrying forward.

This time, he stayed put.

I started trotting up the wooden stairway.

With the pack clutched against my chest, I couldn't see the steps in front of my feet.

So, of course, I fell.

43

No Place Like Home

Rammed myself down on my pack.

It contained my purse and the grocery sack with an open bag of pretzels, four lengths of rope, two denim legs, two sheets and a pillow case, my autographed copy of *Deep Dead Eyes*, and most of my five thousand dollars in small bills. None of which did much to soften my impact with the stairs.

I slammed down hard on top of the pack, mashing my breasts, pounding my ribcage and belly, knocking my wind out.

From the sound of things, I instantly pulverized the pretzels.

From the feel of things, a corner of Murphy's novel tried to punch its way through the gouge in my stomach.

I let out a cry of pain.

A split second after impact, I began skidding down the stairs feet first, knees bumping, thighs scraping, arms being pummeled as they hugged the pack.

The first thing I heard from Elroy was a gasp of, "Oh, dear me!" Then I heard him charging up the stairs below me.

Suddenly, he grabbed the backs of my legs, clamping down hard on them and stopping me.

"I've got you," he gasped. "Don't worry."

"Thanks."

"Are you all right?"

"Fine. I'm fine."

"Just don't move."

I had little intention of moving—at least until I could breathe again and the pain subsided. Even after that, I wouldn't be *able* to move until he let go of my legs. He had a firm grip. And his hands were way up there, almost high enough to touch my butt.

"Don't get fresh," I told him.

"Ha ha, very funny."

"I guess I should've . . . let you carry the pack."

"I'm not one to rub it in."

Oh, sure you are.

"But I did rather expect something of this sort," he added.

I *should've* expected it. I'd had so many falls lately, I was starting to feel like a river.

With Elroy still holding me, I pulled my arms out from under the pack. They seemed to work okay. I placed both hands on a stair to brace myself, then said, "Why don't you sort of ease off my legs, and I'll try to get up?"

"Be careful," he warned.

"Get ready to grab me again, just in case."

When he let go, I pushed at the stair, raising myself off the pack. But suddenly I started to slip.

I gasped.

Elroy grabbed me by the hips.

But I only slipped an inch or two before my knees settled onto a lower stair, stopping me.

"There," I said.

"Okay?"

"I'll be fine now. But I can't get up till you're out of the way."

"Okay."

A true gentleman, he let go of my hips without giving me so much as a squeeze or a pat, and descended the stairs. I got to my feet. With a hand on the railing, I turned halfway around and smiled down at him. "Thanks for catching me," I said.

"Glad to be of service, ma'am."

"See you in a while."

"Are you sure you won't be needing me again?"

"I'll be all right. I'm not due for another fall until about six-thirty or seven."

He laughed. "You fall a lot, do you?"

"Lately. I need to start being more careful." With that, I turned away, climbed up to my pack, bent over it, and lifted it by the straps. It came swinging back and bumped gently against my thighs.

I stayed on my feet.

At the top of the stairs, I set it down, opened its flap, and took out my purse.

Elroy stood at the foot of the stairs and watched me.

"Go on over to the pool," I said. "I'll be down in a couple of minutes."

"Are you sure you wouldn't like to invite me up?"

"Don't make a pest of yourself, Elroy."

"You can't blame a fellow for trying."

"Don't count on it."

With a smirk on his face, he winked an eye, pointed a finger at me, and said, "Later."

Which would've been truly cool coming from Paul Newman or John Travolta. Coming from Elroy, it was sort of sad and funny, but mostly annoying.

As he swiveled around and started swaggering toward the pool, I took the keys out of my purse. I unlocked the door, opened it, then picked up my pack and went in.

I made sure the door was locked.

Then I hauled the pack over to my closet, pushed my way through some hanging clothes, and set it down on the floor. There, it was basically out of sight. You could only spot it by squatting down low and peering in under the clothes. You couldn't spot it that way, either, after I'd shut the closet door.

Good enough.

I wasn't trying to hide the stuff from Sherlock Holmes. My only concern, just then, was Elroy.

Not that I had any intention of allowing him into my room. You can't be too careful, though. Elroy might seem harmless and easy to control, but guys like that will sometimes go nuts on you. I wanted my pack to be out of sight—out of mind—in case he flipped out and came barging in.

Or in case *I* went nuts and brought him in, myself.

Fat chance.

With the pack nicely hidden, I spent a minute or two inspecting my latest injuries. I found minor scrapes on my arms, shins and knees, but no new damage anywhere else—not even where the corner of Murphy's book had jabbed me in the belly. Nothing needed treatment.

I decided against changing any of my clothes.

In the bathroom, I took a few minutes to "freshen up." Which means I washed, brushed my hair and dabbed on a bit of Tropical Nights perfume.

I wouldn't be needing my purse, so I stuck it away inside a dresser drawer.

With nothing except my key case, I stepped outside. Elroy waved at me from a lounger beside the pool. I waved back, then made sure the door was locked before I started down the stairs.

I reached the bottom, still standing.

Elroy got to his feet as I walked over to him.

"Ready for the Happy Hour?" I asked.

"The sun's well over the yardarm," he said.

"Let's go in and concoct something. And I'll see what I can do about finding a couple of nice, thick steaks for dinner."

The sliding glass doors were all locked from inside, so I led Elroy around to the front of the house. Along the way, I kept watch for any telltale signs of Tony.

Everything looked fine.

I unlocked the front door and entered the house. Elroy stepped in after me. I shut the door.

The house felt hot and stuffy.

It was very silent.

I'd left all the curtains shut, so the rooms were filled with murky, yellow light.

"Hang on a second," I whispered. "I'll turn on the air conditioning."

As if nervous about being here, Elroy stayed in the foyer and looked around while I hurried down the hall to turn on the air.

I flicked the switch and heard the blower start.

The sound was good to hear. I hadn't liked that silence.

"Things'll cool off fast, now," I said, returning to the foyer.

"Are you sure it's all right for us to be here?"

"Sure I'm sure. I have the keys, don't I? Come on," I said, and headed for the kitchen. "What do you like to drink?"

"Oh, I don't know."

"How about margaritas?"

"Are we going to use *their* stuff?"

"Sure."

"Is it all right to do that?" he asked.

"Would I be doing it if it weren't?"

"Maybe. I don't know, would you?"

"Nope. Not me. I ain't no thief."

In the kitchen, I went straight for the cupboard where they kept the liquor. I opened it and took out a bottle of tequila.

"The deal is," I explained, "they like me to use their stuff when I'm staying here. They even stock up on my favorite foods and drinks and things. They want me to live it up. They're on vacation, and they want this to be like a vacation for me."

"Really?"

"Don't you believe me?"

"I just don't want to get into any trouble," he said.

"Relax. Everything's fine. What they don't know won't hurt them."

Elroy's face contorted. He blurted, "Oh, my God. I've gotta get out of here."

I burst out laughing.

"It's not funny. I'm leaving."

"I was *kidding!* It was a *joke.* The owners are my best friends. I've got the run of the place. You're not going to get into any trouble. If they walked in the door right now, they'd be delighted to find us here and they'd make the drinks *for* us."

"Honest?" Elroy asked.

"So help me."

After that, he seemed to be all right. He even helped me. Soon, we had a blender full of margarita. While Elroy salted the rims of our glasses, I studied the meat situation.

It came as no surprise.

Except for some hot dogs and salami in the refrigerator, everything else was frozen. The freezer compartment was full of goodies: steaks, pork chops, lamb chops, chicken breasts. But they were as solid as bricks.

"If you don't want grilled weenies," I explained, "we'll have to thaw out something."

"I thought we were having steaks."

"We still *can* have steaks."

"But they're frozen?"

"I'll just nuke 'em till they thaw."

"That'll be tasty."

"Well, we could thaw them out *naturally*, but that might take a few hours."

"I'm not in any hurry," he said, smiling and wiggling his eyebrows.

"Well, let's see how it goes." I opened the freezer compartment again. "We can have anything in here. Would you rather have lamb, or . . . ?"

"You promised me a steak."

For a guest, Elroy seemed awfully damn insistent.

"Then a steak you shall have," I told him, and took out a couple of T-bones.

What is it, anyway, with people and slabs of beef? Hey, I like the things, too. But I'm not wild for them. Steaks aren't the be-all and end-all. If you ask me, lamb and pork have more flavor. And chicken is usually more tender. Besides, steaks are tricky devils. If you don't cook them just right, they get all dry inside. And sometimes, for reasons I've never figured out, you cook up a perfectly good steak and it ends up tasting like liver. I just don't see what the infatuation is.

Anyway, I ripped the butcher paper off the T-bones. Serena was in the habit of freezing her meat in pairs, so the steaks were not only as solid as slabs of concrete, but also stuck together.

I didn't even try to part them.

Smiling at Elroy, I hammered the counter a couple of times and said, "Dinner will be a while."

"No problem," he said.

"These can at least marinate . . ."

"Marinate?"

"You know, maybe some teriyaki sauce."

"No. Perish the thought. Do you want to ruin them?"

Figures!

"Let's not marinate them," I suggested.

"Just a dab of salt and pepper before they go on the fire," Elroy said.

"Excellent. I'll let you take care of it."

Looking very pleased with himself, he said, "Happy to oblige." Then he turned away. He gave the blender a quick buzz that swirled the margarita concoction, whipped it to froth and sent it climbing the sides of the pitcher.

As he filled our glasses, he asked, "Do we have anything to nibble on?"

I thought of Murphy's pretzels.

"What would you like?"

"Tortilla chips, if you have them."

"I'll see if *Serena* has any," I said, and headed for the cupboard where she kept various bags of chips.

"Who is this Serena?"

"She owns the joint. She and her husband."

"Our out-of-town hosts?"

"Right."

"Let's see what they've got," he said, and joined me in front of the cupboard.

There were plenty of nibbles to choose from. Elroy decided on a bag of lightly salted, fat-free, taste-free corn tortilla chips.

"Shall we take it all outside and enjoy it by the pool?" I asked.

"Absolutely," Elroy said.

Carrying the bag of chips, I left the kitchen. Elroy followed with the drinks.

Wanting to avoid the den—I'd never gotten around to cleaning its glass door—I started across the living room. My plan was to open the drapes and let us out through the sliding door.

But along the way, striding by the fireplace, I turned my head to take a look at the saber.

What if it's wet?

What if it's dripping blood?

What if Elroy gets curious and takes a close look . . . ?

But I didn't need to worry about any of that.

The saber was gone.

44

ADAMANT ELROY

Yeah, I thought. Sure it's gone.

I looked away and kept moving.

Where'd I leave it? I wondered. In the den?

I opened the curtains, then stepped over to the sliding door. As I unlocked it, I recalled having the saber with me when I took my bath early that morning. Had I left it in the bathroom?

No.

I slid open the glass door.

Didn't leave it in the bathroom. Wanted everything back in place.

Could've sworn I hung it back over the fireplace.

I DID.

I remembered, now. After breakfast, I'd put the saber on its hooks where it belonged.

So where it is now?

Very quickly, I stepped outside. In my mind, I imagined myself letting out a squeal, flinging my sack of tortilla chips at the sky, and running like hell.

But I simply walked over to the table. From the other side,

I watched Elroy step out of the house, a margarita in each hand. He didn't have a hand to spare for closing the door, so I hurried over and rolled it shut.

Elroy placed the drinks on the table, then pulled out a chair for me. I thanked him and sat down, even though the chair put my back to the door.

He dragged one of the other chairs around the table, and sat down beside me. Then he handed me a margarita and took the other for himself. "Shall I propose a toast?" he suggested.

"Toast away."

"To you and me, and lucky encounters."

"Lucky, huh?"

You'd change your tune if you knew what was going on.

"It most certainly *was* lucky," he said.

"Maybe so," I muttered.

We clicked our glasses together, then drank.

Lowering his glass, Elroy said, "Imagine the odds against me just happening to drive by just the right place at just the right time . . . not to mention *recognizing* you. I call that lucky. I usually don't even pay attention to people on the sidewalks. For that matter, I wouldn't have *been* there if my wristwatch hadn't died on me this morning. It's not my usual route home. Our paths wouldn't have crossed at all except for the fact that I had to make a stop at the mall for a new watch battery."

"I was at the mall, myself."

"Ah! I should've known. We were only a few blocks away when I spotted you." He drank some more of his margarita, then asked, "Are you in the habit of walking to the mall and back? It's a good, long distance."

Nodding, I said, "About six miles each way. It's my chief form of exercise. I try to do it a couple of times a week."

"You certainly dress well for your hikes."

"Well, I like to look good at the mall."

"Aren't you at all . . . nervous about it?"

"About what?"

"Walking that far by yourself. There are so many psychos in this world."

"You're telling me."

"Doesn't it make you the least bit nervous?" Elroy asked.

"A little. But I don't let it stop me. Besides, I've been known to be dangerous, myself."

Elroy let out a laugh. "You can say that again." Then he tore open the bag of tortilla chips and turned it toward me.

I took a handful.

"It didn't occur to me until just this moment," he said, "but look at the irony we've just encountered. *You* fell down the stairs. You, who pushed Mr. Heflin down the stairs. Isn't that just marvelously ironic?"

"Oh, yeah. Marvelously." I popped a chip into my mouth and crunched down on it. It was thin and nearly tasteless.

Do you know what else would be marvelously ironic, Elroy? If our "lucky encounter" ends with both of us getting murdered by a saber-wielding maniac.

I drank some more of my margarita.

And wondered if I should warn him.

I wouldn't need to tell him the whole story, just explain that somebody must've broken into the house sometime today and stolen the saber.

And might be anywhere.

He'll say we should call the cops.

Obviously, that was out of the question.

So what can we do?

Flee.

"This is a *lovely* place," Elroy said. "It must be fabulous to live here."

"It's nice, all right."

"I should imagine that some of our furry friends must wander out of the woods now and again."

"Sure. We get all sorts of critters. Deer, raccoons, squirrels . . ."

Midnight swimmers.

"I'd love to see some deer come out," Elroy said.

"Stick around, there's no telling what you might see."

He leered at me. "Is that so?" he asked.

"You never know."

"Well, well."

"But you know what?"

"What?"

"I think we oughta go *out* for dinner tonight."

"Out? We are out."

"I mean like to a real restaurant."

"You're kidding."

"No, I'm serious. If we have to wait for those steaks to thaw out, we won't be eating till eight or nine. I just don't think I can wait that long. I'm already starving."

"Have some more nibbles."

"It'll be my treat. And you can pick the restaurant. Anywhere you like."

"I like it here. It's so peaceful and pleasant. Of course, I'm sure you're used to it. You live here. But I live in an apartment house. I don't have any lawn at all, much less a swimming pool and a beautiful *forest.* You want to take me away from all *this?* I can eat in a restaurant any old time."

"I'm not trying to cheat you out of the barbecue. Why don't we just postpone it till tomorrow. That way, I'll have time to prepare for it. We won't have to worry about frozen steaks. You can even come over early, and we'll make a day of it. How does that sound?"

"Lousy."

"Lousy?"

"You promised me cocktails and barbecued steaks by the swimming pool. Tonight, not tomorrow. If you'd said tomorrow in the first place, that'd be different. But you didn't, so you got me all set to *expect* it. We can go to a restaurant tomorrow, if you want. But tonight, I want my barbecued steak like you promised."

"When I made the promise," I said, "I counted on being able to thaw the steaks in the microwave."

"Well, you can't do that. They'd be ruined."

"But it was my plan. You can't hold me to a promise if you won't let me follow my plan."

"Why not?"

"It isn't fair."

"It isn't fair of *you* to promise me a barbecued steak by your swimming pool, and get me out here, and then say, 'Oh, dear, I don't want to do this, after all. Let's go to a *restaurant.*'"

"I'm starting to think I don't want to eat with you at all."

"Oh, isn't that just dandy?"

"I'm trying to be reasonable, Elroy, but . . ."

"It's either your way or the highway, is that it?"

"I just think you should cut me a little slack, that's all. This barbecue thing isn't working out, so let's do it another time. For tonight, why don't we just try to make the best of things and go to a restaurant?"

Elroy let out a deep sigh. Then he raised his glass and drained it. Staring into his empty glass, he muttered, "You said it'd be okay to wait for them to thaw. Remember? In the kitchen? We talked about the fact that it'd take a few hours, and you said it wouldn't be a problem. Only now it *is* a problem. Why do you suppose that is?"

"I never said it wouldn't be a problem."

"Maybe not in so many words. But you were all ready to go along with it. You even wanted to marinate them."

"I can still *get* steak teryaki if we go to a restaurant."

He narrowed his eyes at me. "Is that what this is all about? Because I wouldn't let you ruin the steaks with teryaki sauce?"

"No, of course not."

"Then what *is* it about? Why have you suddenly *turned* on me?"

I stared into his eyes.

"I haven't turned on you, Elroy. Though I do think you have a cruddy attitude about all this."

"You promised me, and now you want to take it away."

"There's something going on here that you don't know about."

With a wary look in his eyes, he said, "Such as?"

Don't tell him!

"Somebody was here," I said.

"What do you mean?"

Leaning over close to him, I said quietly, "I think someone might've broken into the house while I was gone. There's supposed to be a Civil War saber hanging above the fireplace. It was there when I left to go to the mall this afternoon. Now, it's gone."

"You're kidding, right?"

"Take a look for yourself. You don't even have to get up."

Twisting in his seat, he peered over his shoulder.

I took a sip of my margarita.

"And where is this saber supposed to be?" Elroy asked.

"You see the fireplace?"

"Yeah."

"There's a framed citation above it?"

"I see that."

"That's where the saber is supposed to be, but isn't. I think somebody must've broken into the house and taken it."

"Hmm."

"For all I know, he might still be in the house. Hiding somewhere. Maybe just waiting for a chance to jump us. That's why I think we oughta get out of here."

Elroy turned toward me. "Instead of running off to a restaurant, shouldn't we call the police?"

"No!"

He smirked slightly. "And why not?"

"Because."

"Excellent reason."

"Because if he's already gone," I said, "the cops won't do any good, anyway. If he's *not* gone . . . well, all the phones are inside the house. I don't want to get chopped up trying to call the cops, do you?"

Elroy's smirk grew. "Don't you have a telephone in your suite above the garage?"

Damn it!

I gave the matter some thought, then said, "Yes, but I can't get to it without my keys. Which I left on the kitchen counter."

"Ah, you have an answer for everything."

"I'm telling you the truth about this, Elroy."

"I'm sure you are."

"You think I'm lying."

"Far be it from me to call you a liar."

"Well, thank you one hell of a lot for believing in me."

"I tell you what," he said. "Just to prove how much I believe in you, I'll go inside, myself, and make the call to the police."

With that, he scooted back his chair.

Grabbing his arm, I said, "Don't you dare."

"Ha! I knew it."

"Okay," I said. "I admit it."

"You admit what?"

He hadn't believed me, anyway. Some people just don't listen, even when you're trying to help them.

"There never was any saber," I said. "I made up the whole business about the break-in."

"Surprise, surprise."

"I just wanted to go to a restaurant, that's all."

He gave my shoulder a squeeze and said, "Maybe tomorrow night." His hand tightened its grip. "But from now on, no more stories. Save them for your books."

"Okay. I'm sorry."

"No harm, no foul," he said, and released my shoulder. "Looks like we can both use refills." Rising to his feet, he said, "Why don't I bring out the whole pitcher?"

"Good idea. And while you're in there, see if you can pry the steaks apart. They'll thaw out a lot faster that way."

"Your wish is my command, my dear."

"Oh, and would you mind bringing out my keys? They should be on the counter near the blender."

"My pleasure." Grinning, he said, "Now, are you *sure* you wouldn't like me to go ahead and dial up the cops?"

"That won't be necessary."

"Thought not," he said, and stepped out of sight behind me.

I heard him slide open the door and enter the house. But I didn't hear the door shut, so I got out of my chair to do it, myself.

As I rolled it shut, I saw Elroy striding across the living room. He didn't so much as glance at the place above the fireplace where the saber should've been.

If he'd bothered to take a close look, he would've seen the hooks.

He could've at least looked, the bastard.

So damn sure of himself.

So damn sure that I'm a liar.

"The hell with him," I muttered.

But I was afraid of what I might see if I kept peering in through the glass door, so I turned away from it.

I strolled over to the side of the pool.

The early evening sun made the surface of the water glare and flash. Even with my sunglasses on, I had to squint. A warm breeze was blowing. It stirred softly against my face and arms, and drifted my skirt against the fronts of my legs. I felt a bead of sweat dribble down my spine.

Elroy'll be fine, I told myself.

45

WHERE IS ELROY?

Or maybe not.

As the minutes went by, I kept expecting to hear the door slide open. But no sounds came from the house.

What's he doing in there?

Playing games, probably.

Payback games. He's staying inside, wasting time, trying to scare me.

I turned my back to the pool and stared at the living-room door. From where I was standing, though, the glass reflected too much. I could barely make out any details of the dim room.

I should probably just go in and see what's keeping him.

Yeah, sure, I thought. That's what he *wants* me to do. So he can jump out and scare the . . .

What if he's dead?

He isn't dead, I told myself. Whoever took the saber is probably long gone. You don't rob a house, then stick around. You get out as fast as you can.

Unless maybe it's not just a robbery.

Maybe the whole idea is to use the sword on me.

Who would want to do that? I wondered.

Judy. She got away, somehow, and now she wants revenge.

But she couldn't possibly know where I live. She knew nothing about me, certainly not my address or my real name.

Maybe my midnight swimmer came back for another try at me.

Get real, I told myself. A guy like that isn't going to show up in daylight. Or any other time, probably, since he had to figure I'd called the cops on him.

Somebody took the sword.

Probably.

But maybe not. Even though I had a specific memory of hanging it back up—had I taken it down again for some reason?

Maybe I'd done it while concentrating on something else. That sort of thing happens to me, sometimes. I suppose it happens to everyone. Haven't you ever, say, started off on a trip but then wanted to turn back because you couldn't recall turning off the stove or locking the front door? Even though you figure you *must've* done it (and you're right), you just cannot remember the act, no matter how hard you try?

It might've been that way with the saber.

Instead of getting all bent out of shape when I saw that it was gone, I should've made a quick search of the house. Maybe I would've found it in the den or bedroom or kitchen—exactly where I'd left it—and saved myself all this worry.

Why not do that now?

Staring at the shut door, I shook my head. This was about as close to the house as I wanted to get.

If Elroy comes out, maybe I'll go in for a look around.

If?

He'll come out, I told myself. Just let him get tired of his little game. He'll quit as soon as he realizes I'm not going to fall for it.

Never should've let him go in there. If he's dead, it'll be my fault.

No, it won't. I told him the truth, and he laughed at me. It'll be his own damn fault.

Anyway, he's fine. Probably wondering, right now, why I haven't come in to look for him yet.

Get used to it, creepazoid. I'm not coming in. You can wait till hell freezes over and our steaks thaw out, I'm staying right here.

Even as I thought that, I realized that it might be a very long wait. Elroy had already shown himself to be childish, stubborn, and inconsiderate. A guy like that would be very slow to quit.

I didn't exactly want to go on waiting.

For one thing, his absence made me nervous; I just couldn't help fearing foul play, even though I knew the odds were against it.

For another, I wanted my margarita refill.

"I'll get you out of there," I muttered.

Then I turned away and walked alongside the pool. I rounded the corner. Stopping near the diving board, I turned to face the house again. The entire rear of it seemed to be glass. I couldn't see in. But Elroy could see out, if he wanted to. At least from the living room, where the curtains weren't shut. Other places, too, if he peeked through gaps at the edges of the curtains.

"Elroy!" I called.

But only once. With the house shut up tightly and the air conditioner on, he probably couldn't hear anything from outside.

Speaking quietly, to myself really, I said, "Come out, come out, wherever you are."

Then I started to undo the buttons of my blouse. I began at the top and worked my way slowly downward. Even though I took my sweet time, I didn't ham it up with any of that stripper stuff you see in the movies. That would've been too silly and embarrassing. I don't mind taking off my clothes, but I'm not going to act like a dork about it.

I slipped my blouse off. I didn't swing it around overhead,

though, and give it a fling. I just dropped it to the concrete at my feet, then unfastened the couple of buttons at my hip and let my skirt fall.

Without looking down, I knew that I was pretty scratched and bruised. But I also knew that there was a lot more to look at than my injuries. My eyepatch panties didn't leave much to the imagination, and neither did my translucent red bra.

Balancing on one foot, then the other, I pulled off my shoes and socks.

Over at the house, there was still no sign of Elroy. The door remained shut.

I took off my sunglasses, crouched, and set them on my skirt. Then I stepped onto the diving board. I walked out slowly over the water. The board bounced a little with each stride. When I reached the end, I stopped moving and the board settled down.

Still, I didn't like standing up there. It was like being perched on a ledge. The slightest loss of balance, and I'd fall.

With my record for falling . . .

This time, at least, I would have a swimming pool underneath me.

I was tempted to go ahead and dive in while I still had control.

Not yet. Just wait. He's gotta see me up here. That's the whole point.

So I stayed put, and turned my head to look at the house. Which upset my balance. Not much, but enough to make me start to tilt. I faced forward quickly, bending my knees and spreading my arms. It was iffy for a second or two, but I managed to get steady again.

After that, I knew better than to turn my head.

I also knew it was only a matter of time before I fell off the diving board.

Are you watching, Elroy? Come on out!

Apparently, he hadn't seen me yet, or he would be hot-footing it out for a closer look.

Maybe he can't see me.

He's down on the floor, dead.

Or maybe he's watching me, all right, but afraid to come out.

Or maybe he's got his face pressed to the glass, somewhere, and he's gazing out at me, spellbound, frantic to watch and see what I do next.

I thought about taking off my bra. *That* would sure give him something to see. But I suddenly pictured Elroy naked and squirming against the glass door, just like the guy last night. Then he *became* the guy last night.

Enough of this nonsense.

I kept my bra on, raised my arms high overhead, bent my knees and sprang off the board.

I'm not much of a diver. I'm not much of an athlete of any kind, really. But I knew I had to be looking pretty good. Even with the worst diving form in the world—and mine wasn't that bad—Elroy had to be drooling and erect watching me. *If* he was watching.

You better be watching, damn it.

I hit the water and went in cleanly and deep. It felt frigid, but only for a couple of seconds. After the first shock had passed, it felt okay. And then it felt just fine, cool and smooth, as I glided along below the surface. When I started to lose power from the dive, I swam underwater until I came to the shallow end of the pool. Then I stood up and turned toward the house.

And found myself looking at the den door.

First, I noticed the pale streaks down the glass.

Then I noticed a gap about ten or twelve inches wide at the door's edge.

It's open!

I hadn't done *that!* I might've misplaced the saber—though I doubted it—but no way on earth had I left the den door unlocked and open.

I hadn't left the curtains open, either.

But they were open now. In spite of the reflections on the glass, I could make out a few vague images inside the den.

Not much, but enough to tell me that someone had opened the curtains.

Elroy must've done it.

Maybe he'd decided to give the house an inspection—just to make sure there really wasn't an intruder. Along the way, he might've opened some curtains, opened the den door . . .

It hardly seemed likely, though.

He wouldn't go around looking for intruders or signs of a break-in. Not Elroy. He hadn't even looked to see if there were any hooks above the fireplace.

I suddenly knew the answer.

He did it as part of his plan to freak me out.

The bastard sure holds a grudge.

Or maybe he's just doing it to amuse himself. Doesn't mean to really scare me. Sees it as nothing more than a fun diversion, like hide 'n seek. A game to help pass the time while the steaks are thawing.

I called out, "Very funny, Elroy. I know what you're doing, and I'm not falling for it. Why don't you stop screwing around and come out?"

No answer came.

Frankly, I didn't expect one.

But I hoped.

"I know you're in the den, watching me."

I knew no such thing.

I only hoped.

Please, let it be a dumb game he's playing.

It has to be.

"I tell you what, Elroy." My voice was shaking. "I'll count to three. If you come out before I reach three, I'll take my bra off for you. Hell, I'll throw it to you. But only if you come out by the time I count to three. One."

Nothing.

I went ahead and reached behind my back, anyway, to show him I meant business.

"Two."

Nothing.

"Time's running out. This'll be your only chance, Elroy. If you don't pop your head out of that doorway in one second . . ."

It didn't pop out.

It rolled.

46

REUNION

Unfortunately, the rest of Elroy wasn't attached.

His head tumbled out of the den like a lopsided, mutant bowling ball, did a little hop over the door's threshold, then dropped to the concrete outside. As it dropped, his tongue was sticking out. The concrete clipped him on the chin, and he bit his tongue nearly off. It hung by a string of flesh as his head rolled a crooked course toward the pool—toward me.

He seemed to glance at me each time his face came up.

The stump of his neck flung blood through the air.

His tongue came off.

He bounced and rolled all the way to the pool. By the time he reached its edge, his nose was flat and his front upper teeth were broken out. He gave me a quick, awful grin, then sailed off the edge and plopped into the water about a yard in front of me.

The water went pink around his sinking head.

I waded backward as fast as I could.

Elroy's head seemed to pursue me.

But I stopped paying attention to it when the den door rumbled open.

Out stepped my midnight swimmer.

He held the saber in his right hand.

He wore nothing but shorts. From face to feet, he was spattered with blood. Except for his left arm, which was *sleeved* with it.

Somewhere in Serena and Charlie's house, he must've made an *awful* mess.

If he kills me, I thought, at least I won't have to worry about cleaning it up.

(You think odd stuff at times like that.)

He walked straight to the edge of the pool, then stopped and rested the point of the sword on the concrete beside his bare foot.

"Hello again," he said. He seemed serious, but calm.

I didn't say anything. I was having trouble breathing. Then I flinched as something brushed against the side of my right leg.

"You must've known I'd come back for you."

I took a step backward to get away from Elroy's head.

"Don't. Don't try to get away from me. You *can't* get away from me. I'm way too fast for you. And today, I'm the one with the sword. I could kill you in the blink of an eye. Or slice off small parts of you here and there. You don't want me to do that, do you?"

I shook my head.

"You be my good girl, then."

I nodded.

"Don't move," he said, then raised the saber, stepped off the edge, and dropped into the pool. As water splashed up around him, I took a single step backward. He didn't seem to notice. But he waded closer to me, and I didn't dare move away from him again. "You're very lucky to have a pool," he said. "I wish I had one."

Lowering his sword, he crouched down until the water covered his shoulders. Then he swished his left arm around, apparently trying to wash the blood off, and the water around it went pink.

"Your name is Alice, right?" he asked.

(Of course, he didn't say Alice. He said my real name, which is my secret.)

"How do you know?" I asked.

"I've heard." He dunked his head.

I thought about making a break.

Before I could decide, his head came up, hair matted flat, water running down his face. With his left hand, which wasn't bloody anymore, he rubbed his face.

"I'm Steve," he said.

"I'm charmed," I said.

He smiled. "Glad to hear it."

"That's sarcasm, Stevie."

His left hand smacked me hard across the face, burning my cheek and knocking my head sideways. My eyes filled with tears.

"That wasn't very nice," I said.

"Depends which side you're on."

"From this side, it sucked."

"If you didn't like it, you'd better learn how to behave."

"Consider me taught," I said.

He grabbed me through the front of my bra, squeezed my nipple and lifted. Both my hands were free. I didn't try to fight him, though. Wincing, I went up on tiptoes and kept my hands down by my sides. Instead of begging him to stop, I hissed through my teeth and glared at him.

"Here's what we're going to do," he said, keeping his grip. "We're going to climb out of the pool, then have ourselves a nice party. Margaritas and barbecued steaks. You have my permission to marinate them. Say thank you."

"Thank you," I gasped.

"This could be a very pleasant experience for both of us."

"I bet."

He pinched me.

I flinched and tears ran down my face.

"You made me do that, Alice. And I *enjoyed* doing it. Did you enjoy it?"

"No."

"Then why did you make me do it?"

"I don't know."

"Would you like me to do it again?"

"No."

"I can even do worse. Much worse."

"You don't have to. I'll be good. I promise."

"You'll be my good girl?"

"Yes."

"My sweetheart?"

"Yes."

"Cross your heart and hope to die?"

"Yes."

He pinched me again. I jerked rigid with the pain, and cried out. He squeezed even harder. Writhing, I arched my spine and threw back my head. Tears spilled down my face.

And I felt his tongue.

Even as he kept pinching me, he licked the tears off my cheeks.

Finally, he let go of my nipple. He put his arm around my back and I sagged against him, sobbing. His hand caressed my back gently.

I thought about taking a bite out of his neck.

I could probably kill him if I did it well.

But he had the sword underwater in his right hand. Even mortally wounded, he could kill me with it in an instant.

Just wait, I told myself. Do everything he says. Be his good girl, his sweetheart, his slave, his whore, his anything-he-wants-me-to-be.

Sooner or later, I'll get him.

I'll get him good.

He doesn't know who he's dealing with.

Hasn't got a clue.

But he'll find out the hard way.

His hand slid down below the waistband of my panties, and gave my bare buttock a squeeze. "So," he said, "are we ready to enjoy our party?"

"I'm ready," I said.

I must've said it okay, because he didn't hurt me.

"Let's climb out of the pool," he said. "You go first. I'll be right behind you. Do everything I tell you to—without hesitation or wisecracks—and we'll have ourselves a merry time. I might even allow you to live."

He let go of me, then stepped out of my way and gestured for me to step past him.

As I waded, I looked for Elroy's head.

I spotted it a couple of yards to my left, hovering just above the tile bottom of the pool, staring straight up as if he were trying to figure the best way of reaching the surface.

Poor bastard.

He'd been a schmuck, but he didn't deserve this.

I glared at Steve, but kept my mouth shut and waded on past him. At the wall of the pool, I braced myself with both hands and boosted myself up.

Steve swatted me across the ass with the saber.

Crying out, I flung myself over the edge and scurried to my feet. I hobbled away from the pool, clutching my buttocks. They felt as if they'd been lashed, but not slashed. There was no cut. He must've used the flat side of the blade.

"Looks count, too," he informed me.

When I turned around, he was just standing up.

I kept rubbing my butt.

"You didn't have to kill him," I said.

"That's a good one, coming from you."

I gaped at him. "What're you talking about?"

"You can't play innocent with me, honey. I saw what you did last night."

"What I did?"

"You're about as cold-blooded as they come." He smirked. "Maybe that's why I find myself so strangely attracted to you. Let's go inside, now. Take me to the kitchen."

I turned around and saw the trail of blood leading to the den's open door. "Okay if we go in the other way?" I asked.

"Suit yourself."

"May I please get dressed?" I asked.

"You may not. I like you just the way you are. Let's go."

I led the way alongside the house, stepped behind the table and chairs, and slid open the living-room door. Steve followed me into the house.

Glancing over my shoulder, I asked, "What do you think you saw me do last night?"

"I saw what you *did* do. Involving the sword and a certain unlucky young man who came to your door."

"I thought he was you."

"Isn't *that* a fine how-do-you-do?"

"Well, you had me scared."

Entering the kitchen, I expected to find Elroy's headless body on the floor. But it wasn't there. Nor did I see any blood or signs of a struggle.

"Go ahead and marinate the steaks," Steve said. "I know you prefer them that way."

"You were spying on us?" I asked, heading for the cupboard where Serena kept her sauces.

"You might say that."

"Where were you?"

"Trade secret."

I took down the bottle of teryaki, found a platter, and stepped over to the counter where I'd left the steaks. I tried to pry them apart, but they were still frozen together. "Can you get them apart?" I asked Steve.

"They'll come apart in the natural course of time."

"Thanks."

"That comes perilously close to a wisecrack."

"I'm sorry. I didn't mean it to sound that way."

"Better watch yourself."

"I will," I said. I placed the steaks on the platter, drenched them with teryaki sauce, picked them up rubbed them with both hands to make sure they were wet everywhere, then put them back into the platter.

My hands were dripping with the spicy brown liquid. As I

turned toward the sink, Steve said, "Wait. I'll lick them clean."

So I held out both my hands, fingers open and spread. Steve licked and sucked them.

It seemed like a weird thing to do—like licking my tears off. But I've got to admit, it felt pretty good. Especially when he sucked each one of my fingers all the way into his mouth. In other circumstances, it might've been a real turn-on. For instance, if someone like Murphy had been doing it to me. With Steve, I was too scared to enjoy it very much.

I had a big worry, for one thing, that he might bite one of my fingers off.

For another, I figured he had terrible plans for me, for later on.

As the last finger slurped out of his mouth, he smiled and said, "Yummy. You're delicious."

I almost said, *"Eat me,"* but stopped myself in the nick of time.

Instead, I said, "Thanks."

"Now you may go ahead and wash your hands, if you like."

I turned to the sink. I used soap and hot water on them. While I was drying my hands on a dish towel, Steve buzzed the blender a few times.

Then he said, "Get me out a clean glass. I wouldn't want to use Elroy's. Might catch something."

"Like what?"

"I wouldn't know. But he must've been gravely ill. He's dead, isn't he?"

Hilarious, I thought.

Keeping my mouth shut, I took down a clean glass for Steve. He lifted the pitcher of frothy margarita off the blender.

"Do you want salt on your rim?" I asked.

"I take my rims without."

"Healthier that way."

He chuckled. "Do you really suppose I'm worried about my *health?* With my lifestyle, I'm looking forward to a lethal injection—or perhaps a bullet—but certainly not hardening of the arteries."

"And what lifestyle is that?"

"I like to think of myself as a 'thrill-killer.' "

"Charming," I muttered.

"Now, march," he said.

"Where?"

"Out to the table. It's time for the Happy Hour."

I stepped past him and left the kitchen. On our way across the living room, I asked, "Did you get a thrill out of killing Elroy?"

"Not particularly, though it was amusing. I killed him because he was an obstacle in the way of you."

"Where is he?"

"Here and there."

"I know where his head is," I pointed out. "Where's the rest of him?"

"Already worrying about clean-up?"

"I just want to know."

"He's in the guest bathroom."

"You killed him in the bathroom?"

"Standing at the toilet, as a matter of fact. Took him completely by surprise. I'm afraid his aim got thrown off when he lost his head. Pissed all over the place. But he finally fell into the tub. Would you like to see?"

"No thanks."

47

THE HAPPY HOUR

"Remarkable woman," Steve said as he filled my glass from the pitcher.

"Who is?"

"You, of course."

"What do you know about it?" I said.

He poured margarita into his own glass, then placed the pitcher on the table. "More than you might think," he said. Before sitting down, he moved his chair around to the other side of the table.

He lowered the saber and leaned it against the side of his left thigh. Probably so he could go for it quickly with his right hand by reaching across his lap. The sword version of a cross-draw.

"I've been watching you," he said, and took a sip. "Very good margarita."

"Yeah."

"You're a fine figure of a woman."

"So I've heard."

"And extremely dangerous."

I smiled sweetly.

"I've never run into a woman like you before. And, I must say, neither had Milo."

"*Milo?*"

"Alas, poor Milo. We were partners, you know. Well, not exactly partners. Let's say Milo was my mentor. Until you killed him."

"Killed him? I don't know what you're talking about."

"Oh, please," he said. Fortunately, he seemed amused, not angry. "Spare me the innocent routine. I saw you do it."

"Where?" I asked.

"Where do you think? At our camp in the woods."

"You were *there*?"

"Oh, yes."

"You must really get around," I said.

A smile spread over his face. "I do, I do. It's my specialty. Getting around. Coming and going. In a most sneaky fashion."

"You weren't very sneaky last night in the pool."

"That doesn't count. I *wanted* you to see me."

"Sure you did."

"Watch out, you're treading close to sarcasm. I may have to hurt you."

"You're going to kill me, anyway."

"That remains to be seen."

"Sure."

He leaned forward slightly in his chair, and something gouged my leg.

"Ow!" I scooted back my chair and looked down. On the side of my left calf, I now had a small, crescent-shaped wound. Made, probably, by the nail of Steve's big toe.

"Real nice," I said.

"Be my good girl and these things won't happen."

"I'm trying."

"Not hard enough. When I tell you something, accept it."

"Okay. I'm sorry. I was *supposed* to see you last night."

"That's right. You *only* see me when you're supposed to."

"Okay."

Grinning, he said, "Do you know that I spied on you yesterday afternoon?"

"No. Did you?"

"Absolutely. For a couple of hours. And you were completely unaware of my presence."

"But I'm sure you were there."

His eyes narrowed.

"Sorry," I said.

"You were sunning yourself by the pool," he said. "A vision. That's when I decided I must have you." He frowned. "Not me so much as Milo, actually."

"You wanted me for *him?* That fat, disgusting slob?"

"He always got firsties. That was our arrangement. I would've gotten you after he was done."

"That's disgusting."

"Cheer up. He won't get firsties anymore, thanks to you."

"Good."

"I could almost feel sorry for him. He was very much looking forward to you."

"Is that so? Was he here, too?"

"Oh, no. I discovered you all on my own."

"Where was Milo?"

"Back at camp with Marilyn."

Marilyn? Must've been the dead woman in Milo's tent.

The woman he'd been eating.

Had Steve been at her, too? I didn't want to think about it. "If Milo was at the camp," I said, "how could he be looking forward to me?"

"Oh, I went back and told him all about you. And, of course, I showed him the photos."

"*What* photos?"

"I took Polaroids of you."

"You're kidding."

"Not in the least. I always take snapshots of our special gals." Grinning, he said, "Before *and* after."

"After?"

"You know."

"Jeez."

"We have quite a striking collection, really. We? Hum. It's just me, now. I'm going to miss that big galoot. There may be lonely times ahead." He drank some more of his margarita.

"So you not only spied on me yesterday afternoon, you also took pictures of me?"

"Exactly. I got several excellent shots, too. Close-ups. For a few of them, I was *this* close to you."

"How close?"

"As close as I am now."

Three feet? "No way," I said.

"Oh, yes way. I'm very good at sneaking about."

"Those cameras are noisy."

"I didn't say you were awake at the time. Let me tell you, your snoring was considerably louder than the camera. You were asleep right *there*," he said, and pointed at the nearby padded lounger where I'd napped, off and on, through much of yesterday afternoon. "When you weren't asleep," he said, "you were drinking Bloody Marys, reading a John D. MacDonald book called *A Tan and Sandy Silence*, and . . ."

"Okay, I get the picture. You were here."

"You interrupted me."

"I'm sorry. Go ahead."

"I was about done, anyway."

"What else did you do while I was asleep?"

"Nothing."

"You didn't . . . touch me at all?"

"I was tempted. You looked absolutely scrumptious. As you do now. But you might've woken up. Anyway, it was my job to reconnoiter, not enjoy. Scout, and return with my findings to Milo."

"So after you took those Polaroids of me, you ran back to camp and showed them to Milo?"

"He was enthralled. We're rarely lucky enough to get our hands on anyone as . . . attractive as you."

"So then what happened?" I asked. "After you showed him the photos?"

"Plenty. But I'm sure you don't want to hear about that. You want to know about my return last night."

"Tell me about it."

"Well, we decided that Milo would stay in camp to keep the home fires burning, and I would pay you a visit shortly after midnight."

"Which is when I saw you."

"I *let* you see me."

"Okay."

"I knew you were watching. That's why I took off my shorts."

"Uh-huh."

"I was hoping to lure you out."

"*What?*"

"Lure you out."

"You're kidding. You thought I'd come out if you stripped for me?"

"Oh, it's a tried-and-true technique." He grinned. "In fact, you were pulling much the same stunt in order to lure Elroy out of the house just a few minutes ago."

"That was different."

"Oh, really?"

"For one thing, I wasn't some stranger. For another, guys are crazy about breasts. It doesn't work the other way around."

"It doesn't? I must say, that comes as a surprise to me. In my own experience, the stripping routine rarely fails. Of course, I don't always get completely naked. That depends on the woman. But I often let myself be seen in various stages of undress. I'm just there, keeping my distance, pretty much minding my own business, as if I've shown up by accident. And I allow them to watch me, to spy on me. The longer they watch me, the more intrigued—and aroused— they become. It works most of the time."

"You're kidding."

"Not at all. It's so easy. I don't have to break in and catch my victims, they come to me. More often than not. But you have to realize, I've already checked them out. They're always women. Always alone. In some cases, it's obvious that they're . . . hungry for romance. You, for instance."

Feeling myself blush, I said, "You had that wrong."

"Did I?"

"You'd better believe it."

"I *don't* believe it. It would've been obvious to anyone who saw you by the pool yesterday. That bikini you had on, the way you rubbed the suntan oil on your body, the way you sprawled on the lounger . . . you wanted *hands* on you. You wanted a man all over you and in you."

"Wrong," I said, and squirmed a little.

"I told Milo, 'This gal's as hot to trot as they come. I might not be able to keep her off me.' So, I must say, it came as a shock to find you calling the cops."

"Couldn't have been *much* of a shock, the way you started humping the door."

He looked confused for a moment, then grinned. "Oh, that," he said. "Afraid I couldn't help it. You looked so . . . ravishing. You were wearing that silk robe. And your breast was out, you know."

"Not on purpose."

"Perhaps not."

"No perhaps about it. It was an accident."

"Are there any such things as accidents? Freud, I believe, said no."

"Fuck Freud," I said.

Chuckling softly, Steve lowered his eyes from my face to my breasts.

"Let me see them now," he said. "Take off the bra."

I gave some thought to refusing. But he would've hurt me. Besides, my bra was wet from the pool and not exactly comfortable. Also, it was a warm night with a soft breeze.

On top of all that, he had the saber. If he wanted my bra off, it would come off whether I refused or not.

I went ahead and took it off and dropped it to the concrete beside my chair.

"How's that?" I asked.

"Spectacular."

I picked up my glass, finished the remains of my margarita, and set it down on the table. Standing up, Steve gave me a refill from the pitcher.

When he was seated again, I said, "I wasn't really calling the police, you know."

"Is that so?"

"I just wanted you to think I was. It was a wrong number. Somebody called the house by mistake. But you had no way of knowing that. For all you could tell, it was me calling 911. I even turned on the light to make sure you would see me."

"What a gal. Gorgeous, tough, *and* tricky."

"Obviously, not tricky enough. Or as tricky as you. You didn't really go away, did you? You just wanted me to *think* I'd scared you off."

"That's right. I ran off into the woods, but then I circled back."

"Weren't you afraid the cops might show up?"

"Not in the least. If they'd come, I simply would've disappeared into the woods. I'm very good at disappearing." He took a sip of his drink, then looked at me. First at my breasts, then at my face. Then he said, "So who *did* show up?"

"You don't know?"

He raised his eyebrows.

"Not as smart as you think you are," I said.

He lurched forward over the table and his hand flew out and slapped me across the face. Then, smiling mildly, he settled back in his chair and asked, "So, who *did* show up?"

I rubbed my cheek and said, "A guy named Tony. I didn't even know him. He was the one who'd called. I'd told him about you on the phone, and I guess he decided to come over and protect me. I *guess* that's what he had in mind. He never told me anything."

"He came to save you from me, and you smote him with your sword."

"I suppose you saw that."

"Sure did. I saw everything, from the moment you opened the front door till you drove away with his pieces. It was a rather amazing spectacle." Shaking his head, Steve said, "I could hardly believe my eyes when you started to dismember him. It seemed—so over the top."

"He was too heavy, that's all. It was the only way I could get him into the trunk."

"I was awestruck. And rather smitten with you, I must admit. Not only was your behavior truly extraordinary, but you were stark naked much of the time. A sight to behold." With a grin, he asked, "Were you naked by accident?"

"I didn't want to get everything bloody, that's all."

"Well, I thank you. It was magnificent to watch you at work, all bare and sweaty. God, how I *wanted* you!"

"So, how come you didn't jump me?"

"Oh, that would've interrupted your show. I wanted to see it through to the finish." With a small laugh, he said, "I *will* be lucky enough to catch the end, though. I'll be a *participant* in it. But I regret missing some of the middle parts. I wanted so badly to follow you when you drove away with poor Tony in pieces in your trunk."

"What did you do, go running back to the woods to tell Milo all about it, show him some more photos?"

"I didn't have the camera. It's no good at night. The flash would give me away. No, I stayed at the house. I wanted to be there when you came back. So I waited and waited. I waited an awfully long time. It was just an agony, the waiting, because I longed for you so much. Finally, I decided to call it a night, and try again tomorrow. So I bid your house a fond farewell and hiked back through the woods to our campsite . . . and who should I find there but *you*? *YOU*, my splendid savage, in the very midst of a life and death struggle with my dear demented friend, Milo!"

"And you did nothing but hide and watch?"

"It was a splendid show. All of it."

"You just . . . let me go ahead and kill him?"

"Certainly."

"Why didn't you try to save him?"

"Oh, I don't know." He shrugged. "Why, oh why? Perhaps because you might've killed me? You had that pistol. I've never much fancied the notion of being shot. I certainly didn't want to risk a bullet for Milo's sake. I'd grown weary of him. He was so bossy. And he always had to have firsties. One gets tired of sloppy seconds."

A thoughtful look on his face, Steve said, "I suppose I was pulling for you to win. That would be a reason for not trying to save Milo, wouldn't it? Also, I was enjoying the show too much to join in. There's nothing like a good fight, especially when a woman is involved. Especially when the woman is you.

"And then, after slaying Milo, you enthralled me with your bizarre treatment of Judy."

"You watched everything?"

"And *heard* most of everything. It was wonderful."

"And then what happened? When I left. Did you follow me then?"

"Ah, no. I gave it some thought, but . . . I was exhausted by then. So I let you go away, figuring I would stay at camp and take care of loose ends and save you for another day." With a languid smile, he added, "A day like today."

"What about Judy?" I asked.

"What about her?"

"What did you do to her?"

"Let me put it this way, darling. I cut her down."

48

BODY HEAT

Steve stuck a tortilla chip into his mouth and crunched it.

"Uck. These are terrible."

"They're healthy chips," I pointed out. "Low fat, cholesterol free, salt free."

"Taste like paper." He took a long drink of margarita to wash the chip down. Then he said, "Are you starving? I'm starving. Why don't we go ahead and barbecue those steaks?"

"They're probably still frozen."

"Let's have a look."

"Fine with me."

Steve and I got up from the table. Holding the saber in his right hand, he followed me into the house. At the kitchen counter, I lifted the T-bones out of the teryaki sauce. They were wet and slippery, and still stuck together. With Steve beside me and leaning forward to watch, I dug my fingertips into the edges where the two steaks met, and pulled hard. Suddenly, they came apart with a sound like ripping cloth.

"Bravo!" Steve said.

I set them down on the platter. "They're still awfully frozen, but . . ."

"I'll thaw them out," Steve said. Taking me by the arm, he turned me toward him. Then, using both hands, he lifted the dripping steaks off the platter and pushed them against my breasts.

I gasped and flinched with their frigid touch.

"This'll warm them up fast," he said, grinning.

"Come on," I said. "Quit it."

"Nothing like body heat for thawing out steaks."

"Please."

"Don't make me hurt you," he warned.

I almost grabbed his wrists, but stopped myself in time.

I *did* back away from him. He came after me, though, grinning and rubbing me with the steaks. Before I got far, my retreat was stopped by a turn in the counter. Steve cornered me and slid the steaks all over my breasts. They felt like slabs of ice. They made my skin burn. My nipples were rigid and aching. My breasts dripped with teryaki sauce, and dribbles ran down my belly.

Finally, he tossed the steaks onto the counter. They thunked the tile surface and skidded a few inches.

Clutching my sides with his wet hands, he crouched in front of me and started to clean the sauce off me with his mouth. First, he licked the dribbles off my belly. Then he slid his tongue over my breasts. He licked and sucked.

After the frigid beef, the heat of his mouth felt good.

It all felt good, especially what he was doing to my nipples with his tongue and lips.

But I worried about his teeth.

What's to stop him from biting me?

What's to stop him from eating me?

His buddy, Milo, ate Marilyn.

Maybe they both did.

I clutched Steve's shoulders, ready to thrust him away in case of trouble.

And stared at the saber.

Needing both hands for his games with the steaks, he'd left the saber propped upright against the counter, five or six feet behind him.

But he was in the way, hunched down, working my breasts with his mouth.

One good shove . . .

He would land on his back within easy reach of the saber.

If he gets it before I do . . .

I couldn't think straight because of what he was doing to me, but I knew this wouldn't be a good time to risk an attack on him.

Wait till it's a sure thing.

What if it's never a sure thing?

Just not now.

He suddenly bit my right nipple. I cried out and rammed my knee up. As it caught him in the chest, his mouth sprang open, freeing my nipple, and I shoved him backward by the shoulders. His back slammed against the kitchen floor.

Just as I figured, he landed beside the saber.

Before he could make a reach for it, I lurched forward between his legs and tried to kick him in the groin. It was a powerful kick. It would've knocked his balls into next Tuesday. But his hand shot down and caught my ankle and stopped my kick cold.

He could stop my foot, but not me.

Even as he gripped my ankle, I dropped onto him, driving my knees down hard into his belly.

He had solid stomach muscles. But not solid enough.

The moment my knees hit him, he let go of my ankle. His lips formed an O. He said, *"Ooomph!"* His eyes bugged out, and his head and shoulders came up off the floor.

For me, it was like kneeling on a raft shooting the rapids. I didn't stand a chance of staying up. Thanks to the fact that Steve had been clutching my right foot, I'd gone down on him with my body slightly turned—facing the saber. So I fell toward it.

As Steve's face got jammed with the left side of my ribcage, I reached high with my right hand and got hold of the blade. Then I flung myself over, trying to roll off him. But he hugged me around the rump. I rolled off him, all right, but he stayed with me. I ended up on my back, Steve on top with his face between my breasts.

His breath was still knocked out, so he was wheezing and gagging and not very strong.

He was trying to pull his arms out from under me.

Clutching the saber where I'd first grabbed it—high on the blade—I pounded the top of Steve's head with the hilt. The blade hurt my hand. That close to the hilt, though, it wasn't very sharp. I didn't think it had cut me.

But the hilt *clobbered* Steve.

I got him with the metal part that curves over to protect your hand during a sword fight.

He grunted and flinched. Then he jerked his arms out from under my ass and I was afraid of what he might do, so instead of worrying about my hand, I hammered him with the hilt about five more times hard and fast. My hand hurt with each blow, but I bashed the crap out of Steve's head and knocked him out cold.

He lay on top of me as if he'd suddenly fallen asleep.

Blood poured out of his torn scalp, soaked his hair, spilled all over my chest.

Bucking and twisting, I threw him off me.

He landed on his back, and I got to my feet. My right hand hurt like mad. I switched the saber to my left, then checked the damage. Not much. The blade had pressed several deep dents across my hand and fingers, but there were no cuts.

I'd gotten off lucky.

In more ways than one.

In *plenty* of ways.

I stared down at Steve. He still seemed to be unconscious. His head was lying in a nice puddle of blood.

I was all bloody, myself. I looked as if a small animal had died a messy death between my breasts.

Steve could've had a jolly time licking me clean.

I thought about waking him up and *making* him do it.

But he might bite me again. Or worse.

Over at the counter, I tore some paper towels off a roll and wiped the worst of the blood off me. I would've liked to take a shower.

But—as usual—I had too many other things to do.

Steve wouldn't stay unconscious forever.

Probably.

Right now, I had a choice to make: either kill him, or not.

No, that's wrong. Letting him live wasn't a real option.

For one thing, he knew too much. He knew my name and where I lived. He'd seen me kill Tony and Milo. He'd seen me abuse Judy, and had probably made her talk before killing her. If the cops got him alive, he would likely "turn over" on me to get a deal.

For another thing, the guy had murdered Elroy and Judy and maybe Marilyn (the dead woman in Milo's tent). God only knows how many other people he and Milo had murdered as a team. He'd called himself a "thrill-killer" and he was probably a cannibal, to boot.

Besides, given the chance, he would try to murder me.

So the real choices were between killing Steve here and now, or killing him somewhere else, later.

I was very tempted to do it here and now. Immediately, he would stop being a threat. (Dead men not only tell no tales, they *get* no tails. They don't rape, torture, or murder anyone ever again.)

But I would be stuck with Steve's body on the kitchen floor. And Elroy's headless body in the guest bathroom. And Elroy's head in the swimming pool. And various other, more manageable messes.

Quite frankly, I'd had enough of that shit.

He made the messes, let him clean them up!

YEAH!

It would be risky. But I had the saber, now.

While I waited for him to regain consciousness, I wondered about tying him up. Some manner of restraint seemed necessary. But how could he pick up Elroy, and so on, if his hands were tied? How could he carry the body away from the house with his feet bound together?

Pretty soon, I came up with a good solution.

I hurried into the laundry room. Serena had a fifteen-foot electrical extension cord that she mostly used for her iron. I unplugged it, gathered it up, and hurried back into the kitchen with it. Steve looked as if he hadn't moved.

I set my saber on top of a counter, then took a small knife out of the butcher block knife holder. In Serena's "junk drawer," I found some heavy-duty strapping tape. The sort that has threads running through it, so it's almost unbreakable.

Kneeling by Steve's bare feet, I tied one end of the electrical cord around his left ankle. I knotted it as well as I could, but cords make lousy knots. You just can't pull them tight enough. So then I unspooled about a yard of tape and cut it off with the knife. I used the tape to wrap his ankle *and* the cord. Then used another length of tape, just to make sure.

When I was done, the cord seemed completely secure.

I had fashioned a "foot-leash" for Steve.

I retrieved the saber. Then I put all the sharp kitchen knives into a drawer so they wouldn't be handy for Steve. When that was done, I picked up my end of the extension cord and gave it a couple of tugs.

"Hey, Steve!" I yelled. "Wake up! We've got work to do!"

49

SLEEPING BEAUTY

Perhaps I'd bashed him *too* hard.

Though I yelled at him and gave him nudges with my foot, he refused to stir.

To make sure he wasn't faking, I gave the crotch of his shorts a couple of prods with the tip of my saber. He didn't react, so I was convinced.

Now what?

In his present condition, he was useless. Worse than useless. Not only could *he* not do any chores for me, but *I* couldn't leave his side.

Well, I could leave his side, but not the kitchen.

At any moment, he might come to. I needed to be nearby when that happened, not off somewhere bringing in the margarita pitcher or gathering up my clothes or cleaning Elroy's assorted fluids off the bathroom floor.

Standing over him, I tried to think . . . plan my moves.

Top priority was keeping control of Steve, so I crouched down and slid his right leg over against his left, then wrapped the cord around both his ankles. Just a simple precaution to keep him from making any quick attacks.

As an added precaution, I placed a kitchen chair on top of him. The chair didn't touch him. With its front legs under his armpits and its rear legs beside his thighs, its job was to keep him from getting up fast and silently.

Now that I seemed to be safe from a surprise attack, I went over to the counter and picked up the steaks. They were still frozen, but seemed to have a slight springiness. Maybe my body heat *had* quickened the thawing process.

I thought about giving Steve the treatment.

But that might wake him up. True, I wanted to get things over with as soon as possible. But if Steve would do me the favor of staying out cold for a while, I could take care of a few matters on my own.

I placed the steaks in the platter of teryaki sauce, turned them over, then washed my hands at the sink.

I wanted to wash my whole body. Even though I'd already done a quick job with some paper towels, I felt incredibly filthy—itchy and sticky from such items as sweat and teryaki sauce and Steve's spittle and blood.

A bath or shower would have to wait.

But now that I had some free time, I went to the kitchen sink, set the saber down on the counter within easy reach, and held a dish towel under the faucet. When the towel was heavy with cold water, I turned around to watch Steve, and mopped myself with the sopping cloth. The water just seemed to flood me. It felt heavenly. It ran all down my body and made a puddle around my feet.

With a fresh dish towel, I dried myself and wiped up the puddle.

I felt so much better!

I felt like celebrating with a drink. Of course, the pitcher of margarita was on the table out by the pool, and I didn't dare go after it. The makings were still on the kitchen counter, though. So I took down a clean glass, tossed in a couple of ice cubes, and poured myself some tequila.

I hopped up and sat on the counter. I was wearing nothing, of course, except my thong panties. The tiles were cool and smooth under my rump.

I took a sip of the gold tequila. It felt cool in my mouth, then seemed to scald my throat and stomach.

I said, "Ahhh."

It is astonishing—and maybe one of life's quiet miracles—how much better every situation becomes as soon as you find a chance to clean up, have a good drink and relax. You might still be in an awful pickle, but you *feel* so much better, regardless.

It also helps if you're alone. With Elroy dead and Steve unconscious, I was alone for all intents and purposes. There was nobody to contend with, nobody who needed to be lied to, tricked or fought. It was such a relief.

I just sat there on the counter with my feet dangling, kept a general eye on Steve, and enjoyed my drink. I'd already knocked down a couple of margaritas. They hadn't been nearly as soothing, though, as the tequila.

Soon, I was feeling fine and lazy.

I wished I could lie down for a nap, but that was out of the question.

I needed activity to keep from drowsing off, so I hopped down from the counter. I set aside my empty glass, picked up the saber and both the dish towels, and went over to Steve. Crouching by his head, I set down the saber. Then I used the wet towel to clean him up. As I wiped the blood off him, I kept a sharp watch for any sign that he might be coming awake.

There was none.

With the same wet towel, I mopped the blood off the floor. This required several trips to the sink and back, but didn't take terribly long. Anyway, it was something to do while I waited.

Next, I folded the other dish towel into a square pad, and placed it against the wounds on top of Steve's head. With long strips of strapping tape (which I cut with the saber), I fastened down its corners to his ears and the sides of his face. It made him look stupid. Which was fine with me.

Pigs deserve to look stupid.

With the mess cleaned up and Steve bandaged, I felt free to relax again. But I was hungrier than ever.

Over at the counter, I checked the steaks. Nearly thawed out, they felt springy and firm, but stiff in the center.

Why wait any longer? I thought. You can't barbecue them on the grill, anyway. Not unless Steve comes to about now.

Well, I could drag him outside.

Right. No way.

I tossed some more ice cubes into my glass, added more gold tequila, took a sip, and sighed.

Squatting and duck-walking, I searched one cupboard after another until I found Serena's wok. I took it to the stove and set it on a burner. Then I hunted out her vegetable oil. I poured some into the wok, turned the burner on, and spent the next couple of minutes cutting the two steaks into bite-sized chunks.

Naturally, I took time out, every half a minute or so, to make sure Steve hadn't moved.

I tossed the two bones into the waste basket beside the stove.

By the time I managed to find Serena's wooden stirring spoon, the oil in the wok seemed good and hot.

I poured in the meat and teriyaki sauce.

Hiss, sizzle, spit, spatter!

"Shit!" I yelped and leaped away, my belly and breasts stinging with a thousand pin-pricks of fire. My skin glittered with specks of oil.

Here's a cooking tip: never stir-fry topless.

Except for a few moments of amazing pain, no real damage was done.

The wok no longer seemed to be erupting, so after a glance at Steve, I picked up the wooden spoon and started to stir the mixture of oil, teriyaki sauce, and chunks of steak.

If they cooked too long, they'd be tough. So I counted to sixty in my head a couple of times while I continued to stir. Then I shut off the burner, hurried over to a cupboard and snatched down a couple of dinner plates.

I piled about the same amount of steak teriyaki onto each plate. Which seemed pretty generous, considering Steve's treatment of me. Also considering it would probably be cold and ruined by the time he might get around to eating it.

I set aside Steve's dinner, then found myself a fork and hopped up onto the counter. The counter made a fine seat. Not only did it feel cool and smooth under me, but I liked having the elevation. Perched up there, I had an excellent view of Steve. And I could jump down and run over to him in about a second if I had to.

With the plate resting on my lap, I sipped my tequila and ate the tasty chunks of steak. There should've been a bed of those crispy, squiggly Chinese noodles underneath the meat and sauce. That would've been great, but I hadn't thought of it. At this point, I didn't want to bother hunting for the noodles.

I wished I hadn't thought of them, though. It's a lousy thing, when you're eating fabulous steak teriyaki, to ruin it by worrying about the noodles that might've been.

Forget about the noodles! Relish the meal you've got!

Words to live by.

Hey, have you ever noticed how much *better* food tastes when you're a little tipsy? For some reason, aromas and flavors seem so much more wonderful than when you're completely sober. If you're not a drinker, you're really missing a treat.

Of course, you're also missing the aftermath, where you feel crummy and may vomit.

I guess it's a toss-up.

Done with my meal, I hopped off the counter. I rinsed my plate and fork at the sink, and stowed them away in Serena's dishwasher. Then I had a little dab more tequila. When the glass was empty, I filled it with cold water and took a good, long drink.

Now what?

Steve was still out cold, and I'd run out of things to keep me busy.

Try to wake him up?

I refilled my glass with water, then added a few ice cubes.

Taking the saber along, I walked over to the chair that I'd placed over Steve's torso. I sat down on it, my feet on the floor just above his shoulders, and rested the saber across my lap. Then I leaned forward and peered down between my knees.

He looked asleep.

"Steve?" I asked.

He didn't move.

I gave his shoulder a nudge with my foot. Still no response.

If he's going to *stay* out cold . . .

Instead of dumping the glassful of water onto his face, I drank it. When nothing was left except for a few ice cubes, I bent way down and set the empty glass on Steve's forehead.

Then I settled back, sliding my rump toward the front edge of the chair. I stretched out my legs, folded my hands down low on my belly, shut my eyes and let my head droop forward.

I know, I know, I know. I had to be crazy to try and take a nap under these circumstances.

But I was so damn worn out by then. I'd had too much excitement, too much stress, too much strenuous activity, too little sleep, and maybe a smidgen too much tequila.

And I figured that Steve was no great threat. Even if he should wake up before me, he was pinned under the chair with his legs bound together and a glass resting precariously on his forehead. He had a slim chance of taking me by surprise.

He *might* get the upper hand, but it didn't seem likely.

It wasn't likely enough to worry me.

Or keep me awake.

After positioning myself for the nap, I must've stayed awake, worrying, for about five seconds. If that.

This was a straight-backed, wooden chair without a seat pad, but I zonked right away. Which tells you how badly I needed some sleep.

I was dead to the world.

Until the noise of bursting glass shocked me awake in the near-dark room and the chair lurched, throwing me off.

50

THE AWAKENING

Earthquake!

That was my first thought. I'd been through some bad ones. They nearly always hit while you're asleep, roaring and shaking you furiously and scaring the crap out of you.

Falling sideways, I was halfway to the floor when I figured out this wasn't any quake.

This was Steve.

My right shoulder hit the floor, and I rolled. Rolled and tumbled as fast as I could, hanging on to the saber. The chair toppled over. Part of it pounded my back, but not very hard.

Clear of Steve and the chair, I scrambled to my feet.

He was already sitting up, but still trying to free his feet from the electrical cord.

"Stop!" I shouted.

He looked up and saw me coming at him.

Even though the kitchen was dim with the gloom of dusk, I must've been quite a sight charging across the kitchen in nothing but my panties, my breasts leaping, my saber high.

One glimpse of me, and Steve let out a yelp.

He quit fooling with the cord and stuck up his hands. "I give!" he yelled. "Don't do it! Please!"

I slid to a halt beside him. Still holding the saber overhead with both hands, I said, "Lie down and don't move."

He sank backward until he was stretched out flat.

Never turning away from him, I sidestepped to the nearest light switch. I flicked it up and brightness filled the kitchen.

As I approached Steve, he lifted his head off the floor. He winced and flinched, but didn't take his eyes off me. Fingering the dish towel that I'd taped to the top of his head, he asked, "What's . . . going on?"

"I won, that's what."

"I don't remember."

"I don't doubt it."

"What happened to my head?"

I shook the saber.

"You chopped my head open? Oh, my God!"

"Don't blow a gasket," I said. "I just gave you a few raps with the handle, that's all. If I'd used the blade, you wouldn't be asking me questions about it. Lie still, and I'll take care of your feet."

"Okay," he muttered.

"I'm not even gonna warn you about trying something."

He eased his head down against the floor.

With the saber in my right hand ready to strike him, I squatted near his feet and used my left hand to unwind the cord. "As long as you cooperate with me, you'll be fine."

"I'll do whatever you want."

"Good. I went ahead and ate, by the way. I couldn't wait for you."

"That's okay."

"But I saved you some."

"Really?"

"Yeah."

When his feet were no longer bound together, I stood up and backed away, the end of the cord in my left hand.

He pushed himself up to his elbows, looked, and saw how I'd fashioned a tether for his left ankle. "Cute," he said.

"It'll let you get around."

"I guess so." Meeting my eyes, he said, "I can't say that I blame you for not trusting me."

I laughed at him. Then I said, "Get up and come over here."

He made it to his feet, and I led him over to the counter where his plate was waiting. I was careful not to let him get close to me.

"Where do you want me to eat it?" he asked.

"Right there."

"What about a fork?"

"So you can stab me with it? Use your fingers."

He started to pick up the plate.

"Put it down," I said. "Leave it on the counter."

He set it down. Then, bending over, he started picking up pieces of steak one at a time. He got a couple into his mouth before he really started chewing. "Mmm," he said. He shoved more in. "Good."

"I know it's not *human*, but it's the best I could do on short notice."

"That was Milo's gig," he said. The words came out mushy because of the meat in his mouth. "Not mine."

"You don't eat people?"

Grinning over his shoulder, he said, "Not that way."

"Very funny."

"He was nuts. Milo."

"He was your mentor."

"Yeah, but he was a fuckin' cannibal. I'm no cannibal. Shit, he did all kinds of weird stuff. Not me."

"Not you. Sure."

"This is really good steak. Really delicious."

"You should've had it when it was still hot."

"Well. Can't have everything." He shoved more into his mouth.

"I want to hear the rest of your story," I told him.

"What do you want to know?"

"You said you watched me in your camp last night. When I took care of Milo and stuff. And then, after I left, you killed Judy. Then what?"

"Did I say that?" He gave me another grin. His lips were shiny with steak juice. "I don't *believe* I said anything about killing Judy."

"Yeah, you did."

"If I said that, I must've been mistaken."

I felt a strange, fluttery tightness inside. I don't know quite what it was. Hope? Fear? Excitement? In some ways, I wanted Judy to be dead. She was a loose end. She could get me in big trouble. But in other ways . . . Hell, I liked her.

"You *didn't* kill her?" I asked.

"No, no, absolutely not."

"Bad choice of words, pal."

"Huh?"

" 'Absolutely not.' Makes me you think you're lying."

"Oh. Jeez. I see what you mean. Protesting too much, huh?"

"What *did* happen after I left?"

He shoved a couple more chunks of steak into his mouth, chewed for a minute, and said, "How about something to drink?"

"The sink's right there," I said.

"A glass?"

"Use your hand."

So he sidestepped to the sink, ran some water, cupped his hand under the faucet and took a few drinks.

"What about Judy?" I asked.

He slurped some more water out of his hand, and said, "What about her?"

"If you didn't kill her, what happened to her after I left?"

Steve sighed, wiped his wet hand across his lips, then shut off the faucet and turned around and grinned at me. "I cut her down."

"You cut her down?"

"The ropes, the ropes. I freed her from the ropes from which she was so cruelly hanging, thanks to you."

"I didn't do that to her."

"But you didn't cut her down."

I didn't need to be reminded of that.

"Are you done eating?" I asked.

"No!" Losing his grin, he turned away and hurried over to his plate and stuffed more steak into his mouth.

"Okay," I said. "So what happened after you . . . took her down from the ropes?"

"Plenty."

"Tell me."

"Fucked the daylights out of her, for starters."

I struck him hard across the ass with the flat of the saber blade. He shrieked and arched his back and clutched his buttocks. For a while, he stood there gasping for air. Then he bent forward a little and braced his hands on the counter top. I could see him shaking.

"You forgot who has the sword," I told him.

"You asked . . ."

"I didn't like your answer. I don't want to hear about that stuff. What *else* happened?"

"We . . . we buried the bodies. Milo and Marilyn."

"Where'd this Marilyn come from, anyway?"

"The tent. Milo had her in the tent."

"Where'd she *come* from? Is she from around here? Did you catch her in Miller's Woods?"

"Huh? No. We grabbed her when we were on the road."

"Tell me about it."

"Well, we spotted her at a gas station. That was a few days ago, when we were up north. We'd stopped for a fill-up, and there she was, pumping gas into her Toyota. A real babe. She wore these short shorts . . ." He glanced back at me and at the saber. Then he went on. "Anyway, we followed her when she left the station. We wanted her to rear-end us, so we got ahead of her, then slowed down. This Marilyn was impatient, so she tailgated us, trying to get us to speed up or pull over. A real bitch move. So then, when we came to a place where nobody was around, Milo suddenly stomped on the brakes. Wham! She rear-ended us. Well, we all got out to check the damage and exchange information. And that's when we snatched her. We threw her into the back of the van, I jumped in with her, and Milo drove off."

"You have a van?" I asked.

"Sure. You've gotta have a van."

"Where is it?"

"Oh, we've got it hidden in the woods. Not too far from a road, but far enough so it's out of sight."

"So you brought Marilyn here to the woods?"

"Right. And put up our camp and had ourselves . . ." He gave the saber an uneasy glance. "We kept her as our guest in the camp for a couple of days, and then she died."

"Died, huh?"

"Well, Milo cut her throat."

"Milo, huh?"

"Yeah."

"How many other people have you two killed?"

"Between the two of us? Quite a few. I couldn't say for sure."

"How long were you together?"

"Milo and me?"

"Yeah. Traveling around in your van, killing people."

"A couple of years."

"My God."

He grinned at me. "Just doing some population control. Environmentally speaking, over-population is a real . . ."

"Shut up."

"Sorry." He faced forward again.

"So what happened," I asked, "after you and Judy dug the graves last night?"

"Nothing. Well, we threw Milo and Marilyn in and covered them with dirt, of course. Then we went to sleep. That's all." Reaching out, he picked up a single piece of steak. He looked at me, then stuck it into his mouth and started to chew.

"But you came back here today," I told him. "What'd you do with Judy when you left camp? Where is she?"

"Still there . . . in camp."

"Alive?"

He nodded.

"Tied up?"

He grunted, then said, "Tied and gagged. In the tent."

"And in what condition?"

"Fine. She's fine."

"She *can't* be fine."

"*I* didn't hurt her."

"Sure you didn't."

"Not much." He leered over his shoulder at me. "I'd be glad to take you to her."

"Not interested," I said.

"Sure you are. You're *very* interested."

"You know what I want?"

"Judy."

"No. I want this house cleaned up. I want you to haul Elroy's body out—and get his head out of the pool. Then we'll take a little trip. You buried Milo and Marilyn somewhere near your camp?"

He nodded and stuffed more steak into his mouth.

"You have shovels?"

"Sure. Tools of the trade. Got a couple of them."

"Okay. Then I guess we *will* go to camp. You can bury Elroy there with the others."

"And you can have a nice reunion with Judy."

51

TEAMWORK

"Cut it out about Judy," I said.

"Whatever you say. You're the boss."

"Finish up with the food. We've gotta get on with this."

He stuffed the last three or four pieces of steak into his mouth. Chewing, his sidestepped to the sink.

"You raped her, huh?" I asked.

He made a garbled sound.

"What?" I asked.

He shook his head and continued to chew. Then he ran the faucet, leaned forward and cupped water into his mouth like before. When the faucet was off, he stood up straight. He wiped his mouth. Then he turned around to face me. "I thought you didn't want me to talk about Judy."

"Yeah. You're right. I don't. Never mind."

"Anyway, I *didn't* rape her."

"But you said . . ."

"I said we fucked. I didn't say anything about rape. A rape requires force or coercion. She was quite willing. After all, I'd cut her down. *You* should've cut her down. Maybe you would've gotten lucky."

"Okay, that's enough. Let's go find Elroy. You lead the way."

Holding the end of the cord in one hand, the saber in the other, I followed Steve out of the kitchen. The rest of the house was pretty dark. As we walked through the foyer, I switched a light on.

"How long have you been here today?" I asked.

"Oh, I arrived around noon. Hoping to find you sunning yourself by the pool like yesterday. I was severely disappointed."

"How did you get in?"

"Sliding doors are a cinch."

He turned to the left and stepped into the guest bathroom. Now that he was no longer blocking my view, I saw a trail of blood drops on the hallway carpet. Steve must've made them carrying Elroy's head from the bathroom to the den. The trail was sure to continue on through the den.

Entering the bathroom, I said, "Nice job on the carpet." And then I saw the mess near the toilet. "Oh, my God."

Steve grinned and shrugged. "What can I say? He made a nice splatter pattern. Could've been a lot worse, though. At least he fell into the tub."

I walked closer to Steve, sidestepped to see past him, and spotted Elroy in the bathtub.

My memory flashed an image of Murphy, also dead in a tub. *Rub-a-dub dub, two men in a tub . . .*

Unlike Murphy, Elroy had his clothes on. And he wasn't sitting sideways in the tub, feet sticking out. He probably *had* been crooked, since he'd fallen from a standing position in front of the toilet. But now he was stretched out on his back, feet toward the drain. His penis was hanging out the open fly of his trousers. His blood-soaked shirt was still tucked in, and his bow-tie, no longer blue, was still in place at the throat of his shirt. Above the bow-tie, he had a ragged stump of neck.

"You want me to pick him up?" Steve asked.

"That's the idea."

"And do what with him?"

"Get him out of the house, for starters."

"He's bound to drip, you know."

"Run the shower on him," I said. "That'll get the worst of the blood off."

"Aye-aye, ma'am." Steve stepped to the foot of the tub, started the shower spraying down onto Elroy, then slid the plastic curtain shut.

"We need something to put him in," I said.

"A couple of plastic garbage bags should do the trick."

"Those'd be out in the garage."

"No problem."

"Yeah, it's a problem," I said. "I'm not taking you all the way out there just to get some garbage bags."

"Afraid I'll make a *break for it?*"

"Something like that."

"Well, we could get a sandwich baggie from the kitchen and put it on his stump."

"Very funny," I said. But his suggestion made me realize that, if the shower did its job, we really didn't need to worry about blood from anywhere except Elroy's neck.

So we marched back to the kitchen. I instructed Steve where to look, and he found Serena's roll of cellophane wrap in the cupboard underneath the sink.

We returned to the bathroom.

While I held the saber and my end of the cord, Steve shut off the shower. He slid open the curtain, stepped into the tub, and got to work on Elroy.

First, he raised the body to a sitting position. Then he removed Elroy's bow-tie and opened the top two buttons of his shirt. After that, he tore off a foot-long section of plastic wrap and draped it over Elroy's neck stump. He squeezed it down firmly so it clung to the raw stuff inside. Finally, he tucked the edges of the cellophane underneath Elroy's shirt collar to hold the wrapping snug.

"That should do the trick," he said.

"I think so," I agreed.

The shower had done a fine job cleaning the blood off Elroy and his clothes. The white shirt was badly stained, but it wouldn't be dripping blood on the way out. With the neck stump secure, he was ready to move.

"Okay," I said. "Now pick him up and let's get him out of the house."

Steve looked at me and raised his eyebrows. "Are you going to lend a hand?"

"No."

"But you're so *good* at body handling."

"I've retired," I said. "You killed him, you carry him."

"What a sweetheart."

"That's me. Let's get going."

Squatting behind Elroy's back, he reached beneath the arms, hugged him around the chest, and lifted.

As Steve hauled Elroy out of the tub, I backed away, giving him plenty of slack with the electric cord. Then I waited while he struggled to find the best way to carry the body. He ended up cradling Elroy in his arms the way you see guys carry their brides over the threshold in movies.

"Ready?" I asked.

"All set," he said. "You ready, Elroy?"

"Cut out the funny stuff," I said. "He was a nice guy."

"Give me a break. He was a pain in the ass. You couldn't stand him."

"Maybe so, but you shouldn't have killed him."

Smirking, he said, "You made me do it. I would chop the heads off an *army* to get my hands on you."

"Go to hell," I said.

Then I led us out of the bathroom. "We'll take him out the front door," I said, turning and moving backward for the foyer. As I walked, I watched Elroy. He dripped onto the carpet, but only water—so far as I could tell. The cellophane on his neck seemed to be working fine. "We'll put him in his car and drive him to the woods."

"Now, *that's* a good idea. I was afraid you might make me walk."

"Can't leave his car here, anyway. We'll park it at the picnic area, and you can carry him the rest of the way to the camp."

I opened the front door, glanced outside to make sure the coast was clear, then stepped out of the way. Turning sideways, Steve carried Elroy past me. I left the door open (since I had no keys on me) and followed them across the lawn to the driveway.

"You'd better put him in the trunk," I said.

Nodding, Steve trudged to the rear of Elroy's car. "How do we unlock it?" he asked.

"Use his keys," I suggested. "They're probably in a pocket of his pants."

"How about coming over here and finding them for me?"

"Thanks, but no thanks. Do I look that stupid?"

"I won't try anything," he said.

"I'm sure I believe you. Just put him down and get the keys yourself."

He started to crouch, then apparently changed his mind. Instead of lowering Elroy onto the driveway, he eased the body down on the trunk of the car. Then he patted both front pockets of the trousers. I heard keys jingle.

The body started to slip, so Steve halted it with one hand. Holding it still, he shoved his other hand into the right front pocket. A moment later, he came out with a key case.

He tossed it to me and said, "Catch."

It sailed toward my left shoulder.

In my left hand, I held the end of the cord that led to his ankle.

I clutched the cord more tightly, and didn't go for the keys.

The leather case smacked me below my left shoulder, slid down my breast and fell to the grass.

"Nice catch," he said.

"Nice try," I told him.

He laughed softly. Then he said, "I know it's asking a lot, but if I pick up your friend and move out of the way, would you be kind enough to unlock the trunk for us?"

"No."

"Please? Pretty please with sugar?"

"Which hand do you want me to use for the keys?" I

asked. "The one with the saber in it, or the one with the cord in it?"

"Either would be fine," he said.

"I'm sure."

"You know what? I've got a terrific idea. Why don't we simply dispense with the cord altogether? In fact, why not forget this entire *captive* routine and work as a team?"

"You're dreaming."

"Let's be partners from now on. How about it? It would make life so much easier for both of us if we start working together instead of fighting each other."

"Only one problem with that," I said. "I'd turn up raped and dead."

"No, no, no. Don't be ridiculous. I wouldn't hurt my partner."

"Forget about it. Come over here and pick up the keys." I gave the cord a couple of quick tugs.

"Okay, okay." Leaving Elroy on the car's trunk, Steve came toward me. I backed away. "I know you want me," he said. "You should've seen the look on your face last night when I was up against the door. *You* wanted to be the door. Not to *mention* in the kitchen tonight when I licked the teriyaki off your incredible, luscious body . . ."

"Just shut up and grab the keys."

He squatted, reached forward into the grass, and picked up the key case. Staying low, he gazed at me and said, "You want me, I want you. We'd be great together. We could go off tonight . . . Hell, we could leave Elroy here and drive away right now. I'll take you to my van, and we'll hit the roads. We'll leave *all this* behind. What do you say?"

"Eat shit and die."

Laughing, he stood up. "That's what I love about you. You're so tough. *And* you've got a sense of humor. Not to mention your killer figure."

"He's slipping," I said.

"Huh?"

"Elroy."

Steve looked over his shoulder just in time to watch El-roy's body slide off the car's trunk and tumble onto the driveway. Facing me again, he shook his head, smiled, and said, "All the guys fall for you."

52

HEAD GAMES

It worked out well. With Elroy sprawled on the driveway, Steve was spared the extra chore of lifting him off the trunk.

I waited near the side of the car while Steve unlocked the trunk. As the lid swung up, he stuffed the keys into a front pocket of his shorts. Then he turned around, picked up Elroy, carried him over to the trunk and dropped him in. The car squeaked and rocked a little. Steve slammed the lid shut.

"Shall we be off?" he asked.

"Not quite yet," I said. "We're missing something."

He grinned. "I suppose we'd forget Elroy's head if it weren't attached."

"Let's go get it."

Worried that Steve might try to shut me out of the house, I stayed ahead of him, walking backward all the way to the front door.

I'd liked it better when he had his arms full.

In the foyer, I said, "Let's make a stop in the kitchen, first."

For that, I let him take the lead.

As we entered the kitchen, he warned, "Careful of the broken glass."

"Thanks," I said.

"You're welcome. What are partners for?"

I stepped around the glass. "We're not partners."

"Maybe not yet. But soon."

"Yeah, sure." I spotted my own keys near the end of the counter, exactly where I'd left them after coming into the house with Elroy. "Step over to the right," I said.

Steve followed instructions. When he was out of my way, I walked toward the counter.

"Need your keys?" he asked.

I didn't bother to answer.

"Which hand will you pick them up with?" he asked. "The one with the cord, or the one with the sword?"

"This may work," I said. Then I tucked the plug under my right armpit. I clamped my upper arm tightly against my side to hold it there. "Now if the cord gets away from me," I said, "I'll just have to chop your head off."

"Hey, we're a team," he said. "Get your keys. I won't try anything."

Watching him closely, I sidestepped to the counter and used my left hand to pick up the key case.

He watched *me* closely as I slipped the case down inside the front of my panties. The leather felt smooth and cool. "Lucky keys," he muttered.

"Shut up," I said. "Let's go get Elroy's head."

Being careful again to avoid the broken glass on the floor, we left the kitchen. From there, we had several possible ways of getting to the pool. I decided on the den door, mostly because I wanted to inspect the carpet damage.

The trail of blood started at the doorway of the guest bathroom and dribbled along the hall toward the den. Not great quantities of blood, but enough. Too much.

"I don't know what the hell I'm going to do about these stains," I said, walking a few paces behind Steve. "They aren't going to clean up. Damn you, anyway. I've been cleaning up after myself ever since last night. I've covered up *everything*. I've worn myself out, cleaning up and covering up and . . .

What am I gonna do about *this*? There's no way to make all these blood stains go away, you bastard."

"Replace the carpet," Steve suggested.

"Yeah, sure. You think my friends wouldn't notice a new carpet?"

He grinned over his shoulder. "Come away with me, and it won't matter."

"No way."

He entered the den. I followed him, pausing long enough to hit a light switch with my elbow. A lamp came on, and I saw the dribble of blood leading to the den's sliding door. "I guess I could tell them I got cut and it's *my* blood."

"Excellent idea. You have such fine ideas. That's one of the things I love about you, darling. Along with your . . ."

"Shove it."

"So sorry."

"Why'd you have do that with his head, anyway?" I asked.

"Cut it off, you mean?"

"And carry it through the house and *roll* it at me."

He chuckled. "I was hoping to bowl you over."

"You're a sick fuck," I said.

"I'm a *splendid* fuck, as you'll soon learn."

"Yeah? Has hell frozen over?"

As Steve neared the sliding door, I quickened my pace. I was about one stride behind him by the time he stepped outside.

I glimpsed the stains he'd put on the glass last night.

Then I stepped out, let him walk ahead, and gave the cord a sharp pull. Its other end jerked his left leg backward. Yelping with alarm, he fell headlong onto the concrete. He caught himself with his hands, but seemed to land fairly hard.

"Just another guy falling for me," I remarked.

On his hands and knees, he looked back at me. I suspect he might've been scowling, but I couldn't see much of his expression because of the darkness.

"That's a lousy way to treat your partner," he said, pushing himself up.

"Knock off the partner crap."

"If you say so."

"We aren't partners. We'll never *be* partners."

"We're already accomplices," he said. "In the eyes of the law."

"I don't plan for the eyes of the law to look in my direction. So just shut up about the eyes of the law and get in that pool and find Elroy's head."

"All right. Partner." Steve took a few steps and halted at the edge of the swimming pool. Then he stood there, slowly turning his head.

Pretty soon, he said, "Oh, my."

"What?"

"It's gotten dark."

"I noticed."

"I can't seem to locate the head."

"It's down there someplace."

"Does the pool have lights?"

"Give me a break," I said. Stepping closer to the edge, myself, I looked down into the water. It might've been a pool of black ink.

"Do *you* see his head?" Steve asked.

"No."

"I suggest we try the lights."

We didn't seem to have much choice. "Okay," I said. "They're over here. Come on." I gave the cord a small tug.

"Don't do that."

"I'll do whatever I want. Let's go."

"Where?"

Using the saber, I pointed out the electrical panel on the wall behind the outdoor table. "You first," I said.

He started toward it, and I stayed a few strides behind him, giving the cord plenty of slack.

The bag of tortilla chips and the margarita pitcher were still on the table.

"Shall we take a break for cocktails?" Steve asked.

"Keep going. Don't touch that pitcher."

"How about this?" he asked. Stepping around the table, he scooped up my bra with his bare right foot. It draped his foot like a huge red mask, flopping about but not falling off as he kept on walking. "Of course," he said, "I prefer you without it."

"Big surprise. You *made* me take it off."

"But I'll let you have it, now."

"Don't bother."

He stopped at the electrical panel and flicked a couple of switches.

Lights suddenly flooded the patio. Glancing over my shoulder, I saw that the pool lights had come on, too. "That'll do it," I said.

"Excellent," Steve said. Turning around, he swung up his foot and flipped the bra at me.

I snagged it out of the air with the saber. It slid down the blade until it met the crosspiece. "Thanks," I muttered.

"Aren't you going to put it on?"

"Maybe later."

"It does look like your hands are full," Steve said. "Would you like *me* to lend you a hand?"

"Let's go get the head."

I backed out of his way. He walked past me.

As I followed him, I lowered the saber. My bra slid down its blade and fell off. I stepped over it.

At the edge of the pool, I stood a couple of yards to Steve's left. The water was brightly lighted, and looked pale blue because of the pool's blue tiles. The hot night breeze ruffled its surface.

"Thar she blows!" he called out, and pointed.

Elroy's head had dropped into the pool at the shallow end. But it hadn't stayed there. It had wandered to the deep end, where it now rested under about twelve feet of water. It seemed to be face-down as if giving the drain a close inspection.

"Now we have a problem," Steve said.

"Do we?"

"Who goes down for it?"

"You do."

"Well, I don't believe the cord is long enough. Not if you're planning to stand here and hold it."

"We'll see. Move over that way," I told him, and gestured to the right with my saber. "We'll get as close as we can."

We both walked along the edge until Steve was adjacent to Elroy's head.

"We're still not close enough," he said. "The cord's too short."

"Go anyway."

"If you say so." With that, he suddenly dived off the edge.

Before he even hit the water, I was leaping out. I held the saber high in my right hand, the end of the cord low in my left. Feet first, I plunged deep.

Through a frothy curtain of bubbles, I saw Steve trying for the bottom. He was in front of me and lower in the water, nearly vertical, kicking and reaching. His shorts had almost come off in the dive. You could see a few inches of his butt crack. From neck to rump, his skin looked very pale and stark and wavery in the underwater lights.

Near his left ankle, his kicking flung the cord this way and that. But he still had slack.

And he still had slack when his right hand thrust down and clutched Elroy by the hair. Hanging on to the head, he curved away from the bottom and began to rise.

Which is when I tried to come up.

And couldn't.

For one thing, the saber weighed me down. For another, I held the cord in one hand and the saber in the other, leaving no hand free to paddle at the water. Though I struggled to kick my way to the surface, I didn't seem to be making any progress.

I didn't panic, though.

I was in no danger of drowning.

Before letting that happen, I would empty my hands and swim to safety.

But what kind of safety would it be if I left the saber at the bottom of the pool?

Just let go of the cord, I told myself.

But I kept my grip on it.

You've gotta let go!

Can't! He'll get away!

Suddenly the cord jerked and nearly flew out of my hand. I squeezed hard and kept hold of it by the plug.

The cord began to tow me through the water.

53

THE GETAWAY

Above me but still below the surface, Steve was swimming toward the shallow end of the pool. He must've known he was pulling me along behind him, but he didn't do anything about it.

He had no idea, I'm sure, that he was helping me.

If he'd known, he would've stayed in the deep water. That would've forced me to drop the cord or the saber or both.

But he towed me to safety.

Just when I was starting to ache for a breath of air, the bottom of the pool suddenly sloped up sharply under me. I tried to lower my legs and stand up. I couldn't manage it, though, with Steve still pulling me forward.

Then he stopped.

I planted my feet on the tile bottom and burst out of the water, gasping for breath and thrusting my saber high. I blinked my eyes clear.

I was standing in water high enough to touch the undersides of my breasts. Ahead of me, Steve turned around in water up to his waist.

The light shimmered on his slim body. He hadn't lost his

shorts, but they were down below the pool's surface. So was Elroy's head. They wavered and undulated the way things do when they're under water.

"Have a nice ride?" he asked.

"Yeah, thanks."

He lifted Elroy's head by its hair. It came up looking at me, water spilling down its face, its eyes and mouth wide open.

When the head was level with Steve's shoulders, he changed his hold on it. He put his left hand under the pulpy neck to act as a platform. Then his right hand let go of the hair and gripped the back of Elroy's head.

He turned the face toward himself. "And how did *you* like the ride, Elroy?"

"It was just super, Stevie boy," Steve responded on Elroy's behalf, speaking in an enthusiastic nasal voice and moving his lips like a lousy ventriloquist.

"Cut it out," I said.

"Stevie alweady cut if OFF, and boy did it hoit! Ouch!"

"That's okay, Elroy," I said, glaring at Steve. "In about two seconds, I'll cut off *Steve's* head. You'll like that, won't you?"

"Oh, dear me, yes! Give him a taste of steel, the bwute!"

Ignoring Elroy, Steve said to me, "You don't want to cut off my head. Not here in the pool. Think of the mess. Aside from the blood, you'd have two heads and a body to haul out."

"Just turn around and get moving. I want to get done with all this."

"Aye-aye." He started backing away from me. I followed, taking a few strides into shallower water.

The level had slipped down to my waist when he suddenly stopped and frowned at Elroy's head. "What's that? A secret?" He brought the head close to his ear and pretended to listen. He nodded. Then he said, "No, I'm not going to ask her that. *You* ask her."

He swiveled Elroy's head so it faced me again.

"Stop this," I said, "and get out of the pool right now."

"But Elroy wants to ask you something."

"I don't want to hear it. Get out."

"Pwease?" Elroy begged.

"Steve!"

"I wubb you, honey. I wub you so bad. Will you wet me kiss you?"

"Shit. Knock it off, Steve. I'm warning you." I raised the saber.

"Juss one wittow kiss on the wips?" Elroy asked.

And Steve hurled the head straight at my face.

I slashed at it, trying to knock it aside. But I swung too soon. The tip of my blade whipped across Elroy's gaping mouth, slicing through both cheeks. His mouth jumped wide open as if he suddenly wanted to take a really *big* bite out of me.

I flung up my left arm in front of my face and started to twist away.

The head crashed against my forearm.

The electrical cord jerked and flew out of my hand.

The head caromed off the bottom of my arm. I looked down just as Elroy's chin punched me in the solar plexus, snapping his mouth shut. I grunted with the sudden pain. He fell almost straight down, gazing up at me from between my breasts until he plopped into the water in front of my belly.

As he sank, I waded backward, doubling over and fighting for a breath.

I knew that I'd lost hold of the cord. But the place where Elroy had struck me is almost like your crazy bone, only worse. Blasted with pain, my main worry was staying on my feet.

Besides, I still had the saber.

And Steve wasn't attacking me, anyway.

While I stood there, hunched over and struggling for a breath, Steve waded for the end of the pool. The shallow end had underwater stairs at the corner nearer to the house, but he ignored them and charged straight forward. He came to the wall, slapped its top with both hands and lunged up. Water sluiced down his body. His shorts dropped, baring his ass and trapping his legs from the knees down. As he tried to spring to his feet, the shorts seemed to tackle him. He let out a yelp and fell sprawling onto the concrete.

By that time, I'd had a few moments to recover.

I still couldn't take a deep breath, but I no longer felt paralyzed by the blow.

Hunched over and gritting my teeth, I trudged toward the end of the pool.

Steve's feet were near the edge. The cord from his left ankle dangled down into the water, and I could see its length below the surface, curling toward me like a strange, skinny snake with a three-pronged head.

Grab it!

I tried to hurry, but the water pushed at me as if it had an urgent need to keep me away from the cord. I leaned forward and kneed my way through it.

Steve flipped over onto his back. He sat up. He saw me coming.

Looking somewhat alarmed, he leaned way forward over his outstretched legs, reached to his ankle and grabbed the cord and snatched it toward him.

Under the water, it darted away from me.

I dived for it, leaping as far as I could, slamming myself down through the water, stretching out my left arm.

And got it!

Tweezed the plug between two fingers.

But then it jumped free.

My hand struck the end of the pool. I reached up out of the water, pawing for the cord, but didn't touch it.

Fast as I could, I got my feet under me and stood up.

Blinking water from my eyes, I saw Steve staggering backward away from the pool. He held the cord in his teeth. It swayed in front of him, its other end still attached to his ankle. His hands were almost finished tugging up his shorts. His penis vanished under the waistband.

I could've been on him in a couple of seconds, except for the saber.

It's hard to climb out of a pool with a sword in your hand.

I wasn't about to let go of it, though.

I guess I could've gone for the stairs, but that probably would've taken even longer than climbing out the awkward way I did, boosting myself over the edge with the saber clutched in my right hand.

Steve never took his eyes off me. He backed farther and farther away while he watched my progress. He even took a few seconds, after his shorts were up, to tighten his belt.

As I got to my feet, he took the cord out of his teeth.

Holding it in his left hand, he whirled around and broke into a run.

"Stop!" I yelled.

Of course, he didn't stop. Why should he?

I went after him.

We sprinted over the warm dewy grass, Steve well ahead of me. I held the saber overhead, ready to strike him down.

If I could only get close enough.

Being built like "a brick shithouse" is never a picnic. But it's a disaster when you're trying to chase someone. You want to be tall and slim and lithe. You want to be flat. And quick.

I didn't stand a chance of catching Steve.

The distance between us kept stretching.

I didn't give up, though. I stayed after him, running as hard as I could, saber waving high and breasts leaping, until he vanished into Miller's Woods.

54

WIRES

Lowering the saber until its tip met the ground, I slouched and huffed for air and didn't go any farther.

My lungs ached from the hard run.

My legs felt heavy, as if loaded with granite.

My heart raced like crazy.

I was drenched. A combination of sweat and pool water, probably. It spilled down my body, dribbles sliding down my skin, all over, tickling me. Drops fell from the tips of my nose and chin and breasts. I used a hand to wipe my face, but it wasn't much help.

I was worn out.

Vulnerable.

Saber or no saber, I would've been easy prey for Steve if he doubled back and jumped me. I was too exhausted. And much too close to the edge of the woods.

When I'd recovered a little, I trudged backward. I was too tired to move quickly, but I put more and more distance between myself and the woods.

I wanted to lie down on the grass.

The grass would make me itchy, though.

So I kept moving, and didn't stop until I reached the apron of the pool. There, I eased myself down and stretched out on the warm concrete. It felt awfully hard against the back of my head. It didn't feel that great under my heels, either. Otherwise, though, it felt okay. I liked that it was solid and dry.

I held on to the saber, my right arm on the concrete by my side, the blade resting across my thigh.

This isn't so bad, I thought. This is pretty nice.

But what do I do now?

Steve got away.

I got away.

We both escaped from each other.

After such a close call, Steve probably wouldn't be coming back. And he wasn't likely to tell any tales, since he's the one who'd murdered Elroy.

Just let him go. Call it even.

What about Judy? She'd promised to keep her mouth shut about me. I couldn't completely trust her about that, but she would probably never get a *chance* to do any damage. If she wasn't dead already (and I figured she might be, even though Steve claimed otherwise), Steve would almost certainly kill her sooner or later. She knew too much. He couldn't just let her walk away.

Maybe I can rescue her.

Yeah, right.

For one thing, you can't exactly rescue someone who's already dead. For another, supposing she isn't dead, why would I want to save her? Dead gals tell no tales.

Besides, I probably wouldn't be able to find the campsite, anyway.

And if I *did*, I'd end up facing Steve again.

I'd been damn lucky to survive this encounter with him. Next time, he might win.

Forget it.

Forget both of them. They're out of the picture.

And I'm almost home free. Just a few little matters to take care of . . .

Such as?

Elroy's head was still in the swimming pool, and the rest of him was locked inside the trunk of his car.

I needed to get rid of them.

Fish out the head, take it around to the car and throw it into the trunk and . . .

Steve's got the keys!

Out front by the car, I'd seen him drop them into a pocket of his shorts.

Without Elroy's keys, I wouldn't be able to open the trunk. Or drive his car away.

When I realized that, I suddenly went all hot and squirmy inside. I sat up. And sat there, head down, groaning.

Doesn't it ever end?

My God, my God.

Killing Tony had been an accident!

All I ever wanted to do was get out from under it—make it go away so I could get on with my life.

It had seemed so simple, at first. Clean up the mess and drop off the body somewhere else. So simple.

But some things aren't simple, and some things can't be undone.

Maybe nothing can *ever* be undone.

That's probably more like the truth.

Once you've done it, it's been done forever and there's no making it go away.

Because too much is attached.

You might think you're dealing with just one matter—like Tony's body—but then it turns out that the body has a dozen wires attached to it. Or a hundred. And every wire leads off into the unknown. One's attached to Judy. Another to an answering machine. Another to poor Murphy. You go to cut those wires, but run into more. Elroy, for instance. And Milo and Steve. Always more wires leading off somewhere.

I guess this might sound like I'm talking about "loose strings."

I don't see them as strings, though. Strings are soft and

you can usually break them with your bare hands. What I mean are thin, steel wires. If you try to break these with your hands, they'll cut into you.

They're everywhere, attached to every word out of your mouth, to your every action, to every person you encounter—and they all lead off somewhere else and drag new stuff into the picture—new stuff with wires leading off . . .

Sitting there by the side of the pool, I felt lost and desperate.

There has to be an end to it, somewhere!

Oh, yeah?

I'd gone through so much. I'd cut so many of those wires . . . A few more, and maybe I'd be free.

Fat chance.

There'll be more. Always more.

It's hopeless.

So what'll you do? I asked myself. Just call it quits, take a nice bath, go to bed, pretend everything is fine?

And go out for the newspaper tomorrow morning and find Elroy's car in the driveway?

I *had* to do something.

Start with Elroy's stupid head.

I sprang to my feet. Standing at the edge of the pool, I spotted his head deep in the water, migrating toward the drain again.

After scanning the grounds to make sure Steve wasn't sneaking toward me, I put down the saber and dived into the pool. The cold of the water shocked me. But then it felt good.

And I felt much better than before.

My despair had gone away.

Apparently, it had been *shoved* away by the mere act of making up my mind to get on with things.

Fuck the wires.

Take care of business.

You know the mistake I'd been making? Why I'd felt such despair a little earlier? Because I'd been looking at the Big Picture. It's the biggest mistake you can make.

Fuck the Big Picture.

Deal with one problem at a time, take care of it, move on to the next.

That's my advice. Take it from me, the deep thinker.

Speaking of deep, I went plunging down through about ten feet of water to reach Elroy's head. He happened to be face up, at the time. I would've preferred to grab him by the hair, but it wasn't convenient so I stuck my hand in his mouth and picked him up by the jaw.

Then I kicked for the surface. I rose at an angle, and came up close to the side of the pool. Holding the edge with one hand, I swung Elroy's head up with the other and set it on the concrete.

I'd left the saber on the other side, so I quickly swam the width of the pool, boosted myself up and climbed out.

As one who learns from her mistakes, I didn't attempt to swim back across. Not with the saber. Instead, I ran around to the side where I'd left Elroy's head. I snatched it up by the hair. With the head swinging by my left side, I jogged over to the garage.

At the side door, I set down the saber. I plucked the keys out of my panties, fumbled with them until I found the right key, then unlocked the door. Inside the garage, I slipped the keys back inside my panties and hurried past my car.

I knew right where to find everything. First, I put on a pair of gardening gloves. Then I went to the cupboard where Serena and Charlie kept their box of plastic garbage bags. I pulled one bag out of the box, shook it open, and dropped Elroy's head inside.

Unfortunately, I should've been holding the bag higher. Its bottom was resting against the concrete floor, so Elroy's head didn't have a nice, soft landing. It made such a nasty *THONK!* that I had to cringe.

Good thing he was already dead.

Anyway, I shut the top of the bag with its plastic drawstring, closed the cupboard, and hurried on out of the garage. I kept the gloves on.

After retrieving the saber, I ran to Elroy's car.

I had no idea whether I would find the doors locked.

But I set down the bag and tried the driver's door. It opened. The car's ceiling light came on. I flicked the lock switch to make sure all the doors were unlocked, then stepped to the back door and pulled it open. I picked up the bag and swung it in. After dropping it onto the floor, I stepped back and shut the back door.

Just for the hell of it, I put down the saber and climbed into the driver's seat to search for keys. You never know. Some people hide a spare set of keys in the glove compartment or under a floor mat or in a magnetic device underneath the dashboard.

Not Elroy, apparently.

And I had not the slightest idea about how to "hot-wire" a car. It sure looks easy in the movies. I'd tried it a couple of times in the past, though, and knew I couldn't do it. So I didn't bother fooling with the wires under the dash.

Unable to find any hidden keys, I used my gloved hands to wipe any areas inside the car that I might've touched on the ride over. Then I climbed out. I left the door unlocked, and shut it.

After picking up my saber, I hurried to the other side of the car and wiped the handle of the passenger door.

Then I whirled away from Elroy's car and ran for the back of the house.

As fast as possible, I gathered up all my clothes. You don't want to be leaving home on an excursion in nothing but thong panties. I carried everything over to the table. I set the saber on top of the table, its handle in easy reach. Then, keeping an eye out for Steve, I got dressed.

Jeans and a dark top would've been more appropriate for the next stage of my plans, but they were upstairs in my room. I was in a hurry. So I wore what I had: my red bra, my bright yellow blouse and long green skirt with the slit up the side. Also, of course, my white sneakers.

All dressed, I picked up the pitcher and treated myself to a few gulps of margarita.

I took a couple of steps toward the switch panel, intending to kill the outdoor lights. But I changed my mind and decided to leave them on. They might help me find my way back, later.

Anything else?

A flashlight? Maybe an extra weapon of some kind?

I glanced into the house through the sliding glass door.

Don't waste any more time. Every minute counts. Get going!

55

INTO THE WOODS

Gasping for air after my sprint across the back yard, I stopped at the edge of the woods. Stopped and listened.

Steve was probably long gone.

But you never know.

He could be sneaky.

Last night, after pretending to run off, he'd circled around to the front of the house and spied on me. He'd actually bragged about it.

So I figured he might be just about anywhere.

After catching my breath and listening for a while, I entered the woods. I moved along as quickly as I dared.

No reason to sneak. If Steve was near enough to hear me tromping through the foliage, the noise wouldn't matter because he was probably already watching me.

I hadn't brought a flashlight, though. A little moonlight came down through the trees, speckling some areas and throwing patches of snowy brightness onto others. But mostly the forest was dark. All around me were dim shapes of gray and black.

Last time, I'd fallen plenty of times in the darkness and even crashed into that broken branch. I didn't want any more accidents like those, so I walked fairly fast but not *too* fast.

I soon managed to find a trail. It was a trail I'd probably used many times in daylight. In the darkness, though, it didn't seem familiar at all. I had only vague notions about where it might lead. All I knew for sure was that it was taking me deeper into Miller's Woods.

Good enough.

I didn't know how to find Steve's campsite, anyway.

And if I somehow found it, he might not even be there. I had no guarantee that he'd returned to his camp after getting away from me.

Maybe he'd gone there, packed up . . . finished off Judy . . . and hit the road in his van.

Taking Elroy's keys with him.

I'd be screwed.

What if I can't get my hands on the keys?

There must be another way to get rid of Elroy's car. That's all I really need to do—move it out of the driveway, leave it somewhere else. Just about anywhere, so long as it's a fair distance from Serena and Charlie's house.

I tried to think of a way.

It helped take my mind off other things.

How heavy the saber felt, for instance. It seemed to grow heavier every minute. Now and then, I had to switch it from one hand to the other.

How hot and sweaty I was, for another instance. I'd been better off without my clothes. They kept the air away from my skin. They clung to me, and seemed to hold the heat in. I didn't have socks on, so the shoes felt slimy under my feet.

I tried not to think about any of that, and concentrate instead on my *real* problem.

What'll I do with Elroy's car?

Can't get it started without the key. So how . . . ?

There must be a way.

Call a tow truck? That'd open a whole new can of worms.

I'd have to contend with the driver, his company records . . . who knows what else? Forget that.

How else can I move it?

I'm not exactly capable of pushing the car myself.

Hire some workers to push it away? But then I'd have them to worry about.

Kill them all. Ha ha.

I lifted my blouse and wiped sweat off my face.

So damn hot.

The heat was fine if you happened to be in an aircondi-tioned house, or sitting around outside or enjoying cocktails or swimming in the pool. But when you're trudging through the woods with a saber in your hand . . .

I took off my blouse. That helped quite a lot. I didn't want to lose it, so I tucked it under the waistband at the back of my skirt and it hung behind me like a tail.

I kept my bra on. Even though it felt wet and uncomfort-able, it stopped my breasts from bouncing and swinging all over the place. I kept the skirt on, too. It was wet and clingy against my rump, but otherwise okay. Besides, I figured it would be easier to wear than to carry. I also kept my shoes on. You don't want to go walking through dark woods barefoot.

With the blouse tucked behind me, I tried to focus my mind again on the problem of Elroy's car.

There must be a way to get rid of it!

How about pushing it with my car? That might work. Push it backward out of the driveway. Once it's on the street, tow it away.

Yes!

Of course, I'd have to do it at night to lower the chances of being seen.

Out on the street in front of the house, I could fasten my rear bumper to Elroy's front bumper with some rope or elec-trical cord—or even pick up a chain at a store tomorrow, and save the job for tomorrow night. Tow Elroy's car into Miller's Woods. Leave it near the picnic area, maybe.

Fantastic!

It would mean a lot of work, and a whole new series of risks, but the plan should succeed fine if I didn't get caught in the act.

I was glad to have a back-up plan. But it sure made me want to find Steve and get my hands on Elroy's ignition key.

So where are you, Stevie boy?

I'd been walking for long enough to be fairly deep into the woods. I might even be somewhere near the camp.

Maybe fifty yards away from it.

Or half a mile.

Or a mile.

It might be dead ahead. Or somewhere to the left or the right.

For that matter, where was the creek? What about the picnic grounds? The parking area?

I'd be glad to find *any* familiar place. But even if I could get my bearings, I still might have trouble locating the campsite. I'd only stumbled onto it by accident, last night. With such a dim notion of where it might be, I probably had no chance at all of finding it again.

There's always *some* chance, I told myself.

Fat chance.

Maybe if Steve has an enormous bonfire . . .

Or if Judy screams . . .

Or I scream?

Shaking my head, I muttered, "How nuts *am* I?"

Nuts enough, apparently.

I stopped walking, then took a deep breath and shouted, "HELLO! IT'S ME! I CHANGED MY MIND! DON'T GO AWAY WITHOUT ME! I'M COMING! CAN YOU HEAR ME? I WANT TO GO WITH YOU!"

In the quiet of the woods, my voice must've carried awfully far.

I listened for an answer.

After a minute or two, I realized that Steve wouldn't call out, even if he'd heard me.

He might *come* for me, but he wouldn't call out.

"WAIT FOR ME!" I shouted.

As I walked on, I was still worn out and sweaty and breathing hard, but now I had fear mixed in.

By yelling, I'd probably improved my chances of meeting up with Steve—but I'd lost any chance of taking him by surprise. From now on, the element of surprise would be on *his* side.

"Idiot," I muttered.

Just keep quiet and maybe he won't find me.

And I for damn sure won't find him, either. Or Elroy's key.

The key isn't worth dying for.

So why am I doing this?

I realized that I could turn around right now and hurry silently away, find my way back to the house and not have to deal with Steve tonight—or maybe ever again. I could take a bath and go to bed. Tomorrow, clean the house. If I couldn't get the blood off the carpet, I'd cut myself and make up a story for Serena and Charlie. They would probably believe whatever I decided to tell them. After dark, I'd tow away Elroy's car with his body in the trunk and his head in the back seat and be done with all this.

I could do that.

But even as it went through my mind, I kept on walking deeper into the woods.

I'm not sure why.

Maybe it was something inside me that didn't like to quit, that needed to see it through to the end, no matter what.

Something that needed to cut the last wires.

Not only did I keep walking, but I started shouting again. This time, I used his name.

"STEVE! HEY, STEVE! WHERE ARE YOU? CAN YOU HEAR ME? I DON'T KNOW WHERE YOU ARE! COME AND GET ME!"

Even if Steve wanted to keep clear of me, I figured he might be tempted to come looking—to stop me from shouting his name through the woods.

No telling how far my voice might be carrying.

Or who might be listening.

More than likely, we weren't the only two people within the sound of my voice. There might be a couple of campers, or someone out for a jog or stroll, maybe some lovebirds or a dog walker or a wino, maybe even a criminal or two using the forest as a place to hide from the authorities or hunt for victims.

Or there might be only the two of us.

I didn't know, and neither did Steve.

"WHERE ARE YOU, STEVE?" I called out. "COME AND FIND ME! DON'T YOU DARE LEAVE ME BEHIND! I'M NOT GONNA LET THEM NAIL ME FOR THIS. IF THE COPS GET ME, I'LL TELL EVERYTHING! I'M NOT GONNA TAKE THE FALL FOR YOU, STEVE! YOU'RE THE ONE WHO MURDERED HIM, NOT ME! I HAD NOTHING TO DO WITH IT. YOU DID IT ALL, AND I'LL TELL THE COPS THAT."

I knocked off the yelling for a while, and just walked along and listened. I heard nothing except the usual sounds you hear on a hot summer night in a forest, such as birds and bugs and frogs and the breeze creeping through the trees and bushes.

"I SWEAR TO GOD, STEVE, YOU'D BETTER NOT LEAVE ME HERE! I'LL SPILL MY GUTS! I'LL TELL THEM ALL ABOUT HOW YOU CUT OFF ELROY'S HEAD! I'LL TELL THEM ABOUT YOU AND MILO, TOO! THE FBI WILL *LOVE* TO HEAR ABOUT YOU GUYS!"

I had a sudden inspiration.

Just in case a stranger *might* actually be listening to me and paying attention—

"I'LL TELL ABOUT HOW YOU CHOPPED UP TONY RO-MANO, TOO! AND HOW YOU SNATCHED AND RAPED JUDY! AND MURDERED HER! I'LL TELL THEM EVERYTHING I KNOW IF YOU DON'T GET ME OUT OF HERE!"

I wondered if I should throw in Murphy for good measure.

No. Why drag poor Murphy into this? He was my own business, my own private loss.

Anyway, I was tired of yelling. I was out of breath and my throat hurt.

And I'd already shouted more than enough to draw Steve's attention—and wrath.

If he'd heard me, he would probably be on his way.

In a rage.

56

I FALL FOR STEVE

A few minutes later, as I went rushing down a dip in the trail, something tripped me. It caught me across the front of my right ankle, then my left. It felt like a taut rope or cord.

With both feet snagged, I plunged headlong.

I flung out my hands, hoping to break the fall. They probably helped a little. But the ground bashed them out of the way and I slammed down hard. By the time my body struck the trail, my feet were free from whatever had snagged them. I skidded down the sloping earth.

The moment I came to a stop, someone rushed out of the darkness beside the trail. A bare foot stomped down on my right wrist, pinning the saber to the ground. I figured it must be Steve's foot. Before I could do anything, he dropped a knee down, punching me between the shoulder blades. Then he clobbered me in the head. I felt an explosion of pain, glimpsed a bright flash, and then I was out.

But not for long.

At least, I don't think so.

While I was knocked out, Steve dismantled his booby-trap, brought it down to where I was sprawled on the trail, rolled me onto my back, removed my bra, and bound my hands together in front of me with the same length of electrical cord I'd used on him.

I woke up to find him standing in front of me. He held the saber in his right hand, an end of the cord in his left. Tugging the cord, he tried to pull me into a sitting position.

"Okay, okay," I said.

"Ah, Sleeping Beauty wakes up."

It sounded like something poor Murphy might've said. For a moment, I thought I was back in his bed . . . but then I remembered he'd fallen into the bathtub . . . with me on him. Fallen and broken his head open.

This wasn't Murphy, this was Steve.

I suddenly felt lost and sick.

"Go to hell," I muttered.

"You don't sound very perky," Steve said. "Hope I didn't break you."

"Fuck you," I said.

Steve hauled away at the cord. It tightened around my wrists and stretched my arms. Leaning forward, I struggled to stand up. It wasn't easy. It wasn't successful, either. When I got to my knees, he jerked the cord and I flew forward and landed hard.

"You must try to be less clumsy," he said.

I wanted to make another crack, but I couldn't because I'd started to cry and didn't want him to find out.

He gave the cord a couple of tugs. "Up we go," he said.

I shoved at the ground with my elbows and knees. I thought he'd probably try to pull me down again, but this time he let me stand up.

"Very good," he said. "Now, let's see. How'll we do this? I don't want to have you behind me, so . . . You take the lead." He stepped to the left side of the trail and pointed the way with the saber. "Ladies first," he said.

As I walked by, he swatted me across the ass with the

blade. I flinched and gasped. Then he came in behind me, holding the cord low. It dangled from my wrists and hung against the side of my left leg.

"We'll just stick to the trail for a while," he said. "I'll tell you where to go."

Pretty soon, he asked, "You weren't satisfied with getting out alive?"

"I . . . want to go away with you."

"So I heard. So *everyone* must've heard in ten counties. But I figure you were lying about that. Just like you were lying when you said I killed Tony. I didn't rape or kill Judy, either. Bad enough you were yelling your head off like a lunatic and accusing me of all kinds of shit, but making *false* accusations . . . That really takes the cake. How could you do that to me?"

"I'm sorry," I muttered. "I just figured . . . I don't know . . . I thought if I said enough really awful things about you, you'd *have* to come and get me."

"It worked," he said, and laughed.

"I was telling the truth, though, about going away with you. I want to be your partner."

"I don't think so."

"You said you wanted me."

"Still do, hon. And I aim to *have* you. But maybe not for my partner. I happen to think you're playing games about that. You'll be all nice and chummy till you get the upper hand, then you'll nail me."

"No, I won't. We'll hit the road together. I'll help you . . ."

"No, you won't."

"I will! I want to!"

"You're just saying this to save your sweet rear end. That's about all you're interested in. You don't want to be my partner. You hate me."

"I do not."

"I've got a nasty wound on my head that says otherwise."

"I only did that because you were hurting me. You *bit* me!"

"Ah, yes. I was enjoying a taste of tit teryaki."

Real cute.

"We could be great together," I told him. "You know damn well how tough I am."

"Tough? Not at all. I've rarely put my lips around such nice, tender tits. Love 'em."

"They go where I go," I told him. "Take me on as your partner, and we'll all be together."

"Or I could take them *without* you."

Don't let him get to you!

"I won't be much good to you dead."

"Oh, I wouldn't say that."

"I mean as a partner."

"Oh, that. True."

"You're going to need a partner."

"Now that you've killed Milo?" he asked.

"Right. Exactly. And you owe me for that, don't you?"

"Owe you how?"

"No more sloppy seconds."

"True, true," he said. "I thank you."

"And now you need a *new* partner, and I'll be it. I can drive for you. I can do all sorts of stuff. Like help you get girls. I can even . . . you know . . . help *do* stuff to them."

"*Do* stuff?" he asked.

"Like tie them up, help you kill them or whatever, help you dispose of their bodies. Whatever you want." I looked over my shoulder at him. "You *know* I can do that sort of stuff."

"Yeah, you're a bad cat."

"Bad enough."

"Not *nearly* bad enough, honey."

"I am, too."

"You're a pussy."

"Tough enough to kill Milo and Tony and knock *your* brains half out of your head."

Again, I couldn't bring myself to mention Murphy. I didn't want him to be part of this.

"If you had what it takes," Steve said, "you would've taken care of Judy. You left a living *witness*."

"She didn't know enough to get me in trouble."

"Bullshit. She knew plenty. You didn't kill her because you're not as tough as you think you are. You *liked* her, so you let her live."

"No."

"You had the hots for her."

"Did not."

"You fell for her, so you didn't have the heart to take her down."

"You're nuts."

"That so?"

"Yeah. So maybe I didn't kill her, I beat the crap out of her and left her for dead. I figured she'd never get out of the woods alive."

"Who are you trying to kid?" Steve said.

"Nobody."

"*She's* probably the real reason you came out here tonight. You never had any intention of hitting the road with me, you came out here to save that girl's ass."

"You're nuts."

"Or maybe *whip* it," he added, and laughed softly.

"Judy had nothing to do with this," I insisted. "I came because I want to go away with you. That's the only reason. After you got away . . . never mind."

"No, no. Please, don't stop now. I can't wait to hear it."

"Why should I waste my breath? You won't believe me, anyway."

"Oh, try me."

Looking over my shoulder again, I said, "I missed you."

"How sweet."

"I figured we'd probably never see each other again, and I suddenly realized how much I . . . I wanted to be with you. I know it sounds crazy. And you probably don't believe me, anyway. But there's something about you. I can't explain it. All I know is that I suddenly felt this horrible emptiness inside after you were gone. And I knew that the emptiness was because . . . I was afraid I might not be able to find you, that I might have to go the rest of my life without you."

"I'm deeply moved," he said. "You loved me so much that you came after me with a sword."

"It wasn't meant for you."

"But I've got it, and I thank you."

"That isn't what I . . . I only brought the saber along for protection. I never intended to use it against *you*."

"And you never will."

"That's fine. I would've *handed* it to you, if you'd asked. You didn't have to ambush me for it."

"You know something, Alice?"

"Plenty."

"You *are* marvelous. I've mentioned that before. But the more we're together, the more I discover. Now I find that you're not only sexy and stacked and gutsy and witty and tough—but you're a quite a fine liar, too."

"I don't lie."

A laugh burst out of him. "You could be President!"

"I just want to be your partner."

"There you go again. But you know what? Considering your many wonderful attributes, I might just be willing to let you have a go at it."

"At being your partner?"

"Exactly."

This was pretty much what I'd been hoping to hear, but I sensed trouble. "What's the catch?" I asked.

"No catch. There will be an audition, though."

"What do you mean?"

"You don't know what an audition is?"

"Of course I do. But I don't see the point. I mean, you've already seen me in action."

"My dear, I've *felt* you in action."

"So why do I have to prove myself?"

"It's simple. You're not the only sweet young thing interested in the role."

"You're kidding."

"Judy."

"*Judy?*"

He laughed. "Of course! Who else *would* it be? Marilyn? Marilyn's a looker, but she's much too stiff for the part. Of course it's Judy."

"She really is alive?"

Steve had claimed, before, that he hadn't killed her. But I'd figured he must be lying. *Now* I believed him. Now that I'd have to be going up against her for the "role" of Steve's partner.

It made me feel strange, somehow, to find out she wasn't dead. Relieved, I guess. Nervous. Excited.

I felt dread, too.

Because I would probably *have* to kill her, this time.

"What makes you think Judy wants to be your partner?" I asked.

"Told me so, herself. Fact is, until *you* came along shouting all that shit for the whole world to hear, I'd say that Judy pretty much had it in the bag. I don't think she'll be very pleased to find out she has competition."

"She'd make a lousy partner for you," I said.

"Oh, I'm not so sure of that. I happen to think she'll make a spectacular partner. Better than you, in some ways. She's younger than you, certainly more beautiful. Though she's lacking your magnificent figure, she has a certain innocence that I find very appealing, tremendously sexy."

"Yeah, well, that's her problem. She can't be partners with a *thrill-killer*. She's a fuckin' goody-two-shoes."

"Which is why we need the audition," Steve said. "She'll have to prove that she has what it takes."

57

SEARCHING THE DARK

"Let's head over in that direction," Steve said. Stepping up close behind me, he pointed to the right with the saber. "We don't have much farther to go."

I could see nothing over there except more dark forest. I stepped off the trail, though, and started hiking through the undergrowth. The ground was rougher, littered with rocks and fallen limbs. There were also plenty of unexpected dips and rises. I walked very carefully. I'd already had too many falls, and sure didn't want to go down with my hands tied together.

As I made my way along, low bushes clawed at my skirt and pushed at my legs as if trying to keep me back. Higher limbs slid their moist leaves against my bare arms and breasts and face. Some limbs scraped across my skin like dull claws. Others poked and scratched me, drawing blood. I couldn't see the blood, but felt it dribbling down my skin, here and there.

Every so often, Steve gave me instructions about which way to turn. I tried to do what he said. Sometimes, though, I displeased him. Either I didn't move fast enough, or my turn wasn't exactly what he wanted. He'd jerk the cord, hurting my wrists and twisting me around. Or he'd smack me with the flat of the saber blade. Once, he even jabbed me in the right buttock hard enough to make me bleed. The seat of my skirt got so wet that it stuck to my rump, and I felt blood trickling down the back of my leg.

After he did that, I said, "I'll make you a better partner if you don't wreck me."

"But I enjoy wrecking you. Anyway, I need to soften you up a little for Judy."

"What do you mean, soften me up?"

"You're bigger and stronger than she is."

"So?"

"We need a level playing-field."

"What for?"

"The audition, of course."

"What're you gonna do, have us *fight*?"

"Among other things," he said, sounding very chipper. "Winner becomes my partner. Loser loses."

"But I've got to be 'softened up'?"

"Exactly."

"That's not fair."

"We've got to be fair to Judy, don't we? You have all the natural advantages. Besides, she's been through a lot."

"*I've* been through a lot."

"Not as much as Judy. She was rather roughly used by Milo, myself *and* you. In her present condition, she wouldn't stand much of a chance."

"Then let's just skip this 'audition' crap, and you can declare me winner by default."

"Not a chance. I think you'd better hang a left about now."

"If I'm so much better than she is . . ."

He jabbed my other buttock.

"OW!"

I turned left and kept on walking.

He kept giving directions.

After a while, he kicked one of my feet sideways, tripping

me. As I stumbled forward out of control, he said, "Oops!" Then I fell. With my hands bound together, I couldn't catch myself. I struck the ground hard.

"What a klutz!" he said, and laughed.

I pushed myself up, and we continued through the woods. Finally, Steve took the lead. He stayed well ahead of me, pulling the cord so it stayed taut between us. This went on for a while.

"Are we lost?" I asked.

"We'll find it. I know we're close. I had no way to keep the fire going, though. I was gone most of the day, and Judy was certainly in no position to add any wood."

"How'll we find it if there isn't a fire?"

"I know the area pretty well."

"Not well enough, apparently."

He gave the cord a rough tug. It jerked my wrists, stretched my arms, and made me lurch forward, staggering. This time, though, I didn't fall.

We kept walking.

After a while, I said, "Do you mind if I make a suggestion?"

"Suggest away."

"Not if you're gonna hurt me for it."

"What have you got in mind?"

"Maybe you should try calling out to Judy."

"I don't think she'll answer."

"What kind of partner *is* she?"

"I left her with a gag on."

"Maybe she got it off. Why don't you at least *try* calling her? These are big woods. We might *never* find your camp."

Stopping, Steve turned around and faced me. "You call her," he said. "She's more likely to answer if it's you."

"After everything I did to her?"

"It's not half what I did. Tell her you ran into me and killed me and now you want to help her get free."

"She won't believe that."

"Make her believe it."

I gazed through the darkness at Steve.

If I refused to call Judy, maybe we *wouldn't* be able to find her.

It might save her life. Or mine.

"Do it," he said.

"What if I don't?" I asked.

Steve walked slowly toward me. "You want to find her as much as I do," he said.

"So she and I can have some sort of *fight to the death*?"

"Against her, you stand a chance." He raised the saber blade and moved it slowly torward my chest. Because of the way my wrists were tied, my breasts were pushed close together by my upper arms. They had a deep, narrow crevice between them. Steve slipped the blade in. Then he flicked it from right to left to right to left, paddling the sides of my breasts a few times. Not very hard. Gentle slaps that didn't hurt much, but made me flinch anyway. And worried me.

If he turns the blade . . .

"Think you stand a chance against *me*?" he asked.

"Not at the moment," I said.

"Call out to Judy. Make her answer."

He gave the saber a quick, hard flick. It slapped the side of my right breast.

"JUDY!" I shouted. "IT'S ME! ALICE! WHERE ARE YOU?"

Steve and I stood in silence, listening.

Nothing.

"CAN YOU HEAR ME? STEVE'S DEAD. I TOOK HIM BY SUR-PRISE AND KILLED HIM! HE CAN'T HURT YOU ANYMORE! I WANT TO SET YOU FREE! ARE YOU AT THE CAMP? WHERE ARE YOU? MAKE SOME SOUNDS SO I CAN FIND YOU!"

No sounds came.

Just the breeze and the birds and the bugs.

"You'll have to do better than that," Steve whispered. He slipped the blade deeper into the crevice until its point met my chest.

"COME ON, JUDY! I'M SORRY ABOUT EVERYTHING, OKAY? I KNOW I HURT YOU. I WENT TOO FAR, AND I'M SORRY. NOW LET ME HELP YOU."

Nothing.

"Maybe she couldn't get the gag off," I whispered to Steve.

"Or she might be afraid to speak up," he said. "I knew the gag might not be enough to keep her quiet, so I gave her a gentle warning. I said if I heard her yelling, I'd come back and do some very nasty things to her. You know. With my teeth. With burning sticks." I couldn't see Steve's smile, but I knew it had to be there. "In tender, intimate places."

"You pig."

He stuck me.

"*OW!*"

"Be nice to the man with the sword. Now, try again."

I felt a thin stream of blood sliding down between my breasts. "What do you want me to say?" I asked.

"Whatever works."

"Maybe she can't hear me. Maybe she's already gotten away."

"I don't think so. Try again."

"JUDY!" I shouted. "HE'S ALIVE. HE'S GOT ME. KEEP YOUR MOUTH SHUT, AND MAYBE HE WON'T FIND . . ."

"Fucking . . . !" he blurted, and jerked the blade up.

While I tried to back away, the point sliced a vertical slit up the middle of my chest, missed my throat, and nicked the front of my chin. Then I was falling backward.

I slammed the ground. It smashed my breath out, but at least I didn't land on anything terribly hard or sharp.

Steve lunged at me with the sword.

Its tip popped through the front of my skirt, pierced my panties and poked me.

"No!" I cried out.

And Judy, somewhere not very far away, shouted, "STOP IT! I'M OVER HERE!"

Steve turned his head toward the sound of her voice.

"LEAVE HER ALONE, STEVE! DON'T HURT HER! I'M RIGHT HERE IN CAMP WHERE YOU LEFT ME."

"Okay," he called. "Stay put, and keep talking till we find you."

He raised the saber and stepped away from me. When the slack was gone, the cord grew tight and pulled at my wrists. To save myself pain, I didn't resist. I sat up, then struggled to my feet.

"Speak to me, Judy," Steve said.

"I'm over here."

He towed me in that direction.

"Speak up."

"Are you okay, Alice?" Judy asked.

"Sure. Dandy. How about you?"

"I've been better."

"What'd Steve do to you?"

"He . . ."

"All right, all right, ladies. Knock it off. Just count, Judy."

"Just die," Judy said.

"Count. One, two, three, four . . ."

"Go to hell."

When she said that, Steve jerked my cord. I stumbled forward. Arms stretched forward like a diver (thanks to the cord), I flew off my feet.

Not again!

I cried out, "*AHH!*" and crashed down to the ground in front of Steve's feet.

"What'd you do to her?" Judy called.

"*I* didn't do anything to her—*you* did."

Instead of giving me time to stand up, he trudged backward, pulling the cord, dragging me.

"Alice?" Judy asked.

She sounded no more than a few yards away.

"RUN!" I shouted as Steve dragged me closer to her. "GET AWAY!"

"I can't."

58

THE AUDITION

He made me lie flat on the ground, face down, my legs spread wide apart and my arms stretched overhead. "Don't move," he told me.

Crouching just beyond my bound hands, he worked on the fire. He got a small blaze going, then added sticks from a nearby pile. The flames grew. I could feel their warmth. The fire crackled and hissed and popped. He added larger chunks of wood. Soon, he had a roaring, hot campfire with flames leaping two and three feet into the air.

"Okay," he said. "Get up on your knees."

I pushed myself up. Kneeling, I settled back on my haunches.

And scanned the campsite. It looked pretty much the same as last night, but Judy was no longer hanging by her wrists from the tree limb. I didn't see her anywhere.

Leaving my hands tied together, Steve shoved my wrists in against my belly, then wrapped the cord around me a couple of times like a belt. He drew it backward and looped what was left of it around my ankles.

"Now," he said, "stay put."

He picked up the saber, then headed for the tent. Twisting sideways, I watched him. He flung one of the tent flaps aside, poked the saber into the ground nearby, then ducked into the dark opening.

A few moments later, he scuttled out backward. He was bent over, straddling Judy, dragging her by her upper arms. Her head was between his feet. She had it raised and turned sideways, trying to keep her face off the ground.

She was naked, of course.

And hogtied with rope—hands bound together behind her back, feet forced up and tied almost within reach of her hands.

As Steve dragged her toward me, she strained upward, arching her back. She managed to get her upper body off the ground so she was skidding along on just her thighs.

About six feet away from me, Steve hoisted her to her knees. Leaving her, he hurried over to the tent and retrieved the saber. With the weapon in his right hand, he took up a position midway between us but slightly off to the side where he wouldn't obstruct our views.

Judy and I stared at each other.

The old, red bandana hung around her neck.

She looked awful. And beautiful.

Her sweaty body was smudged with dirt, smeared and streaked with blood. She gleamed like gold in the firelight. She was a battered ruin of welts, bruises, scratches and cuts. I'd given many of them to her myself.

Including a bullet wound to the right side of her head. The gouge from that was out of sight, hidden under the curls of her wet, blond hair. I knew she had it, though. And knew I'd done it.

Shot her. My God. Tried to kill her.

What's the matter with me?

"I'm so sorry," I whispered.

"Shut up," Steve said. "You can look, but don't talk."

So I kept on looking.

In spite of all the damage to her body, Judy didn't seem beaten. Hurt, badly hurt, but not beaten.

She knelt like a proud soldier at attention, her body straight and rigid, belly sucked in, chest out, shoulders back, chin up. She had a fierce look in her eyes. The only sign of weakness or vulnerability—her lower lip was clamped between her teeth.

My throat felt tight and thick, but I managed to say, "I wish I'd never gotten you into . . ."

"Shut up," Steve said.

"Go to hell," I told him.

He smiled at me. "Better be nice. Only one of you gets to be my loyal sidekick. The other stays here, toes up, ticket cancelled, farm bought, dead as dirt. And I'm the sole judge. In other words, you'd better start kissing up."

"Kiss my ass," I said.

"I'm sure I'll get to it sooner or later," he said. "Now, let's start the audition. Is everyone feeling well rested and fit as a fiddle?"

Judy and I looked at each other, but said nothing.

"Good!" Steve blurted. "Let's begin. Who would like to go first?"

"Go first?" I said. "I thought we were supposed to have a fight."

"All in good time, my dear. This'll be a multi-part audition, with the fight as the finale." Grinning, he added, "We'll work our way up to it."

"So what else do we have to do?" I asked.

"Anything I say. Now. Who would like to start? Do we have a volunteer?" He turned his grin from me to Judy. "How about you, sweet thing?"

She glared up at him, but didn't answer.

"Remember, ladies, cooperation counts."

"What do I have to do?" Judy asked.

"Competition number one?" Raising the saber high, he used his other hand to unfasten his belt. "The Great Suck-off!" he announced. His cut-offs dropped around his ankles.

Even though I despised him and he disgusted me, I've got to admit he had a wonderful body. All slender and smooth, with sleek muscles and a small, tight rear end. His penis stuck out straight in front of him. It was only about half-erect, but already seemed pretty huge.

Resting the saber on his shoulder, he stepped out of his shorts and walked over to Judy.

She stared straight forward, her lips pressed together in a tight line.

Steve stopped by her left side.

"Turn and face me," he said.

She turned. It didn't look like an easy task, the way she was tied. But she managed.

"Excellent," Steve said. He moved closer to her. When he stopped, he was almost touching her lips.

Judy's mouth was shut. Apparently breathing only through her nostrils, she sucked in air as if she'd just finished a sprint. The quick panting made her chest swell and contract, her breasts lift and fall. She looked as if she'd been dipped in melted butter.

"Open wide," Steve said.

She didn't.

He prodded her lips, but she kept them shut.

"Do you want to lose by forfeit?" he asked.

"*I'll* do it," I told him.

"I'm talking to Judy," he snapped. All the tease was gone from his voice.

"Do me instead! She doesn't want you. I do. Come on over here and put it in. I'll suck your brains out."

"Your turn'll come. Now butt out." To Judy, he said, "Open up, honey. Right now."

She shook her head.

So then Steve grabbed her by the hair and jerked her head back. Her mouth stayed shut.

"Don't!" I cried out.

Ignoring me, he did a little prance. I couldn't tell exactly what was going on, but he must've knocked her in the belly with either a knee or a foot. She suddenly grunted and her mouth sprang open. With the hand clutching her hair, he jerked her head forward.

He shoved himself in.

"Yes!" he cried out. "Now *suck*, honey, *suck!*"

He waved his saber high.

Judy wheezed and gagged as he thrust.

"Stop it!" I yelled. "Leave her alone!"

"You're next!" he shouted.

"Bite him, Judy! Bite his fucking cock off!"

Maybe afraid she might follow my advice, Steve suddenly flung her away. She fell onto her back, her tied arms trapped beneath her and her knees in the air.

Steve tossed the saber aside. Hands free, he threw himself on top of Judy. His hips shoved her legs even farther apart. He clutched her shoulders to pin her down. Then his ass rammed forward and she gasped and I knew he was in her.

"NO!" I shrieked. *"STOP THAT!"*

He hadn't done much of a job securing me.

I had no trouble at all working my feet free. By the time I'd managed to stand up, the cord that Steve had wrapped around my waist was hanging in a couple of loose coils down my rump and legs.

But my hands were still lashed together.

I struggled to jerk them free. The cord had no give, and only dug into my wrists.

But I didn't intend to let it stop me.

Steve was still on top of Judy, grunting and thrusting.

I couldn't take the risk of going for the saber. It was in his line of sight—if he happened to look up from Judy. Besides, it'd be a tricky weapon for someone whose hands are bound together.

Whereas the carving knife was conveniently located high on the inner side of my right thigh—and just the perfect size for one-handed use.

It had come from Serena and Charlie's kitchen.

Before setting out to hunt for Steve, I'd decided against a flashlight but in favor of a knife.

Hurrying toward him now as he raped Judy, I used both hands to reach in through the slit of my skirt. With my left hand, I drew the knife downward, freeing it from the single strip of tape that held it to my thigh.

The way Steve was huffing and thrusting, he must've been just about ready to come.

I changed the knife to my right hand and twisted my wrist so the blade pointed forward.

Judy was writhing and sobbing under him.

Steve's firelit ass bobbed up and down, buttocks flexing.

I dropped toward him, my hands low, the blade straight out like a steel version of his penis and aiming for the shadowy crack between his cheeks.

The blade slid in easily and deep.

Suck this, asshole!

Steve squealed.

I gave the handle a hard twist, turning the blade, and his squeal jumped an octave higher. My ears hurt. He jerked and thrashed under me. Hot fluids flooded out over my hands. Mostly blood, I suppose.

He tried to throw me off, but he didn't stand a chance. Not the way he was caught between Judy and me. Not the way his nervous system had gotten trashed with the first thrust of my attack.

I'd nailed him but good.

As badly as I wanted to climb off and escape from Steve's gushing ass, I wanted even worse to keep at him until the job was done. So I stayed on him with the knife buried deep, and went on working its blade around, really ripping him up inside.

For quite a long time, he shuddered and twitched and screamed.

Finally he settled down.

59

AND THE WINNER IS . . .

Underneath me, underneath Steve, Judy wept.

"It's okay," I told her. "It's over."

"Is . . . is he dead?"

"If he isn't, he wishes he was."

"Could you . . . get him off me? He's . . ." She started crying too hard to go on.

I shoved myself off Steve's back. On my feet behind him, I bent over and grabbed him, clutching his right ankle with my right hand. As I dragged him off Judy, his face rubbed between her breasts and down her belly. About the time his mouth got to her navel, I gave his ankle a strong jerk and stumbled backward. His face sped the rest of the way. The slight rise of her pubic mound must've acted like a ramp. Going over, his head jumped up as if he needed to take a last peek at her. Then he dropped off and his face struck the ground.

I kept staggering backward as fast as I could, dragging him by the foot, until our momentum ran out. Then I let go and stood above him and tried to catch my breath.

Judy rolled onto her side. She lay there sobbing quietly.

Crouching, I pulled the knife out of Steve's butt.

Then I stood up straight. I raised my hands and studied them in the firelight. They were crossed at the wrists and tightly wrapped with the electrical extension cord.

Right away, it was obvious that I wouldn't be able to reach the cord with the knife's blade.

I could think of only one way, without help, to free my hands from the cord.

By loosening it *with my teeth*.

Both my hands were bathed with blood and filth from Steve. I brought my hands toward my mouth, anyway, but the stench made me gag.

Forget it.

Maybe there was a way to use the knife, after all.

Bending over, I spread my skirt open and clamped the knife's handle between my knees so that the blade pointed upward. Then I lowered my arms, easing my wrists down until the blade slipped between them.

I moved my hands up and down, rubbing the cord against the blade's edge.

The coating of the cord—rubber or plastic, I guess—was so hard that the blade didn't have much effect on it.

Maybe try it with the saber.

This'll work. Just gonna take a while.

I tried to apply more pressure, but my knee-grip wasn't secure enough so the knife slipped.

"What're you doing?" Judy asked, her voice quiet and shaky.

"Trying to cut this damn cord off me."

"Can't you . . . just untie it?"

"Not with my hands tied."

"I'll do it for you."

"Thanks anyway," I said, and kept rubbing. Pretty soon, my legs began to tremble from keeping such a tight hold on the knife. Also, my back started to ache.

"Are you afraid of me?" Judy asked.

"Give me a break."

"Then why won't you let me help?"

"I'd have to cut you loose."

"So . . . now I'm *your* prisoner? Again?"

"I don't know."

"Just great," she murmured. "I thought . . . after all this . . . you've saved my *life*, Alice. Twice."

"I know."

"You just . . . killed Steve for me."

"For both of us."

"I'm the one he was raping."

"Yeah."

"You're the best friend I've ever had."

"Sure."

"And you're afraid I'll . . . *jump* you?"

"You might," I said.

"I won't."

"Sure."

"So what are you going to do, kill me?"

When she said that, I pushed too hard or flinched or something. I'm not sure exactly what went wrong, but my knees let go of the knife and it fell to the ground. I blurted, "Shit!" and almost felt like crying, myself.

"Just come here and I'll take care of you," Judy said.

"Okay. Okay." I squatted, picked up the knife, and walked over to her with the long end of the cord trailing behind me.

"Do you know what I think?" Judy asked.

"What?"

"I think we should go away together."

"Huh?"

"Just disappear. You and I."

"Yeah, right." Crouching behind her, I slipped the knife blade under the taut line connecting her hands and feet. With one hard tug, I severed it.

Judy said, "Ah." She straightened her legs. "Oh, God," she said, and stretched. "That feels so good. Thank you."

Her feet were still tied together. I decided to leave them that way, and started to cut through the rope binding her wrists together.

"No funny stuff," I said, "or I *will* kill you."

"I mean it about going away together," she said.

I stopped cutting. "The hell you do," I told her.

"These guys have a van," she said.

"I know."

"Maybe we can find it. They sure as heck don't need it anymore. We can use it for our getaway."

"You don't want to run away with me. Hey, I was pulling the same stunt with Steve. So were you, apparently. It's not a bad ploy if you can pull it off, but . . ."

"This is different."

"Oh, yeah? How?"

"I hated him. I don't hate you."

"You should. Everything I did to you."

"You were just scared, that's all. Trying to protect yourself."

"By killing you."

"But you didn't kill me," she said. "And you saved me from Steve *and* Milo. I owe you."

"No, you don't. You don't owe me for anything. After all the awful things I did to you . . ."

"Forget about that stuff, Alice."

"Sure."

"I think we'd be great together. We could take their van and hit the road."

"Why?" I asked.

"You know why."

"You tell me."

"Because we're in this whole thing too deep," Judy said.

"*You're* not. You're just a victim."

"The cops won't know that. My ex-boyfriend's body is in the trunk of his car—in the parking lot of *my* apartment building. I'll be a suspect right from the start. And one look at me, they'll know I've been tangling with someone."

"Right. Milo and Steve. And me."

"That's the point, Alice. I can't tell the truth without telling on you. And I won't do that. So I'll be in deep trouble if I stick around."

"I guess you're right about that," I admitted.

She *was* right. We'd gone way past the point where all might be explained by a few simple lies.

The truth would get Judy off the hook—if the cops believed her—but it would destroy me.

"You'd really . . . give up everything and go away with me?" I asked.

"What's to give up? I've got no family, no boyfriend, a crummy job. We can drive off and start all over, just you and me. Change our names, maybe dye our hair . . . Wouldn't it be great?"

"Sounds pretty good to me," I said.

If we went away together, I supposed I would miss my room above the garage, and Serena and Charlie and their kids. But my life hadn't really been all that spectacular so far, anyway. I wouldn't be giving up much, that's for sure.

And the idea of going off with Judy . . . I felt almost like a kid on the eve of a great adventure.

Not that it's going to happen.

"Do you really mean it?" I asked.

"Yeah. I mean it."

I went ahead and finished cutting her hands loose. "Oh, that feels so great," she said. She rolled onto her back. Sighing, she rubbed her wrists. "Thanks. Give me a second or two, okay?"

"Sure."

While she stretched and rubbed her wrists and tried to recover, I crouched by her feet and sliced through the rope between them.

She said, "Ah," and "Thanks." Then she sat up and rubbed her ankles. "Feels so good." Smiling up at me, she said, "Now, let's take care of that cord."

On our knees, we faced each other.

I still held the knife in my right hand.

"What're you gonna do with that?" she asked.

"It's just in case."

Leaning forward, Judy put her hands gently on both sides of my face. She gazed into my eyes.

God, she was so beautiful.

"What kind of friends are we going to be?" she asked. "If you feel you need a knife . . . ?"

"You don't really want to go away with me," I said.

"Yes, I do."

I swallowed hard, and said, "Bull."

"Trust me, Alice."

"I'd like to trust you," I said. "But I can't."

"Yes you can. You *can* trust me. You can *depend* on me. We'll be best friends, now and forever."

"Yeah, sure," I said. My eyes filled with tears.

Judy put her hands on my shoulders. "You won't have to be lonely anymore. Neither will I. We've both been so lonely . . . and hurt. But no more. We have each other, now." She leaned in closer and gently kissed each of my wet eyes and then the tip of my nose.

I let the knife fall from my hand.

Judy sighed as if very relieved. Then she whispered, "Thanks," and leaned back and picked up the knife. With a strange smile on her firelit face, she said, "Now *I'm* the one with the weapon and *you're* the one tied up."

"That's right," I said.

I suddenly felt cold and sick inside.

"You believed me?" Judy asked. "You really *believed* you could trust me?"

"I guess," I said, my voice shaking. Her beautiful, golden face was blurry through my tears.

"You really thought I wanted to be your best friend? And *run away* with you?"

"Yeah. No. I guess not. But . . . but I *wanted* to believe you. I wanted it so badly."

Then I was bawling like a kid with a crushed heart and I couldn't stop.

Not even when Judy tossed aside the knife and freed my hands from the electric cord.

Not even when she pulled me against her and hugged me tightly and stroked my hair.

Not even when she whispered, "Believe," in my ear.

EPILOGUE

How do you like that?

Judy had *meant* it.

When I was finally able to settle down and stop crying, I found myself to be about the happiest I'd ever been in my whole life. Filthy, worn out and hurting all over, but . . . *spectacular!*

So that's pretty much where the story ends.

I've got to stop it somewhere, right? This seems like a good place, since all the bad guys are dead, Judy and I are safe, and we've agreed to hit the road, together, for parts unknown.

There are still a few things that ought to be told, but I'll try to be brief.

For starters, there at the camp when I finally finished crying, I took off my skirt and we both used it to wipe most the blood and assorted yuck off our bodies.

Then I searched the pockets of Steve's shorts and gathered all the keys.

We buried Steve. Now, that was a chore!

When he was underground, we took down the tent and made the whole campsite go away.

We searched out the van, tossed the tent and some other odds and ends inside (including an astonishing and horrible collection of Polaroid photos that we'd found in the tent), started up the van with Steve's keys, and drove back to Serena and Charlie's house.

There, we took a quick shower in the master bathroom. (How wonderful to be really clean again!) Then we helped patch each other with an assortment of bandages, pads and tape. You should've seen us. We ended up looking like a couple of mummies.

We got dressed, borrowing shorts and tops and footwear from Serena.

By that time, it was about one o'clock in the morning. We still had quite a lot of night left. So we shuttled Elroy's car (with him in it), back to Miller's Woods and left it in the parking area near the picnic grounds.

Then we drove the van over to Judy's apartment building. Scouting around, we found Tony's car in the parking structure. The neighborhood seemed quiet. Maybe the body *had* been discovered and the place was staked out by cops. But we doubted it.

If I'd had Tony's keys, I might've moved his car to a new location. But I'd long ago (the previous night), thrown them into the campfire. I could've dug them out while Judy and I were breaking camp, but it hadn't occurred to me. Anyway, I suppose it's just as well. Trying to move Tony's car might've set off a whole new series of problems. You know how it is: everything is connected. Wires, wires, everywhere. So his car stayed put.

Up in Judy's apartment, I helped her pack. We made several trips down to the van. Though we had to leave a lot of her stuff behind, we took everything that was truly important to her. Then we drove on back to Serena and Charlie's house.

We parked the van in the garage.

Judy hurried upstairs with me, and helped me pack. We made a few trips down to the van. When I was satisfied that I had everything truly important—including the tapes from the answering machines, the five thousand dollars in cash from poor Murphy, and the autographed copy of his book— I locked up my room for the last time. Downstairs, I removed the license plates from my car and put them on the van. I also spent a couple of minutes in my car, signing it over to Serena.

Then, with me carrying the saber, we went to the main house. The sun was rising. We desperately needed to sleep, but we couldn't risk it. Before too much longer, one of the bodies was sure to be discovered.

They were all over the town and woods, like bombs that might go off at any moment.

So we didn't even try to sleep. Instead, we went to work cleaning up the mess that Elroy had left behind, thanks to Steve. In the guest bathroom, we scrubbed the walls and toilet and tub and floor. Then we worked on the carpet stains.

Which were pretty much hopeless.

I'd known they would be.

There was just no easy way around those stains. Lies would probably work with Serena and Charlie, but if the police should get involved . . .

Anyway, I would be gone. They could make whatever they wanted of the bloodstains.

By the time Judy and I finished our attempts to clean things up, it was about eight o'clock in the morning. Together, we made coffee and breakfast for ourselves, for each other. We had a delicious, leisurely meal.

While Judy cleaned up the breakfast mess, I wrote a note. It went like this:

Dear Serena and Charlie,
Great news! An old friend dropped by—someone I hadn't seen in years. We really hit it off. The upshot is, I'm going away with him. Whatever I've left behind, in-

cluding my car, is yours. I've signed the pink slip for you. It's in the glove compartment.

I'm not sure when I'll be back this way again. But thanks for everything. You've been great friends and landlords. I'll miss you and the kids.

Give my love to Debbie and Jeff.

When I get settled, I'll give you a call.

Love and kisses,
Alice

P.S. I'm so sorry about the blood stains on your carpet. I had a minor accident with a beer bottle. Jim and I did our best to clean the stains, but you may need to replace the carpet. Maybe you can pay for it by selling my car.

Bye,
Me

I propped up the note in the middle of the kitchen table.

Just before leaving, I cleaned the saber, dried it thoroughly, and hung it up on the wall above the fireplace where it belonged.

On our way out of town in the van, we stopped at our bank. We both had accounts at the same branch, which was not very strange when you consider the size of Chester. We went in separately, ten minutes apart, and withdrew our money. It didn't come to much. But added to the cash from Murphy, we had enough to get by on for a while.

Back in the van, we headed for the city limits.

During our travels, we followed the newspaper, TV and radio accounts of what came to be known as the Miller's Woods Massacre. It was a big story. A huge story. I mean, you're not supposed to have that sort of slaughter in quiet, small towns like Chester.

Here are the basics.

Elroy's body, found where we'd left it, triggered a major search of Miller's Woods. Which led to the discoveries of several shallow graves. They not only dug up Milo, Steve and

Marilyn, but two more female corpses that *we* knew nothing about.

When they found Tony's dismembered body in the trunk of his car, they figured he'd been done in by the same culprit who cut off Elroy's head. This connected Tony to the Miller's Woods Massacre, even though his body was discovered several miles away, in a parking space at Judy's apartment building.

Which dragged Judy into the picture.

Judy, missing and presumed dead. The authorities seem to think that she's buried somewhere in Miller's Woods, but they eventually quit looking for her body.

Murphy Scott, the manager of Tony's apartment complex, may or may not have been murdered in connection with the Miller's Woods Massacre. His death might've been an unrelated murder, or an accident. They just don't know. Nicely ironic, if you ask me. The mystery writer's death, in the midst of so much mayhem, remains a mystery.

In the course of the entire investigation, so far as I know, my name has never come up.

As for all that has happened to Judy and I since leaving Chester, I could make another whole book out of it. But I won't. Not for now, anyway. Maybe never.

There are a couple of items I should mention, though.

For one thing, I was in the doctor's office last month and read in *Entertainment Weekly* that this really major actor has signed on to star in a film version of a movie called *The Dark Pit,* from the novel of that title by the late Murphy Scott.

Cool, huh?

He would've liked that.

It made me awfully sad, though.

The other thing is, Judy and I are going to be mothers. Both of us. We're due at about the same time, early in April. Sounds corny, I know. I mean, like a soap opera or something. But you might say it's sort of a mixed blessing.

The father of my baby has to be Murphy. Which is wonderful, I think. Wonderful and sad, like the fact that they're going to make a movie of his book, only better than that, and worse. Him being dead . . .

But Judy's child—well, we don't know who the father is.

Possibly Tony. But he's a long shot, considering the time element. The father is almost certainly Milo or Steve.

Not exactly the best news.

Genes count for plenty. Do we really want to bring a kid into the world if half his genes come from a vicious rapist, a sadist, a thrill-killer, a cannibal?

Judy and I talked about terminating the pregnancy.

But we decided against it.

For one thing, we wanted nothing more to do with killing.

For another, half the baby's genes will be from Judy, and that's got to count for plenty.

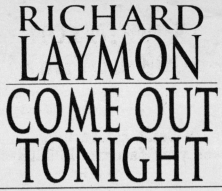

RICHARD LAYMON
COME OUT TONIGHT

Sherry's getting nervous. When Duane left for the 24-hour Speed-D-Mart, he said he'd be back in ten minutes. But that was twenty minutes ago, and that store isn't someplace you'd generally want to go at this time of night. Then Sherry hears a noise from up the street. It could have been a car door slamming. Or a backfire. But it sounded like a gunshot.

Sherry tells herself she has nothing to worry about. Still, she puts on her clothes and heads out into the night. She's afraid of what she'll find, but she has no idea of what's really in store for her. If she did, she never would have left the safety of her home. And she never would have met a madman named Toby Bones....

Dorchester Publishing Co., Inc.
P.O. Box 6640
Wayne, PA 19087-8640

_5183-4
$7.99 US/$9.99 CAN

Please add $2.50 for shipping and handling for the first book and $.75 for each additional book. NY and PA residents, add appropriate sales tax. No cash, stamps, or CODs. Canadian orders require an extra $2.00 for shipping and handling and must be paid in U.S. dollars. Prices and availability subject to change. **Payment must accompany all orders.**

Name: _____

Address: _____

City: _____ State: _____ Zip: _____

E-mail: _____

I have enclosed $_____ in payment for the checked book(s).

CHECK OUT OUR WEBSITE! _www.dorchesterpub.com_
_____ Please send me a free catalog.